To Ginny & Bill

# *The Moon War*

---

BOB DAVEY

Bob Davey

Laguna Niguel, CA 2/17/19

Create Space Independent Publishing Platform

***The Moon War***



Create Space Independent Publishing Platform

ISBN: 978-1-48018-721-4
1-4801872-1-6

Printed in the United States of America

*For Julie*

*my inspiration*

*my mentor*

*my loyal fan*

# Prologue

---

## Ignition

**Kurchatov Institute, Moscow**

Only Dmitri Nikolaevich Vorotnikov, Senior Research Fellow for Fusion Energy, could run the test by himself. Only he knew every component of the machine and every line of its software. Of course, it would be easier with the technicians, but tonight he would work alone. Tonight there would be risks.

He scrutinized the graphs displayed on the computer monitor and whispered to himself, "Definitely some enhancement. But not enough for the Ministry. The bastards!"

A few touches of the light pen brought a test plan to the display. Vorotnikov adjusted his bifocals, studied the values and muttered, "Still won't do."

After clearing the screen, he loaded the gain matrix and scanned the entries. Moving to an adjacent computer, he entered some numbers, then ran a simulation program.

"Check the soft X-rays," he thought, returning to the first monitor. He stroked his heavy brown beard. "Peculiar concentrations. Could be interactions." He shrugged. "Not much."

With the processing complete, the simulation presented its conclusions. Vorotnikov examined the screen, then smiled and thought, "Yes. Better."

Now more than an hour since the last shot, the T-15's torus had been pumped to a hard vacuum. Large enough to drive a car through, the hollow metal doughnut lay buried at the heart of the tokamak. Girding its shell, superconducting magnets created one dimension of a confining magnetic field. Coils circling the circumference generated a crossing counterpart. Combined, they forced atomic particles into a narrow beam, safely away from the walls.

In a separate building, massive flywheels whirled at their maximum speed. Coupled to powerful generators, they would provide the tremendous pulse of energy needed to heat and confine the particles. Without them, firing the T-15 would dim lights all over Moscow.

Vorotnikov checked the status of the instruments and initiated the shot sequence. When the magnetic fields reached their required strength, the computer commanded a small valve to open, releasing a tiny puff of deuterium into the vacuum of the torus. Immediately, a rapidly increasing current was drawn from the generators. Concentrated by giant iron rings, the building magnetic field transferred the power to the wisp of deuterium.

The current raised the temperature of the gas to tens of millions of degrees, forming a plasma. Its ions, now colliding violently, were squeezed toward the axis of the torus by the magnetism, creating a beam of increasing density and pressure.

Antennas filled the inside of the torus with powerful electromagnetic waves while particle accelerators, each larger than a bus, bombarded the ions with streams of high-energy deuterium atoms, increasing the temperature to more than one-hundred-million degrees. But the process triggered instabilities, causing the beam to undulate, threatening a collision with the wall.

A control computer sent correcting commands to a series of saddle coils. Looking like rings of icing draped over the top of a doughnut, they modified the magnetic field and damped out the instabilities.

As the temperature neared its maximum, turbulent plumes appeared at the edges of the beam. Without further action, the plasma would diffuse and cool. But Vorotnikov's new system could deal with the problem. Analyzing thousands of measurements in millionths of a second, a massively parallel computer sent commands to an array of ring coils blanketing the torus.

At first, the new coils seemed to work. The edges of the beam regained their uniform shape and the temperature continued to increase. But then the undulations reappeared. Suddenly the plasma slammed into the side of the chamber, transferring its energy to the wall, jolting the torus and sending shocks through the entire tokamak and all its instrumentation.

From start to finish, the experiment had taken less than two seconds.

Vorotnikov knew precisely what had happened. "Damn!" His anger was entirely self-directed. "Should have known I'd get a disruption. Better check for damage."

Back at the control console, he called up the measurements made by a broadband spectrometer. Wringing his hands, he scanned the information. "Not too bad." His anxiety diminished. "Mostly carbon. Hit the inner wall. May have damaged the instruments."

After turning on the vacuum pumps, he examined the data. "Lost the interferometer. Might get by with a realignment."

Vorotnikov left the control room, walked down the stairs to the main floor and entered the tokamak hall. Under ordinary circumstances, the interferometer would have realigned itself. But at a temperature close to two-hundred-million degrees, the disruption had not been ordinary.

The procedure went quickly, thanks to his years of practice. In less than an hour, everything had been returned to normal.

He pondered his next move. "Must be the time resolution. Feedback isn't keeping up. Why didn't I model that?" He located the proper module. "There. Twice as fast. Should be enough."

Modifying the simulation took a few more minutes, but before long he was examining the display, pleased with the results. With the flywheels up to speed and the pumping complete, he restarted the process. Current flowed, magnetic fields filled the torus, the transformer fed power into the deuterium and the temperature increased. Fifty-million watts radiated from the antennas and the temperature increased. Deuterium atoms collided with the plasma and the temperature increased. But this time there were no undulations, no plumes. The plasma stayed centered in the torus, its temperature now greater than three-hundred-million degrees.

The computer removed the power from the antennas, then from the particle accelerators. The test was over. But the temperature increased!

The screaming alarm startled Vorotnikov. He sat in disbelief, staring at the monitor, his hand over his mouth. It took almost a minute before he regained enough composure to silence the alarm and inform the computer that all was well.

He displayed the values of neutron flux that had triggered the warning. "My God!" he gasped. "It can't be true. The shot was finished."

Still not willing to believe the data, he examined more and more measurements. There was absolutely no doubt.

"I think I did it!" he whispered, allowing himself a cautious measure of elation. "Ignition! I must have had D-D ignition."

He stood, then paced rapidly back and forth along the long, narrow control room, the clicking of his heels on the brightly waxed floor assaulting the pristine silence of the laboratory.

"Fifty years—nothing but failures," he said aloud. "All those people. Now, finally, everything—field-reversed mirror, helium three—everything." Breathing rapidly, his mind leaping from one repercussion to the next, he struggled to assimilate the event. "Suppressing the plumes—nonlinear feedback—had to be the answer. But no one saw it—until now."

He stopped at the center of the control panel, then turned to face the tokamak, tears trickling from the wrinkled corners of his eyes. He raised his arms, fists clenched and yelled, "I did it!"

But concern tempered his exhilaration. "I wonder what the neutrons did to the machinery?"

After removing a radiation counter from its cabinet, he hurried around the tokamak hall. Encased within thousands of tons of magnets, the torus itself couldn't be examined, but the nominal readings he observed in the outer structure allayed his apprehension. The small quantity of gas hadn't produced significant radiation. Relieved, he scrambled up the stairs to the control room.

"What now? That should convince the ministers. But maybe not. They want a powerplant and I can't give it to them. Not for a lousy million rubles. Might get a bit closer, though."

With the vacuum pumps working and the flywheels spinning up, Vorotnikov again turned to the simulation. "Maybe I can replenish with the neutral beams—prolong the ignition. Eliminate contamination with the diverters."

He modified a section that evaluated the removal of impurities, altering the parameters so they matched the characteristics of the tritium and helium three produced by the fusion. Finished, he ran the program.

"Aha! Says it will work. Radiation shouldn't be too bad. Just need enough fusion to convince them I've produced some power."

Barely able to control his trembling fingers, he entered the information that would determine the sequence of the test. He paused at the termination mode. "Better do it manually. Not sure what will happen here."

The events unfolded in precise order. Studying the monitor, Vorotnikov could scarcely believe the numbers. Ignition was marked by a huge jump in electron temperature. Once again, the alarm sounded but this time he ignored its warning. The reaction continued. Vorotnikov watched transfixed.

Suddenly, he realized what was happening and pressed the trackball button to terminate the shot. "My God!" he shouted. "Let that get away." He silenced the alarm.

Trembling with excitement and apprehension, he picked up the radiation counter. Even in the control room, the instrument showed the effect of the fusion. Gripping the handrail, he stumbled down the stairs to the main floor, then inched toward the tokamak. The counter indicated a continual increase in radioactivity. As he neared the door to the T-15's chamber, it became clear. He had killed himself.

# Madman

**Over Southern Nevada**

Streaking across the patchwork of restricted airspace, the trio of attack aircraft raced west beyond the salt flats of Groom Lake toward the Belted Range. The early morning sun transformed the dull shades of the desert terrain into a mosaic of earth tones, bringing a stark beauty to the faces of the jagged mountains. Along the arid valley floor, long shadows of sagebrush and ocotillo speckled the tan backdrop, the resulting pattern's uniformity broken only by a few arroyos and a sprinkling of Joshua trees.

With little thought or effort, Colonel Brandt Strickland kept his TF-22F in perfect position as he mentally reviewed the performance of his pupils. After four years together, he and the airplane had fused into a single entity, each thoroughly comfortable with the other. The sequence of thought, movement and response now blurred into a smoothly flowing unity as if he controlled the machine directly with his mind.

Despite its Trainer/Fighter designation, Brandt's plane had

only one seat, mute testimony to the extraordinary evolution of combat-pilot training. Now simulators of mind-numbing complexity generated situational realism sufficient for the development of all the dexterity and knowledge needed to control the vehicle and fully exploit its weapons. But it still took the pressure of in-flight training to hone the analysis, judgment and teamwork skills needed to become an effective warrior.

"Well, Kesler managed to stay alive through two passes," he muttered to himself. "But that's flying against a sorry excuse for a range."

Denton's voice interrupted his thoughts. "Hacker Flight approaching range entry. Go full data link."

Responding to his pupil's command, Brandt touched one of the twenty gray buttons that ringed the left multi-function display, ending all radio communication and tying the computers of the three planes together with undetectable laser beams. They would now function as one, an almost infinitely flexible system of destruction.

The Wolf-Pack concept emerged from the Chad War. The system could link as many as eight F-22s, all but one of which could fly unmanned. When fully implemented, the technique created an integrated offense, defense and reconnaissance capability of truly awesome potential. But on this day, the weapons bays carried only electronics. As the students selected and deployed devices, the modules would determine the effectiveness of their decisions.

Brandt's TF was equipped with additional computers and secure transmitters. With these, he would create a complete target environment on the ranges below, collect information from the other planes, integrate it with responses from the ground, and develop comprehensive performance evaluations.

Brandt's training-panel display demanded instructions. "Time to find out how much they learned last week," he whispered into his dead mike, his voice blending with the hiss of gas and the quiet clicks of the oxygen-mask valves.

"Range crypto channel. Multi-sensor array activation. Call up the LIDARs. Range weapons armed."

Brandt manipulated the trackball on the side of his stick to place the cursor on the desired items of the range-configuration display. He had long ago mastered the trick of flying in an exact relation to another aircraft while watching both the terrain and the many displays that cluttered his field of vision.

"Sure love going at this range," he thought. "Best we've got. Best in the world!"

Twenty miles ahead, dozens of electronic detectors came alive as the range-control computers decoded Brandt's commands. Simultaneously, laser designators rotated to their default firing angles.

The planes passed north of Yucca Flat and started descending into the Kawich Valley. Brandt kept his fighter just below the turbulence from Kesler's engines, feeling the slight buffet as her thrust vectoring tickled the tops of his twin vertical stabilizers.

With another touch of his trackball, he turned over the operation of his plane to the computers. They would maintain his relative position through the rapid maneuvering of the low-level attack.

"Okay, down we go. Denton's pretty smooth this morning. He'd better be. South-to-north pass. Really a monster."

Brandt eyes caught glimpses of the display as it reported the progress of the attack. "Passive micro activated. Passive laser; IR. Watch this. Not one return. This range is unbelievable."

Amber flashes caught Brandt's eye.

"LIDAR hits, dummy. Come on. Don't give them a track. Down, dang it! Make them dig it out of the ground clutter."

Brandt checked the offensive status.

"Let's get some weapons up, Kesler. Thatta girl. ARMs? You'll never use them. Not with this setup. Directed energy? Might get lucky.

"Okay Denton, where's the target? That's right, you need the radar. Burst mode so they won't have time. Agility on. The kid's learning!"

Denton commanded the computers to generate a random pattern of turns, climbs and dives. Brandt felt his g-suit inflate and release as his plane followed the gyrations. "That's it, push up the jink. Don't give 'em anything but random hits. Come on, work the radar."

Red flashes appeared at the side of the left display. Startled, Brandt's mind raced to determine the meaning of the icons.

"What the heck? Continuous interrogation? What is this? Range screwup? Blast! It's us! It's me! Radar's on continuous! What are you doing Denton?

"Dang! Here we go. Multiple tracks—range lasers. They've got us. Missile hits—two, three. We're dead. Game's over."

Brandt selected the abort command and heard his breathing

over the reactivated sidetone.

"Hacker flight, this is Madman. Stealth lost. Break attack. Climb to flight level two-one-zero. Form on me."

He pushed the throttle forward, moved ahead of the other planes, turned east into the sun and headed for Nellis.

**Nellis AFB, Nevada**

Sighting down the tops of the certificate holders that hung in a row along the side wall of his office, Brandt noticed that the third frame had tilted a few degrees. After realigning it, he stepped toward the back of the room, rearranged the American flag that stood in the corner until its folds draped perfectly, then adjusted the spotless blinds covering the rear wall's single window until the entering light reached just the right intensity.

He moved to his government-issue gray desk, checked that its front face precisely followed the line of the floor tiles, then nudged the rectangular table that butted against the desk's left side into perfect perpendicularity. Satisfied with the table, he adjusted the position of its two plain chairs until the gap between their backs and the table's edge measured exactly two finger widths.

He looked down at his trousers to verify that the creases, which were barely flattened by his sinewy legs, remained razor sharp. Stepping up to the unframed mirror attached to the inside of the office door, he confirmed that his short-brown hair flowed back smoothly from his temples.

He went to his desk, sat erect in the plastic-upholstered swivel chair and patted the three small stacks of documents into perfect rectangles. Satisfied, he lifted Denton's training folder from the top of the center pile and began to leaf through it.

The intercom buzzer sounded. "Lieutenant Denton to see you, Colonel." The secretary's voice revealed nothing.

He touched the intercom select. "Send him in."

Brandt heard the knob turn and watched as his office door opened slowly but deliberately. He rose, pushed his chair under the desk and stood behind it.

As Denton's eyes met his, Brandt said quietly, "Close the door."

"Lieutenant Denton, reporting as ordered." The words were automatic. An inch shorter than Brandt's six-feet, Denton was forced to look upward just enough to aggravate his apprehension. Brandt stared at him without blinking.

"Well, Denton, you not only managed to get yourself killed this morning, you also took care of Kesler and me. Why, may I ask, did you feel so kindly toward the range personnel as to assist them by turning on my radar full blast?"

"Sir, I thought I had preset all modes to threat-analysis during preflight. Apparently, the agility mode was still on manual-continuous so when..."

"You thought!" Brandt walked around his desk and stood face to face with Denton, inches away. "Didn't you ever hear of verification? The status was displayed on the HUD, right in front of your nose."

"Yes sir, but..."

Brandt hissed into Denton's face. "Do you think you're going to get through your whole career playing video games on the HUD? Do you?"

"No sir."

"Dang right you won't. This stuff about the Russians not wanting to attack American interests is horse manure. Believe this, mister. We'll be fighting those bastards—and soon!"

"Yes sir."

"They're going to rebuild their economy by making new weapons. Good weapons! Their sensors will make that range you screwed up look like a Sunday picnic. Try that assuming business and we'll be sending you back to your mommy in a blotter. You reading me?"

"Yes sir."

"Frankly, I don't give a cow pie if you turn yourself into a puddle of apple butter, but by God you're getting paid to defend this great country and I will not allow you or any other screwup to risk lives, equipment or mission success."

"Yes sir."

"Tell ya what we're gonna do, Lieutenant." Brandt's voice took on an air of excitement. "We're going up again tomorrow morning. Just you and me. Same range, only this time you do it all. Weapons. Sensors. Everything."

Denton swallowed. "Yes sir."

"And I expect perfection. In and out. No tracks. Not one. Assured target destruction. Clear?"

"Yes sir."

"Six-o'clock takeoff."

"Yes sir."

"That's all."

Denton saluted. "Good afternoon, sir."

Brandt followed Denton out the office door and stopped at the secretary's desk.

"Liz, have Ops set up a mission for Denton and me tomorrow morning. Six-o'clock takeoff."

She smiled knowingly. "Certainly Colonel Strickland."

He watched Denton disappear across the Wing Headquarters area. "You know, Liz, that lieutenant's going to develop into a really fine fighter pilot. I just need to temper his arrogance with some judgement. Have to be careful, though. Don't want to crush his self confidence. Takes a fine balance of criticism and praise."

Liz had heard it all before. "You really worry about them, don't you?"

"Sure do. That's why I take the time to fly with each and every student. After all, someday I may have to depend on one of these clowns to keep me alive."

Brandt laughed and stepped back to his office. He closed the door, returned to his desk, and started to examine a report. His hand moved unconsciously to the left side of his neck.

"Danged Gs. Danged neck bones," he mumbled.

Failing in his attempt to rub away the pain, he reached into the bottom desk drawer and removed a bottle of pills.

"Hope nobody catches me taking these," he thought. "But it's this or no more flying. Doggone flight surgeons. Make cheaters out of all of us." He removed two pills and swallowed them.

Brandt noticed an envelope at the top of his in basket. He opened it and began to read. "Pentagon?" he said aloud. "Study group? What the do they want me for? Three months! Dang it all!"

# Tigrytsa

**Russian Space Station**

"There they are! Same place as the IR returns." Svetlana adjusted the range settings, trying to improve the image. Set at its highest resolution, the Priroda-9 easily discriminated between the sand dunes and the camouflaged covers hiding the tanks. Four hundred kilometers below, Moslem fanatics sweltered in the heat of the Muyun Kum Desert, anxiously awaiting the darkness that would cloak their escape back to Dzambul.

Satisfied with the picture, she studied the screen, thinking to herself, "This should help finish them off. No way the commanders could get this detail from the satellite—even if was working perfectly—which it sure as hell isn't."

After selecting the necessary commands from the menus, she waited while the computer recorded the images. When it had finished, she commanded the system to transmit the encoded message. Within hours, strike forces armed with detailed location and strength information would crush the rebel threat.

"I'd appreciate it if your military friends would give me some time to do research," Razin complained. "You certainly don't need a materials scientist to help you spy on the Moslems."

"We're both here to do whatever is required," Svetlana replied curtly. "In any case, if I'm successful tomorrow, you'll be able to get back to your tests. No more imaging tasks and I'll take care of running the station."

Somewhat chagrinned, he responded, "Sorry to complain. I know you've got a tough one ahead of you. Don't want to add to your problems."

***

Despite having spent more than two years in space, Engineer Colonel Svetlana Zosimova had maintained the hard, tautly muscled body of her track-star days. Fanatical about physical fitness, she ran the space station's exercise machines to the point of breakdown. But the upcoming activities would tax even her extraordinary strength and endurance.

After checking out her modified Sokol suit, Svetlana donned

the complex garment in the large portion of the base block. Then she moved through the rear port into the orbital module of the docked Soyuz and asked Razin to hand her the YMK manned maneuvering unit. Svetlana placed it in its storage rack and tried to secure it.

"Not so easy with the suit on," she muttered.

Peering down through the helmet's faceplate, she struggled with the clamps, unable to see them clearly. But, after a few tries, she managed to snap them together and complete the loading.

Her familiarity with the task made closing the Soyuz docking port a routine affair. She quickly locked it and checked the seals. Inside the base block, Razin closed the receiving cone, cranked the locks into place and activated the test sequence. Communicating through his headset, he told Svetlana the space station was ready for separation.

She moved into the descent capsule and strapped herself into the commander's couch. After completing the preparation checklist, she transmitted to Razin, "Initiate the undocking."

As the automatic sequence concluded, the Soyuz-TM slowly receded from the station. When the separation distance reached three-hundred meters, Svetlana felt the attitude control thrusters fire and watched through the porthole as the spacecraft rotated to point its main engines along the direction of the orbit.

Thirty kilometers above and a fraction of an orbit ahead, a Khorek satellite made final orientation and velocity adjustments. As large as a semi-trailer, it housed a comprehensive array of imaging, detection and storage systems capable of monitoring any activity on the earth's surface.

Buried deep within the behemoth, three large inertia wheels rotated in nearly frictionless bearings. Used to conserve propellant, the wheels were connected to the satellite by torque motors. After receiving a command, the motors attempted to increase or decrease the velocity of the wheels. But in the weightless vacuum of space, the reaction torque rotated the spacecraft in the opposite direction, thereby accomplishing attitude control without the use of thrusters. If everything went perfectly, when the reverse torque was applied to stop the satellite, the wheel stopped as well. Of course, the system wasn't perfect. Small amounts of friction left the wheels with some residual spin. When the spin became too great, it was eliminated by firing small rockets.

But now the satellite was in trouble. Its nearly continuous use during the Kazakhstan war had depleted the supply of fuel and despinning operations around the primary axis had been halted. As a result, one wheel now rotated faster than its design maximum and any further torquing could cause it to fail, sending the entire satellite into an uncontrollable tumble. And the replacement was still a month from launch.

The range rate gradually dropped toward zero as the Soyuz positioned itself some five meters from the Khorek's solar panels. After unstrapping, Svetlana pushed away from the couch and moved into the orbital module. Once inside, she closed the hatch and verified that her EVA suit was functioning normally. Then she activated valves to vent the module's air into space. As the pressure dropped, she felt her spacesuit inflate and stiffen, making every movement awkward and tiring.

After opening the outer hatch, she attached her safety lanyard and floated into the star-filled blackness of space, catching a last glimpse of the sun as the Soyuz moved into the earth's shadow. She would perform her first tasks in the dark, using small lights on the sides of her helmet. Time in the sunlight had been reserved for the greater challenges that lay ahead.

She worked deliberately, unloading the tools and equipment, moving the containers outside and attaching their tethers to special fittings protruding through the green thermal blankets that covered the exterior of the Soyuz. Because of its size, the YMK required extra care but she managed to ease it through the hatch and secure it.

Passing over the inky blackness of the South Pacific, she pulled herself toward the YMK and tried to grab an attachment clip. But even touching the unit caused it to rotate. She gently pushed herself away from the Soyuz and waited until she and the YMK reached the end of its tether. With one dimension stable, she managed to attach the right side of the YMK and align it with her body. Then she made the remaining connections at her side and on her legs. Satisfied that she and the YMK were one, she released its tether.

To save the satellite, she had to attach small rockets at specific locations on its surface. But first she needed to install the mountings.

She released the components unit and its tool set from their tethers and clipped them to her suit. Then, using the YMK's thrusters, she moved toward the Khorek. The mission plan called for her to use a set of threaded holes that held a small backup antenna.

Still in the dark with only a sliver of a moon to help her, she eased toward the satellite. Carefully threading her way between the solar panels to an area on one of the eight flat sides, she found the antenna, fitted a friction-antitorque tool to a mounting screw, then braced herself by holding the antenna with one hand while activating the tool with the other. She watched with satisfaction as the tool slowly accomplished the extraction, then pulled the screw from the tool and placed it in a clip provided for the purpose.

The remaining three screws proved equally cooperative. She removed the antenna, then stowed it in a pouch on the left leg of her suit.

The lights of Honolulu passed by in the distance, but Svetlana hardly noticed.

She removed the first thruster mount from its container and placed it over the screw holes. This time she had only an electrical connector to grasp while she inserted the screw and maneuvered the tool and the mount into place.

Just as she activated the screwdriver, she lost her tenuous grasp of the connector and twisted away from the satellite. Still holding the tool, she grabbed a propellant port to stop her motion. "Damn!" she yelled, her heart pounding. "Lucky I didn't hit the panels."

Repositioning herself above the Khorek, she once again aimed the screw at its target. With a single motion, she grasped the connector and activated the tool. Her timing was perfect and the screw threads engaged. With the mount secure, she quickly inserted the remaining screws and tightened them down.

Because no antenna had been attached to the opposite side of the Khorek, creating the second thruster mount involved placing a metal strap completely around the satellite. As she reentered the daylight, Svetlana removed the strap from its container and attached one end to the thruster mounting.

"Now comes the fun part," she whispered to herself.

Holding the free end of the strap, she used the YMK to move away from the satellite. As the strap slowly unfolded, she tried to fly herself around the Khorek, taking care not to damage any of the antennas and sensors protruding from its surface. But the YMK rockets fired unevenly and she began to rotate. She tried using the arm thrusters but the strap began to twist. More attempts to stabilize the motion only made things worse. Realizing she was moving backward toward a solar panel while placing an increasingly hazardous stress on the mounting, she released the strap, then moved away from the satellite to reevaluate the situation.

Breathing heavily under the combination of exertion and stress, she spoke to herself. "Okay! Motion is stopped. Concentrate on the strap. Maneuver toward the end. Keep a bit of tension." She felt her skin become clammy as her labors exceeded the suit's cooling capability.

After grasping the free end of the strap, she moved slowly away from the satellite. Then she began a careful encirclement, winding the metal sections around the Khorek. Six minutes later, she had returned to the mounting flange.

"Missed! About three centimeters. Have to back away." She unwound four sections, then repositioned them to improve the alignment. Finally, she mated the attachment clip to the mount.

"Not perfect, but close enough," she panted.

With the most difficult tasks completed, she returned the tools to their containers, trying to reduce her heat output so the suit could catch up. Still panting, she mumbled, "Time for round two," and moved back toward the Soyuz.

Feeling more confident and with renewed energy, she released the second tool package and the two rockets, attached them to her suit and moved back toward the Khorek. For the first time, she allowed herself a moment to experience the grandeur of her situation. A vast swath of Russia lay below her, blocked only by dots of clouds. She easily identified one feature after another as she raced over the earth. But she still had things to do.

After centering herself over the first mount, she moved one of the rockets into position in front of her waist. Then, using the inertia of her body, she pushed the mounting flange of the rocket sideways into the attachment. Finally, she moved to the opposite side of the satellite and mounted the second rocket. With her work complete, she returned to the Soyuz, nearly exhausted, drenched with perspiration, but enormously satisfied.

Back in her couch, with the YMK and tools stowed, hatches sealed and orbital compartment repressurized, Svetlana breathed normally for the first time in nearly two hours. By touching a few selections on her communications screen, she sent a coded message to Razin and the Space Agency announcing the success of her EVA. Soon, signals would be sent to receivers in the rockets commanding them to fire. The life of the satellite would be extended and Razin would return to his research.

She initiated the departure sequence and watched the distance between the Soyuz and the Khorek gradually increase. The computers determined the commands needed to reintercept the space station's trajectory and, after the required delays, she felt the main engines fire.

As Svetlana approached the base block, she was surprised to see that another Soyuz had arrived. Her automatic docking went by without incident and she soon floated inside the space station, grateful for Razin's help as she removed the EVA suit.

"Welcome back," Razin said. "That job should get you another medal."

Svetlana smirked. "Right now I'll be happy to get some rest. Who came up in the TM?"

"I'm afraid you can forget about relaxing—at least for a while."

A third cosmonaut appeared from the opposite end of the base block. Svetlana recognized him immediately.

"Vadim! What are you doing here? You weren't supposed to launch until next week!" She pushed herself across the module and embraced her former classmate.

"Good to see you, Svetlana. Came up early to replace you. Afraid we won't have much time for catching up."

Razin pointed to a block of text on one of the displays.

Svetlana, upset by the message, blurted out, "What? Why would they terminate my mission? There must be someone else who can serve on this advisory board. When did they tell you about this?"

"Notified me three days ago," Vadim replied.

Angry, Svetlana said, "Why didn't they notify me? And how did they get the vehicles ready that fast?"

"Don't know. But it looks as if you're finished about three months early."

Svetlana sighed. "Frankly, after what I've just been through, I should be happy. Don't know if you heard about the Khorek repair."

"I did hear, and I hope you got it right. I'm not fond of solo EVAs."

***

Still baffled by the unexpected turn of events, Svetlana donned the light-weight pressure suit used for transit between earth and the space station and made her way back toward the Soyuz.

After a brief farewell, she entered the nearly empty orbital module, closed the docking port, then floated into the descent capsule and secured the hatch.

The undocking passed without incident and, after moving away from the base block, the Soyuz positioned itself for reentry. A short time later as it approached the south Atlantic, the primary engine fired, slowing the vehicle's speed and initiating its descent into the atmosphere. Its work complete, the large service module separated along with the orbital module. Lacking protection, they would burn up before reaching the surface.

Now facing opposite the direction of motion, Svetlana felt the small orientation engines adjust the flight path angle. Then, with the air density increasing, she felt herself being pushed into the couch as the module decelerated. The opening of the primary parachute pushed her down harder. Suddenly, the descent module began to swing wildly back and forth as it dropped through the edge of a thunderstorm. Blown almost a kilometer from the intended landing site, it descended toward a hillside. A few meters above the ground, rocket motors fired to soften the impact but the steep terrain deflected their thrust, upsetting the vehicle and causing it to tumble end over end. Despite being strapped in, Svetlana bruised her legs and arms as they slammed against the controls.

The module came to rest upside down, its nose imbedded in a narrow ravine. Now hanging from the seat harness, wincing in pain, and with little hope of early rescue, Svetlana fumed, "Well, shit! Great end to a great mission. What next?"

## Chapter 1

# Special Study Group

**The Pentagon**

The flashing appointment reminder at the top of his computer screen caught Brandt's eye. He glanced through the office window, across the desks of the Special Study Group into an office on the adjacent wall. Darrell had already left.

Taking an envelope from his desk drawer, Brandt left the office and wound his way through a maze of cubbyholes, finally trading the tomblike silence of the Joint Intelligence Center for the commotion of the D-Ring corridor. Now a month into his temporary assignment, he still wasn't comfortable with life in the Pentagon. Missing the challenge of commanding a fighter wing came as no surprise. As for the seventy-hour work weeks, he'd been on priority 1A programs before. But the people here were different—guarded, political, with hidden agendas. He felt isolated, with no one he could talk to—except for Darrell.

A left turn brought him to the entrance of a Level-R Briefing Room. He peered into the lens of the iris scanner, then waited for the security computer to open the electrically operated door. A typical Level-R, it had four rows of six seats, divided symmetrically by a center aisle. Inside, all surfaces were flat, unadorned and undecorated, assuring that any attempt to plant a sensor would be immediately detected.

Four people had arrived before him. At the left end of the

front row, a woman scanned messages on a video pager. Darrell sat behind her.

At the opposite end of the row, a balding man slouched, his hands clasped behind his head. In back of him, an Air Force captain punched the keypad of a pocket computer.

Brandt took an aisle seat in the second row. A minute later, Rear Admiral Gerald Fletcher, Defense Intelligence Officer for Russia and Eurasia, entered and walked to the raised platform at the front of the room.

"Good morning folks." The Admiral's tone was relaxed. Of average height and slightly overweight, Fletcher's ruddy complexion, thick gray hair and broad smile made him appear more like a corporate sales executive than a senior military officer.

"I brought you here this morning to exchange reactions to the Russian moon mission. No agenda, really. Just want to swap ideas about where this might be headed.

"Some of you probably know each other, but let me make the introductions anyway. On my right in the first row is Anita Montgomery. She heads up the CIA's Slavic and Eurasian Analysis Office.

"Behind her is Lieutenant Colonel Darrell Wilkins, the Shuttle Commander you read about in the papers, and across from him is the head of DIA's Special Study Group, Colonel Brandt Strickland. He usually makes his living running a fighter wing at Nellis but ended up here because he worked with the Russians on the Super Shuttle program.

"On my left is Doctor Raul Cardenas from the Space Flight office at NASA Headquarters and behind him we have Captain Yasunori Mashita from the Air Intelligence Agency's outfit at Fort Belvoir."

The participants nodded briefly as they were identified.

"Colonel Strickland, let's start with your presentation."

Brandt removed a memory module from his envelope. He traded places with Fletcher on the dais, then slipped the module into the flat-panel display on the front wall and entered the identification number of the decoding algorithm.

"Everything we've looked at," he began, "tells us the Federation wouldn't stand a chance going it alone. Their manned-space program is a shambles."

Using the display, he reviewed the demise of the original Mir complex and the limitations of its recent replacement.

"Their support of manned-space activities has been minimal for at least five years. Remember, they had to halt their contributions to the Space Station almost a year before it was mothballed. About the only thing they've accomplished in the last decade is the launch of the new base block."

"Wasn't a woman cosmonaut involved with that?" Fletcher asked.

"Zosimova? Yes, sir. In fact, she proposed it—then flew some real hairy missions, all by herself, to get it operating. She's probably the only reason they've got a program. But they have no capability for a moon mission. No heavy-lift booster, no suitable upper stage, no lander. And limited resources for serious development."

"Miss Montgomery," Fletcher interrupted, "suppose you take it from there."

Brandt ejected his module from the display and headed for his seat as the CIA executive stepped forward. When she turned to address the group, Brandt found himself looking into the most intriguingly beautiful face he'd ever seen. Anita's soft, delicate features and large brown eyes were accented by just a hint of makeup.

"African-American," he thought. "But different somehow." A glance at Darrell confirmed that her charm hadn't been lost on his colleague.

"Thank you, Admiral Fletcher," she began. "At the CIA, we started working on this as soon as the announcement came through. Frankly, what they're proposing makes absolutely no sense."

She went through a set of graphics that provided an overview of the political and economic situation in the Federation, then concluded by stating, "So, here they are, on the verge of economic disintegration, the whole country ready to explode and they decide to send a man to the moon. Figure that out!"

"What about diverting attention from the economic problems?" Darrell asked.

"Obvious explanation," Anita replied, "but it doesn't stand up. As I pointed out, things are so bad that nothing is going to appease the people except food, clothing and jobs. The spirit-building idea is also contradicted by their proposing an international program. If they wanted to build pride and gain prestige, they'd be going it alone."

Fletcher nodded. "Thanks Anita. Colonel Wilkins?"

Anita moved toward her seat. Brandt noticed Darrell hurrying a bit, then brushing against her as they exchanged places. Anita glanced back, looking annoyed.

"I don't have anything formal to present," Darrell began. "Just some ideas.

"The only justification we've been able to come up with is a desire to steal technology from the West. We think their defense honcho, Belyaev, may be trying to develop a new weapon and needs a peek at American and European capabilities. We'd expect them to be very active in the R-and-D phase of the program—host conferences, conduct joint tests. Then, after they get what they want, they'll start objecting to a bunch of trivial details and eventually drop out."

"So you think the whole thing's a ruse?" Cardenas asked.

"Only explanation that holds together."

Mashita interrupted him. "Colonel, we just received some satellite images that may contradict your theory. Some time back—could be fifteen years—we spotted some construction activity near the Plesetsk missile-launch complex. Ended up being a large building—rectangular, no windows, flat roof. Never saw anything go in or out. Back then, if the Russians were careful, they could get things past our Keyholes.

"Anyway, last week we finally saw something. Two large missile transporters entered the building. Never imaged anything like them before. Two days later they emerged carrying massive loads and drove to the airfield. Both times, the operation was done at night, under cloud cover and at our worst observation angles. No question they were trying to keep us from getting a good look.

"We also saw two old Antonov 225s parked on the ramp. We don't have confirmation, but we think whatever was on the transporters ended up on top of the Mriyas."

"I'm not up on the aerospace details," Anita said. "What's a Mriya?"

"Sorry, Ms. Montgomery," Mashita replied. "It's a gigantic cargo plane. Six engines."

Anita nodded. "Thanks. Guess I should have known."

Returning to the primary issue, Brandt said, "Interesting, but what does this have to do with the moon program?"

"Nothing so far, Colonel. But yesterday we were analyzing some images of the Moscow area and guess what? The 225s showed up at Kaliningrad—obviously delivering something to RSC Energia. That's where they build manned spacecraft."

Brandt raised his eyebrows. "Okay. Now I'm interested. Did you see what they unloaded?"

"Nope. They must have worked hard to avoid observation. Timed it just right."

"Any guesses?"

"Size and mass estimates point toward some kind of booster. "

"SL-17s!" Cardenas shouted. "Must be cores for Energia boosters."

"Except there are no more Energia boosters," Brandt objected. "Remember? We offered them hard currency for another Space Station launch and they had to turn it down."

"Maybe they didn't want to give up the ones at Plesetsk. Maybe they were keeping them for some military program."

Brandt looked back, puzzled. "What would the military want with something that big?"

"Hey, Colonel," Cardenas chuckled. "That's your business, not mine."

Fletcher stepped forward as Mashita worked his way back to the second row.

"Folks, you can check out the military details later. For now, let's assume the objects really are SL-17s and let's assume they're being delivered to RSC Energia. So what? Dr. Cardenas?"

Keeping his seat, the space expert answered, "It's certainly possible they'd want to use them for a moon mission. In fact, having an Energia might be the key to making the whole thing feasible."

Mashita was satisfied. "Sounds like you've solved the puzzle."

Cardenas smiled and continued. "At this point, with the multinational talks barely started, I'd guess they're doing some preliminary design work, probably trying to determine what modifications will be needed."

Anita interrupted, "I'm sorry gentlemen, but this still doesn't make sense. We haven't resolved the fundamental problem. Getting involved in a manned-moon expedition isn't going to help the Federation's domestic situation. Whether or not they have this SL-17, which I assume is some sort of rocket, they'll still have to spend many, many rubles—and they can't afford it. This puts us right back where we started. Why do they want to go to the moon?"

The room remained silent for an uncomfortable interval. Fletcher tried to restart the discussion.

"Let's try this. Is there anything on the moon they might be interested in?"

Cardenas slumped in his chair and answered, "I can't imagine what. NASA used to justify its manned-moon proposals in terms of surface exploration, setting up telescopes and mounting manned missions to the planets. But it was all nonsense. We can accomplish any of these things much more easily and much less expensively with robots."

"What about the minerals we brought back?" Fletcher probed. "Anything valuable?"

"Not a thing. Same stuff you'd find on earth."

"Even that fusion-energy fuel?" Darrell remarked offhandedly. "I seem to recall a Shuttle operation that had something to do with mining the moon and bringing it back to earth?"

"Oh, you mean helium three?" Cardenas laughed. "Just another gimmick to maintain employment. We actually got funding for some research programs. Generated lots of papers, several conferences. Amazing what you can sell to technically ignorant Congressmen."

"Really?" Anita replied. "Well, Doctor, how about helping a technically ignorant political scientist understand what you're talking about."

"Sorry, Ms. Montgomery," Cardenas said. "Helium three is the perfect fusion-energy fuel. Lots of advantages. Non-polluting, very efficient. But the technology is light years away. Proposing studies to develop mining methods was really preposterous."

"Especially since you said everything you found on the moon is available on earth," Brandt reminded him.

"Oh, but helium three is the big exception," Cardenas responded. "There's virtually none of it on earth. Has to be made in a nuclear reactor which generates radioactive waste. If there was a use for the stuff, getting it from the moon wouldn't be unreasonable."

Tiring of the discussion, Brandt replied, "But there isn't any use for it, right?"

"Certainly not for fusion power. I don't know of any other use."

Brandt summed it up. "So as far as we know, there's no good reason for anyone to go to the moon, and lots of reasons for the Federation not to go. But there's at least some evidence to suggest they're doing it anyway."

"Maybe they figured out how to make fusion energy from

helium," Mashita suggested. Cardenas replied, "I guess anything's possible, but it'd be one hell of a breakthrough. Truth is, I'm not qualified to comment—out of my field. Anybody else got an opinion?"

His challenge evoked no response. Finally, Fletcher said, "Looks like we're not going to figure it out this morning, which is hardly surprising. But we've eliminated some possibilities and supported our conclusion that something very strange is going on.

"First of all, I gather no one here thinks the Russians are really trying to initiate an international moon expedition. Any disagreements?" Fletcher scanned an array of expressionless faces.

"Okay. Second, we seem to have concluded they're engaged in some sort of significant activity at RSC Energia, possibly involving SL-17s. What about that?" Again, no one raised any objections.

"Finally, it's possible they're actually preparing for a moon mission and their motivation has something to do with helium three. Anybody have strong feelings about that one?"

Brandt decided to stick his neck out. "Sir, that's only one of many explanations. For example, what if the Mriyas weren't carrying SL-17s?

"Then there's the helium-three idea. That objective wouldn't require a manned expedition. If they really wanted to mine the moon, they'd be developing robotic systems. Frankly sir, I'd like to see some verification before pushing this any further."

Now Fletcher received nods of approval. "Fair enough, Colonel. Captain Mashita, any idea when we can get some more spy-sat input?"

"Should be any time now, sir. Air Intelligence has already requested close-up monitoring of Kaliningrad."

"Have them look for An 124s, Captain," Cardenas suggested. "They use them to transport SL-17 strap-ons. If they're really overhauling the boosters, they'll need four strap-ons for each core."

"We'll do that, Dr. Cardenas. Thanks for the information."

Fletcher continued with his wrap-up. "Anita, think we'll be able to get any help from your people in the Federation?"

"I can make the request if you wish, but somebody in this building will have to back it up. I don't think anyone at Langley will risk a compromise. Not for a study group."

"And at this point, I wouldn't blame them," Fletcher added as he headed for the door.

Brandt picked up his envelope and turned to leave. He noticed Darrell moving toward Anita.

"Impressive presentation, Ms. Montgomery," Darrell cooed. "You filled in a number of areas I've been struggling with."

She turned, looked at him without smiling and said, "Colonel Wilkins, from what I know of your background, I can't imagine you struggling with anything."

Brandt laughed. "Better watch what you say, Darrell."

He stammered, "I'm afraid the intelligence business is a new world for me." Then, becoming charming again, he added, "Say, do you have any plans for lunch? By now, everyone in the office will have left and I hate to eat alone."

Sounding surprised, Anita replied, "Sorry, Colonel, I have a plane to catch."

"Right away?"

Although obviously uncomfortable with being pressured, she answered, "I've got about three hours before takeoff."

"Need a lift? I'd be glad to drive you."

"I just use the Metro to get over to Reagan."

"Best way at rush hour, but the traffic won't be a problem now. Why don't we eat at a hotel in Crystal City and then I can take you to the airport?"

"Pretty pricey for a working gal."

"Come on, Ms. Montgomery. It's on me."

Anita thought for a moment, looked up at the handsome astronaut, then shrugged. "Okay. Sounds too good to pass up. Will you be joining us, Colonel Strickland?"

Noticing Darrell's pleading expression he replied, "Sorry, I've got a busy afternoon."

Grinning with gratitude, Darrell said, "Us TDY peons park in the boonies. Up to the hike, or should I bring the car around to the front of the building?"

Anita laughed, a lyrical laugh, the loveliest Brandt had ever heard. "No, I'll walk with you."

Brandt followed them through the automatic door into the noisy corridor but lost them in the crowd. He felt the pangs of his chronic loneliness emerge as he headed toward his office and a brown-bag lunch.

* * *

Several rings, spokes and flights of stairs later Anita and Darrell arrived at the south entrance. As they stepped outside in the cool fall air, she stopped to put on her coat. He took advantage of the opportunity to touch her shoulders as he helped her slide the sleeves over her arms, then said, "We'll have to walk about half a mile."

Panting, she replied, "I'll manage, if you'll slow down a little."

Darrell laughed. "Sorry about that. I seem to have succumbed to the Pentagon practice of racing everywhere. Say, what did you mean about *knowing my background*?" The question was a gamble, but he couldn't think of any other.

"Col. Wilkins, I'm sure you're well aware of your worldwide fame."

"Please, it's Darrell."

"Okay. Everyone calls me Nita."

"Nita." He quickly whirled the name around in his mind. "I'm still surprised you'd know anything about an astronaut."

"Are you looking for compliments or something? You're a lot more than just an astronaut. Or is all that stuff about your growing up in Harlem just media hype?"

"Nope, it's all true. Momma really was a crack addict and I never knew my father."

"And you grew up in foster homes?"

"Yup—until I left for the Academy."

"It's incredible you got into the Academy. How did you do it?"

"Teachers. A few of them believed in me. Got on my case. Hounded me about taking school seriously. Pushed me to get good grades. That got me into Bronx Science and out of the neighborhood."

"You moved away?"

"No, but I was gone all day and had to study all night. Just dropped out of sight. The gang bangers forgot about me."

"Sounds pretty lonely."

"It was, but I was determined."

"Incredible!"

"Not really. I always felt I wasn't doing anything special—that lots of other kids could do as well or better."

They had arrived at Darrell's bronze Corvette. As he opened the door, Anita teased, "Does NASA issue these to reinforce the image?"

"Oh, sure! Absolutely! If it was up to me, I'd be driving a Honda."

Buckled in, they moved slowly through the huge parking area, wound their way to the Jefferson Davis Highway and headed south.

"Now you know all about me," Darrell said, trying to restart the conversation. "What about you?"

"Less traumatic upbringing, thank God. Born in Kenya. Father was in the diplomatic corps. Worked at the embassy. Mother coordinated economic-development activities."

"Was she Kenyan?"

"If she had been, I wouldn't have my job. She was from Los Angeles. Went to UCLA. She was African-American, by the way and my father was Eurasian. I'm a mix of everything."

Darrell looked over at her, now understanding her uniqueness. "Did you grow up in Africa?"

"That's where I went through elementary school—a special school for the kids of missionaries. Then I was shipped off to a prep school in Connecticut." She paused, then added with little emotion, "Two years later my parents were killed in a plane crash."

Darrell gasped, "That's terrible! Must have been devastating."

"Certainly frightening at that age. But my father had done a good job with the finances and the people at the school looked after me. During the summers, I visited my grandparents in L.A. It all worked out."

The parking attendant opened Anita's door as they stopped in front of the hotel. Valet parking was a luxury Darrell rarely allowed himself but this was a special occasion.

Lunch went smoothly, filled with inconsequential chatter, gentle probing, lightweight humor. By the time it was over, Darrell was dazzled. Anita seemed intrigued.

Not wanting to spoil an almost perfect interlude, Darrell said very little as they drove to the airport. He carried her suitcase as they walked to the security gate. After he placed it on the conveyer, she thanked him for the lunch and turned to go.

He blurted out, almost desperately, "Say, if you don't mind, I'd like to keep in touch. Really could use your ideas as we put the moon reports together."

Anita seemed disappointed by his bringing up business. "No problem. I'm in the WATS directory, but let me save you the trouble."

She took a card from her purse and handed it to him.

Darrell stumbled, "Uh, I might need to talk with you after hours."

Anita laughed with the same wonderful lilt, searched for her pen and took back the card. "Why didn't you just ask me for my number?"

While Darrell blushed, she jotted down the information and pressed the card into his hand. And then she was gone.

**Alexandria**

"Brandt, you bastard! You don't look a day older than you did in Chad."

"Clean livin' and regular crappin'. That's the secret." He looked across the hot tub at Darrell's muscular body. "Of course, you ain't too shabby yourself, but you work at it." He splashed some water at him.

"Hey, watch it, man! You'll dilute my drink. Damn, it's sure hard livin' it up with you along. When are you going to take up booze?"

"Heck, Darrell, if I started drinking you'd kill yourself trying to keep up."

"Bull! You wouldn't be able to drink any better than you fly."

"My point exactly. I beat you flying, I'd beat you drinking."

"You beat me flying? Brandt, you're so full of it. You're lucky everything's computer controlled in that 22F. If they ever let you touch the stick, you'd buy the God-damned farm. Hey, does that thing wipe your fanny for you too?"

"Careful, buddy. You're gonna make me remember some fun times at N'Djamena."

"You shit! You know damned well that wasn't my fault."

"Never forget watchin' you taxi out—seeing that missile pickle off your wing and head right for the General's C-21."

"Bored a nice neat hole in the vertical stab."

"Good thing it didn't explode!"

"Until it hit the tree on the other side of the runway."

The two men laughed uncontrollably.

"Christ, Darrell, I never did hear such an ass chewing as you got. That man was downright poetic."

"And then he had to apologize!"

"Now those were the days."

Darrell's alcohol level had reached the sentimental range. "Except for the guys who didn't make it back."

Brandt saw tears form in Darrell's eyes, then felt a wave of depression flow over him. "Amen, pardner." He sat silent, looking up at the stars.

Darrell brought him back. "Get you another—what the hell is that stuff?"

"Caffeine-free Diet Coke, the thinking man's drink. And yes, you can."

Darrell lifted himself just far enough out of the water to reach into a cooler and extract a can of soda.

"Man, it's cold when you get out of the tub." He tossed the can to his host.

"Thanks, buddy. And thanks for taking me to dinner."

"Thanks for letting me stay here."

"Least I could do—after dragging you away from Houston."

Sitting there with Darrell, Brandt felt better than he had at any time since coming to the Pentagon. With the background research under way, the study group was finally making progress on its first report and his schedule had eased to the point where he could spend an evening with his former wingman without neglecting a stack of paperwork.

He popped open his Coke. "Hope this business doesn't last too much longer."

"Fletcher said another month."

"Maybe. Depends on what the Russians do. By the way, how did the lunch go?"

Darrell grinned. "With Anita? She's fantastic. Would you believe she grew up in Africa?"

"Think you'll see her again?"

Sounding like a teenager with a new girlfriend, Darrell responded, "Sure hope so. She gave me her number!"

Brandt laughed. "There goes my plan to work your fanny off."

Darrell finished his scotch. "Shit, when did you ever worry about my love life? Only way I'll get any consideration is to find you a woman."

For the second time, Brandt felt the depression well up. He replied in a whisper, "No thanks, pal. Not yet."

Darrell nodded and said, "Sorry to bring it up. But punishing yourself won't bring Nancy back. Don't you every get out?"

"I have dinner with friends every now and then—mostly people you've met. Their wives seem to think I need a home-cooked meal."

"Not much entertainment."

Brandt smiled. "Heck, you know me. As long as there's some open desert left and a horse to ride, I'm happy. I'll never get over being a ranch kid."

Darrell yawned. "Ready to turn in?"

"Sure am, buddy. Need at least four hours of sleep or I can't function the next day."

"Gees Brandt," Darrell said, "now you've got me worried. Sure you're not too old for this business?"

Brandt's aim was off and the empty soda can barely grazed Darrell's arm before it clattered across the patio. He closed the cooler, followed Darrell into the house, then went to his room and changed into pajamas. After brushing his teeth, he turned out the lights, sat on the end of the bed, his face in his hands, and quietly wept in the darkness.

**The Pentagon**

Brandt took the envelope from the Section Chief and signed in the space next to his name at the bottom of the *Eyes Only* list. From the cover sheet, he knew the video memo had originated at the office of the Secretary of Defense, assembled from other intelligence reports specifically for the Special Study Group. After walking to a small booth at the corner of the office complex, he sat on the built-in bench and closed the door. He opened the envelope, extracted an unmarked memory module, and loaded it into the wall-mounted player. Then he touched the start button and watched the screen as the first message appeared.

*Item Number One*
*Classification: TOP SECRET SPOKE RYBAT*

*Operatives observed arrival of two Antonov 225 aircraft at airfield near RSC Energia in Kaliningrad. Unloading operations not observed. Also detected arrival of four An-124 aircraft at same location.*

A map showing the location of the airfield appeared below the text.

"Fits together," Brandt thought.

*Item Number Two*
*Classification: TOP SECRET UMBRA REDWOOD*

*Unconfirmed report of clandestine plan to develop weapons system from Energia launch vehicle. Report claims the program was initiated by the government of the Soviet Union to offset the reduction of their ICBM capability resulting from the implementation of SALT disarmament treaties. Preliminary analysis concludes:*

*1. Weapons system was to be a super-MIRV ICBM with at least 50 warheads.*

*2. Only a very small number of vehicles were to be built, possibly as few as two.*

*3. Program was abandoned at a very early stage. No evidence of upper stage or post-boost-vehicle development.*

*4. Weapons were to be stored at and launched from Plesetsk facility.*

Astounded, Brandt hit the Pause button. "Dang! Looks like those old Commies got cold feet and then didn't know what to do with the Energias. No wonder the Federation didn't want us spotting 'em."

He restarted the player.

*Item Number Three*
*Classification: TOP SECRET MORAY RYBAT*

*Command Cosmonaut Svetlana Zosimova ordered to return from space after only 46 days. Cover story justification was participation in special advisory board. Preliminary analysis concludes Zosimova was brought down for a secret military purpose possibly related to the manned-moon initiative.*

Brandt paused the machine again and thought, "Bet she's gonna organize their crew training."

*Item Number Four*
*Classification: TOP SECRET SPOKE GAMMA RICHTER*

*Message intercepted by German intelligence indicates the Director of the Federation Space Agency, Yevgeni Tsvigun, has assumed direct responsibility for the upgrading program of the Khorek-class spy satellite. Failure to employ current coding procedures indicates message may be a diversion. Absence of Tsvigun from high-level government meetings confirmed. Unverified sighting of Tsvigun at Central Design Bureau of Experimental Machine Building (TsKBEhM) facilities in Kaliningrad.*

Brandt nodded. "Darn right it's a diversion. If he was working on a Khorek, he'd be in Kuibyshev. But he's at RSC Energia—and at the branch that builds one-of-a-kind spacecraft."

*End of information*

He pressed the eject button and withdrew the module, then inserted it into a special erasing slot. The machine filled it with random numbers, conducted a series of reading tests to assure no intelligible information remained and then ejected it.

Brandt left the booth, took the envelope to his shredder and converted it into confetti, then dropped the scraps into a paper bag marked *BURN*. Within the hour, it would be picked up, carried to an incinerator and turned into ash.

***

Brandt touched the icon to activate the video-conference center and said to Darrell, "I want to get a better handle on the fusion-energy aspects. We'll be talking to a physicist from Lawrence Livermore."

The screen at the front of the room followed the setup program as it went through the interconnect process. Then it showed a thin, gray-haired woman wearing small, oval-lensed glasses.

"Are we linked?" a reedy voice asked from the speakers.

"Seeing you just fine," Brandt answered. "Darrell, this is Doctor Paula Lenrick."

Turning toward the video camera, Brandt continued, "Doctor Lenrick, I've got Lieutenant Colonel Wilkins from my staff with me.

As you know from our telephone discussion, we have reason to believe the Socialist Federation is planning to send a crew to the moon. One possible explanation has to do with obtaining helium three for use in fusion powerplants. Is that reasonable?"

Lenrick responded, "You should be talking to someone from Princeton. Their fusion research has concentrated on the type of reactors that might someday use helium three. At Livermore, we study laser fusion."

"Typical scientist," Brandt thought before responding, "We need to communicate over a secure link."

Lenrick tilted her head to the side. "I see. Well, I'll do my best. As for laser fusion, we're just now reaching the energy levels needed to react deuterium, much less helium three."

"What about the Russians?" Darrell asked.

"They used to do world-class work, mostly at the Kurchatov Institute in Moscow. In fact, they invented the approach that's used by almost everyone else for fusion-power research. But because of the economic problems, their work has been second rate for years."

"Could they have stumbled onto some sort of breakthrough?"

"Not likely. Fusion reactions involving helium three are far beyond anything that's being reported. In addition, their primary facility is antiquated—even lacks the shielding needed for sustained fusion."

"What have they done recently? Any new equipment?"

"Nothing I know of. And the few papers they've presented have been quite unsurprising—almost embarrassing. In fact, the facility I referred to has been shut down—supposedly for maintenance, but probably for lack of funds. Oh yes, one other thing. Their two top physicists didn't even show up at the last Fusion Energy Research Conference. First time they've missed it for as long as I can remember."

Intrigued by her last remark, Brandt asked, "What do you think happened?"

"No idea. Maybe they couldn't afford the trip. That would mean things are even worse than I'd imagined."

Darrell had another explanation. "Or perhaps they're working on a major breakthrough related to helium three?"

Lenrick seemed tired of making the same point. "As I said, that's very unlikely. Listen, why don't I just ask them what they're doing? I know them personally."

Pleasantly surprised, Brandt replied, "Great. How would you do that?"

"No problem at all. I just have to get to a Videonet port. Let's see. It's about three in the morning in Moscow. Won't be anyone at Kurchatov, obviously, but I can leave a video-mail message. We should have a response in a few hours. While I'm at it, I can check their personal pages. Give me about five minutes."

The monitor showed her leaving the Livermore facility. Brandt took advantage of the interlude to update Darrell on Russian spaceraft-design capabilities. As he finished, Lenrick reappeared on the screen. She looked rather perplexed.

"I'm not quite sure what to conclude from my Videonet query. I had no trouble connecting with Kurchatov. As expected, neither Vorotnikov nor Usachev was available in the middle of the night. But neither of them had a greeting strip, which is rather odd.

"Anyway, I tried their personal communication blocks next. They both contained identical statements saying they were on extended vacations and would update their information files as soon as they returned.

"This is very unusual. These are world-famous physicists—people who never take vacations. Even stranger, they left no contact information.

"Then I tried the home page for the T-15 tokamak section. This is the facility that's been shut down for maintenance and is where the physicists spend most of their time. The page said the modifications were nearly complete and the T-15 would be returning to operation next week.

"That's really odd. If this piece of equipment has just completed a major modification program, I'd expect the scientists to be there sixteen hours a day. I'd guess they're off working on a different program."

Brandt said, "The obvious question is whether this has anything to do with the moon initiative. Dr. Lenrick, does their absence change your opinion about a fusion-energy breakthrough?"

She removed her glasses and rubbed her eyes. "A breakthrough is always possible—and these two scientists are as good as anyone else in the world."

Brandt nodded. "Something to think about. Thanks for your help." With two touches, he shut down the video system.

"So, where does that leave us?" Darrell asked.

"Almost in the barn, buddy," Brandt replied. "Just need to figure out why they're sending a crew up there."

**The Pentagon**

Although certain the interim summary would raise some eyebrows, Brandt was surprised when he got a memo to report to Fletcher's office the day after it had been distributed.

"Colonel," Fletcher began, sounding uncharacteristically formal, "your report created quite a stir at the JCS. Next time, I'd appreciate it if you'd go over something like this with me before you send it out."

That caught Brandt off guard. "Sorry, sir. I sent the report up through the chain of command as it was explained to me."

"Sure, sure. I know. But your DIA chain is really just a formality for the TDY. Truth is, you're really working for me and we're all working for the Joint Chiefs. If you go through the DIA route, you end up with the Secretary of Defense and all the politics that go with it."

Feeling both confused and chagrinned, Brandt replied, "Understand, sir. Won't happen again."

Fletcher smiled, then continued, "Now it seems to me you've leaped over a lot of missing information to arrive at these conclusions. At our last meeting, you seemed pretty skeptical about the very things you're now proposing."

Brandt replied, "Sir, we eliminated every other possible explanation. All we had left is what's in the report. That they're going after the helium three. That they've made some sort of fusion energy breakthrough and have an urgent need for the stuff. They'll certainly want to exploit the discovery. Sell the powerplant technology, perhaps even the plants themselves and the fuel to power them. If they get to the moon right away, they'd have a big head start. Then they could develop the mining technology, build the spacecraft and dominate the business."

Fletcher put his feet on the desk, leaned way back and looked at the ceiling. "Suppose you're right. What should we do about it?"

"Get started on our own moon program. Develop the technology. Set up a pilot plant."

Fletcher sat up. "That's what I was afraid you'd say."

"Sir? What do you mean?"

"That's not the politically preferred response."

Again feeling confused, Brandt replied, "Don't follow you, sir."

"Use your head. This administration is trying to reduce military and space expenditures. The Special Study Group was established to provide them with justification for ignoring the Federation challenge."

"How could we do that?"

"Easy. You conclude there's no good reason for anyone to go to the moon, just as you did at our meeting. Remember?"

"How could our saying so help? They'd get contradictory recommendations—at least from NASA."

"But you and Wilkins are national heroes. Test pilot engineer who saved the Super Shuttle program and NASA's top military astronaut. If you two say it's a waste of money, that's all they'd need."

Now becoming angry, Brandt blurted out, "Except we don't say that!"

Fetcher sat up, looked into Brandt's eyes and shrugged. "Too bad! Too bad for you, anyway."

Brandt looked at him, expressionless.

"Think about it! You'd be the darlings of the administration. If you play ball, they'll open doors. High-level appointments. Name it."

Brandt was appalled. "Sir, you know we don't care about that. The truth is, the Russians are putting together a manned lunar landing, by themselves, as fast as they possibly can. And getting their hands on an economical supply of helium three is the only reason we've been able to come up with."

Fletcher replied, "I figured you'd say something like that. Trouble is, I don't run the show any more than you do. I'm afraid your conclusions will be ignored."

"Ignored?" Brandt replied. "By now, they've been seen by the whole Defense Department."

"Not really," Fletcher argued. "You're forgetting about the classification level. Only the top people know what you think, and they're all political appointees."

Brandt felt defeated. "What do you want me to do?"

Fletcher's eyes narrowed. He stared at Brandt as if threatened by the question. Then his manner changed abruptly. Smiling, he said in a condescending voice, "Tell you what I'd do, Colonel. I'd play it straight. Analyze the information and do everything possible to determine what's going on. Then report it. But run everything by me before it goes out."

Brandt bit the inside of his cheek to stifle his frustration, then replied, "No problem with that, sir."

Fletcher smiled approvingly. "That's all I ask."

***

Brandt loaded the module, started the machine and watched as the messages were decoded.

*Information Origin: CIA*
*Routing: OSD/JCS/DIA*

*Item Number One*
*Classification: TOP SECRET SPOKE RYBAT*

*Significant increase in engineering activity reported at the Central Design Bureau of Experimental Machine Building (TsKBEhM) in Kaliningrad. More than four-hundred engineers transferred from other RSCs within the past month. No information concerning the nature of the design project. Considering the primary activity at TsKBEhM, projection is a unique space vehicle, possibly connected with the manned-moon initiative.*

Brandt smirked as he thought, "Yeah, no kidding."

*Item Number Two*
*Classification: TOP SECRET MORAY REDCOAT*

*Cosmonaut Svetlana Zosimova observed entering Star City cosmonaut training center near Moscow.*

Nodding as if in agreement, Brandt thought, "Probably there to work on simulator development—maybe even crew selection. They're moving very fast."

*Item Number Three*
*Classification: TOP SECRET SPOKE RUFF*

*Activity observed at the Energia launch complex of the Baikonur Cosmodrome. Effective camouflage prevents positive identification. Best estimate is overhaul of work platforms.*

"Hah!" Brandt felt a bit self righteous. "Not much doubt about the launch vehicle."

*End of information*

Brandt removed the module, placed it in the envelope and carried it to the Army major who had just joined the Special Study Group. It was the last time he would touch an *Eyes Only* package.

## Chapter 2

—

# Go to the Moon

**The White House**

President Alfonso "Alf" Torres, now halfway through his first term, enjoyed meetings of the National Security Council. They remained among the few occasions when he truly experienced the power of his office.

The 52-year-old son of a wealthy New Mexico businessman, he had risen rapidly through the political ranks from the Albuquerque City Council to the Governor's office. At each level, he had demonstrated a remarkable ability to build effective coalitions from representatives of diverse communities, credentials that made him an obvious choice for the Democratic Party's first Hispanic presidential candidate.

The President centered his tastefully patterned silk tie as he watched his Air Force Chief of Staff settle into a wooden armchair and pull herself toward the rectangular table. "Good evening, General Cushman," he said dryly. "We're just getting to the moon question."

Along the table to the President's right sat his personal Chief of Staff, Martin Herrera, the National Security Advisor, Lawrence Chambers, and the new arrival, General Linda Cushman.

Although she had vigorously opposed the President's force cutbacks, Cushman's uniqueness as a female chief of staff, and an extremely supportive press, prevented Torres from implementing the sort of retribution he considered appropriate.

On the opposite side of the table sat the Secretary of Defense, Jeffrey Farrand, the Director of Central Intelligence, Pamela Windham, and NASA Administrator, Dr. Phong Nguyen.

Chambers opened the discussion of the second agenda item.

"Mr. President, although there's reason to doubt the sincerity of the Federation's initiative, some evidence shows they're already preparing for the mission. General Cushman's got some satellite pictures."

The matronly woman, resplendent in a uniform bedecked with an array of ribbons rarely seen on a female chest, moved to the new Integrated Communication and Intelligence Display and entered her identification number. The first page of preloaded information appeared on the large flat-panel screen.

She used recently acquired satellite observations to show the latest activities at Baikonur and RSC Energia, then finished with a description of existing Russian space hardware accompanied by detailed drawings and photographs.

"What would you conclude from this?" Torres asked.

With no expression in her tone or on her face, Cushman replied, "The activities indicate that the Federation is preparing for a major space program. Anything beyond that would be speculation."

Torres turned to the head of NASA. "Dr. Nguyen, can the Federation put a man on the moon?"

Speaking softly, Nguyen replied, "Mr. President, with Energia booster available, they have two major pieces of hardware. They still need upper stage, spacecraft and lander."

"Could you estimate how long it would take them to complete the program?"

"I understand they do not have money."

Chambers intervened in his classic southern drawl, "We don't know that for certain, so let's just figure they've got the bucks."

Sounding a bit frustrated, Nguyen replied, "Even with unlimited funds, they have an enormous program to assemble. Lander alone would take several years to develop and test. And what would they use for second stage? Might finish development in three or four years."

Chambers tapped the point of his pencil on the table a few times. "Just for comparison, tell me how long it would take us to get a crew to the moon."

With a troubled expression, Nguyen said, "Because the space initiative was cancelled, we have no components. We have to develop spaceship and lander, boost into earth orbit with Shuttles, refuel and get crew on board, do moon mission, return to earth orbit, then use Shuttle to come down. Extremely complicated. Maybe four or five years."

"You're saying it would take us a year longer than the Russians?" Torres asked.

"Best estimate I can make at this time."

"Suppose we use the International Space Station?" Herrera suggested.

Shaking his head, Nguyen answered, "Don't see any role. First, it would take significant effort to get it back in operation, even if other Consortium members cooperate. But what would we do with it? We never built facilities needed for launching deep-space missions—fuel storage, crew transfer."

Chambers sighed. "Anyone else have questions?"

Seeing no one respond, the President thanked Nguyen and turned to his CIA Director. "Pamela, have your people figured out why the Russians are interested in the moon?"

"Not yet, Mr. President, but we did locate one of the fusion-energy physicists." She walked to the display console and made a few entries. A picture of a bearded man in a rumpled suit appeared.

"This is the gentlemen as he appeared four years ago at a fusion-energy conference. We've confirmed that he was relocated to Akademgorodok." A map emerged showing the location of the city and its street pattern.

"Akademgorodok?" The Defense Secretary repeated. "That's a closed city, used for military research. Could mean he's been reassigned to weapons development."

"You'd think so, wouldn't you? But we can't relate any of his previous research to weapons. Most likely he's still investigating fusion energy but, for some reason, it's become a secret project."

"Which fits the breakthrough hypothesis."

Windham nodded. "Yes it does. And the proposal that they're going after helium three."

"Marty, would that create a problem for us?" the President asked his Chief of Staff.

"It could, Mr. President, if they were able to control the

market for helium three. As fusion energy replaced fossil fuels, it would cause severe economic disruptions, possibly a major depression throughout the Free World."

Chambers argued, "Don't think so, Marty. Remember, you're talking about the Russians. They'd play hell competing. I mean, if we wanted to, we could set up a moon-mining operation in no time. As far as controlling costs, marketing the product, distribution—we'd put them out of business in a month. For that matter, so would the Europeans—even the Japanese."

"Sounds like we'd have a helium rush on the moon," Herrera said.

The President winced. "Let's get back to reality. As I see it, we have no clear evidence that the work in Russia has anything to do with the moon. It could be for another piece of their space station or a satellite. Who knows? Therefore, I see no justification for a response.

"Now I'm not saying we ignore the situation. We'll support the international program and we'll increase the surveillance by our intelligence agencies. I need reliable information that clears up the question once and for all."

**Arlington, Virginia**

It was a whole new Anita, not at all the polished professional but an excited schoolgirl on her first big date.

"Oh, Darrell, the Ritz-Carlton!"

They entered a small chandelier-lit lobby, turned right and walked down the hallway that led them to the unpretentious sign that signified their arrival at *The Grill.*

"Reservations for Wilkins, please."

The *maître d'* led them across the elegant dining room. Softly illuminated by delicate wall lamps, it embraced its guests with grace and charm.

The dinner was a dreamy haze of sauté fois gras, playful banter, poached lobster with a ginger-lime sauce offset by a dry chardonet, playful banter, a buttery dark-chocolate terrine in *crème anglaise*, playful banter. By coffee, he was convinced she was the most witty, most articulate, most delightful woman alive.

Darrell managed to calculate the appropriate gratuities and sign the charge slip without thinking about the financial damage. An attendant appeared with their coats and, after slipping them on, they departed through the rear door. The exit opened into the *Pentagon City Fashion Centre Mall* where he hoped to work off some of the dinner's calories by strolling along the endless balconied walkways.

Dazzling in its full complement of Christmas decorations, the four-story atrium shimmered as the reflections of tens of thousands of lights glittered from tinselled decorations while surrealistic reindeer soared toward the rafters.

As they sauntered hand in hand, Darrell agonized, hating to risk spoiling the magic of the moment, yearning to prolong the shear ecstasy of pursuing Anita, yet desperate to share his quandary. Her sensitivity ended his dilemma.

“Darrell, why don't you tell me what's on your mind? You got a business problem?"

Surprised, he answered, "Is it that obvious? The truth is, I need your help."

Her elation gone, she responded, "Okay, Darrell. What's up?"

"Nita, we've been cut out of the loop."

"What do you mean?"

"I mean we're not being copied on essential information. Seems like we came to the wrong conclusion about the moon business. We're sure the Russians are going for it."

"Doesn't surprise me, Darrell. What's the problem?"

"It's not what the politicians want. They're looking for justification to ignore the Federation initiative. We're telling them they can't do that."

"And they're keeping you away from information that supports your case?"

"Exactly."

"Where do I come in?"

"You're my only hope for getting the information."

Nita stopped, looked squarely into Darrell's eyes and said firmly, "You're not asking me to violate the espionage laws."

"Of course not Nita. What we need is the same information that's in the classified reports, but from unclassified sources. Even if you can only identify the publications, we can handle the rest."

"Isn't that pushing the rules a bit?"

"I don't think so, Nita. But if you feel uneasy about it, just say no. I'll understand completely."

Her hands thrust deeply into the pockets of her long wool

coat, Anita seemed cold. "This is from Strickland, isn't it?"

"Brandt handed me the problem. I'm trying to solve it."

Anita smirked. "His file makes him sound like a fanatic."

"You checked his file?"

"To get some background for the meeting. You know about his father?"

Surprised by the question, Darrell said, "That he disappeared? Of course. Brandt's convinced the Communists got him."

"Which explains why he hates them."

Darrell shrugged. "Could be."

"There's something strange about him," Anita continued. "His eyes, maybe. Distant, sad."

"Been that way since his wife was killed. Never got over it."

"So he's alone now."

Darrell nodded. "Yup. But he's used to it. Grew up an only child on a remote Montana ranch."

"While his father chased around the country giving right-wing speeches."

"Just the same," Darrell argued, "he's not a nut. Just a very hard-working, absolutely straight-arrow guy. And he needs your help."

Anita sighed. "I'll do what I can, but there's no hope of finding everything you want in open publications."

Greatly relieved, Darrell tried to rekindle the enchantment. "Hey, you never know—and you're an angel for trying."

But the magic was gone. They made their way back to the lobby, retrieved the Corvette and headed for Anita's town house, saying little, absorbed with their own concerns.

**The Pentagon**

Brandt pushed the stack of reports to the side of his desk. His tired eyes could no longer focus on the words, not that it mattered. Despite the painstaking work of his group, aided by Anita's research, he still had no answer. Why were they sending people to the moon?

He looked into the dimly lighted bay beyond his office window as if searching for an explanation. But every study confirmed his conviction that machines could perform every function and do it at much lower cost. What was it that only a crew could accomplish?

He left the office and walked slowly up and down the dark aisles, sometimes pausing and closing his eyes. For what seemed like the thousandth time, he thought through the activities on the moon, each action by each member of the crew. He envisioned the Apollo astronauts, stepping off the lander, playing golf, riding the rover, planting the flag.

He had it!

Brandt felt his emotions run away—anger, elation, smug satisfaction. He slammed his fist into his palm.

"Those dirty bastards! My God, it's hard to believe they'd do it. Proves everything I've ever thought about 'em."

He raced back to his desk and, through blurry eyes, began to write.

**The Pentagon**

"Colonel, where the hell did you get this stuff?" The Admiral had reacted even more strongly to the report than Brandt had anticipated.

"Sir, all the sources are listed at the end. I'd be happy to get you copies, if you wish."

"Don't give me that crap. You know damn well what I mean. How were you able to locate this bizarre collection of information? Bills of lading from Samara, for God's sake!"

"Sir, that's the location of the Progress OKB. We were looking for evidence that a significant number of personnel might have been transferred to Kaliningrad."

"And you found it, didn't you? Or did you know about the transfers first—before you went looking for the shipping data?"

"Sir, we found all the documents in unclassified data banks. We never violated a security procedure."

"Okay, Colonel, relax. I'm not going to push you about it. But you've put your ass in a vise. You don't seem to understand that the JCS can't just ignore what you put out. These reports are official—on the record. If this thing blows up some time in the future and they dig out your analysis—find out you predicted everything—heads will roll."

Brandt stood at attention in front of the Admiral's desk without replying. Fletcher glared at him.

"Yeah, right Colonel. You're no dummy! You know what

you're doing. I just hope you know the price you're going to pay."

No reply.

"Oh, for Christ's sake, sit down. I'm trying to help you."

Brandt sat stiffly, facing the Admiral.

"This is really going to make people mad. Do you honestly think the Russians are going to claim the moon?"

"Sir, everything points that way. You've read all the evidence. What's missing in the report? Is there something I don't know?"

"Maybe there is. Did you ever think of that?"

"Sir, when I came here, you told me I'd have access to everything—absolutely everything."

"Yeah, Colonel, I know. But then you got off on this obsession about the Russians."

"It's no obsession, sir. It's the truth."

Fletcher slapped his desk. "No it isn't! We have no proof that the Federation is planning a unilateral moon expedition. That's the truth!"

"No proof? Sir, what do you want? Engineers are streaming into Kaliningrad. The head of the Space Agency is there along with two Energia boosters and they're rebuilding the launch complex at Baikonur. Their top cosmonaut is in Star City. What do you think they're doing?"

Fletcher sighed. "Colonel, the problem is, you lose either way."

"Sir?"

"If you're wrong, you end up looking like an idiot. And if you're right, you end up pissing off most of the administration and the Joint Staff. You're going to leave here with no friends."

"What am I supposed to do?"

"Truth is, it doesn't matter anymore. You've already burned your bridges. In two weeks, you go back to Edwards, but the reports stay here. I just hope you haven't done too much damage."

"No chance of getting extended so I can see this through?"

"You must be kidding. I'm being pressured to terminate your TDY immediately."

"Because I've tried to do the job you brought me here for?"

"Overdoing the job—and not being sensitive to some political realities."

"Sir, you're absolutely right. I'm not a politician. But if I was, I'd be very, very concerned about the Russians. How's it going to look when they've taken control of the world's energy supply and we're four years away from being able to do anything about it?"

"Frankly, Colonel, I can't be concerned with unlikely contingencies. I have to deal with the here and now—and that means a President who wants to terminate space programs."

"Sir, does this mean you won't be distributing the report?"

"Haven't decided yet. It's hard to justify squelching it. You did a good job—well researched, logical, nicely written. Not even classified. The JCS probably ought to see it. Besides, if I sit on it and it turns out you're right, I could end up on the shit heap instead of you."

Barely able to contain his outrage, Brandt blurted out, "Is there anything else, sir?"

The Admiral looked at him with a mixture of sympathy and disappointment. "Guess not, Colonel. Sorry this didn't work out better. Just try to put it behind you and get back to being a fighter pilot."

**The White House**

"Damn it, Marty! I thought we'd put a stop to this."

Only when very angry did the President's demeanor depart from the refinement and polish portrayed in the caricatures of political cartoonists.

"Mr. President, this wasn't a leak. The material was unclassified. The DOD had no choice but to hand it over."

"I want to know why it wasn't classified and how the God-damned *Post* found out about it. Jeff, who screwed up?"

Sounding defensive, the Defense Secretary replied, "Mr. President, no one did. The report was prepared by Colonel Strickland. He based it entirely upon unclassified material."

"I don't care. These conclusions are clearly sensitive information. General Cushman, what are you doing to hang that son-of-a-bitch?"

The Air Force Chief of Staff looked stunned. "Mr. President, I can order an investigation if you wish, but that certainly wouldn't be my recommendation."

"You haven't even started investigating this?"

"Sir, Colonel Strickland is a national hero who is getting very favorable treatment in the press. He prepared the report as part of his temporary assignment and, as far as I can tell, it was extremely well done. What is there to investigate?"

"How about his loyalty to the country?"

Herrera intervened. "Mr. President, I know you didn't mean that. I'm sure he had nothing to do with the newspapers."

The President glared at him, then smiled, emerging as the professional politician. "Of course, Marty. Of course."

The Defense Secretary joined the rescue operation. "Mr. President, I think we need to discuss our response to the article."

"Absolutely right, Jeff. Absolutely right. That's why I called this meeting. Now, as I see it, our first objective must be to disprove this *claim-the-moon* crap. Could they do it?"

"Not really, Mr. President," Chambers replied. "By treaty, the moon belongs to all nations. But countries are permitted to exploit the moon's resources."

"And the Federation signed the treaty?"

Taken aback, Chambers replied, "No, they didn't. Fact is, neither did we. But it was ratified by enough other countries to become official."

"Wait a minute," the Defense Secretary interrupted. "What other countries? Is this a UN treaty?"

"Of course," Chambers answered.

"Then the Federation isn't bound by it, right?"

Chambers thought for a moment, then said, "Technically, no. Not since their expulsion. But they've been observing all their UN obligations except for paying the fees. After all, they want to be reinstated someday."

"I wonder," Farrand said. "If the stakes were high enough, don't you think they might try claiming some part of the moon?"

"No, Jeff. Not really. Stakhanov's more responsible than that. He may be a Communist in Socialist clothing but he knows that sooner or later he'll have to reestablish trade with the West."

Herrera interjected, "What good would it do anyway? Suppose they claim the whole moon? How would they stop us from going there and setting up our own mining operations? Shoot us?"

Farrand shrugged his shoulders. "Why not? Wouldn't put anything past them."

~~"Then you're convinced Strickland is right?"~~

"How the hell would I know? That's what makes this so damned frustrating. We won't know if they're going to claim the moon until they do it."

Turning to his Director of Central Intelligence, Torres asked, "Pamela, have you learned anything since the last meeting?"

She looked up from her notes. "Only one significant item, Mr. President. An operative inside RSC Energia confirmed that at least some of the activity is related to the development of a manned soft-landing vehicle."

The Defense Secretary stood up, placed his hands on the table and leaned toward Torres. "Mr. President, we have to stop kidding ourselves. There's no doubt whatsoever that the Federation is racing to get to the moon. They've diverted major resources away from their defense buildup and they must be squeezing every ruble to prevent a civil uprising. For some reason, they want to get there very, very badly—and I think Strickland came up with the answer."

Torres stared at him. "What do you propose we do about it?"

"I think we have to get there first. Get Americans on the moon and claim it for all mankind." Farrand sat back down.

Before the President could respond, Chambers argued, "I'm afraid that wouldn't work, Jeff. If you apply the old rules dealing with claiming territory, we can only claim it for ourselves. Of course, we'd be free to negotiate treaties allowing other nations access—even give them parts of the moon. But first we have to claim it and be prepared to defend the claim."

Confused, Torres probed, "But Larry, you said we were prevented from making claims by a UN treaty."

"Not quite, Mr. President. Remember, we didn't sign it. But, unless we wanted to brew up a hurricane of protests, we'd have to make our intentions very clear."

"And what did you mean about defending our claim?"

"Sir, if we simply land on the moon and return, and the Federation also lands but establishes some sort of base, they could say we abandoned our claim. Ultimately, we'd have to be able to prevent anyone else from occupying our territory."

Sounding exasperated, Torres asked, "So we have to set up a moon base?"

"Only before someone else does, sir."

Torres shook his head, then continued. "Marty, how is this playing in the press?"

"Mixed bag, sir. The conservative papers are howling about

our weak space program and the potential for losing the moon. Our papers, and most of the TV stations, are saying that the whole thing is ridiculous and that the report was planted by the DOD and NASA to win support for manned space."

"What about the foreign press? Larry?"

"Attacking us for questioning the Federation initiative. Accusing us of being paranoiac. Demanding apologies."

Torres nodded. "Not surprising. How do we handle it?"

Chambers responded, "Sir, I'd suggest we go slow. With everything out in the open, the Federation will be under a lot of pressure to share information about their program. Sooner or later, we'll know what their plans are."

"You recommend doing nothing?"

"We'll need to put out some statements about the viability of the Super Shuttle program, our commitment to maintaining a leadership role in space, the stuff we're doing for the international effort—that sort of thing."

Herrera interrupted. "Mr. President, with all due respect, I think that approach would be courting disaster. At their current pace, the Russians may be getting ready to launch in two years. That puts us right in the middle of the reelection campaign. If the Russians claim the moon, this administration is toast."

The President wrinkled his brow and narrowed his eyes. "Larry?"

"Doing nothing is a risk, Mr. President. But so is every other response. Suppose we try to beat them—pour eighty billion into a crash program? That would wreck our social welfare efforts and it could trigger double-digit inflation. Not only that, we might not make it. In a crash program, anything can happen."

The President stood and slowly walked around the table. His advisors looked down at their notes until he had completed the circuit. He stopped behind his chair.

"Very well. We'll take a middle path. Marty, I want you to announce an enhanced study effort to be conducted jointly by NASA and the DOD. The objective will be to develop contingency plans for the most rapid, but also the most cost-effective, lunar-landing program. Emphasize our intention to continue with the international effort—that we're simply increasing our support. That should keep the right-wing idiots quiet for a while.

"Jeff, I want this run like a weapons-development program.

Tight control of all information—and I mean tight. NASA will be there primarily to maintain the proper public image.

"Larry, I want to propose a multilateral conference to discuss the implementation of the UN treaties. Let's take the initiative on this—show ourselves as a world leader interested in preserving the rights of all nations. If the Federation actually plans to take the moon, this should build worldwide opposition—maybe change their mind.

"Pamela, I don't have to tell you how important it is for the CIA to stay on this. We have to know what the Russians are doing and why.

"Any questions?"

The Air Force Chief of Staff hadn't received her instructions. "What should I do about Colonel Strickland, Mr. President?"

Torres snorted, "General, you can put the son-of-a-bitch in charge of the whole damned thing for all I care."

**The Pentagon**

Not since he marched to the last discipline board of his cadet career had Brandt felt this way. Not during the war. Never during a test flight. Clammy hands, dry mouth, knotted stomach. Anxiety symptoms. Worse than fear.

Brandt closed the door behind him, crossed the large, blue-carpeted office to a spot in front of an imposing desk and saluted smartly. "Colonel Strickland reporting as ordered, ma'am."

Already standing, Cushman quickly returned the salute, walked around the desk and pointed toward a brown leather chair. "Have a seat."

The General joined him, sitting at the opposite side of a small, round coffee table. Brandt found her more attractive in person than in her pictures. Her official Air Force portraits looked wooden and news photos always showed her as stern, almost hard. But face to face, she looked more human. Her medium-length gray hair fell pleasantly along the sides of her round face and she used makeup effectively. A perfectly tailored uniform flattered her figure, which was more sturdy than stout.

"Colonel Strickland, I guess you know your report created quite a stir. Can't remember when I've seen the President so upset."

Astonished, Brandt blurted out, "The President? Ma'am, let

me assure you, I had nothing whatsoever..."

"I know, Colonel," she interrupted. "Any number of people had access to the document and any one of them could have read it and called the paper. Clever of you to keep it unclassified."

"Ma'am, I had no intention..."

"Yes, yes. I know. But it worked just the same."

Not quite sure how to interpret her remarks, and still a bit nervous, Brandt decided to stick with, "Ma'am?"

"The President asked me how I was going to punish you. I politely reminded him that you're a national hero, very popular with the press. I guess that changed his mind. He decided that we needed a joint NASA/DOD effort to develop contingency plans for a crash lunar expedition. Sarcastically suggested that I put you in charge. So that's what I'm going to do."

It took Brandt an awkward moment to recover. The lady general, although never cracking a smile, seemed to enjoy every second.

"Ma'am, I don't know what to say. How to thank you."

"I should be thanking you, Colonel. You've got more brains—and more guts—than the whole Joint Staff. And, by the way, I agree with your conclusions."

"Ma'am, it's the only scenario that fits the information."

"I know. I read your report. Let's talk about the project. For now, I want you to stay at the Pentagon. I'll establish another study group, directly under AFCVC.

"I want you here for two reasons. First, even though this is a joint effort, I don't want to leave any doubt about who's in charge. You'll certainly need NASA people to help with the technical work, but they won't be making any decisions.

"Second, this must be kept quiet. The country will continue to participate in the international program. That's for the public. Yours will be the real show. But there can't be any leaks. Everything is classified. One more story in the *Post* and your career goes down the toilet. Understood?"

Brandt swallowed, then said, "Absolutely, ma'am!"

"Okay. First thing we need is an estimate of the earliest possible Federation launch date. Then you get to figure out how we'll beat it."

"Ma'am, there's just one problem."

"Yes?"

"I need access to all available information."

Cushman looked puzzled. "That's been taken care of."

"*Eyes Only* reports?"

She chuckled. "You'll get the information before it goes into the reports."

**The White House**

"Twenty-two months?" The President immediately grasped the implication. "That's preposterous! Is this another attempt to commit this administration to an unwarranted crash program? Because if it is, I'm going to have to make some staff changes."

Seemingly unconcerned by the veiled threat, Cushman continued with her presentation. "Mr. President, let me assure you, these estimates are not biased."

"Are they backed up by intelligence? Do we have something from the Federation that identifies a target date?"

"No sir. As Ms. Windham pointed out, the FSA has clamped down hard, obviously in response to the newspaper story."

"So this is just guesswork by that pilot."

"Sir, Colonel Strickland is leading a team of experts—people from all branches of the armed services, NASA, CIA. They're putting in long days—and nights—trying to prepare the best possible estimates."

"Estimates that always seem to support their objectives. Marty, what do you make of this?"

"My concern, Mr. President, is still the prospect of a Russian blockbuster right in the middle of your reelection campaign. I think we have to accept the possibility that Strickland is right and take steps to limit the potential damage."

Torres sighed. "All right, then. What's the next step? General Cushman, have Strickland's geniuses come up with any ideas?"

"They're proceeding as you requested, sir, examining different approaches to completing a lunar landing in the shortest possible time—and at minimum expense, of course."

"I'm almost afraid to ask, but do you have any idea what this will cost?"

"I'm sorry, Mr. President, but the preliminary cost analysis hasn't been completed."

Torres turned to his National Security Advisor. "Larry, care to venture a guess?"

Chambers thought for a while, then said, "Well sir, I figure at least five Shuttle launches. That's three billion right there. Module development would run another five billion, maybe more. Then there's the cost of testing and, of course, the operation itself. Sixty billion?"

Shaking his head in disbelief, the President asked, "Where would we get it?"

"That kind of money?" Herrera responded. "Not much choice, Mr. President. We'd have to go to Congress. Ask for an increase in the deficit. That'd brew up a cyclone."

"Larry, what's the Federation going to do when they find out we're mounting a competitive program?"

"Mr. President," Farrand replied, "they'll probably use it to justify scrapping the international initiative—going it alone. It's possible they might even accuse us of trying to claim the moon for ourselves. Old trick. Accused becomes the accuser. Then, if they beat us there, they might claim the moon and say they're only keeping us from doing it. Could be quite a mess."

"And what are the chances of them beating us?"

The Air Force Chief of Staff responded, "Mr. President, unless we initiate an all-out crash program tonight—not tomorrow, tonight—there is no way we can be on the moon in twenty-two months. Even if we start immediately, it's a slim chance at best. But don't forget, without a lot of luck, they won't make it either."

Smirking, Torres quipped, "That's the first hopeful thing I've heard you say.

"What about our proposed moon-treaty conference? Larry?"

"Not much enthusiasm, Mr. President. Even our closest allies aren't ready to believe there's a problem. We're getting polite expressions of general interest in discussions at some future date."

The President rose and walked around the table. It took three complete circuits before he finally stopped at his place.

"Frankly, I don't like anything I've heard here this evening. This whole business is still based on speculation. We have no idea whether we'll be able to win another space race, even if we pull out all the stops. On top of that, we'll probably end up hurting our relations with other countries. Can it get any worse?

"Now, I'm the first to admit that my technical knowledge is limited, but the missions you're suggesting seem ridiculous. We have trouble orbiting one Shuttle a month. How are we going to accomplish five launches in a short time with only two vehicles?

"All things considered, I should probably stop this thing right here. Gamble that the Russians won't succeed or, if they do, they won't actually try to control access to the moon. But Marty's right. It's too much of a risk. So once again, I have to find a reasonable approach.

"General Cushman, tell Strickland to propose a mission that makes sense. Hell, we got to the moon in the 1960s with a lot less falderal. The plans must be around somewhere. Just build another one.

"And get the damned cost under control. I want to see this thing done for no more than forty billion. I think we can safely divert that much from military programs."

His face reddening, the Defense Secretary shouted, "Mr. President, I don't..."

Torres interrupted, "Jeff, let's not get into another argument over defense needs. Hell, this thing will probably be a dead issue in a month. Chances are we'll never need the money.

"Okay, where was I? I want public announcements integrated into the program plan. Estimate how long we can go before the press figures out that something's afoot. As far as the media is concerned, I want to be ahead every step of the way.

"Then let's decide what we're going to say. My first inclination is to get everything out in the open as soon as we go public. Assuming the international initiative has fallen apart, we can announce our continued participation through a joint mission. We launch our people about the same time they launch theirs. Push the Russians about cooperative scientific objectives. Make plans for the crews to meet on the moon. That may wring some information out of them. Hell, the Federation might even back off, assuming they really wanted the moon in the first place.

"Next, I want an analysis of this fusion energy business. Get our people at the government labs—Los Alamos, wherever—to figure out whether a breakthrough is actually possible. There's a good chance that everything we're proposing is idiotic.

"Finally, I want to stop operating in the dark. Pamela, I can't accept any more excuses. Kick some butts over there at Langley if you have to, but find out what's going on in Russia.

"General Cushman, since you seem to have taken this on,

I'm giving you overall responsibility for the time being.

"All right then. Let's get this settled down. I'm sick of tying up every meeting with the damned moon problem.

"Larry, what the hell are we going to do about Brazil developing nuclear weapons?"

**The Pentagon**

Flight tests had always been challenging, sometimes disappointing, occasionally frightening, but never this frustrating. Brandt had organized the Study Group into five sections dealing with mission design, flight hardware, ground support, systems integration and program planning. Exploiting Darrell's NASA contacts, he'd recruited outstanding managers for each of the sections and then quickly staffed them with equally competent analysts. But the work was floundering.

Study after study produced the same result. Project Constellation and its Crew Exploration Vehicle had been cancelled too early along to produce any useful hardware and the two Super Shuttles couldn't do the job. Not in twenty-two months; not in four years. Brandt worried that this morning's meeting would bring more of the same.

He'd assigned Jerry Hensfeld, a mission-planning specialist from Huntsville's Marshall Space Flight Center, the most critical task: finding a realistic overall approach. Hensfeld, who'd joined NASA after finishing his doctorate at Georgia Tech, was thought of as rather a free spirit, albeit a brilliant one. Since arriving at the Pentagon, he'd developed and rejected one concept after another. Now he sat in Brandt's office, dressed in green slacks and a plaid flannel shirt, going over his latest ideas.

"So the mothballed Shuttle serves as the transfer vehicle and stays behind in lunar orbit," Brandt summarized. "I don't think NASA is going to like giving up a Shuttle."

"Why not?" Hensfeld replied. "We'll never get the money to upgrade it. It'll just fall apart someday and be turned into scrap."

"What about leaving it in lunar orbit? I can see the environmentalists having a fit."

"We'll call it the first lunar space station. Tell them it's for future missions."

Brandt looked at him, not smiling, and replied, "I wasn't joking. What do you think of the Federation's approach?"

Hensfeld's expression brightened. "Brilliant! Absolutely brilliant! Another triumph for Ligachev. He's building the whole vehicle from available components—except for the lander. Not only did he find the Energias, he's rounded up an old Cryogenic Upper Stage and mated it to a Proton Block DM. That's the whole booster. Then there's the spacecraft—built entirely from Soyuz modules."

"But they'll have to be extensively modified," Brandt argued.

"The Orbital Module will certainly be different but the Descent and Service Modules just need to be extended a bit."

"What about the lander? That's a ground-up development."

"Ligachev's smartest move. There is no lander. Just the legs and the engines he's attaching to the Descent Module. Very simple to build."

Brandt turned away and spoke to the wall. "Then they might meet our worst-case forecasts."

"As far as hardware is concerned, I don't see any reason why they can't be on the moon in two years."

Brandt shook his head. "Got anything else?"

Hensfeld taped a new drawing to the wall. "Just one more idea for today."

"This is pretty far out, but I thought it was worth looking at. Since we started this exercise, we've been beating our heads against a wall trying to overcome a non-negotiable, three-year minimum for developing any new component. What stops the show every time is the lander. We've always assumed that, except for the Apollo Lunar Module, we've never developed a manned vertical lander. But we have.

"We forgot about the old McDonnell Douglas DC-X vehicles. It takes a real space hound to remember this, but the company designed a single-stage-to-orbit version called the DC-XB. It was supposed to be the X-33 but they lost the contract.

"Incredibly, it makes a pretty good moon ship." Hensfeld pointed to his drawing. "With this scheme, we develop mechanical interfaces to strap on two SRBs. The vehicle lifts off from the Cape and goes into earth orbit. Next, we do a refueling using the Super Shuttles. That's still a problem because we need so damned much propellant, but it's the only major problem.

"Once the DC-XB is refueled, it can do the rest of the mission all by itself—get to the moon, land, boost back into a return trajectory. Then it can use aerobraking to enter earth orbit. From there, it can be refueled for the descent or left in orbit for future use. Pretty wild, huh?"

Brandt wasn't impressed. "Doesn't sound real to me—using Shuttles as tankers. How much weight are we talking about?"

Hensfeld raised his eyes toward the ceiling. "Hoped you wouldn't ask. For the complete mission, I'm estimating between a hundred-fifty and two-hundred-thousand pounds."

"Christ Jerry, that's three Shuttle missions!"

"Sorry Brandt, it's four. We have to carry the propellant in tanks, provide pumps, valves, conduit. Talking about big-time fluid handling. Takes up a fair percentage of the payload."

Brandt frowned. "I think that kills it. Even if you could get the money, it would take too long. Four months at our maximum launch rate. Cryogenics would boil away."

"Afraid you're right. Unless we can get a faster launch rate, we're stuck with storables and that means at least a quarter-million pounds. Still might get by with four Shuttles. And the transfer operation would be easier."

"Except for the toxicity," Brandt reminded him. "You can bet Transpace wouldn't like it and, since they operate the Shuttles, they may be able to veto the proposal."

Hensfeld seemed surprised. "Could they do that?"

"I'd have to check their contract to be sure."

"Why not use military flight crews?"

"Probably can't. Have to establish a national-security requirement."

"Just the same, Brandt, this is the first approach that actually has a chance to beat the Russians. I think it's worth pursuing."

"Won't argue, Jerry. We'll need more information about the DC-XB design. What's it got inside? Life support? Avionics? Guidance? And how much Boeing will want for building it."

"Considering the financial status of their Aerospace Division, I think they'll be ecstatic at the prospect of a contract—any contract."

"Let's hope so. Oh yeah, before you go, I need an update on the President's directive."

Hensfeld looked disgusted. "For God's sake, Brandt, we can't go on chasing that sort of nonsense. It's taking every bit of

Cynthia Tontini's time and I need her for the serious options."

"Sorry, buddy. He's the Commander in Chief. He's pressing Cushman for answers and she's pressing me."

"But there's no way we're going to build another Apollo. That's really stupid."

"Maybe it is, but we'd better have a well-prepared report to back up that conclusion."

"Brandt, everything we've been doing centers on the use of existing hardware. It's the only way to get close to the deadline. And we have absolutely nothing from Apollo."

"Nothing left in storage somewhere?"

"It's all in museums—or in open-air displays. Maybe we should use that stuff. Clean out the birds nests and the mouse turds. You volunteering to be the command pilot?"

Brandt laughed. "No thanks!"

"Besides, even if we had a perfectly mothballed Saturn, it would be hopelessly out of date."

"Just the same, the President wants to know why we have to spend money on a new design. He thinks it would be cheaper to build another Apollo since we already have the plans."

"Does he have any idea of the manufacturing operations it would take to build those components? The tooling?"

"I'm sure he doesn't."

"Uh huh. Well, I'll try to get some closure on this in the next few days. Maybe Cynthia can throw something together that will bury it."

**The White House**

"And so, Mr. President, I can say with confidence that the Federation is preparing to send a crew to the moon and that the expected landing time is within two years." The Director of Central Intelligence cleared the display and returned to her seat.

The President scowled. "So, where does that leave us? Larry?"

"Sir, it's unlikely we'll ever know for sure whether the Federation plans to claim the moon, but the evidence is pretty overwhelming."

Torres pursed his lips and shook his head from side to side. "All right, all right. Let's figure out what our response should be."

The President's Chief of Staff answered first. "Sir, I believe the concept you presented at our last meeting is right on track—profound, actually."

"Thanks for the flattery, Marty, but what are you talking about?"

"Mr. President, I mean the idea of announcing a joint mission. Having the crews meet on the moon. It's absolutely perfect. Takes the wind right out of the Federation's sails."

"Marty, you know damned well I meant that as a bluff to get the Federation to forget about claiming the moon."

"And that's the beauty of it, Mr. President. If they do back down, there's no reason for us to pursue a space race."

"And if they don't?"

"Then we're no worse off. We just continue with our program, beat them to the moon and claim it ourselves—with the clear understanding that we'll share it with other nations."

"You've just committed this country to a moon-landing program. Do you realize that?"

Herrera nodded and said almost apologetically, "I don't see that we have any choice."

The discussion stopped while Torres evaluated the information. He knew everyone at the table had reached the same conclusion: that Strickland's report was correct and that he had stubbornly refused to believe it. He saw them all looking back into his eyes as he slowly accepted the inevitable. The welfare programs he had struggled so hard to implement would be sacrificed by events beyond his control.

The tension at the table became almost unbearable. Finally, Torres broke it.

"All right, God damn it!" He spat out the words like a curse. "Go to the moon!"

## Chapter 3

---

# A Spacecraft and a Crew

**The Pentagon**

More than two months! Brandt's anxiety increased every day. His NASA engineers seemed unable to find a solution that made sense. But he hadn't been able to come up with anything better. Sitting at the edge of a thinly padded metal chair, he waited for Hensfeld to present his latest ideas.

"Still looking for a way to get the XB into orbit and fill it with propellant," Hensfeld began.

Although he knew the answer, Brandt asked, "Transpace still giving you a hard time?"

Hensfeld nodded. "Seems to get worse instead of better. We've given up on cryogenics. Can't do that many missions in the time we've got. And the Transpace contract is absolutely clear about the quantity of storables they're required to carry."

Brandt smirked. "But for money, they'll do anything, right?"

Hensfeld shook his head. "Not this time. They're really spooked about transferring toxics in orbit. You know what a spill would do."

Brandt shrugged. "The stuff's nasty. So what?"

Ignoring the remark, Hensfeld continued, "What we need is a big, two-stage booster. Something that will push the fully loaded XB to a point where it can complete the mission on its own."

Recalling their last meeting, Brandt asked, "What about your plan to use SRBs?"

"It's not perfect, but we may have to go that way. Look, I think you need to hear something from Cynthia Tontini."

"The one who's doing the Apollo analysis?"

"Yup. I think she's come up with an interesting idea."

"Christ, Jerry, don't tell me you want to build another Saturn."

"Not exactly. She's waiting at her desk. It'll only take a few minutes."

Brandt sighed, "What the heck, go get her."

Hensfeld returned with the young woman following. More than pleasingly plump, Tontini's cherubic face and straight blond hair made her look like a teen-aged choirgirl.

Forcing a half smile, Brandt said, "Jerry tells me you've come up with something."

Tontini nodded. "It's possible the President is correct—at least partially. We need to get the fully loaded DC-XB to a speed and altitude that will allow it to complete the rest of the mission. It turns out that the Saturn S-IC and S-II stages would be just about perfect."

"Problem, Cynthia! We're fresh out of Apollo boosters," Brandt reminded her.

"Yes, Colonel, I know that. But we can make new tanks fairly easily by replacing the metal with composites."

Hardy impressed, Brandt asked, "Aren't you forgetting something?"

"Sir?"

"Engines. What are we going to do for engines?"

"That's certainly a problem for the first stage. I haven't talked to Rocketdyne about building the F-1s."

"Who'd want them, Cynthia? That's ancient technology."

"But known technology. What we need is an existing design that can be quickly duplicated. And we can use Shuttle engines on the second stage."

Brandt sighed. "Cynthia, we need to use existing hardware. Jerry's worked out an approach using the Shuttle's solid-rocket boosters."

Tontini wrinkled her brow. "I've analyzed the configuration. I think it's marginal."

"Jerry?"

"I disagree. But I think we need to pursue both approaches. It's just two different ways of accomplishing the same thing."

"And the Shuttles?"

"Forget 'em."

Brandt shook his head and said, "I'll say this for your idea, Cynthia. It's politically smart. What could be better than having the President think our space ship was his idea?"

Hensfeld laughed. "Hadn't thought about it that way."

After Tontini left, Hensfeld tried to continue his presentation but Brandt interrupted.

"Jerry, you've just told me we've got one plan that's marginal and another that uses ancient, unavailable junk. That doesn't cut it, pardner! And we're running out of time."

Hensfeld retorted, "We've been busting our butts seven days a week analyzing configurations. The constraints make this mission damned near impossible and here you are bitching that we're not moving fast enough."

Brandt yelled, "I'm not setting the deadlines, Jerry. The Russians are. And they've got a spaceship designer named Ligachev who's doing a fine job meeting those deadlines. You're supposed to do even better."

Hensfeld turned his back to Brandt and said, "As you well know, the Russians have a few significant advantages. No one in my group—including me—asked to be here. Just say the word and I'll gladly go back to Huntsville where I belong."

Brandt hissed, "Can't get off that easy, pal. You're supposed to be the best we've got and it's time to prove it. Beating those lousy Russian bastards isn't optional."

"I haven't exactly been sloughing off, Colonel."

"You haven't solved the problem, either."

Brandt marched back to his office, fully aware that his outburst had jeopardized the success of the program. He hurled his foot into the side of his desk, not feeling the pain.

**NASA Headquarters**

More time had only added details to the two flawed concepts but Brandt realized he couldn't wait any longer. He had to present the group's results to the NASA leadership so they could start planning support activities.

And they were all there to listen—directors from Kennedy, Stennis, Lewis, Langley, Johnson and Marshall, and the Associate Administrator for Space Flight, Dr. Warren Baxter. Brandt's moon program had become the hottest property in the space business.

Hensfeld and Tontini went through their presentations. As always, the briefings reflected painstaking attention to detail, anticipating every objection and providing a solution to every obstacle.

The NASA supervisors listened attentively but asked few questions and seemed unimpressed. As Tontini left the podium, Baxter stood up and walked to the front of the room.

"Dr. Hensfeld, Ms. Tontini, my congratulations. These are outstanding proposals. Extremely well presented. But, of course, they're not acceptable. You've assumed NASA will accomplish the infrastructure modifications necessary to support a new vehicle. Either of your configurations will require a completely new mobile launcher.

"Furthermore, you've proposed stacked vehicles that are incompatible with the Shuttle facilities. That would require the complete refitting of a high bay in the Vehicle Assembly Building. Even if we could make the modifications in the time you've mandated, we'd refuse. It would completely disrupt our ability to operate the Super Shuttles.

"Right from the beginning, you were told by NASA how to accomplish this operation. The Administrator laid out a plan based entirely on the use of the Shuttles, a plan you found unacceptable."

"A plan that could not possibly meet the time constraints," Brandt shouted from his seat.

Baxter replied, "The problems you identified can be addressed by adding the necessary fueling and crew-support capabilities to the International Space Station. That's what NASA proposes and it's the only approach NASA will support."

Brandt fell back in his chair. "So that's what this is all about," he thought. "NASA wants to use the moon program to finish the danged Space Station."

"Let me make this absolutely clear," Baxter continued. "The only manned-space operations that are going to be launched from Complex 39 will be aboard Super Shuttles. If it doesn't look like a Shuttle, weigh like a Shuttle, fit like a Shuttle, operate like a Shuttle, then you'd better forget it—or build your own launch facility."

With that, he picked up his briefcase and walked out the door. The other NASA managers followed close behind. Brandt sat back down, put his elbows on the conference table and held his head in his hands. Hensfeld and Tontini sat looking at him, saying nothing.

After several minutes, Hensfeld said, "Well, Colonel, what now?"

"You heard him, Jerry. Shuttles and the Space Station. Might get to the moon five years after the Russians."

"Which means forget the whole thing," Tontini concluded sadly.

"Afraid so," Brandt replied. "They'll use this to discredit the group—say NASA should have been put in charge right from the start."

Hensfeld's eyes suddenly popped wide open. "Hang on, folks. He didn't say we had to use the Shuttles. We just can't change the Shuttle facilities. What was it? Look like a Shuttle, fit like a Shuttle? But it doesn't have to be a Shuttle. Hensfeld slapped the table. "Damn! Should have come up with this two months ago. We've been thinking about the Shuttle as a single vehicle, but it's really two vehicles. The back end is the engine portion of a second stage that goes with the external tank. The front is a reusable spacecraft, totally independent."

Brandt picked up the train of thought. "So we keep the engine section—leave it right where it is—and replace the rest of the orbiter with a lunar spacecraft."

"With the DC-XB!" Tontini exclaimed.

"But with all of its interfaces rearranged to match the ones on the Shuttle," Hensfeld reminded her.

"Damn, why did it take us so long?" Brandt moaned. "The answer was right under our noses. Cynthia, are you on board with this?"

She hesitated, obviously reluctant to abandon her cherished concept, but quickly surrendered to the unimpeachable logic.

"Of course," she sighed. "It's the only way. But there are some old guys at Rocketdyne who are going to be very disappointed."

"And a President named Torres," Brandt observed. "But we can blame it on NASA."

**Alexandria**

Slouching in an armchair, Darrell sipped his scotch, then looked across the living room of Brandt's rented townhouse and asked, "How did your meeting go?"

Brandt lifted his head from the couch. "With Cushman? She was happy about the configuration decision. Wanted me to stay with the moon program. Help coordinate the military aspects."

"You'd be great! Did one hell of a job with the Super Shuttle."

"This is different, Darrell. The military's role will be very small. Most of the decisions will be made by NASA."

"Scary thought!"

"Truth is, they're the only ones left who can run a big space program. The Air Force doesn't operate at the cutting edge anymore."

"Where does that leave you?"

"Couldn't get the top slot. It'd take a star and I doubt if I'd get through the politics."

"Even after all this time?"

"So I've been told."

"Just for saving my ass. Makes me feel like shit."

"Nothing to do with you, Darrell. The trouble is, I won. Got the press behind me when they threatened the court martial. That's what hacked off the brass. Really had nothing to do with jumping out of the bird to help you."

"Just the same, you should have a fair shot at running this."

"Trying to tell you I don't want to."

"So you're back to Edwards?"

"Hope not. Told Cushman I wanted to command the mission."

"Go to the moon?"

"Yup."

Darrell hesitated for a moment, then said, "I want to be there with you."

Brandt grinned. "I'd love it, but I don't think the string pullers will want two Air Force types."

Darrell raised an eyebrow. "Hadn't thought of that. But I'm assigned to NASA. Might make a difference."

"Maybe, maybe not. But the third crew member would have

to come from another service."

"Or be a civilian. Maybe a woman. I'm sure the selections will be very political."

"No doubt about it. But I wouldn't want a woman along."

"Why not? Had some great gals in Chad. Remember Norma?"

"Who could forget? Tore me up when she got killed. But this is different. Too public. They'd want to put a movie star in the spacecraft."

Darrell laughed. "Not many of those in the astronaut corps. In fact, after Kim Standel retires, we won't have any women in the military group. Anyway, the quarters are going to be a bit tight for coed operations. We'll be lucky to have as much room as the Apollo crews."

"You know the astronauts, Darrell. If it was your call, who would you choose?"

"Hard to say. Barely enough military people left to handle the classified launches. And the Transpace crews are a writeoff."

"Check the contract to see if they have to get up in the morning?"

Darrell smirked. "You got it. And there's not enough time to train someone who's never been in space, so the military astronauts are probably it."

"Who does that leave?"

"What about Brian Howe?"

"The Marine?"

"Why not? Damned good pilot. Two master's degrees—electronics and computer science."

"That'd help," Brandt replied, genuinely impressed. "Anybody else?"

"Only Andy Yang."

"Don't know him."

"Navy. Lieutenant commander. Physics major from Stanford . Graduate degree in systems engineering."

"Flying experience?"

"Some combat—close-air support flying off a carrier. Five years in flight test at Pax River."

Brandt laughed. "Guess that ought to do it."

"But that's the end of the line. The other astronauts are all pretty senior—looking to move into a command slot within a year or two."

Brandt sat up and stretched. "Heck, the politicians will probably choose people we never heard of."

**The Pentagon**

It seemed as if years had passed since he first walked the corridors of the Chief of Staff's complex, but it had been only five months. In that brief interlude, the last traces of a late snow had melted and the cherry blossoms had come and gone. And, as others put it, he had matured, understood better his capabilities, and his limitations. Experiencing an odd mixture of relief and nostalgia, Brandt entered what had been the Special Study Group's office space. Now all but empty, it showed few signs of the frantic activity that had taken place.

Certain Brandt's organization would be short-lived, the Pentagon staff had given him a disorganized collection of vacant offices along with whatever furnishings happened to be in them. Given their brutal work schedules, it wasn't surprising the group's members had never really moved in. Now, except for the wastebaskets, still filled with hastily discarded memos and notes, there were no traces of their stay. Most had already left Washington, scattering across the country to catch up on the tasks they'd been forced to postpone.

Brandt had just finished emptying the last few items from his desk drawer when Hensfeld poked his head in.

"Glad I caught you. Didn't want you to get away without saying goodbye—and to thank you for the party last night. Nice of you to foot the bill."

"Least I could do after the effort the group put out. Glad to hear you'll be handling the DC-XB development."

"Turns out to be more of a spacecraft-design program."

Brandt laughed. "Yeah, we were stretching it a bit with some of those presentations. What about Cynthia? Think she'll be able to handle the engine segment?"

"Absolutely!" Hensfeld replied with uncharacteristic enthusiasm. "She's a dynamo. You saw what she can do when she gets committed to an idea."

Brandt flopped into a chair. "Just thinking about the last five months. You know, I never took a day off. Not even one. What a madhouse."

"Sure got a lot accomplished. The program's on a sound footing."

"Up to you NASA guys now."

"And Congress."

Brandt nodded. "Any word on the funding? I've been too busy to keep track."

"Still arguing. Good thing the President made the emergency allocation. It'll keep us going through the preliminary design reviews."

"I hope they stop talking and start acting. Doesn't help having NASA Headquarters telling the subcommittees they should be funding the Space Station."

"Heard you were going to straighten them out."

"My next stop, Jerry. Don't know how much luck I'll have—me against Nguyen."

"Planned your strategy?"

Brandt wrinkled his nose. "Strategy? Nah, I'll just play it straight. Answer their questions as best I can."

"Doing anything else while you're there?"

"Getting interviewed for a possible crew slot."

"Really? Didn't know you were interested."

"You kidding? A chance to walk on the moon? That's every pilot's dream."

"In that case, good luck. Got to run."

"Thanks, Jerry." Brandt ignored his extended hand and gave the surprised Hensfeld a bear hug.

**NASA Headquarters**

The interview left Brandt extremely thirsty. He got off the elevator, walked by the security counter tucked across the end of the narrow lobby and stepped into the adjacent convenience store. After pulling a cup from the dispenser and paying for his can of iced tea, he went outside and sat at one of the round, wrought-iron tables that filled a small courtyard between the NASA Headquarters building and the street.

Barely a minute later, a bronze Corvette pulled into the no-parking zone in front of him. He ran to it and jumped inside.

"Perfect timing, Darrell. I just finished."

Darrell laughed. "This is my sixth time around the block."

"Sorry about that."

"So, how did it go?" Darrell pulled into the heavy afternoon traffic rushing down E Street.

"Asked lots of questions, but most had obvious answers. I got the impression they'd already made up their minds."

"Favorably?"

"Probably shouldn't say so, but it seemed pretty positive."

"Can't imagine who else they'd choose. You virtually created the program, you have astronaut experience, a graduate degree in engineering . Is anybody else even close?"

Laughing, Brandt replied, "Just you. Did they give you any trouble?"

"Pretty much the same deal. But they pushed me about taking a program management position instead."

Brandt raised his eyebrows. "Probably be a good move—career wise."

Darrell shook his head. "Not for me. Mostly public relations and putting out fires. Drive me crazy."

"Know what you mean."

Darrell asked, "How did it go with the congressmen?"

"They were surprisingly friendly, especially when you consider all the pork-barrel projects we're threatening."

"Think you convinced them?"

"If they have any sense at all. Only an idiot would believe that expanding the Space Station is the fastest way to get to the moon."

"In a way, it surprises me they'd still consider us for the crew. Doesn't NASA resent our spoiling their party?"

"I'm sure some people do—like Baxter. But they're in charge now—responsible for success or failure. And even the President doesn't want to fail. From now on, they'll do what's best for the program."

"And that puts us inside the XB."

"Hope so."

After turning on South Capitol, Darrell asked, "You still have to get to Houston right away?"

Brandt nodded. "Yeah. Coordination meeting with the Center Director first thing tomorrow."

"Sorry to make you fly back alone."

"No problem. I'll enjoy the solo time. When are you picking up Anita?"

"Soon as I drop you at Andrews. Haven't seen her in almost a month."

Brandt shrugged. "Going to the moon is tough on romance."

**East Potomac Park**

Darrell spotted Anita's metallic-green Corolla and slid his Corvette into the adjacent parking space. She was standing under the trees looking out over the Potomac, her back to him. Because it was the middle of a workday, only a few others were privileged to take advantage of the perfect May weather and the beautiful setting. As he approached, she said, "The trees around the Tidal Basic are still beautiful, even without the blossoms." Darrell reached for her hand. She grasped his mechanically, without showing any emotion. In her billowy white dress, tied at the waist with a red sash, Anita was the personification of springtime. Darrell looked at her lovingly, suddenly realizing how much he'd missed her.

"What happened at the interview?" she asked, sounding only mildly interested.

"Went well. I think I've got a good shot."

"And that puts you inside the spaceship?"

"With Brandt, I hope."

The soft breeze off the Potomac rustled the leaves. Darrell wanted to hold her, kiss her, pick up where they'd left off. But she seemed different, acting more like a good friend than the love of his life.

"And now you're off to Houston?"

"Tomorrow night. Where would you like to go for dinner?"

Anita looked at him, expressionless. "Think I'll pass."

The rejection hit Darrell like a blow to the stomach. "Really? What's the problem?"

"No problem. I have other things to do."

"Nita, look at me. I love you. I need to be with you."

She laughed sarcastically. "You need to be with me? Where have you been for the past two months?"

Feeling frustrated, Darrell snapped, "You know where I've been—and what I've been doing."

In a soft voice, she replied, "Yes, Darrell, I do know—and I understand."

"Then what's the problem?"

"How can I keep this from sounding petty?" she asked

herself. Then, after a pause, she answered slowly, "I just don't see any future for us. The moon program is going to completely consume you—for years. There'll be nothing left."

Darrell struggled to find an answer, desperately wanting to tell her she was wrong, that they'd have plenty of time together. But he knew it would be a lie. In a voice filled with agony, knowing he might be killing one dream so another could survive, he said, "Guess I've got a tiger by the tail, Nita. And I don't want to let go."

Her eyes filling with tears, knowing what the answer would be, she asked, "It means that much to you?"

He held her by the shoulders and said, "Yes it does. This is once in a lifetime. A chance for me to be everything I've ever dreamed of. Push myself to the limit."

She cocked her head and replied coyly, "How could a silly little romance compete with that?"

Releasing her, he answered, "Please don't say that, Nita. You know I love you—want to spend the rest of my life with you."

"After you get back from the moon."

In desperation, Darrell gambled. "Nita, come to Houston with me. Marry me!"

She started to protest, but he stopped her.

"Let me finish. I know it wouldn't be great. My schedule is going to be horrible. But we'd still be together. Having you there, even for a few hours a day, would be wonderful for me."

She looked away. "You know better than that, Darrell. I'd just be in the way. One more thing for you to worry about. But even if that wasn't true, you're asking too much."

"I know Nita," he said softly. "You've got your own career—and a life here."

"It's not just that. I wouldn't have a role in Houston. What do you expect me to do? Sit around the house all day and half the night waiting for you to stagger home and fall into bed?" Angry with herself, she added, "Damn it! Why can't I say what I feel without it sounding like a soap opera?"

She wiped her eyes, then stood erect with her head high. "All right Darrell. Brutal honesty. Even if I had no career to worry about, even if I had nothing to keep me here, even if I could find work in Houston, I wouldn't marry you."

He turned away from her and looked across the river.

"Look at me, Darrell." She waited until he faced her. "If you were going to Houston to manage the program, even if it meant not seeing you for months at a time, I'd be willing to work things out. But you're getting ready to fly to the moon, the grand finale of this insane program. I know you won't admit it, probably not even to yourself, but there's a good chance you won't get back. I cannot—will not—let you make me a thirty-eight-year-old widow. That's why you're asking too much."

His mouth opened to disagree, but he uttered nothing. It was pointless to argue. All the safety procedures, all the redundancies, all the statistical computations couldn't disprove her perception. He could only look at her longingly and say, "I understand."

They started back towards Anita's car but, after walking only a short distance, Darrell stopped, grasped her shoulders again and said, "Nita, I can't accept not having you in my life. Last fall, two wonderful things happened to me. There's no way I can choose between them. Giving you up would be devastating, something I'd never get over. But giving up a chance to walk on the moon would be just as bad. Either way, I'd spend the rest of my life regretting, second guessing. Please help me. Meet me half way."

With tears once again filling her eyes, she asked, "What do you want me to do?"

"Just ride out the moon program. We're talking two years."

"Will I ever see you?"

Darrell smiled, feeling an enormous sense of relief. "Nita, we'll make it happen. I'll squeeze out days, hours if that's all I can get. But we'll be together. Here, in Houston, maybe places in between. We'll be together."

She hugged him as tightly as she could, pressing her head to his chest. "Darrell, I do love you. You know that. But I'll worry every day until it's over. Damn! Why did you have to be an astronaut?"

"If I hadn't been, we'd never have met."

"I know. But it's still not fair. I want all of you, not the piece left over after NASA is finished."

He gently brushed a tear from her cheek. "Well, right now you've got all of me. Can I talk you into dinner?"

She kissed him gently and ran her fingers through his hair. "Vietnamese take-out. My place."

**Clear Lake City**

Brandt had every reason to feel ecstatic. NASA had given him everything he'd asked for—Darrell as pilot, Brian as mission specialist, Andy as backup. And they'd selected him to be the commander. But now he had to get the crew trained, a task with its own set of challenges.

Brian was preparing for an upcoming Shuttle operation and Andy had just returned from a visit with his grandparents in Taipei. Although the crew selections had been announced two weeks earlier, this evening marked Brandt's first opportunity to get the crew assembled in the same place at the same time.

Having decided an informal get together would be the best way to ease into what would surely become close-knit relationships, he'd asked Darrell to host a dinner at his house near the Johnson Space Center. After eating on the screened patio, the group strolled inside, heading toward Darrell's cozy living room.

Arriving first, Marine Major Brian Howe flopped himself into an overstuffed chair opposite the stone fireplace. He had the barrel-chested build only rigorous exercise can maintain. His short, blond crew cut and wide-set blue eyes exaggerated the squareness of his face which, when he wasn't smiling, could appear quite intimidating. But now he looked completely relaxed as he called to Darrell, "Damn, that was one fine dinner!"

His host joined him, taking the adjacent seat. "Hell Brian, there's no trick to steaks. Just find some good meat, wait until the charcoal's hot and don't overcook."

"Don't give me that", Brian argued. "What'd you put on 'em that tasted so good?"

"The sauce? It's the shitake mushrooms."

Brian shook his head in wonder. "Where do you latch on to stuff like that? Must be part of staying single."

Darell shrugged. "Being a bachelor ain't all bad."

Lieutenant Commander Andrew Yang entered and stretched out on the leather couch. Only five-foot-nine, his chunky build made him look even shorter. Once a college wrestler, he retained the thick neck and burly arms of his former athletic career. Short black hair, a thin mustache and an almost perpetual impish grin helped make him appear younger than his 35 years.

Sitting on the hearth sipping a Seven Up, Brandt redirected the conversation. "Darrell, how are we supposed to organize this training program if NASA keeps dragging you back to Washington every week?"

Darrell smiled, remembering certain advantages to his Sunday T-38 flights. "Really hasn't slowed things down, at least not so far. But you've got a point. Now that everyone's available, we should probably go full bore."

That caught Andy's attention. "Doing what? We don't even have a mission profile."

"That's coming Andy," Brandt said. "Meanwhile we can get started studying the moon. We've got scientists coming out of the woodwork with ideas about what we should do while we're up there."

"I suppose they'll want to stuff the spacecraft full of experiments."

"Won't be room for many. Just the same, I'm sure we'll have some science tasks."

Brian asked, "Do we know where we're going to land?"

"Not yet, and that's another problem. The President wants us to meet up with the Russians but they won't discuss their program plans."

"So screw 'em. Let's do what's good for us."

Brandt laughed. "Brian, I'm hardly the one to give advice, but you might need to polish your political sensitivity. Anyway, we'll manage to stay busy. Of course, you'll be part time until you get back from the Shuttle mission."

"Emphasis on the part," Brian reminded him.

Brandt nodded and continued, "But what's really going to keep us hopping is having only one backup crew member instead of a complete second crew. That means we're all backups. Everyone will have to be proficient in every task—including mission control. Whoever stays behind plays CapCom."

"But the operation itself doesn't seem that difficult," Andy commented. "From what you've told me, it sounds as if almost everything's automated. Until we land on the moon, we might just as well be asleep."

"Only if everything works perfectly, Andy. Still need to monitor the operation and handle system failures."

Brian said, "Brandt, I'm not too happy with what you told us about the simulator deliveries. If we can't get them before next February, we'll only have seven or eight months to train together."

Brandt looked around as if expecting to find someone listening in, then said quietly, "Maybe not that much," then asked, "Darrell, you made any progress with getting us a mock-up?"

"In the works. My guess is the program office will go for it. If we have a problem, it'll be with Boeing. They still claim their virtual-reality simulator will do the job."

Not impressed, Brandt grumbled, "Computer baloney!"

Andy asked, "What about the neutral-buoyancy tank? When are we going to get the mock-ups for that?"

"The mockups aren't the problem," Brandt replied. "It's Transpace."

Darrell's brow wrinkled. "Now what?"

"They don't want to give up the tank at Marshall. Say they need it for Shuttle training, including our recovery mission."

"But that's just grabbing the damned spacecraft and stickin' it in the cargo bay," Brian said. "They can practice it tomorrow."

"I agree, but they want timely training. Claim they'll need the tank for the two months preceding the launch."

Darrell snapped, "Come on, Brandt! We're going to the moon. We'll be using the tank right up to the day we leave for Kennedy."

"They say we should use the tank here at Johnson."

This time Andy reacted. "At Johnson? It's not deep enough. If anything, they should be using it."

"Another little difficulty. They say they'll need it most of the time for their other missions." Brandt leaned back into the soft couch. "But, as they say in the business, we're working the problem."

Then his expression turned bright. "Good news about the landing trainer. Everyone at the program office supported it. Didn't have any trouble convincing them a manual landing was a real possibility."

"Somebody trying to tell us something?" Darrell quipped.

"Are you saying we'll have a full-scale thrusting simulator?" Brian asked.

Brandt replied, "Too much to hope for. Probably have to get by with whatever the software wizards come up with."

"So what've we got?" Darrell said. "Classroom stuff about the moon, experiments, systems engineering, simulator training for the entire mission, buoyancy-tank work for the time on the moon.

What else?"

Brandt thought through his still incomplete knowledge of the training requirements. "That's about it, except for emergency procedures."

Deciding they'd done enough work for the evening, Brandt asked, "Anybody need another beer?"

The others waved him off.

Brian broke the brief revere. "Hey Brandt, what'd you mean when you said the training time wouldn't be even eight months?"

Brandt drew the group together by speaking in a very soft voice. "You'll get this at tomorrow's briefing. We finally got an intelligence report out of the Federation. Looks like they're planning to launch some time during October or November next year."

His announcement brought whistles of amazement.

"Apparently, they want to have it coincide with an anniversary of the Russian Revolution. That moves up our best estimate by several months."

"Any possibility of this killing the program?" Brian asked.

"I think they'll let everything continue until the critical design reviews. Then they'll go through a plan-to-completion exercise to see if we can make it."

"So we're good until the end of October," Darrell added.

"Wait a minute," Andy interrupted. "If the CDRs are scheduled for October, all the manufacturing, testing and integration has to be finished in one year. That's impossible, Brandt."

"That's why fabrication will have to start prior to CDR—at least for the major components. It's a gamble and I'm sure there'll be some rework, but it's the only way to beat the long-lead-time items."

Darrell rolled his eyes. "Guys, I've seen some wild ones, but this is the wildest."

Brandt said, "I'm still hoping the Federation runs into trouble. That may be our only real chance."

Brian worked himself out of the chair. "And on that happy note, I will take my leave. Eight-o'clock briefing and a long day after."

As the group drifted toward the front door, Brandt patted Darrell on the back, saying, "Buddy, you keep cookin' like that and we're all gonna move in."

## Chapter 4

---

# Zvezdny Gorodok

**Star City**

Even on the bright spring day, Zvezdny Gorodok's zero-gravity-simulator building felt chilly. Svetlana left her jacket on as she and Tsvigun rode the elevator to the upper-level-access platform.

Leaning over the railing that rimmed the top of the empty tank, she watched four technicians carefully guide the descent-module mock-up into place on top of the lander. Although more than nine-meters high, the spacecraft replica reached barely three-fourths of the way to her feet and, even with its legs fully extended, occupied only a fraction of the tank's soccer-field-sized floor.

"Looks insignificant," she said.

Peering into the tank, Tsvigun replied, "Looks are deceiving, Svetlana. That little spacecraft will do more for the Federation than all the Mir modules combined."

She walked along the rail to get a better view of the operation. "We were pleased to receive the mock-ups early. It gives the technicians more time to lay out the hose paths and plan the interior training activities."

Tsvigun replied, "Interior? I thought you were going to use the tank to practice unloading the experiment."

"The experiment!" she huffed. "Yevgeni, sometimes I think that's all you're interested in—as if our primary mission was scientific research. My main concern is getting the crew down to the surface and back into the spacecraft. Not easy when you're wearing an EVA suit designed for weightlessness.

Tsvigun nodded and asked, "How closely will you be able to duplicate the conditions?"

"Everything will be weighted to simulate lunar gravity, but the water provides a resistance we won't have on the moon."

"I'm still concerned about the experiment, mostly about handling that much weight."

"We'll need plenty of practice, working as a closely coordinated team."

Tsvigun smiled. "With you in charge, that won't be a problem."

Until this point, Svetlana had managed to control her anger, but his remark unleashed it. She glared at him and retorted, "Won't be a problem? Let me assure you Yevgeni, it will be a very challenging problem. At this point, I have serious reservations about the success of the mission."

Sounding as if he'd been expecting her outburst, Tsvigun replied, "Bakatin?"

"You're damned right, Bakatin! Is the President insane, or does he want us to fail?"

"I can assure you he is quite sane and thoroughly committed to the program's success," Tsvigun replied coldly.

"Then why did he force that lazy, arrogant playboy down my throat? I need Alexander Dubinin—as a primary crew member, not a backup. Instead of a seasoned cosmonaut, you give me an irresponsible drunk!"

"Svetlana, he can't be that bad," Tsvigun replied firmly. "He's been on the national aerobatics team four times, he has a fine technical education and he's extremely enthusiastic about the mission. Begged for the assignment!"

"And he's Kirilenko's son-in-law. Tell me that had nothing to do with the President's decision."

"Obviously, that's why he was selected. Kirilenko adores him and Stakhanov needs the Chairman's support. I'd hoped to avoid bringing this up, but Bakatin has some complaints of his own."

"Complaints? What does he have to complain about?"

"He claims he's being treated like an outcast—that you and Vadim ridicule him. Says you're angry about not getting your way and are taking it out on him."

Trying to sound objective, Svetlana replied, "I'll admit to some degree of disappointment, even some prejudging of his character. However, my criticism of his performance reflects his continual failure to make a serious effort. His attitude has been utterly uncooperative, even antagonistic. There is no way to justify his lack of professionalism."

Tsvigun listened, but replied firmly, "Nevertheless, you're stuck with Bakatin and your job is to make the best of it."

"Easier said than done. The concept of discipline seems to be missing from his upbringing and he has no respect for the experience of the cosmonauts."

"Meaning you?"

"Meaning me, Vadim, Alex, the technical staff at Gugarin and everyone else I've seen him interact with."

"I've heard he's a little headstrong."

"Headstrong? That's not the point. He refuses to follow instructions—doesn't even show up for training sessions. I tell you plainly, Yevgeni Grigoryevich, he puts the program and the rest of the crew in serious peril."

Tsvigun crossed his arms and looked straight into her eyes, his expression communicating both annoyance and concern. "Svetlana, there's no way I can have Bakatin removed, but I'll speak to Belyaev and he'll speak to Stakhanov who'll speak to Kirilenko. This may take some time, but I'm sure the situation will improve. No one expects you to make a cosmonaut out of him. Just get him to the point where he can do the job and then get him back in one piece. Understood?"

Svetlana knew when she'd been given an order, even when it came from a friend. "Of course, Yevgeni. You know I'll do everything possible."

"For which you'll have my sincere appreciation—and my continuing admiration."

Taking a deep breath, Svetlana quickly changed the subject. "Suppose we look in on Vadim and Alex."

They made their way to the front door where Tsvigun's chauffeur met them for the short drive to the new lunar-surface-training facility.

"You used the old gymnasium," Tsvigun observed.

"That's right, Yevgeni. You have a good memory."

As they entered, Svetlana waited while Tsvigun surveyed the gridwork of beams suspended twenty feet above, his eyes following the mesh of cables as they snaked their way down to a gimbal-mounted harness. She shouted as he approached the edge of the walkway, "Careful, Yevgeni. You're about to step on the moon."

He stopped just short of a large dirt-covered area and watched as Alex, who was wearing a complete EVA suit, hopped clumsily across the rock-strewn surface, his weight partially supported by the overhead cables. Computer-controlled motors spun rapidly back and forth as they accommodated the motion of the harness, striving to support precisely eighty-four percent of his weight. Vadim ran next to him, communicating through a headset.

Suddenly, the edge of Alex's boot came down on a large rock. His leg flew outward and he tumbled, landing on his side. Vadim tried to break his fall, but managed only to prevent him from becoming entangled in the cables. Almost immediately, Alex jumped to his feet, ready to try again.

"You see the problem, Yevgeni? The boots are made for extra-vehicular activity. They're almost useless for walking on a rough surface."

Tsvigun asked, "What have you done to correct the problem?"

"We're trying different sole designs. But, as you see, there's still a problem. We may need to stiffen the boot—provide more ankle support."

"Has Vadim experienced the same difficulties?"

"Essentially the same. He had problems getting traction on the dust."

"What about Bakatin?"

"What about him? He hasn't shown up for any of the training sessions."

"Where is he now?"

Trying not to sound angry, Svetlana stated, "In Moscow. At a meeting."

Tsvigun nodded.

"Of the Black Sea Yacht Club. It seems he's the Vice President and the meeting concerns rules that affect his sailboat."

Tsvigun's brow furrowed and his lower lip jutted forward. He blurted out, "That's clearly unacceptable, Svetlana. I'll try to speak with the Chairman myself."

Relieved that she'd finally gotten through to him, Svetlana felt it best not to reply. Instead, she returned to the moon-walking discussion.

"There may be a problem with the harness. It reduces our weight correctly, but it also changes our inertia. I'm considering using the Ilyushin to simulate lunar gravity."

"The IL-76? I thought we'd scrapped it."

Svetlana laughed. "Probably should have, but it's still around. We use it to give cosmonaut trainees some experience with zero gravity."

Svetlana spotted Alex removing his helmet and called, "Vadim, Alex! Come here for a minute."

Ippolitov arrived first, wearing his cooling-and-ventilation undergarment. Only 178 centimeters tall, he was forced to look sharply upward as he greeted Tsvigun. "Nice to see you, sir. Want to try some moon walking?"

Shaking his head emphatically, the Director answered, "Not after watching Cosmonaut Dubinin lose his balance. How are you, Vadim?"

"Very well, sir, although our training schedule is demanding and it follows almost four months in orbit. I'm worried my daughter will forget me."

"Now you joke with me, Vadim Eduardovich. No one could ever forget you. How many others can boast of feats like yours? Just saving the Sukhoi prototype puts you in a class by yourself and now you do solo space-station missions!"

Vadim laughed self consciously. "Unfortunately, none of that impresses my family."

With the help of a technician, Alex freed himself from the harness and walked slowly toward the group, waddling awkwardly in the space suit.

Svetlana made the introductions. "Director Tsvigun, I don't believe you've met Alexander Grigoryevich Dubinin, our backup crew member. Alex, this is Yevgeni Tsvigun, the Director of the Federation's Space Agency."

Alex, who had already removed the bulky spacesuit gloves, shook Tsvigun's hand. With his boyish face protruding from the oversized helmet ring and his blond hair thoroughly matted by the head covering, his appearance was hardly impressive but he made up for it with an ideal salutation. "It's a great honor to meet the man responsible for developing the Mir modules."

Tsvigun beamed and joked, "Vadim tells me Svetlana is overworking you."

"We work hard, but I enjoy it. I must be prepared to take over any role on the mission."

"That's true," Tsvigun replied thoughtfully. "In a way, you have the most difficult training requirements."

"Not at all, sir. Each of us must be able to accomplish all the assignments and Colonel Zosimova has the added burden of supervision."

"Then I mustn't keep you from your work."

Tsvigun started back toward his car, then asked, "May I take you somewhere?"

"Yes, thank you," Svetlana answered. "My office is in the simulator building."

Once seated in the back of the limousine, she decided to take advantage of Tsvigun's undivided attention.

"I'm worried about Ligachev's projected arrival date for the simulator. If we get it in November, we'll have only ten months until we leave for Kazakhstan. That's not much time."

Sounding annoyed, Tsvigun countered, "It seems adequate to me Svetlana, and I'm certain Ligachev will exert every effort to meet the schedule."

"Of course, Yevgeni. I didn't mean to imply otherwise. Actually, I was wondering if our departure to Baikonur couldn't be delayed. We're scheduled to spend almost a month there. Don't you think we could accomplish more here at the Training Center?"

Tsvigun looked at her as if trying to determine whether she knew more than she should. "In part because of the problems we've encountered in Kazakhstan, I want the crew monitoring the entire assembly and checkout sequence. And there may be some additional training involving equipment at Baikonur." Then he added, "Of course, you could always fly back to Zvezdny Gorodok if you felt you needed more simulator work."

Although she couldn't pinpoint the reason, Svetlana had the feeling the offer wasn't genuine—that Tsvigun was keeping something from her.

The driver pulled up in front of long, two-story building. "Here you are, Svetlana. I appreciate your frank appraisal of the training program. I'm sure, between us, we can resolve the problems."

"Of course, Yevgeni. Thank you for your help. I know you

have many other matters to deal with."

"All too true. In fact, I wanted to give you a brief review of the hardware development. I met with Ligachev two days ago and he told me all the segments of the first SL-17 have been tested successfully at Baikonur."

"Excellent news!"

"Yes it is. The core and all the strap-ons are back in the assembly building being integrated into a complete booster. While that's being done, the segments from the second SL-17 will be tested."

"And then they'll test the complete Energia?"

"They'll have to finish upgrading the test stand, but as soon as it's ready they'll do a run at full-thrust."

"When is it scheduled? I might be able to go."

"They're saying mid-September, but I wouldn't fly there unless you can spare at least a week. We're having problems with the workers—delays, defects. They don't have the same dedication we're used to here in Kaliningrad."

"Sounds as if they need better supervision."

"That's a problem. The Director, Nazarbayev, is a bit lazy. More concerned with appearances than with productivity."

"Nazarbayev? Is he a Moslem?"

"I presume so. He's a Kazakh."

"Could he be a rebel sympathizer?"

Tsvigun shook his head. "No. His loyalty is unquestioned."

"What about the people who've been hired to handle the SL-17 work? How many are Kazakhs? Have they been properly screened?"

"You're raising important questions, Svetlana, questions I'll certainly discuss with Belyaev at our next meeting."

Svetlana remembered she'd interrupted him. "You were talking about the hardware development."

"Ah yes. Ligachev tells me things are going well. He conducted a design review earlier this month and the results were quite satisfactory. Good enough, in fact, to begin the manufacturing phase. Of course, he'd already started to build the spacecraft and the upper-stage boosters were available. The only problem seems to be the software, as usual." Tsvigun checked his watch. "Well, I believe that gets you up to date."

Svetlana wasn't quite finished. "Before you go, I wanted to ask about the lander. I know Ligachev has complete confidence in the automatic system, but I still feel we should have some type of manual backup."

Tsvigun sighed, then said, "Svetlana, look around. The grass is green, the trees have leaves, flowers are blooming. It's a beautiful June day in Moscow. Try to think of something besides the moon program, at least for a moment."

It had been many years since she'd heard him speak of anything but his work, many years since he'd manifested even a hint of sensitivity. In fact, she'd come to assume he had no interest other than his career.

She studied his face while she replied, "The moon program has become my life, Yevgeni. There isn't time for anything else."

Sounding upset, he contended, "Yes there is, Svetlana. There must be! If you exclude everything else, you'll lose your perspective—become less effective, not more, and alienate those who depend upon your leadership."

For the second time in an hour, he'd made a comment hinting of criticism, something Svetlana had never before experienced, something quite unlike him. She thought he looked tired, but something more than physical exhaustion. His cheeks were sunken and his eyes were ringed with darkness. "You're trying to tell me something, Yevgeni, something that has nothing to do with getting to the moon."

He smiled and said quietly, "Perhaps I am, Svetlana. Perhaps I am. Tell me, do you see your daughter?"

Disturbed by his probing into a painful part of her life, she answered defensively, "As much as I wish to, which is very seldom."

"When was the last time?"

"A year—maybe longer. I don't remember. We have little in common."

"I think you need her—or someone. Someone in your life. You're still young and attractive."

She looked at him again, at this person who had once been the center of her world. He was thinner, less animated, strangely more at peace. At once, she knew.

"You're ill, Yevgeni. Seriously ill."

Her perception startled him. "It shows so much? I must be more careful."

"I'm right then! What is it?"

"I have cancer, Svetlana. It's being treated."

Svetlana could see the sadness in his eyes, the look of resignation. "But the future is not bright."

"This will be my last program, Svetlana, but I'll live to see it completed."

"And Yekaterina? Does she know?"

"That I'm ill? Of course she knows. How ill? She doesn't want to know. But oddly, we grow closer now, trying to make up for years of isolation, each living our own lives. We spend more time at the dacha."

Svetlana reached over and took both of his hands in hers. "I am so saddened by this news, Yevgeni, but grateful we may still share some time together."

Unable to continue, she got out, turned, and waved as the car pulled away. As she walked slowly toward the building, she felt a sickening cramp in her stomach, a slight dizziness, a wrenching sadness. She could scarcely believe what she was experiencing. She was still able to care, still able to feel. For the first time in many years, she felt hers eyes fill, felt a sob well up within.

## Chapter 5

# Test at Baikonur

**Baikonur Cosmodrome**

She had driven by the Energia Assembly Building many times, even marveled at pictures of its cavernous interior, but nothing had prepared her. Standing on the seventh-floor balcony of the nine-story office structure that served as the facility's room divider, Svetlana looked out across the enormous bay, awed by the sight that sprawled before her eyes.

A complete Energia booster, suspended horizontally from the cables of a gigantic bridge crane, slowly descended toward the cradle of its transporter-erector. Flanked by its four strap-ons, the SL-17's core stretched half the length of a soccer field.

But the transporter, a steel behemoth as crude as the rocket was sleek, dwarfed the booster. Its perimeter, a frame of massive girders, was laced with dozens of walkways which, in comparison, looked like so much filigree. The monster rested on an array of 160 railroad-car wheels that bore its tremendous weight as it moved the few kilometers to the launch pad. Incredibly, it fit comfortably into a quarter of the building. Although dozens of technicians labored below her, the vastness swallowed up the sounds of their activities leaving only a low, unintelligible murmur.

"Quite a sight, isn't it?" Tsvigun asked in a way that required no answer. "Makes you realize how much the Soviet Union could accomplish when it focused its resources."

"Breathtaking, Yevgeni! A monument to Russian technology."

"And once again a functioning facility." The observation came from a well-groomed gentleman standing at Svetlana's left whose meticulously contoured beard and carefully trimmed black hair framed a pudgy, smiling face. His perfectly tailored light-gray suit, hand-stitched dress shirt and tastefully decorated cravat looked absurdly out of place in the industrial setting, but Askar Nazarbayev's success had been built on impressions.

Ligachev had moved further down the balcony toward the bay doors so he could examine the engine sections of the booster. Svetlana spotted him studying the vehicle through a pair of binoculars. He abruptly returned to the group and addressed the Cosmodrome's director.

"Mr. Nazarbayev, I've detected several discrepancies—safety wires not properly terminated, vents not properly secured. I insist upon performing a thorough inspection prior to the test and I'll need your best technicians to resolve any problems."

Most solicitously, the director assured him, "It will be just as you wish, Doctor Ligachev, although I'm certain my staff will be most happy to reinspect the booster, if you so desire."

Stiffly, Ligachev responded, "It's apparent your staff isn't capable of assuring the satisfactory completion of the preparations."

Although, on paper, Nazarbayev worked for Ligachev, distance and culture precluded close supervision from Moscow. Consequently, he enjoyed a remarkable degree of independence. He answered, "Then it will be necessary to postpone the firing. Would an extra day be sufficient?"

Ligachev glowered. Nazarbayev was toying with him, forcing him to pay for his insults with an embarrassing delay.

"There will be no need to reschedule the test," Ligachev said. "I'll complete my inspection today—starting immediately. Have your technicians meet me at the center of the bay doors. We'll start with the transporter-erector."

It was Nazarbayev's turn to squirm. "But Doctor Ligachev, it's only four hours until the start of the party honoring you and our other distinguished guests."

"Which means I'll arrive a little late. Please make my apologies to your managers. Let me see, was it this way to the elevator?"

Scrambling to catch up, Nazarbayev called to him, "Please, allow me to accompany you." Then he looked back and stammered, "Director Tsvigun, Colonel Zosimova, please excuse me for a few minutes."

As their host followed Ligachev down the balcony toward the end of the structure, Tsvigun and Svetlana watched the workers ease the Energia into position and mate it to the erecting mechanism.

"What was that all about?" Svetlana asked.

Tsvigun broke into quiet laughter. "A mix of things, Svetlana. Vladimir's concerned about the test, but whether he actually found problems looking through those binoculars..." Tsvigun raised his eyebrows. "He'll feel better after he's gone over the vehicle, although he can't possibly inspect everything.

"But there are other agendas. He's never been comfortable being responsible for Baikonur. Simply no way he can control it from Moscow. But he can't bring himself to turn the work over to Nazarbayev. Doesn't trust his management capabilities. This, of course, rankles Nazarbayev. So Ligachev's trying to show he's on top of things and Nazarbayev's trying to show he's in charge."

"Could be a problem."

"On the contrary. If they get into a contest with Ligachev trying to find discrepancies and Nazarbayev trying to eliminate them, the program will benefit."

"As long as someone checks up on the workers."

"Exactly."

Tsvigun started to laugh again.

"What's funny, Yevgeni?"

"The party tonight. Ligachev hates them. Can't stand getting drunk when he has work to do. I wouldn't be surprised if he set up the whole thing just to get out of going."

"You think he won't come?"

"He'll get there eventually—probably very late. Then he'll eat his dinner while the rest of us toast each other. Tomorrow morning he'll be back here by six, fresh as a daisy while everyone else nurses a hangover."

They heard the elevator door open and walked toward it, joining the director as he emerged. Somewhat winded, Nazarbayev apologized, "I'm terribly sorry to have left you here." A few deep breaths later he added, "It's time for our tour of the launch pad. If you'll follow me."

Emerging at the floor level next to the transporter, they made their way toward the end of the building. As she walked by, Svetlana looked up at the erecting mechanism, a complex triangle of massive beams and hydraulic actuators. She estimated the main pivot to be at least fifteen meters above the floor.

After boarding a dented van, the group bounced along the kilometers of poorly maintained road that separated the Energia Assembly Building from the launch pad. Looking out across the flat, barren terrain, Svetlana noticed several launch towers in the distance, jutting upward into the cloudless sky. Closer to the road, she saw the usual splatter of small buildings, pipes, tanks and machinery that seemed to accumulate around every launch facility.

Through the windshield, she spotted the four towers that marked their destination. Three were flimsy-looking structures used to hold the hundreds of high-intensity lights needed for night operations. The other was the permanent service tower, a column twenty-five stories high that looked like the framework of an unfinished skyscraper.

As they neared the pad, its decrepit condition became increasingly evident. Many of the small support buildings had been abandoned, their doors now hanging limply from loosened hinges. The pavement had broken into fragments and debris littered the area—rusty barrels, dirty sections of ducting, coils of wire, old electric motors, all covered with the tan dust of the desert.

Walking from the van toward an empty concrete building that occupied a corner of the pad, Svetlana felt uneasy about being launched from the dilapidated structure. She followed Nazarbayev up some stairs and down a corridor to the base of the tower. As they emerged, he resumed his apologies.

"It's a mess, I know. Still much work to do, but we're concentrating on the items needed for the tests." He pointed upward. "The swing arms were in very poor condition, but they're working perfectly now. All the fueling umbilicals have been overhauled and tested."

"What about the rest of the propellant equipment?" Tsvigun asked.

"We're still having problems with a liquid-hydrogen valve. Sometimes it doesn't respond to a command."

The trio snaked across the pad, detouring around standpipes

and protrusions, toward the set of concrete pillars that would support the rocket.

"We will deactivate the release mechanism for the test," Nazarbayev explained. "Otherwise, the hold-down system will function just as it will for the launch."

Tsvigun grumbled to Svetlana, "Release mechanism? Look at this! I wouldn't be surprised if the booster rips itself loose."

Having heard more than she cared to, Svetlana decided to explore the rest of the area. She worked her way to the edge of the pad and peered down into the flame trench 30 meters below. The exhaust from the rocket engines would roar downward through an opening in the pad's surface, be deflected by a sloped concrete wall, then blast along the trench into the open area beyond. Once again, she found herself overwhelmed by the enormity of the structure.

As she turned around, she saw her companions heading back toward the van. She walked quickly to rejoin them for the drive to Leninsk.

**Leninsk**

The next morning, the van returned to pick them up in front of the newly renovated visitors' lodge. Blinking in the sunlight, Svetlana stepped through the open door and found Tsvigun already inside, sitting behind the driver.

"Good morning, Yevgeni. You look better than I expected."

"I have a confession to make, Svetlana. My vodka was really water. I'm not permitted to drink alcohol."

After leaving the lodge, the van crossed the railroad tracks at the edge of the small town of Tyuratam, drove under the highway leading southeast to Tashkent and stopped at the entrance to the Cosmodrome. A few words from the driver got the gate opened and soon they were motoring past an array of tracking antennas toward a cluster of office buildings. In the planters around their entrances, a few hearty shrubs had managed to survive years of neglect, providing a tiny green contrast to the tan sea that stretched in every direction.

The van continued past the Energia Assembly Building and turned right toward the launch pad, passing the transporter-erector on the way. They stopped alongside the service tower where they found Ligachev and Nazarbayev watching the locomotives ease the transporter into position.

"Now comes the most impressive part," Nazarbayev said.

As they watched, the massive girders of the erector began to move, rotating and unfolding, gradually raising the huge booster. Finally, the machine shuddered and stopped. The Energia stood upright.

Prolonging the suspense, Nazarbayev said, "It still must be lowered onto the stanchions."

Almost imperceptibly, the booster crept down toward the supports. Only soft clunking sounds announced the completion of its journey as heavy steel clamps engaged fittings on the rocket.

Nazarbayev heaved a sigh of relief. "It's in position. We can start the fueling operation."

"First get the transporter out of the way," Ligachev ordered.

Taken aback, Nazarbayev replied, "The procedure calls for leaving it in place until the fueling's complete. It provides additional support as the weight increases."

Ligachev said firmly, "I'm aware of the procedure but, given the state of your propellant-handling equipment, I don't want to risk the transporter."

Nazarbayev looked over at Tsvigun for support. Tsvigun stared back, expressionless.

Sounding dejected, Nazarbayev said, "Very well. As you wish," and walked to the side of the transporter. After a brief conversation with some technicians who were standing outside the control room, a discussion punctuated with numerous shrugs and pointings, he returned to the group. Within a few minutes, the semi-circular clamps that girdled the rocket began to open and soon after the erector lowered to its horizontal position. The Energia stood alone, a giant spire resting on its concrete supports.

"I want it at least a half mile from the pad," Ligachev ordered.

Nazarbayev nodded, then addressed the group. "I'm sorry but, for safety reasons, you must leave during the fueling. You can watch from the blockhouse, if you wish, but you'll see more in the engineering building on the closed-circuit television."

Svetlana and the others accepted his offer and made their way back to the vans for the short drive. Soon they were crowded around a monitor in the second-floor meeting room of a drab, dirty building.

By the time they'd all found chairs, the swing arms had pivoted from the service tower toward the Energia. Nazarbayev became noticeably agitated as they neared the rocket, but relaxed once they made contact.

"I believe the propellant connections are complete," he said. "They'll put the kerosene into the strap-ons first. You won't see anything."

As he predicted, the picture remained unchanged even as eighty-six tons of fuel flowed into each of the four rockets that surrounded the core.

After a few minutes of inactivity, Tsvigun inquired, "How long is this going to take?"

"The kerosene transfer? About four hours." Nazarbayev provided the information with neither comment nor sentiment.

"Four hours?" Tsvigun said. "I'm not going to sit here looking at the same picture for the rest of the day."

"I didn't think you'd want to, Director Tsvigun. And the cryogenics will be transferred tonight so, once again, there won't be much to see. For that reason, I've arranged a little entertainment in Leninsk—some local entertainment. I'm sure you'll enjoy it."

"That means Kazakh folk dancers," Tsvigun whispered to Svetlana.

She whispered back, "Think positively, Yevgeni. If it's a Moslem party, you won't have to worry about the drinking."

**Baikonur Cosmodrome**

Contrary to their host's wishes, all three of the Moscow visitors had elected to watch the test from the blockhouse. As the van drove toward the launch pad, Nazarbayev reminded them of the comforts they were foregoing.

"I wish you'd let me take you back to the engineering building where we have suitable accommodations," he argued. "There'll be refreshments and the television monitors are larger. You'll actually see more. Inside the blockhouse, you'll have to stand in the back."

"I'd rather watch the measurements as they're being recorded," Ligachev replied. "And I want to be able to speak directly to the test engineers."

Svetlana had no logical reason for her decision. She just wanted to be closer to the action.

Nazarbayev emitted a whimper of frustration, then pleaded, "We're well within the danger zone here so please get inside the blockhouse as quickly as possible."

The van stopped alongside an ugly concrete monolith. Ignoring Nazarbayev's request, Ligachev walked around it to get a better view of the booster, now standing fully fueled about a half mile away. Svetlana decided to tag along.

Using his binoculars, Ligachev slowly scanned the vehicle. "Surprising how much frost forms, even here in the desert. But not much else to see." He led the way back to the entrance and through the heavy steel door to join the others standing along the rear wall of the one-room building.

Svetlana was appalled by the crudeness. She noticed the smell before anything else, the acrid stench of rancid tobacco tar that overpowered even the fresh smoke emanating from three ashtrays. She remarked to Tsvigun, "Doesn't look very sophisticated, does it?"

Overhearing her, Nazarbayev responded defensively, "Elegance is of no value here. We need simplicity, ruggedness, and minimum cost."

Svetlana knew the explanation had some validity. The industrial-grade equipment, although rather dated, had been designed to withstand harsh treatment and was tough enough to survive the vibration and shock of an explosion.

Instrument racks covered the front wall, most of them partially filled with aging electronic equipment that converted signals from hundreds of sensors into a usable form. Adjacent to the equipment, an assortment of dials, lights and charts displayed the values of the measurements. Other panels held banks of switches that controlled the operation of the test stand. Many empty spaces, some revealing the ends of unused wires, attested to the time that had elapsed since the building's last upgrading.

Within and between the stacks of instruments, eight small television monitors displayed different sections of the booster from a variety of perspectives. Another two monitors provided longer-range views of the entire launch pad.

Seated at plastic-topped tables facing the instruments, three test engineers scanned the displays. At the center table, the lead engineer studied the screens of two computer terminals. He turned to Ligachev, who was standing behind him.

"We're having problems with a liquid-hydrogen valve. Makes it difficult to keep topping off the core."

"The test must be conducted with full tanks," Ligachev said. "That's the maximum-stress condition and I want to verify the dynamic response."

The engineer replied, "Very well, sir. I'll try again." A

moment later, he turned to Ligachev and said, "Worked that time, sir. Resuming the firing sequence."

Addressing a string of questions to his crew, the lead engineer worked through his checklist. The technicians verified each item—instrumentation sets, propellant transfers, umbilical disconnects. Finally the swing arms were retracted and the engineer called out, "Prepare for ignition."

The technician put his fingers on two large red buttons located near the right side of the center panel as the engineer commanded, "Start ignition sequence."

The technician pushed both buttons, sending a command to the control computer to begin the complex process that would start the Energia's eight engines.

Within seconds, the strap-on engines reached their rated thrust. The power of the four huge rockets penetrated even the thick, reinforced-concrete walls of the blockhouse. Everything shook, amplifying the low-frequency rumble that made direct communication difficult.

Ligachev studied the television screen that showed the rocket exhausts, apparently satisfied the test was proceeding normally.

As the strap-on engines progressed through their starting sequence, a similar series of events began in the four core engines. On the television monitor, however, their ignition was less evident because the reacting hydrogen and oxygen produced no flame. Nevertheless, Ligachev seemed able to recognize the subtle changes in the pattern of the exhaust. He bellowed, "Core-engine ignition!"

With the entire booster producing its maximum thrust, the vibration caused the unoccupied tables to creep across the floor and the television images to blur. Propellants poured into the engines at the rate of twelve metric tons per second.

With intense concentration, Ligachev scrutinized the exhaust pattern. Suddenly he called out, "Fire! There's a leak in one of the core hydrogen lines. Stop the test!"

The lead engineer leaped up and jumped to the monitor.

"Here! You can see it—flame shooting out."

Only Ligachev's practiced eye would have detected it. Barely visible, the light-yellow streak extended outward from the center of the booster. After watching for less than a second, the engineer shouted, "Yes! You're right!" Then he turned and ordered, "Emergency shutdown! Now!"

The technician already had his fingers on the switches.

Above each of the engines, propellant valves rotated toward their closed positions. The strap-ons stopped first, their fiery exhausts shrinking and then disappearing. The core engines followed immediately but, as the ball valve on one of the liquid-hydrogen lines rotated, it jammed. The increasing force pushed the valve stem against its bearings. The valve body fractured.

A red light flashed and warnings blinked on the computer monitors. "We're still flowing LH2," the technician screamed.

Liquid hydrogen gushed from the line, pushed out by the pressure in its tank. As it flowed over the hot engine, it vaporized and a large bubble seemed to envelop the booster. For a few seconds, nothing happened as the light gas floated upward, but as the bubble increased in size, some hydrogen drifted into one of the strap-on thrust chambers. Covered with a thin film of carbon deposited by the burning kerosene, the walls of the combustion region remained extremely hot. At one point, a tiny spot of carbon glowed red. It was all the hydrogen needed.

The flame spread instantly, engulfing the entire booster. Staring at the monitors in disbelief, no one in the blockhouse made a sound.

Once the initial volume of gas had burned, the flame died down, but the respite was short lived. At the rocket's base, the propellant continued to pour out, vaporize and ignite, creating an inferno. It took only a few more seconds for the flames to melt through the thin walls of the tanks, releasing kerosene and liquid oxygen from the strap-ons.

Although it had been built to withstand the explosion, the blockhouse lurched violently as the shock wave hit. Inside, all the lights went out, the computer monitors bounced off the table and the technician was thrown into the control panel. The engineers flew off their chairs, bruising themselves as they fell. Knocked off their feet, the four visitors collided with each other as they crashed to the floor.

When the emergency lights came on, Svetlana saw Ligachev kneeling on the floor, his face in his hands. He was shaking uncontrollably.

Tsvigun crawled over and put his arm around him.

Somewhat unsteadily, Svetlana stood up, immediately feeling the soreness in the shoulder she'd landed on. As she looked around, she saw two of the engineers slowly getting to their feet. The third writhed in pain under one of the tables. On the floor near the equipment racks, she spotted the technician lying in a pool of blood. Nazarbayev, apparently unhurt, stood over him, staring down.

"Is he breathing?" Svetlana yelled, shocking Nazarbayev into action. He leaned over, looked at the man and answered, "I don't think so."

Shoving an overturned table out of the way, she went to see for herself. The technician bled from several head wounds, made by the switches and knobs he'd collided with. Blood trickled from his ears. She knelt over him, took his wrist and felt a rapid pulse.

"He's alive, but seriously injured. We have to get him to a hospital. Give me your jacket."

Surrendering the garment reluctantly, Nazarbayev watched in dismay as she folded it and then gently placed it under the technician's bleeding head. Then she grabbed a chair, laid it on its back and used it to elevate his feet.

Kicking pieces of the shattered computer monitors out of her way, she crossed the room and lifted the table off the third engineer. He looked up and moaned, "Arm! Can't move it. I think it's broken."

Seeing his blood-stained shirt sleeve, Svetlana concluded she could easily do more harm than good.

"You may have a compound fracture," she said. "Best not to move. But your technician's been badly injured. We've got to get him out of here."

The engineer yelled at her, "You can't go outside! You must wait!"

Svetlana looked at him, not comprehending.

"Debris! It'll rain down. The explosion blew pieces of the rocket miles high."

Indeed, as she listened, Svetlana thought she could hear things hitting the roof of the blockhouse.

"What can we do? Do you have any medical supplies?"

"First-aid kit on the far wall, next to the equipment racks. Don't think there's much in it. Try the telephone."

She called to the other engineers, "Call for help. A doctor."

The closest engineer groped under a table, found the phone and contacted the security office. He told her, "They're already on their way. They'll have us out of here in a few minutes."

Moments later, a dull pounding on the door marked their arrival. The engineer picked his way across the room and released the latches.

As she stepped outside, Svetlana felt as if she'd emerged from a bomb shelter. The air was thick with dust and smoke and small pieces of metal fell around her. She looked toward the launch pad but could see very little. With the others right behind her, she climbed into the back of a truck. Ligachev sat across from her, his head bowed, his eyes closed. No one spoke all the way to Leninsk.

**Leninsk**

A storm system had moved toward Baikonur and the day started overcast and cool. The three visitors trudged from the lobby of the lodge to a waiting van.

Ligachev looked a mess. Wearing the same suit he had on in the blockhouse, still dusty and wrinkled, he had neither bathed nor shaved. Entering first, he chose a seat in the back of the van.

Tsvigun looked little better. Haggard, his eyes bloodshot, he showed ample evidence of a sleepless night. He dragged himself to a seat next to his disheveled program manager.

As the van moved off, Svetlana said angrily, "I hope you've been up all night working on a recovery plan because if you haven't, you've wasted precious time."

"For God's sake," Tsvigun exploded, "we may not have a program anymore and we'll almost certainly be removed from our positions."

"That's absurd, Yevgeni. We lost one booster. You're overreacting."

Ligachev explained, "It's a matter of credibility, Svetlana. I made a serious error, an error of judgment. Tried to rush things, skipped important crosschecks."

"And we lost much more than the Energia," Tsvigun added. "The test stand must have been badly damaged. I doubt if it can be repaired in time for a launch next year."

"We don't know that, at least not yet. And there's always the other stand."

Ligachev shook his head sadly. "Which is a long way from being operational."

"Any idea what went wrong?"

"That's the most humiliating thing, Svetlana. Some part of the liquid-hydrogen line must have failed. Completely ruptured. I can't find any explanation for it."

"Didn't you inspect the core engines yesterday?"

"Of course I did, but not the ducts upstream from the shutoff valve. They're behind the flame shield. But, as I said, I don't understand how a duct could fail."

"The point is, it did," Tsvigun interrupted, "and that calls into question the reliability of the entire booster. We're faced with a complete requalification—at least another year's work. If we find major design flaws, it could be two years."

"Here we are," Svetlana announced. "I guess we'll know the status of the stand soon enough."

As the van slowed to a stop, Nazarbayev ran up to meet them. Svetlana opened the door and stepped out with the others right behind her. The Baikonur Director had a bandage on his right cheek but otherwise looked as immaculate as ever.

"Director Nazarbayev, you were injured," Tsvigun said sympathetically.

"A scratch, Director Tsvigun, nothing more."

Svetlana asked, "How are the rest of the people?"

Nazarabayev's head dropped. "I'm sorry to report the technician died from his injuries. However, the engineers are fine. The lead engineer's arm was not broken—only badly cut."

"He died," Ligachev said. "Terrible. My fault."

Nazarbayev looked at him, obviously surprised by the expression of concern, then said, "I presume you wish to see the launch pad," and led them through the concrete building to the pad's surface.

Svetlana's first impression was that little had changed. Other than a sprinkling of small metal pieces, the area didn't look much worse than it had two days before. The service tower seemed unharmed and the concrete pillars appeared intact.

"Is there a damage assessment?" Ligachev asked.

Nazarbayev replied, "As expected, the tower is structurally sound and the test stand itself is essentially undamaged. However, most of the wiring that had just been installed was destroyed, as was all of the propellant-transfer ducting."

"What about the swing arms?" Tsvigun asked.

"Structurally sound, but the bearings must be replaced. All greases and oils were burned. The umbilical fittings melted, as would be expected."

As they spoke, the lead engineer ran across the pad toward

Ligachev yelling, “The valve! We found the valve! You must come and examine it."

"Which valve?” Ligachev asked. “What do you mean?"

"Liquid-hydrogen valve. It failed. Broke in half."

"That's impossible,” Ligachev responded. “It must have been damaged in the explosion. Where did you find it?"

Catching his breath, the engineer answered, "Down in the flame trench—but I think it broke before the explosion. Probably caused it. Can you handle the stairs down to the bottom?"

He replied, "Down? Yes, that's probably okay," then turned to follow the engineer, walking toward the edge of the pad. Only some twisted stubs remained of the handrail that had been used to support someone descending down the ladder to a landing about a meter below.

Realizing Ligachev might have difficulty, Svetlana ran to join him. She held his arms as he stepped back over the edge and groped with his foot for the first ladder rung. Two rungs down, he was able to grasp the sides of the ladder and work his way to the landing, the first of twelve connecting as many flights of stairs as they zigzagged down the nine-story-high face of the test stand. Ligachev handled the rest of the descent as well as could be expected for a man of his age.

Next, Svetlana assisted the engineer, taking care not to squeeze his injured arm, and followed him down to the bottom.

The explosion had blown the core's propulsion section several hundred feet down the flame trench. The trio walked along the sloping side until it met the floor of the channel, then continued another forty meters, passing larger and larger pieces of debris. Finally, the engineer stopped at the mangled remains of a large rocket engine.

"Here it is," he said, "one of the core engines. And there's the LH2 line."

Ligachev knelt down to examine the duct. Emerging from a jumble of twisted tubing, the foot-wide conduit turned ninety degrees to point away from the engine's nozzle toward the fuel tank. Just beyond the engine, a large globe valve lay ripped almost in two.

He probed the valve body with his fingers mumbling, "Can't be. Can't be." He remained there almost motionless, staring at the valve, seeming to need time to convince himself of the reality of his perception. Finally, he turned to the engineer.

"Will your telephone work here?"

"I can reach the control center."

"Tell them to get here at once. Bring whatever equipment is needed to lift this engine and what's left of the connecting components—without doing any more damage. Tell them I'm ordering it and I want maximum security."

The engineer walked about a hundred meters to one side of the trench, completed the call and returned.

"They're bringing a truck with a fork lift. It may take an hour to get here. If you'd like, I can probably get a helicopter to take you back to the engineering building—or Leninsk, if you'd prefer."

"The engine won't leave my sight until it gets to Kaliningrad. Where's the rest of the core propulsion system?"

The engineer pointed further down the trench.

Ligachev examined the wreckage of the other engines, then returned. "Can you reach Director Nazarbayev with that?" He pointed to the telephone.

"On the test stand?" the engineer answered. "No problem, sir."

After being handed the phone, Ligachev asked to speak with Tsvigun.

"Yevgeni? I found the answer—the cause of the accident. I must get an engine back to Kaliningrad immediately. Can we commandeer the Antonov that's sitting at the airport?"

"Yes, damn it, it's that important. And make sure the plane is secure. Have my things packed, will you? I'm staying with the engine to supervise the loading."

He handed the phone back to its owner and returned to the engine. "Svetlana," he asked, "would you mind flying back to Moscow with me in an Antonov?"

"A cargo plane? Of course not, Doctor Ligachev, but why?"

"I need to stay with the engine and I think it would be a good idea if you and Yevgeni went along."

**Leninsk**

Moving the remnants of the engine had gone more easily than Svetlana would have guessed. Following Ligachev's directions, the Baikonur workers had constructed a cushioned pallet to support the wreckage without distorting it. Then, working with the flight crew, they'd loaded it into the plane and strapped it down.

Seated on the extended flight deck in an area normally reserved for a backup crew, Svetlana felt relieved as the plane left the ground. She looked across at Ligachev. Although still unshaven and even dirtier and more rumpled than at the start of the day, his expression had changed from that of a defeated old man to a stern, determined, administrator.

She turned to him, raised her voice so she could be heard above the engine noise, and asked, "Since the valve caused the accident, can the problem be corrected in a reasonable amount of time?"

Motioning for Tsvigun to lean toward him, Ligachev said, "There is no problem. Nothing needs correcting."

"I don't understand, Vladimir," Tsvigun responded.

"It was sabotage. Some rotten bastard, probably a damned Kazakh, weakened the valve housing."

Tsvigun asked, "How could they do that?"

"Don't know yet, Yevgeni. We'll find out when we get the engine back to Kaliningrad. As soon as we take the valve apart, we'll know exactly what they did."

"It sounds as if this required sophisticated engineering," Tsvigun commented.

"The most troubling aspect. The explosion was the result of careful planning and daring work by a team of dedicated professionals. Must have been people on Nazarbayev's staff—only way they could have done it without being detected."

Feeling almost elated, Svetlana said, "Then the cause was a security failure. It had nothing to do with the program. There's no reason why we shouldn't be able to continue—almost uninterrupted."

"We still have many problems, Svetlana," Ligachev reminded her. "First, there's the damage to the test stand. That will take a great effort to repair. And we have only one booster left. If anything happens to it, the program will be delayed for years."

"But those are not the most serious difficulties," Tsvigun added. "We have to deal with the security breakdown."

"Isn't that the FSA's job?" she asked.

"Their job, but our problem," Tsvigun continued. "It means they'll have to investigate every person involved in the moon program—assure absolute loyalty. At Baikonur, this may mean the loss of a good portion of the work force, even if they're innocent."

"And Nazarbayev is already short of skilled personnel," Ligachev added.

Svetlana said firmly, "Minor delays. Nothing more. We'll still be on the moon before the Americans!"

## Chapter 6

---

# Critical Design Review

**Huntsville**

Seated at a table near the front of the hall, Brandt thumbed through the last pages of his presentation and thought, "Well, they said it'd be different."

Looking like a war room in the midst of battle, the Huntsville Hilton's conference center had been transformed into a bustling workplace. Contractor teams huddled over tables covered with layers of drawings, documents and scribbled notes. Portable computers were everywhere, connected to the outside world through wireless networks.

In response to the Federation's announcement that their lunar expedition would be launched the following fall, Roland Singleton, the recently appointed Program Director, had convened an unprecedented event. In place of separate design reviews, the contractors would make their presentations to the entire team. Sensitive items would be openly debated by all contributors, even potential competitors.

Singleton justified the aberration with a single word: time. He demanded that every potential delay be eliminated before the end of the design review. To emphasize the point, he'd plastered the walls with four-foot-high banner plots of the master program schedule.

As Brandt took notes, Jerry Hensfeld presented an overview of the projects he supervised. He'd already covered the status of the third-stage booster, a presentation that brought applause when he announced that the design activity had been completed almost a month early. He continued with a description of proposed landing-system tests and, after some discussion, agreed they were unnecessary. This evoked another round of applause.

Disturbed by the decision, Brandt picked up the microphone at the center of his table and said, "Doctor Hensfeld, the simulator's all we've got for practicing manual landings and you just scrubbed the only tests that can provide data for its design."

Having been down this path before, Hensfeld replied, "Colonel Strickland, as I stated previously, testing the shell won't improve the data base. There are too many differences between its dynamics and the moon vehicle's."

That gave Brandt the opportunity he'd been looking for. "What about this? Suppose you cobble together a vehicle that weighs a sixth of the actual but has the same dynamics. Keep the same landing gear and engine section we'll use on the moon."

Hensfeld thought for a moment, then replied, "Sounds like a good idea. Of course, you've just proposed an entirely new activity we'll have to add to the program."

This brought a chorus of good-natured boos.

"Not added," Brandt objected, "replaced. Do this instead of the other tests. It's cheaper, faster and it'll give better information."

With the training problem resolved, Hensfeld moved to the aerobraking test, an expensive but essential experiment designed to assure the survival of the spacecraft as it skimmed the upper atmosphere after returning from the moon.

"Boeing Aerospace is building the upper portion of a DC-XB aeroshell. This will closely duplicate the condition of the actual spacecraft as it approaches earth. Their biggest problem is not knowing the final mass distribution of the crew compartment. Except for that, the test vehicle should be ready by the milestone date."

Apparently sensing criticism, Ron Collen picked up his microphone. "I'd just like to remind everyone that Boeing Space Systems is still waiting for final specifications on communications requirements, scientific payloads, and lunar-surface operations. When I get my numbers, Boeing Aerospace gets their numbers."

With that, Singleton jumped up from his place at the front table, walked rapidly to the podium, which Hensfeld hastily surrendered, and stared down at Collen.

"Mr. Collen, that attitude is unacceptable. Passing the buck will not be tolerated. If your lack of information is impacting the schedule, then use this opportunity to resolve the problem. I trust Boeing Space Systems talks to Boeing Aerospace."

Collen shrugged and said, "Yeah, we talk. Of course we talk. We'll get it straightened out."

Having made his point, Singleton apologized to Hensfeld for the interruption and returned to his seat.

Concluding his discussion of the reentry test, Hensfeld said, "What we need are best-estimates, then refinements as the program goes along. We can always make last-minute adjustments."

Miriam Raddock of Transpace interrupted. "Doctor Hensfeld, Transpace is very concerned about the ever-expanding support you expect from the Super Shuttle. This started as an optional retrieval operation tucked in after a routine mission. Now the retrieval's mandatory, we've added the repair activity for the X-ray Telescope, and we're supposed to carry the entire moon crew as observers. That puts us outside the payload envelope. In order to guarantee retrieval, we'll have to double the propellant supply for the OMS which makes it impossible to carry four passengers."

"Because you need four Transpace people to do the repair mission?"

"Exactly."

"Why not have the moon crew help with the repairs?"

"That's a contract violation, and there's no way we can train them. Not with only four months until the launch."

Brandt picked up his microphone. "Crew training supports Transpace on this. We can't pile that much mission preparation on top of the lunar work."

Hensfeld turned back to Raddock. "What do you recommend?"

"Either eliminate the repair activity or reduce the passenger requirement to one person."

"I can't speak for Goddard," Hensfeld replied, "but I'm sure the repairs have a high priority." Then he asked, "Colonel Strickland, can you help?"

"We need enough familiarity with Shuttle operations to accomplish the recovery. I'm the biggest problem. Haven't been in space for some time."

Hensfeld responded, "Then we could get by with one

passenger."

Shaking his head, Brandt argued, "What happens if I get sick? We should have at least one other crew member covering the mission."

Addressing Raddock, Hensfeld asked, "Can Transpace handle two passengers?"

After a short conference at the Transpace table, she replied, "We'll work it out."

Sounding relieved, Hensfeld said, "Okay, I think that's it for the aerobraking test. We've got some action items for Boeing Aerospace and some cleanup details for Transpace. Otherwise, we're go for launch next January."

His assertion brought scattered applause.

"Which brings us back to the spacecraft." He brought up the next chart. "There are three interrelated activities. The first involves the propulsion section. We're getting the OMS engines from Aerojet and, as of yesterday, the delivery date hasn't slipped. Because the subsystems have been adapted from either Shuttle or Apollo, the risk level is low. The details of the aeroshell design will be included in the formal CDR. At this point, I'll just say things look pretty tight.

"The final segment is the pressure-vessel that houses the crew. It includes crew accommodations, guidance and navigation equipment, instrumentation and displays, controls, communication equipment, EMU support, and data-acquisition modules."

This time, he displayed no detailed graphics. Instead, as he rattled off the component names, the words appeared along the right side of the screen.

Brandt wasn't happy. "Doctor Hensfeld, it's obvious the actual design hasn't been completed, but isn't there anything that shows the basic layout? The crew training schedule calls for having a mockup in two months and a full-blown simulator by next February."

Hensfeld looked toward the Boeing Aerospace table and asked, "Mr. Collen?"

Sounding disgruntled, Collen picked up a data-storage module and walked to the stage. "Okay if I load this over your stuff?"

Hensfeld nodded permission.

After a few seconds, Collen's first drawing appeared showing a flat-topped cone with several cutouts.

"You'll get more of this tomorrow, but let me get Jerry off the hook by giving you some hints. This is a drawing of the pressure shell—pretty-well finalized. The design's an Apollo derivative. A little heavy, but it'll work.

"The window and hatch locations have been finalized. Hatch is pure Shuttle—same hardware, located to line up with the White Room on the Orbiter Access Arm."

He selected another drawing. "Couch design is almost complete—similar to Apollo, except they need to flip over for aerobraking so the astronauts can face backwards."

His next display page looked more like a rough sketch. "As you see, this is work in progress. We've made some preliminary decisions about subsystem placement. Now let's talk about what's missing. I can't show you an instrument panel. Why? Because nobody seems to know what the astronauts will need or what functions they want to control. The truth is, we can automate the whole mission—just have the astronauts along for the ride. But they'd have a temper tantrum if we tried that, so we need to give them some buttons and switches and levers to play with. Question is, which ones do they want?

"Let's talk about the nose—that empty space on top of the pressure shell. What goes there? Nothing? That's fine with me, because we don't need the volume for any identified mission equipment. Some difference from Apollo, eh? So what's the problem? I'll tell you what's the problem. NASA abhors a vacuum!"

The comment brought laughter from several tables.

"Wait long enough and someone from the program office is going to come up with a dandy new subsystem we can stick into that space—and there goes the schedule.

"Oh yeah, one more little hangup. We don't know where the hell we're going! Less than a year until the launch and NASA hasn't figured out where to land. Makes it kinda hard to generate mission-dependent software.

"So, Mr. Singleton, you tell me what you want and I'll do my level best to deliver it. Until then, we're a week late on all milestones and slipping day for day."

After removing his data module, he returned to his table, allowing Hensfeld to continue.

"Mr. Collen, we've already addressed the issue of displays and controls. The stated design policy is to provide all status information on the multi-function displays. The guidelines for controls were also discussed. There should be soft switches on the displays for every actuator in the spacecraft."

Collen responded loudly, "That's a cop out, Jerry, and you know it. You're saying since you can't decide what you want, we should provide everything—and do it with software. You just added a year to the program. And you still haven't said where you want actuators."

Brandt watched Hensfeld's face redden as he replied, "Those are design decisions, Mr. Collen, decisions you're being paid to make. That's supposed to be your company's area of expertise, isn't it?"

"And we're making the decisions. The question is, are you going to come back and second-guess everything?"

Interrupting the argument, Singleton said, "Mr. Collen, why don't you just do your job and stop worrying about what NASA might or might not do in the future?"

Apparently impatient with Collen's griping, others in the room applauded. Before he had a chance to react, someone from a table toward the rear announced, "Mr. Singleton, in keeping with the open format of this meeting, I'd like to say that, after consulting with my management, the staff at Northrop-Grumman would be happy to bid on a parallel contract to develop the crew module."

The announcement brought a barrage of guffaws mingled with shouts of, "Better watch your ass, Ron!" and "Northrop's gonna get ya!"

When the outburst died down, Singleton responded, "Thanks for the offer, but I hope that won't be necessary."

Then, addressing the Boeing Aerospace table, he added, "Mr. Collen, we're here to get this program on schedule. What we need from you is a plan to accomplish that."

"Fair enough," Collen replied. "You'll see our proposals at the CDR. But we can't decide where to land."

Hensfeld asked, "Anyone from mission planning want to comment?"

Norm Hoang answered from the Marshall Space Fight Center table. "We're still facing the same old problem. If we're going to meet up with the Federation crew, we'll have to land where they land—except they aren't saying where that will be. Anyway, we've come up with a baseline mission which I'll describe this afternoon. To keep everyone from dying of curiosity, it calls for a landing on Mare Tranquillitatis."

As he uttered the words, the room buzzed with side

conversations.

"Okay, let me explain why. Granted, it's the region we already know the most about. But the primary purpose of this mission is getting the crew there and back, not scientific research and, operationally, the Sea of Tranquility is the safest bet. That's why it was the destination for Apollo 11.

"Just the same, there are some major scientific payoffs. Among other things, it's the number-one site for mining helium three and we'd like to know more about the regolith. So, with JPL's help, we're hoping to have a small rover ready for the mission—basically the same concept we used for Mars but with more emphasis on the mineralogy.

"The other objective is a long shot. If we can land close enough to the Apollo 11 site, we may be able to recover some samples from the lander platform. They'd provide an outstanding opportunity to study the effects of long-term exposure to the lunar environment. I guess you could describe the mission as *ahead to the past*. More later."

Hensfeld thanked Hoang and said, "That completes my overview of the vehicle design."

Brandt interrupted, "Excuse me Jerry. We still haven't resolved the problem of getting down to the surface."

From his chair Collen replied, "Good point, Colonel! I've even got an answer. First of all, there's no problem with the lower portion of the vehicle—the part that stays on the moon. It'll have a conventional ladder. But we can't do that for the upper section. An external ladder would burn off during the aerobraking—might make for some strange aerodynamics. But Boeing has a solution." He grinned. "You're gonna love this one! We subcontracted the task to a company in Portland and they've come up with a rope ladder."

That brought laughs from around the room.

"Of course, it's not made of rope, but it works the same way. It's a very high-tech gadget that rolls into a remarkably small cylinder. You secure it to the hatch opening and then just let go. It unrolls down the side of the spacecraft and lines up with the ladder on the lower section. Isn't that sweet?"

"It just dangles from the hatch?" Brandt asked, somewhat dismayed by the prospect.

"Not quite, Colonel," Collen replied. "It has clips that will latch into fittings located at several points along the side of the vehicle. Now get this. As you climb down, you'll be kicking these things into place with your boot. Told ya you'd love it."

An angry voice intervened as the owner of Advanced Technology Products grabbed his microphone. "Mr. Collen, your description is a gross disservice to the engineers who designed this device. They've done a first-rate job meeting some very challenging size and weight constraints while devising a safe and effective solution. We'd have appreciated being given the courtesy of presenting our own work to this audience. But, as we've all seen, courtesy isn't something you know much about."

After a short but awkward silence, some applause trickled from a few tables.

"Hey, lighten up Zaki," Collen laughed. "This is as much my system as yours." Then, turning to Brandt, he said, "Seriously, Colonel, I think ATP's done a great job with this. If it works, and I think it will, they've saved us some real headaches. But we're gonna have to test the hell out of this baby and if it craps out, we've got another delay."

Brandt still felt uneasy. "Okay. We'll have to add that to the training schedule. Sorry for the interruption."

At this point, Singleton returned to the podium to announce the lunch break and admonish everyone to be back on time.

Brandt followed the crowd out of the ballroom and into an adjacent area where buffet tables had been set up near the side walls. The center of the room was filled with round tables, each ringed by eight chairs.

After guessing which of the four lines would reach the food first, he picked up a small tray and a set of plastic utensils folded inside a paper napkin and joined the slow shuffle.

He spotted Hensfeld sitting with Hoang and Tontini. "Might as well join my innkeeper," he thought as he selected a prepackaged salad.

After settling in and getting the foil-packed dressing blended with his lettuce, he downed a few mouthfuls, then said, "Jerry, I sure appreciate your putting me up—and Jill's breakfasts are out of this world."

"Glad to have you, Brandt," Jerry replied. "You're a first-rate baby sitter."

Tontini noticed Singleton approaching. She whispered, "Uh oh, wonder what we did wrong."

The Program Director bent over and said, "Doctor Hensfeld,

sorry to interrupt your lunch but I need to talk with you for a moment."

Caught with his mouth full, Hensfeld mumbled, "No problem. Just finished."

As they left, Tontini said, "Wonder what that's all about?"

"Probably a change in the afternoon's schedule," Hoang guessed.

Brandt grumbled, "Hope they don't bump me. I want to get this over with."

"What are you going to talk about?" Tontini asked.

Finishing his last piece of cucumber, Brandt replied, "Overview of the training schedule—classroom work, moon-walking trainer, neutral buoyancy tank."

"Anything time critical?" Hoang asked.

"Just the simulator—what we talked about this morning. Wish there was a way to build a fire under Collen."

"Don't worry about him," Tontini said. "If anyone's going to meet the launch date, he will."

"That's right," Hoang agreed. "I've been watching him operate. He's got the Boeing plant humming—lots more going on than he'll admit. They're already cutting metal."

"Then why is he griping?"

"Just his way of getting NASA to pay attention. He's absolutely right about needing a mission plan."

Tontini looked at her watch. "Time to get back."

They picked up their scraps, dutifully dumped them into a large cardboard trash container, and headed for the ballroom.

As Brandt returned to his place, he noticed Singleton and Hensfeld already on the stage, waiting for the group to settle down. Singleton spoke first.

"Ladies and gentlemen, if you'd please take your seats, I have an important announcement."

The room gradually became quiet. Speaking slowly, Singleton said, "I have just been informed that one of our imaging satellites detected an enormous explosion at the Energia launch pad in Kazakhstan."

He barely got the words out before the room exploded in pandemonium. Senior engineers and vice-presidents high-fived; business owners jumped up and down in the aisles; marketing managers danced on the table tops; women executives kissed government representatives they'd never met before. Singleton tried to restore order but the celebration went on for a good five minutes.

Brandt slapped a stranger on the back yelling, "How 'bout that, buddy? I knew those dang Commies would trip up sooner or later."

Finally able to continue, Singleton said, "The Socialist Federation has acknowledged that the accident destroyed one of their SL-17 boosters..."

Another round of cheering ensued, but ended much more quickly.

"...destroyed one of their SL-17 boosters. The report stated there were no injuries."

As the room buzzed with conjecture, each attendee speculating on the impact of the event on his or her program, Hensfeld moved up to the podium.

"If I may have your attention. Obviously, the most important question is the effect this will have on the Federation's schedule. Their biggest problem will be repairing the test-stand, but our best hope for an extended delay comes from their announced launch date. Even a one-month postponement puts them into the winter-storm season which raises the possibility they may wait until spring."

Hensfeld's optimistic speculation brought more enthusiastic responses from the audience. Brandt, however, was anything but elated. He spoke into his microphone.

"Jerry, as you know, I spent some time analyzing the Federation's capabilities. Much as I hate to throw cold water on this, I must express my doubts about the accident having much effect on the Federation's program."

His clearly unpopular hypothesis evoked grumblings and a few boos.

"Let me explain. First of all, there's no reason to believe they don't have other boosters available. This means, as Doctor Hensfeld stated, their biggest problem is going to be getting the stand back into operation. Looking at the time they have available, I don't think it's going to cause a launch slip. Most of the primary structure is built to withstand an explosion—just like our launch pads.

"Don't get me wrong. They'll have to scramble to get things fixed. But we can't use this as an excuse to ease off. Not for a minute. If we do, we'll be looking up at a red moon."

## Chapter 7

# Aeroshell Test

**Super Shuttle Atlantis**

Drawn toward it by forces beyond his control, his dread grew more intense with each step. The back of an immense bird, an owl, scarlet, silhouetted by a shimmering golden aura. The head, slowly turning, turning toward him. But the eyes. He dared not look into them. Anxiety became terror. The head still turning. His heart pounding. Unbearable horror. Screaming. Pounding.

Brandt's eyes snapped opened. The next bang jolted him fully awake. He slid open the privacy panel and saw Darrell's face smiling back at him, his fist ready to hit the sleep compartment again.

"Get-up time already?"

"Pretty close, Brandt. Sounded like you were having one hell of a dream."

"Oh yeah?" he responded, trying to sound nonchalant as he worked himself out of his sleeping bag.

"Shoutin' up a storm. Sounded like swahili. What was it about?"

Pushing himself out of the cubicle, Brandt lied, "Danged if I know. Never can remember dreams. Must be this Transpace crap they're feeding us."

Darrell chuckled as he zipped up his cobalt-blue NASA jacket. "More likely all that Tabasco sauce you pour on it."

Brandt stretched. "Got to do something. After the first day in orbit, I can't taste a thing. Time to tackle the john."

For the next thirty minutes, Brandt entertained Darrell with a comedy of clumsy eating, dressing and hygiene activities. Having logged many days in Super Shuttles, Darrell completed the tasks with far less effort.

"What are they doing up there?" Brandt asked as he placed his food tray in the galley compartment.

"Getting ready to capture the satellite."

"Wish they'd let us help. I'm sick of just hanging around."

Brandt took his wireless-intercom unit from a storage bin, attached the control box to a strip of velcro on his wasteband and placed the headset frame over his right ear. He worked the small earphone into position and moved the microphone to the corner of his mouth.

Gently propelling himself up through the interdeck access, he arrived at the back of the flight deck just as the Transpace Shuttle Commander, Monica Guerrera, turned to her crew members and said, "Approaching apogee. Prepare for circularization burn."

Less than a minute later, she announced, "Starting burn," and Brandt felt a slight push, like an underpowered car pulling away from a stoplight.

Then Guerrera called, "Stand by for OMS shutdown," and seconds later he was once again weightless.

After selecting the primary intercom channel, Brandt turned the control box's function switch to *VOX*. That put him on a party line with the other crewmembers.

"How long until we rendezvous?" he asked.

The payload specialist, Henry Sanden, looked over and answered, "A few minutes."

"Okay folks," Guerrera said as she pushed out of the left seat and moved aft, "now we earn our pay. Hank, you ready with the arm?"

"System check's complete," Sanden answered. "Everything's go."

Brandt noticed that the pilot, Dae-Sung Le, and mission specialist Janice Tyson had already donned cooling-and-ventilation garments. They were also wearing oxygen masks, finishing the hour of prebreathing needed to flush nitrogen from their bodies before starting their EVAs.

Aided by a pair of binoculars, Sanden peered through the aft crew station's remote-manipulator window, out across the open cargo bay and into space. "Got a visual." he reported.

Guerrera searched the sky through the orbiter-controller's window, waiting patiently for the distance between the two spacecraft to diminish. "Got it," she said as she placed her hands on the control sticks.

"Doing a manual rendezvous?" Brandt asked.

"The Germans don't want their satellite irradiated, even by our little radar. Afraid they'll lose data."

Initially only a bright dot, the image of the spacecraft gradually grew larger. Looking over Sanden's shoulder, Brandt squinted, trying to discern its shape. At first appearing to be spherical, it emerged as a cylinder with small panels extending outward.

"Reducing closing velocity," Guerrera said, the tension in her voice becoming noticeable as she adjusted the Shuttle's position, stopping with the satellite twenty feet above and to her right. She turned to Sanden. "All yours Hank."

The fifty-foot arm, resting along the edge of the cargo bay, lifted from its supports and began a slow rotation to the right, folding its elbow as it moved. Sanden maneuvered the end until it pointed toward the satellite. Then he stopped to adjust a small television monitor until it showed a clear image of the satellite.

"End-effector camera looks good," he reported, then returned his hand to the controller.

Watching the monitor, he brought a tubular device at the end of the arm closer to its target. Inside the tube, a set of three wires waited to close around a rod protruding from the satellite's surface.

"I've got the grapple," Sanden reported as the image appeared. He used the wrist joint to make small adjustments as he slipped the wires over the rod.

"End effector's closed." Sanden released the stick and stepped back to relax.

Sanden's next commands were supposed to push the satellite toward the back of the Shuttle where a large ring-shaped structure protruded from the cargo bay. It was designed to hold the satellite while the crew performed the repairs.

Sanden gradually extended the elbow. With the satellite nearing the support ring, he attempted to slow its motion but the wires in the end effector slipped off the rod and the arm jumped back.

"What the hell?" he shouted as he checked his status

indicators. Seeing nothing amiss, he scanned the satellite with the television camera.

"Damn!" he exclaimed. "Look at this, Monica!"

The commander moved to the screen and studied the image. "Knob broke off the grapple."

Sanden moved the end effector closer, then zoomed in on the rod.

"Sheared off," Guerrera exclaimed. "Looks like something hit it. Try backing off the zoom and scanning to the left."

Sanden complied, then said, "Debris hit. Got the electronics module too. Took a piece off the edge of the cover."

"Doesn't that beat all?" Guerrera sighed as she adjusted the velocity of the Shuttle to keep the satellite in position. "What do we do now?"

"Have to work in free space." Sanden answered.

Shaking his head, Le responded, "Forget it, Hank. Look at that damned thing. Probes sticking out all over. You'd play hell replacing those modules without breaking something and if you did, the company'd have your ass. Besides, we're not getting a hazard increment for this operation."

"Need input from mission control," Guerrera said. She returned to her commander's position, made some selections on the audio panel above her head and dropped off the intercom. A few minutes later, she rejoined the group.

"Bad news. Boss says we have to do it."

"Jesus!" Le shouted, spinning himself around. "What's with those assholes?"

"Big incentive award riding on the repair."

"Did you explain the risks?"

"Yup. He said not to break anything."

"Aw, shit!" Le muttered.

"No use bitching. Put the suits on and let's get this thing over with. Oh yeah," she added, "they wouldn't authorize the extra pay."

"Then screw 'em," Le snarled. "I'm not gonna risk it."

"Goes for me too," Tyson said. "I'm tired of sticking my neck out to protect the company's profits. Contract says we don't have to do this. Mission plan calls for a captive repair. That's that."

"Jesus!" Guerrera fumed. "That leaves me with a crappy mission eval."

"What about maneuvering Atlantis around to align the

mounting ring with the ROSAT?" Darrell suggested. "Then Le and Janice could bring it in manually and lock it down."

"Move the whole damned Shuttle?" Guerrera gasped. "Are you crazy? One slip could cause an impact."

"It's really not that hard. Had to do it with a spy sat. Heck of a lot bigger."

Guerrera thought for a moment before responding hesitantly, "Okay. I guess if you can do it, so can I.

"Janice? Le? That okay with you?"

"Not the same as having the satellite on the arm," Tyson complained, but then acquiesced. "What the heck, as long as you can get it close enough, bringing it down on the ring shouldn't be any different."

Tyson and Le dropped through the interdeck access to the mid-deck section.

Brandt followed Darrell to the back of the flight deck, standing behind Guerrera and Sanden, looking past them into the cargo bay. Le called, "Opening the outer hatch," then quickly appeared, emerging from the airlock exit. A few minutes later, Tyson joined him.

Brandt watched Le move through the cargo bay, checking the items that had been stowed along its walls. Tyson released a large piece of equipment from a storage area and said, "Let's get the work platform mounted."

Sanden brought the end of the arm down into the bay. With Le's help, Tyson removed the end effector and replaced it with the platform.

"Monica," Le's voice said, "we're approaching the terminator. Need the cargo-bay lights."

"Roger," Guerrera replied as she turned on a bank of floodlights to illuminate the satellite.

Using a control stick on her right, Guerrera slowly rolled the Shuttle until its vertical axis lined up with the axis of the satellite. Then, using the stick in her left hand, she moved Atlantis sideways to place the satellite directly above the cargo bay.

Her last task was to move it farther back. With the left-hand control, she fired thrusters to move the Shuttle into position. But when she tried to stop the motion, she over controlled and the satellite moved forward again. Trying once more, she commanded the thrusters, but developed too large a relative velocity.

"You're going to hit it!" Sanden shouted.

She reversed the commands and the satellite drifted forward.

"Always have trouble in the dark," Guerrera complained, then announced, "I'm pulling away to a safe distance," as she brought the Shuttle down until the satellite hovered well above the top of the tail. Certain the danger had passed, she caught her breath, then stated, "That's it until we get back into the light."

"Tell you what," Darrell offered, "let me give it a try."

"Can't allow it," Guerrera responded firmly. "Major contract violation."

He gently but deliberately eased her away from the pilot's position and put his hands on the control sticks. "I won't tell if you won't."

Guerrera started to protest, but Darrell had already moved Atlantis much closer to the satellite. Once he had it lined up over the mounting ring, he eased the Shuttle upward, bringing the bottom of the satellite within inches of clamps that would hold it in place.

"Nice going!" Le's voice came over the intercom. "Just about perfect."

Gently pulling and pushing, he and Tyson brought the base of the satellite down on the ring and closed the latches.

"Colonel," Guerrera said, her voice reflecting a mix of resentment and relief, "you've just committed yourself to pulling Atlantis away again once they're finished."

Grinning, Darrell replied, "Love to!"

The speed of the repair work surprised Brandt. Supported by the work platform, Le selected tools from the equipment post and used them to remove and replace the inoperative components. As soon as he removed something, Tyson took it to the storage area and exchanged it for its replacement.

"That does it," Le announced as he tightened the last fitting.

"Let's get rid of it," Guerrera ordered. "Colonel, you ready to back us away?"

"No problem, Commander. Soon as they get it loose."

Le and Tyson released the latches, held on to the mounting ring and pushed on the satellite. "It's moving almost exactly upward," Tyson reported.

"I'm going to let it drift as long as I can," Darrell said. "No use tempting fate."

Once the satellite had cleared the tail, he turned the control station over to Guerrera. "Hell, you don't need me."

"Nice job," Brandt said to Guerrera. "You deserve a bonus."

She sighed, "We won't hold our breath."

**Super Shuttle Atlantis**

Floating next to Darrell, Brandt listened to the report from the Range Operations and Control Center with growing concern. Although the launch had gone well, an apparent programming error in the upper stage had left the aeroshell with a large crosstrack error. Now Brian, who had gone to Florida to observe the operation, relayed more bad news from the Boeing engineers.

"Data drop-outs?" Brandt said. “How serious?”

Brian's voice answered, "Can't tell. Could mean a big data loss."

Brandt switched off his intercom. "Dang it, Darrell, that's the whole mission."

"Unless they can use the aeroshell's lift to correct the trajectory," Darrell replied.

"They'd better. Otherwise we're looking at a six-month slip."

Activating the intercom, Brandt asked, "How soon does that thing enter the atmosphere?"

"Already has," Brian replied. "Velocity's starting to decrease; crosstrack error's being reduced."

Brandt tapped his palm with his fist, anxiously waiting for the next report.

Brian's voice returned. "Into negative lift now. Trying to maintain constant Gs. Looks like the program's doing the job."

"Come on, baby. Come on," Brandt whispered.

"Back out of the atmosphere," Brian announced. "Getting the numbers. Not perfect, but the final burn should put it close enough for the recovery."

"Wahoo!" Brandt yelled into the intercom. "If the XB can pull that off, it'll sure as heck get us back from the moon."

Darrell yanked off his headset and rubbed his ear.

***

Brandt had joined Darrell in the mid-deck area to complete the prebreathing. Growing restless waiting for the rendezvous with the aeroshell, he listened to the progress of the operation over his headset.

"Delta-v values coming out of the computer," a voice from mission control stated. "Should be seeing them as they load."

"Roger, Houston," Guerrera answered. "Flight computer's acknowledging the data transfer. Working on the burn parameters."

Two minutes went by before Brandt heard her call, "Houston, we may have a problem. The propellant estimate brings us right down to the minimum for reentry."

"Roger that Atlantis," the voice responded. "We've been looking at the numbers. You'll have to push the reserve requirement, but it looks okay."

"Those bastards," Le's voice said. "They've got the damned spacecraft off trajectory and they're gonna risk our necks trying to complete the rendezvous."

"Contract specifies our propellant margins," Sanden commented. "They're taking a big chance if they violate the minimums."

"What chance?" Le retorted. "They're down in Houston having a doughnut. We're up here hoping they'll leave us enough delta-v to get back."

"Atlantis, this is Houston."

"Go ahead, Houston."

"Our calculations show you won't have a problem. Even with the two burns, you'll satisfy the reserve requirement."

Now off the communications radio, Guerrera snarled, "Fat chance we could do anything about it, even if they're lying."

Cutting his throat with his finger, Brandt switched off the intercom channel, then verified Darrell had done the same.

"Happy bunch, these Transpace folks," he quipped.

Darrell grinned. "Inspirational!" Then asked, "About ready to step outside?"

"Yup," Brandt said. "Wondering if I can still get the EMU on inside the airlock." He switched back to the party line.

"There it is." It was Tyson's voice. "About eleven o'clock."

"Got it," Guerrera replied. "Should have ignition any time."

As she spoke, the OMS engines fired, accelerating the Shuttle to match the orbit of the aeroshell.

"Want to go upstairs?" Darrell asked.

"Why not?" Brandt switched to the portable oxygen supply, then followed him up the accessway.

Le and Sanden were prebreathing in the back of the flight

deck while Tyson ran through the Remote-Manipulator-Arm checklist.

Brandt peered through the forward windows. He asked Guerrera, "Where is it?"

She laughed and pointed at the window above his head.

He looked toward the earth and saw a long, white cone drifting slowly toward the rear of the Shuttle, its nose pointed toward them. "Looks too big to fit into the cargo bay," he said.

"It is," Guerrera replied. "Still has the propulsion section attached."

He looked at her, puzzled.

"Must have slept through that part of the briefing, Colonel. We have to disassemble the damned thing."

"Sounds like a lot of work."

Guerrera shrugged. "Lots of bolts to unscrew. Janice, you ready with the boom?"

"Everything's green," she replied, now standing at the operator's station waiting for Guerrera to match velocities.

"Plenty of daylight this time," she said to Darrell. "Don't think I'll need your help." She smirked as she grasped the orbiter hand controls, brought Atlantis down closer to the aeroshell, then stopped the relative motion.

"There's the grapple, Janice," she said. "Let's hope this one stays together."

Tyson moved the arm out of the cargo bay. Switching her gaze to the television monitor, she brought it toward the grapple until the end effector closed, then called, "We've got it!"

"Ready to head out?" Brandt asked Darrell.

"Not just yet, Colonel," Guerrera interrupted. "I want you in here until they get that thing locked on the mount."

Raising his eyebrows, Brandt responded, "As you wish, Commander."

Le moved toward the rear of the bay to work with the ring mount that had been used to support the ROSAT-B. Meanwhile, Sanden completed the airlock procedure, emerged through the hatch and joined him. Together, they extended the support ring from the mount and tilted it to a forty-five-degree angle.

Tyson used the arm to bring the spacecraft toward the proper position, letting it slowly rotate to the desired angle. As it entered the bay, Le and Sanden guided it toward the mount, finally easing its nose into the ring.

"Inflating the clamp," Sanden announced. An elastic tube inside the ring filled with nitrogen, pressing itself firmly against the surface of the aeroshell's nose. Satisfied with the fit, he said, "Release the arm."

The elbow bent toward the bay allowing Le to replace the end effector with a work platform. He slipped his feet into the restraints and rode toward the interface between the nose portion of the XB and its propulsion section.

"Okay for us to get going?" Brandt asked Guerrera.

She nodded. "Any time, Colonel."

He descended to the mid deck, verified the airlock pressure, opened the inner hatch and floated inside the telephone-booth-sized cylinder, closing the hatch behind him.

He inspected the EMU, which hung from a frame on the airlock wall, unfastened its lower-torso section and slid his legs through the trousers and into the boots.

After checking the upper-torso section, he took a deep breath, removed the mouthpiece and nose clip of the portable breathing unit, then wriggled his way in, got his head through the neck ring and grabbed for the oxygen. At this point, he realized that the sleeves of his undergarment had bunched up above his elbow.

"Dang! Darrell told me I'd forget the loops."

He found squirming out no easier than getting in, ending up almost out of breath before he managed to grab the mouthpiece. He slipped the retainer loops over his thumbs and was ready to try again.

"Better," he thought as his hands emerged from the wrist rings, but the rounds of interrupted breathing were wearing him out.

Grasping the umbilical from his cooling-and-ventilation garment, he pushed it into the back-pack supply tube. Satisfied with the connection, he joined the two torso sections by closing the waist ring.

With the hardest part behind him, he donned the head covering. Then, after setting the oxygen-control switch, he slipped on the gloves and snapped them into place.

He held his breath one more time, got rid of the portable oxygen, lowered the helmet over his head and locked it to the neck ring. He felt the suit pressurize and started to breath normally again. A quick look at the suit's status panel verified there were no leaks.

"Brandt, you fall asleep in there?" It was Darrell.

He answered, "Thanks for checking my intercom, Darrell.

You reading me?"

"Loud and clear, but I'm sure getting bored waiting."

Brandt's next task was to depressurize the airlock so he could move into the vacuum of the cargo bay. On the airlock control panel, he found the *AIRLOCK DEPRESS* switch, rotated it first to *5*, waited until the pressure stabilized, then rotated it to *0*. Within a few minutes, the pressure had dropped enough for him to open the outer airlock hatch and move into the cargo bay.

Looking up at Le, he could see why Guerrera had been so blasé about the uncoupling procedure. The pneumatic wrench made short work of disengaging the connecting bolts. Meanwhile, Sanden used a different tool to remove the engine.

As Brandt moved carefully toward the back of the cargo bay, Guerrera's voice stopped him. "Colonel, I want you on a tether at all times."

He responded, "Roger, Commander," then released the end of a nylon strap from a reel that slid along the cargo bay and attached its fitting to a clip on his waist.

Using a handrail to propel him, he moved toward the domed nose of the XB. It looked as if the epoxy material had ablated to a fraction of its original thickness. Although the tiles on the side were discolored, none appeared to be missing or broken. As he examined them, Darrell appeared.

Brandt eased his way back along the cone, being careful not to touch the surface. As he approached the propulsion section, Darrell cautioned, "Better stop there until they finish with the disassembly. Tethers get wound around things."

Hearing the warning, Le responded, "I'm finished with the bolts. We can get the arm out of your way."

Tyson moved the platform away from the vehicle back into the bay where Le exchanged tool sets. Taking advantage of the opportunity, Brandt moved along the propulsion section toward the end of the vehicle. Sanden was still hard at work.

"Did you video this area before you started the disassembly?" Brandt asked.

"Yeah," Sanden answered. "Still have to do the propulsion section."

Having overheard the conversion, Le arrived with a camera and began to record the condition of the rear portion of the vehicle.

"We'd better get out of your way," Darrell said, moving in

front of the interface. "How do you get the segments apart?"

"Mechanical separators," Le answered.

"Any other connections?" Brandt asked.

"An electrical connector," Le replied as he picked up a separator.

"Just need to push these into the cutouts and release the catches." He inserted the devices at four points around the spacecraft and said, "Hank, you about finished?"

"Everything's disconnected," he replied.

"Okay, let's pop them." They disengaged the latches that held the separators in their compressed condition.

"Now the others," Le ordered.

As soon as they released the last latches, the segments began to move apart. Sanden reached into the opening and tried to rotate the shell of a large electrical connector. After a moment, he said, "Can't get enough torque on the damned thing!"

Le tried but had no better luck. "We got any tools for this?"

"Nothing," Sanden replied.

"Damn!" Le fumed as he tried again. "If we can't get it apart, we'll have to release the whole vehicle. Let it reenter."

"Hank, you have to recover it!" Brandt yelled. "The telemetry didn't work. We need the vehicle."

"Relax, Colonel," Sanden said. "There was an on-board data recorder. We already removed it."

"I still want to bring the aeroshell home. Let me give the connector a whack."

"Don't think you'll have much luck, Colonel," Le said. "Have to push the shell toward the connection, then rotate it to release the retaining pins."

"Gotcha," Brandt replied as he reached for the device. With nothing to brace against, his first attempt was comical, requiring Sanden to stop his spinning to prevent a serious encounter with the tether. When everyone stopped laughing, Brandt said, "Need to use my left hand to push the shell while I hold the other side with my right hand."

"Yup," Le replied, still chuckling. "That's the way."

With real determination, Brandt shoved the shell down and then wrenched it loose.

"Think I got it."

"Damned if you didn't," Le observed, sounding impressed.

"You've got strong hands, Colonel."

Now completely free, the engine segment drifted away from the Shuttle.

"Colonel Strickland. Colonel Wilkins." It was Guerrera. "That's it for your EVAs."

"Roger," Brandt answered, starting to move back toward the bay. He quickly retracted his tether, freed himself and then reversed the airlock procedure, hurrying so he'd be able to watch Tyson bring the aeroshell into the cargo bay.

Still in his EMU undergarment, he went to the aft crew station and stood behind Guerrera. The vehicle had already rotated to a lower angle.

The arm gently pushed while the mounting ring held the nose in position. Finally, it slid into the clamps on the sides of the bay and locked itself in place.

"Good work," Guerrera said, sounding more relieved than elated. "Let's go home."

## Chapter 8

# Crew Training

**Marshall Space Flight Center**

"Not gonna make it," Brandt fretted to himself as he floated in Marshall's Neutral Buoyancy Simulator. "Not in the time we have left."

Wearing clones of Shuttle space suits, his crew moved clumsily about the spaceship replica. Usually, the suits were ballasted to simulate zero-gravity, but additional weights had been added to match conditions on the moon. This meant the astronauts sank to the bottom of the tank unless supported, a situation that made the job of the safety divers considerably more difficult.

Brandt peered through the mockup's observation port, watching Brian struggle with the manual release lever. "Should be able to do this in his sleep," he thought.

Finally, the hatch popped open just as Andy returned from the nose bay with a large, cylindrical package. It was the ladder.

Brandt listened over the intercom as Brian tried to unfasten a fabric strap that held it closed. "Damn!" he fumed. "Still can't work it."

Darrell reached to his left and lifted the ladder onto his chest. He managed to squeeze one of his glove's thimble-shaped fingertips under the catch to release it.

Brandt shook his head, worried by what he'd seen. Even in baseline activities, the crew hadn't reached an acceptable level of proficiency. He floated to the side of the mockup and watched Brian move the ladder outside, snap its retaining clips to edge of the exit port and release the catches. The ladder unrolled down the side of the mockup.

Freeing himself from his couch, Brian tucked and pivoted, then pushed his legs through the opening. Holding the edge, he groped for the ladder rung three feet below. With one foot supported, he eased his shoulders and helmet out, grabbed the side rails and began to walk down. Every few steps, he kicked the latches on the rails into sockets on the side of the mockup.

"At least he's got that down," Brandt thought as he watched him descend toward the bottom of the tank.

"Ladder's secure," Brian called.

Darrell moved through the hatch and stood on the ladder looking back inside. Meanwhile, Andy retrieved a mockup of the JPL rover from the nose and maneuvered it toward the hatch.

Darrell bent over, trying to align his backpack with the lower edge of the opening. Then, as Andy slid the rover through, he tried using one hand to push it into place while holding on with the other. Meanwhile, Andy secured it to the suit with two small lanyards.

Very carefully, Darrell stood erect on the ladder and began to step down. Everything went well for the first ten feet, but then his foot missed one of the rungs. He leaned sideways and, before he had a chance to recover, the load slipped off his backpack. Badly off balance, he was unable to regain his footing and fell off the ladder.

Two safety divers rushed in to grab him. They released the rover and let it drop to the bottom of the tank. Then, with Brandt's help, they pushed Darrell back on the ladder and held him until he was secure.

"Colonel Strickland, from now on you'll have to use a safety tether." It was the voice of the facility director, speaking from the control room adjacent to the tank.

"Roger that," Brandt answered. "Looks like we need a better approach."

Darrell completed his descent to the bottom of the tank, albeit a bit more slowly.

With the ladder secure and having only a small television camera to carry, Andy had the easiest task. Nonetheless, he slipped twice on the way down.

The crew moved toward an open area where Andy

methodically unfolded the legs of the dummy camera. He set it on the bottom of the tank and pretended to photograph the others as they assumed a variety of inappropriate poses.

"Hey gents," Brandt interrupted, his patience wearing thin, "we've still got a lot to do."

With Andy leading the way, the trio returned to the spacecraft mockup, climbed to the open hatch and pulled themselves into their couches.

Reaching around to his left, Brian flipped two releases, looked down the side of the mockup and watched the ladder slowly roll back up into a cylinder. Everything went well until it reached the floor of the tank. The last set of latches failed to disengage.

"Did it again," Brian said. "Hope the company's right about that not happening on the moon."

Brandt sighed and said, "Time to shed the weights." The safety divers floated to the access port and unfastened lead-filled straps from the astronauts' legs, arms and chests.

"Okay, get ready for aerobraking," Brandt ordered.

Brian and Andy flattened their couches. Still strapped in, they turned themselves over so they faced the floor of the tank.

"Now for the fun part," Darrell said stiffly. After moving to the bottom of the module between Brian and Andy, he grabbed the sides of his couch and pulled it toward him. As it came down, it flattened. At that point, Darrell rotated it and locked it in position.

"Okay guys, here we go." He tried to turn over to put his back into the couch but got stuck half-way around. Brian and Andy each took one of his arms and pulled him the rest of the way. "Ain't pretty, but it seems to work," Darrell said as he finished strapping himself into the couch.

Brandt winced as he thought, "Probably wasting time. Not much chance we'll have to wear EMUs during aerobraking."

"And now, the same thing backwards," Darrell grunted. Minutes later, he and the others were once again in their normal positions, ready to simulate the final stages of the mission.

Brandt appraised the exercise. "Not too bad, people. Got a ways to go, but we're making progress." Taking a deep breath, he continued, "Guess it's my turn. Brian, I'd like you to observe while I go through this with Darrell and Andy."

"Jesus, Brandt," Andy complained, "we've been at it for four hours. Isn't it about time for lunch?"

Trying not to sound annoyed, Brandt replied, "Breathing the nitrox, we can work for six hours. Don't know about you, but I hate going through all the preparation more than twice a day. Suppose we break after the next round?"

"Sounds good to me, Brandt," Darrell answered, ending the argument. "Let's get the weights back on."

An hour later, Brandt rode the tiny open elevator up the side of the tank. As soon as he emerged from the water, technicians lifted off his helmet and began to help him out of the upper-torso section. Before he'd finished removing the pants and boots, the technicians were already working to free the other astronauts. With his helmet off, Darrell remarked, "Thought that went pretty well."

"Best so far," Brandt agreed, "but we haven't figured out how to get the rover down without risking someone's neck."

By this time Brian had his helmet off and was able to join the discussion. "Why don't we lower it on a tether. Just slide it down the side and set it on the ground? Do it before we deploy the ladder."

"Might damage the tiles," Darrell replied.

"Thought about that. Just need to change the case so the edges are rounded. Then it won't catch on anything."

After picturing the operation, Brandt said, "Brian, as long as JPL goes along, I think you've got the answer. Everybody feel they'll be able to handle the weight?"

Darrell said, "What's it weigh on the moon? Sixty pounds? I'd sure rather lower it hand over hand than try to climb down with the thing on my back."

"Amen to that," Brian said.

Brandt thought for a minute. "Might be able to have the mockup modified for the Friday session. If not, then for Saturday."

Darrell replied, "Saturday? We're supposed to fly back Friday night."

"Don't see how we're going to make it, Darrell," Brandt responded. "Just too many things to iron out. And once we leave, we're gonna play hell getting back. Next week Transpace gets the tank. All our stuff gets pulled out."

"Which is bullshit, Brandt, and you know it. The tank at Johnson is plenty big enough for their work."

"Hey Darrell, I'm not calling the shots here."

"Yeah—sorry Brandt. But I've got a serious problem with Saturday."

"I'm afraid you'll have to tell Anita to come another time," Brandt replied stiffly.

"Damn it, it's not just Anita. We're set to work with a bunch of underprivileged kids. And NASA's lined up press coverage. It's not something I can walk away from."

"PR bullshit," Brandt mumbled. Then, looking at Darrell, he continued, "Just tell me how we're gonna reach an acceptable level of proficiency in two days."

"Work like hell. Schedule night sessions for today and tomorrow."

"You're assuming we can get the technicians."

"Easier than bringing them out on a weekend."

Brandt turned to Brian and Andy. "Okay with you?"

They both nodded and Andy said, "Frankly Brandt, I could use a couple of days with my family. Sure rather bust ass while I'm here and then get the hell home."

"Then that's what we'll do," Brandt replied wearily.

**Johnson Space Center**

"How'd it go with the kids Saturday?" Brandt asked as he and Darrell relaxed between simulator sessions.

"Great, Brandt. They couldn't get enough of Anita—boys and girls alike—blown away by the beautiful lady spy. You know, I think they ended up more interested in the CIA than the astronaut corps."

"Make you jealous?" Brandt asked.

"Maybe a little," Darrell replied, laughing. "Seriously, I'm sure they were intrigued with the novelty of her position. Super role model for the girls."

"She go back yesterday?"

"Late afternoon. We had a picnic lunch at the Nature Center."

Brandt glanced across at the simulator technician and saw he was waiting. "Ready to get back to work?"

Darrell nodded. "I'll play commander."

Brandt called to Brian, "How about taking systems? Try a manual aerobraking."

Finishing his last gulp of coffee, Brian replied, "Let's do it," and climbed into the simulator, scooting across to the right-hand couch. Darrell followed and Andy settled into the pilot's position.

Brandt studied the display, waiting for the first signs of aerodynamic forces. Mentally urging Andy on, he mumbled to himself, "Okay buddy, you're coming in steep so you need to establish the lift early."

As if in response, Andy said, "Entry angle's high. Establishing maximum angle of attack." He commanded the pitch thrusters to rotate the nose upward.

Brandt stared at the display, muttering under his breath, "Don't overshoot, damn it!"

"Reducing alpha," Andy called as he tried to lower the nose. "Damn! Going too high."

Pitching further down to generate negative lift, Andy fought to keep the spacecraft on track. But he overcontrolled again. Just as he began another pitch reversal, he noticed he'd drifted left of the track. He used another set of thrusters to point the nose to the right and watched the attitude indicator slowly confirm the effect of his control inputs, but the distraction proved disastrous.

"Diving below track!" he yelled, desperately trying to raise the nose, but it was too late. By the time the ship started up again, it had slowed too much. Warning lights flashed and a computer-generated voice told him, *Committed to Reentry*.

The technician terminated the simulation and commanded the computers to reset the conditions for another attempt. Brandt looked at the floor.

"Guess we burned up again." Brian broke the silence.

"Yeah. Still haven't got the hang of the manual system," Andy admitted. "Brandt, isn't there something we can do with the software to generate some lead points?"

Looking up, Brandt spoke into his microphone. "Andy, the whole idea of manual operation is simplicity. As soon as we start to add processing, we risk software errors."

"I know," Andy sighed, "but this is almost impossible to control."

"It's not all that bad," Darrell argued, "but you can't expect to fly as precisely as you do with the full system. Just set the angle of attack, watch the response, and be ready to correct immediately."

Brandt wanted to move on. "Let's get back to emergency procedures."

After turning off his intercom, Brandt instructed the technician to simulate an electrical overload.

"Overload on primary electrical." Darrell caught the failure the instant the annunciator switched on.

"Bringing up the checklist," Brian said as he manipulated the trackball on the armrest of his couch. He quickly ran through a series of tool-kit icons, stopping when the electrical-system symbol appeared followed by a list of procedures.

*1. Non-essential systems: OFF*

He moved the cursor to the item and touched the trackball button to select the automatic procedure. The software disabled dozens of devices while illuminating their caution lights.

*2. Verify load reduction.*

The indicator still showed an overload and the annunciator started to blink, warning of a more serious problem.

"Looks like an increasing current drain. Must be a motor jamming up," Brian said.

*3. If overload persists, Secondary Bus Transfer Switch: ON*

Brian made the selection. Immediately, all displays went dark.

"Aw, blast it!" Brandt fumed.

Darrell threw up his hands. "How are we supposed to get proficient if the simulator keeps screwing up?"

Turning to the technician, Brandt asked, "Can you tell what happened?"

Scanning through numerous display pages, he replied, "Afraid not, sir. Looks like the whole thing crashed."

Pulling off their headsets, the astronauts climbed out of the simulator, down the short flight of stairs, and walked in circles, stretching and twisting to work the cramps out of their muscles.

"Darrell," Brandt said, "you got any idea what's going on with Boeing?"

"Probably no more than you do."

"If these screwups are any indication, the spacecraft's gonna be a piece of horse dung."

"Doesn't breed confidence," Darrell conceded and added, "but don't forget, manual operations aren't their highest priority."

"I hear ya, buddy, but I'm determined to be prepared."

"Ready to go, Colonel," the technician said.

"Okay. Set us up for manual landings. Brian, your turn."

The trio clambered back into the simulator with Brian in the pilot's couch, Andy handling the systems, and Darrell back in the middle.

"Starting at ten-thousand," the technician informed them over the intercom. “Landing zone two.”

Coming alive, the simulator's displays raced through the mission sequence, finally settling at the last stage of the descent to the moon's surface.

Brian scanned the information and called, "Got it."

With the autopilot in control, the simulator showed a gradual reduction in the height of the spacecraft. The left display showed an image of the lunar surface as it would be seen by one of the downward-facing cameras. In the center of the instrument panel, a smaller display showed the orientation of the vehicle as well as the altitude, rate of descent, and horizontal velocity.

As expected, the indicator began to tilt and a red annunciator labeled *Auto Control* flashed. Brian moved the cursor over the warning and punched the trackball button. Then he selected the override icon.

His left hand was already on the sidestick controller, commanding the thrusters to right the spacecraft. With the altitude diminishing, the display of the surface showed ever greater detail.

"Boulders!" Using the stick, he directed the vehicle first to the right, then to the left. "Looks worse." He tried moving it forward. Almost immediately, the terrain appeared smoother. A slide switch on the top of the stick controlled the thrust of the main engines. Brian adjusted it to maintain a steady descent. As he passed through a hundred feet, he added thrust. At fifteen feet, the left display began to blur.

"Blowing up dust," he noted as he transferred his attention to the other screen. He reduced the descent rate until the height indicator read two feet, then one foot, then zero. He slid back the thrust switch, simulating the cutoff of propellant to the engines.

"We're down," he said as he called up the shutdown checklist on the left display.

"Nice going," Brandt said. "That's about as good as it gets—in the simulator anyway."

"Still worried about it being too easy?" Darrell asked.

"Wish we could practice on something closer to the real thing. Simulators can fool you."

"What about that boiler-plate thing they're building?" Andy asked. "The one you recommended."

Darrell said, "I talked to Boeing about the tests when we were in California and they told me they're adding a backup manual control system."

"Not the same as the spacecraft," Brandt replied.

"We could get them to change it. Use the same software."

Brandt nodded. "Think you've got something there, Darrell. I'll give Hensfeld a call."

**White Sands Missile Range**

It was White Sands all right, but not the National Monument. The blinding gypsum dunes with their bus loads of tourists lay far to the north, beyond the interstate that would soon be closed, delaying the visitors' return to Las Cruces. This day, the moon program had priority.

Brandt surveyed the desolate terrain, wondering how the landing system could possibly cope with its endless mounds and gullies. Hensfeld had told him about the skunk bush, how its roots clung tenaciously to the sandy soil. But around them, the relentless wind and powerful flash floods had free reign to erode, cutting away the surface, eventually leaving the plant isolated and the land a labyrinth of furrows.

Looking toward the launch platform, Brandt felt embarrassed about being responsible for such an ugly vehicle. Boeing had built it just as he proposed, a single pipe extending upward with arms jutting out at several levels, each one terminating in a ball. It looked like a huge Tinker Toy creation painted slate gray.

He stated the obvious. "Sure ain't pretty."

Hensfeld nodded and replied, "They call it the *Strickland*."

Chuckling, Brandt replied, "Guess that's as close to immortal as I'll ever get."

"To be honest, you came up with a winner."

"How many flights so far?"

"Only the two we did yesterday. But you were right. They turned up some plume problems."

"Got a fix?"

"Already on the vehicle." He looked at his watch. "We'll find out if it works in a few minutes."

They got in Hensfeld's rented SUV, drove the two miles of dirt road back to the trailer and joined the rest of the crew.

"Look any better than it does on TV?" Darrell asked.

"Worse. Would you believe they named the thing after me?"

Darrell laughed. "Heard about that."

"Which reminds me," Hensfeld said, "we need a name for the

spacecraft. NASA public relations says *Manned Lunar Landing Vehicle* has to go. Any ideas?"

Darrell replied, "I've given it some thought, Jerry. What about *Artemis*—sister of Apollo and goddess of the moon?"

"Sounds perfect," Hensfeld replied. "Okay with you, Brandt?"

He shrugged. "Why not?"

Hensfeld smiled, then turned toward the control console and asked, "Are we ready to go?"

The technician answered, "Waiting for confirmation on the telemetry."

"I'm surprised range safety will let us get this close," Darrell said. "How much distance can that thing cover?"

"More than enough to get here," Hensfeld replied. "But it's got a destruct package on board. If it goes haywire, we'll blow it up."

"Telemetry's green," the technician declared, then entered the launch command into his computer and followed it with the confirmation password.

Watching on the television monitor to the left of the instrument panel, Brandt saw his creation lift from its platform and climb rapidly into the bright sky.

"That's ten thousand," the technician reported. "Coming back down."

"Brandt," Hensfeld said, "I want you to watch this carefully. The lower monitor shows the terrain as the downward-looking cameras see it."

As he spoke, the display showed the ground growing closer.

"The autocorrelator's processing the image, trying to get a match to an ideal pattern. The computer selects the most attractive site, then calculates a descent profile toward the touchdown point."

Brandt saw the altimeter readout drop to one thousand.

"As we get closer, the computer looks for the best orientation as well as position. There! See that? It just commanded a roll to put the landing pads down in the gullies. Now it'll move around to keep the plumes away from the mounds."

Images on the monitor grew larger and more easily identifiable. Finally, specific plant pedestals could be seen. Then the image blurred, obscured by tan dust.

"Touchdown. Engine shutoff." The technician confirmed what the monitors showed.

Hensfeld said, "You'll be trying to duplicate what you saw the computer do."

"Make you nervous, Brandt?" Darrell asked.

Brandt raised his eyebrows. "Don't want to break the toy."

"Don't worry," Hensfeld said. "If you try to land on an unacceptable site, the computer will take over. In fact, while you're operating the vehicle, it'll be figuring out the best way to recover from your errors."

"Appreciate your confidence in our capabilities," Brandt said, smirking.

"How long before they get it turned around?" Darrell asked as he watched the servicing truck head toward the rocket which had landed about fifty feet from the dirt road.

"Won't be long," Hensfeld said. "Better get you into the controller."

He led them to the opposite end of the trailer where the left side of the crew module had been replicated.

"This is the same setup you've got in the simulator except we've only provided the pilot's station. The displays will reproduce what you were just watching on the monitor. Shouldn't be too much different from the images you've been practicing with."

"Except what we've got here is a lot rougher," Darrell noted.

"That's true," Hensfeld said. "The chances of your encountering something this bad on the moon are essentially nil."

"Which makes it ideal for practicing," Brandt said, trying to sound confident.

"Want to go first?" Hensfeld asked.

"Since I got us into this, I guess it's only fair." Brandt slipped into the couch, got comfortable and began to touch the controls and switches, assuring himself that everything felt familiar.

The technician called back, "Ready when you are, Colonel."

Brandt gave him a thumbs up.

As the engines started, the display was obscured by the dust cloud but seconds later it cleared to show the ground dropping away. Brandt glanced at the right-hand screen, checking the height. As it approached ten-thousand feet, he put his hands on the controls. At the top of the display, the words *Manual Control* blinked in red.

Brandt searched the camera image, trying to locate a particularly promising spot, but everything looked about the same. He decided to let the vehicle descend for a while. As it passed through four-thousand feet, he saw what looked like an open area. Using the control stick, he steered toward it, studying the pattern of dark green patches, trying to find the place with the fewest mounds. The altitude showed one-thousand feet, then five hundred. He still couldn't pick out specific gullies.

Finally, when below two-hundred feet, he found a pattern that looked about right. He twisted the control stick to roll the vehicle, aligning it with the points he'd selected for the landing gear. But as he neared them, he saw they were too far apart.

Halting the descent with the thrust control, he moved the vehicle right, then forward, frantically searching for a usable arrangement of plants and channels. Finding something that looked promising, he continued the descent, reorienting the rocket as he went. Finally, the display was blocked by dust and he watched the altitude decrease, using the thrust to achieve the proper rate.

Suddenly, the flashing red message disappeared and the altitude began to increase. At fifty feet it stopped, then decreased as the computer completed the landing.

"Hey, I had that one," Brandt said as Hensfeld appeared.

"Sorry about that. Had to let the computer finish the job. You'd have survived the landing, but the engines would have ended up right over a mound. Might have damaged one of the nozzle skirts."

Brandt shook his head. "That's not even a little bit easy. Darrell, you ready to give it a try?"

He wrinkled his brow. "Don't know. Jerry, you sure the computer can recover if I screw things up?"

"No problem. Besides, we've already got all the data we need."

"Which is the only reason you're letting us play around, right?"

"Bingo!"

After the astronauts had each completed two flights, Hensfeld summed up their efforts. "You guys did better than I thought you would. Darrell's first try was marginal, but the others were definitely survivable."

"Gotta be careful around here," Brandt snickered. "With praise like that, you might end up with ego problems."

"Maybe we should make him fly the damned thing," Darrell suggested.

Hensfeld's eyes opened wide. "Not a chance! It's obvious you've spent a lot of time in the simulator. Which brings up a good point. How did this compare with the sim's dynamics?"

Darrell replied, "I thought the pitch control seemed a little sluggish."

Hensfeld nodded. "We've added an additional component. Put it in the empty space in the nose."

Brandt asked, "What is it?"

"The thing you all put at the top of your wish lists."

"The toilet!" Brandt shouted ecstatically. "You got us the toilet!"

"Yup," Hensfeld grinned. "Had the room, had the weight, so why not?"

"Boy," Darrell said, "bet Collen loved you for that!"

Hensfeld laughed. "It was the *I told you so* heard 'round the world. But he got over it."

"Buddy, you have no idea how much you've improved this operation—not having to use those blasted bags."

"I'll ditto Brandt on that," Darrell agreed. "You're a real hero."

"Glad you're pleased. Ready to try another flight?"

The technician interrupted them. "Telephone for Colonel Strickland."

"For me? Who'd be calling me here?" He walked to the other end of the trailer and picked up the receiver.

After a brief conversation, he put the phone down and returned to the group. "Darrell, you're not gonna believe this. We've got to be in the Pentagon tomorrow—nine a.m. sharp."

"You're putting me on."

"Told ya you wouldn't believe it."

"What are we supposed to do about this operation?"

"Guess we could work in one more round, then hightail it back to Houston. I need to get home. Didn't bring a dress uniform along."

"How thoughtless," Darrell joked.

"Know what this is all about?" Brandt asked coyly.

"Haven't a clue."

"Career-impact counseling."

Darrell looked back in disbelief. "Bullshit!"

"Nope. Got a call from Chief of Staff's office last week. Said they wanted to discuss assignment preferences—for when we get back from the moon. Never thought they'd force us to make a special trip."

"Great timing." Darrell muttered. "And they want us in

blues?"

"With all decorations. Something about an official portrait with General Cushman. We'll get the orders at Ellington base ops after we land."

"Incredible!"

"No use complaining. Let's see if we can nail a landing before we go."

## Chapter 9

# Weapons

**Pentagon**

"Unbelievable!" Brandt thought. "Absolutely bizarre!" Looking at their faces, he knew the other three astronauts felt the same way. He wanted nothing more than to share his exasperation, but the anteroom of the Chief of Staff's suite was hardly the place for a bitch session.

A master sergeant entered the room and held the door while a photographer carried in a tripod-mounted camera and a leather bag. He scanned the name tags, spotted at Brandt's and said, "Colonel Strickland, if you're ready, I'd like to get you posed before General Cushman comes in."

The next ten minutes were spent rotating torsos, lowering chins and touching up Brian's nose with a dab of powder. Finally, Cushman arrived and, after greeting the astronauts, began her own ordeal with the photographer. A few minutes later, it was over.

"As long as you're here," Cushman said offhandedly, "why don't you give me an update on the training program." She led them into her office, closed the door and walked to her desk.

Brandt watched as she opened the lower left drawer, bent over and reached inside. A panel behind the desk slipped open to reveal an eight-foot-square room with a plain metal table in the center. Six plastic chairs completed the furnishings. The tan walls were perfectly flat, as was the brown, painted floor and the white ceiling. A single lamp in the center of the table provided the only light. Brandt noticed it had no power cord.

"Son-of-a-gun!" Brandt thought, both surprised and fascinated. He'd heard of these rooms but had never seen one.

"Please go in," Cushman said.

After they'd left her office, she tapped something on the device in her desk, closed the drawer and stepped into the room. A few seconds later, the door slid shut.

After walking to the far side of the table, she said, "This is a Security-Level-M Briefing Facility. Its location—its very existence—is top secret. Please sit down."

Brandt scanned the room. There were no vents, no outlets, no telephone jacks—in fact, no connections whatever to the outside world. As he sat down, he noticed something mounted on the underside of the table. He stole a quick glance and saw the louvered ports that answered his question. "Atmosphere regenerator. Like a spaceship."

"Gentleman," Cushman began, "the official classification level of this briefing is top secret. However, the material requires much more than routine precautions.

"We've just received some intelligence from a CIA agent operating in the Federation. The unauthorized disclosure of the information would lead to ramifications more serious than any I've ever encountered. It is only after careful deliberation that I've decided to add you to the handful of people who know of these findings." She paused to let the words sink in.

"One of our few functioning operatives has been working in Akademgorodok, the research center near Novosibirsk where the Russians do most of their advanced weapons development. In recent months, this agent has been following two activities related to the moon mission.

"First, we've been trying to find out what happened to two physicists who were sent there from the Kurchatov Institute—the ones Colonel Wilkins felt might have made a fusion energy breakthrough. To the best of my knowledge, we've learned nothing.

"Second, we've been curious about the experiment the Russians are bringing to the moon. In particular, we've been wondering why it's being built in Akademgorodok rather than at a university or research institute. Two days ago, we got our first information.

"The beginning of the message contained a reasonably detailed description of the device. Except for its size, there were no surprises. It appears to be a mineralogy laboratory with the capability of coring rather deeply into the lunar surface. This part of the message ended saying the second portion was also related to their moon program.

"Unfortunately, it is virtually undecipherable. Apparently, the agent either selected an unusable combination of scrambling algorithms or the encoding device failed. For obvious reasons, we can't contact him to find out what happened. In fact, it's quite possible he's been picked up by the FSA.

"As I indicated, the CIA's attempts to decode the message have been unsuccessful. So far, only a few words have been recovered, most of no consequence. One word, however, was enough to bring you to this meeting. In several instances, the analysts identified the word *weapon*.

"Obviously," Cushman continued, "we don't know what this means. It could refer to some future plans, uses for lunar materials. Who knows? But it might refer to arms being carried by the cosmonauts. That deeply concerns me and, because it could possibly threaten your personal safety, I wanted to discuss the matter with you."

"Ma'am, I find it very hard to believe that any cosmonaut would carry a weapon," Andy said. "It's against everything that's been done in space."

"My initial reaction also, Commander. However, after discussing this with the Director of Central Intelligence, I've been forced to concede that, given the circumstances surrounding the Russian program, the possibility cannot be dismissed.

"I agree with Colonel Strickland's conclusion that the Socialist Federation is determined to get to the moon before we do, claim it and then exploit the helium three. If we arrive first, it is not inconceivable that they'd use force to establish their claim."

Brian blurted out, "Ma'am, are you saying they'll try to kill us?"

"Only that they might."

"But we probably won't land in the same place."

"Remember Major, if we get there first, they'll know where we are. If they wish to, they can land nearby—claim they're responding to the President's invitation."

"Could be why they won't announce their landing site," Darrell suggested.

Cushman looked at her watch. "I'd like to hear your thoughts about our response."

No one spoke.

"Our options are rather obvious," she prompted them. "We can do nothing. Just hope the message has a benign explanation or they really won't resort to force."

"Which would leave us at their mercy if we guess wrong," Brandt responded.

"Or, we can provide you with some protection."

"Carry guns?" Andy was obviously uncomfortable with the idea.

"Probably not guns. If we decide to develop some form of defense, it must be absolutely secret. No one involved in the preparation of the spacecraft can know."

"Ma'am, that'll be awfully hard to pull off," Darrell said. "The technicians examine every square inch of the vehicle."

"We'll have to be very careful. But first, do you want weapons?"

Once again, the astronauts were unable to answer.

"Gentlemen, the door opens in three minutes. That will conclude this briefing."

Brandt tried to respond. "Ma'am, this is very hard to decide. Depends on how you feel about the Russians. Personally, I wouldn't put anything past their government. But the cosmonauts—that's another matter. Hard to believe they'd agree to carry weapons."

"They're military officers," Brian reminded them. "They'll obey orders."

"What about the third one?" Andy asked. "He's not in the military."

"He's related to a high government official," Brian replied. "I'd trust him least of all."

Without much conviction, Darrell said, "I guess we should look into developing some type of defense, just in case. If they get the message decoded and it turns out we don't need it, we can always stop."

"Very well," Cushman said, trying to conclude the meeting. "Obviously, this isn't something we can put out for open bid. We'll have to rely upon a special weapons unit in the CIA. They develop devices for operatives.

"I must caution you once more." She spoke slowly and distinctly, emphasizing every word. "You will not speak of this again after you leave this room. Not even to each other. You will discuss this with no one, under any circumstances. Have I made myself clear?"

Four heads nodded silently.

"The level of Federation espionage has increased dramatically since the start of the moon program. With few exceptions, this room being one of them, there is no location where you can be completely confident of security.

"I intend to keep the number of people aware of this to an absolute minimum. This means excluding even high-level government officials. I can think of nothing worse than having this fall into the laps of the politicians."

At that moment, the door opened. Her manner changed abruptly to that of a cordial hostess.

"That's about it," she said brightly as she led them back into her office. "Sorry to pull you away from your work. Hope the briefing helped make the trip worthwhile."

They left as a group, making their way through the Pentagon corridors back to the staff car that would take them to Andrews and their T-38s.

**Baikonur Cosmodrome**

Tsvigun looked out across the wasteland. In every direction, the scrub plants of the Kirghiz Steppe withered and the crust of the dry earth cracked. The van's air conditioning had lost its battle with the August sun. As they made their way toward the headquarters building, sweat dripped from the foreheads of its occupants and soaked the underarms of their short-sleeved shirts.

Sitting next to Tsvigun, Belyaev continued his glowing account of the government's success in gaining funding from the Duma while suppressing dissent from the populace. Responding with enthusiasm to the Defense Minister's bombastic bragging aggravated Tsvigun's fatigue and the dizziness brought on by his medical treatments.

Ligachev sat in front, next to the driver, saying nothing.

"Ah, here we are," Tsvigun said as they stopped in front of the only attractive building in the Cosmodrome. He hurried from the van into the comfortably air-conditioned lobby and followed Belyaev down a hallway to a small but well-appointed office.

"My home in Kazakhstan," Ligachev remarked as they settled into the light-green overstuffed chairs.

Belyaev opened the discussion, asking Tsvigun, "Yevgeni, how would you rate the training of the cosmonauts? I am concerned about the way the crew functions together. Assuming Bakatin is able to go, do you think he'll work well with the others?"

Tsvigun answered, "I believe any problems of that nature have been resolved. At least Zosimova doesn't refer to them anymore. If she still has reservations about Bakatin, she keeps them to herself."

"I asked you about Bakatin, not Zosimova," Belyaev said stiffly.

Flinching imperceptibly at the inappropriately curt retort, Tsvigun replied, "Yes, you did. I understand he's worked very hard to meet the highest standards of proficiency."

Belyaev seemed surprised. "Can he really accomplish the necessary tasks?"

"Necessary?" Tsvigun responded. "Yes, absolutely. Zosimova abandoned the idea of having every crew member capable of performing every function. They each have a primary assignment and a backup role."

"And they've accomplished that?"

"I'd say they're on schedule. There's still a lot of work to do—mostly joint simulations with control-center personnel. That started last week."

"Which gives them only three weeks to practice."

"If we want them here a month before the launch."

Seeming puzzled, Ligachev asked, "Why must they spend so much time in Baikonur? They could accomplish a lot more at Zvezdny Gorodok."

Tsvigun looked at Belyaev for a nod of approval, then said, "They'll have some additional equipment to work with, Vladimir. Highly secret equipment."

Picking up the explanation, Belyaev continued, "We shouldn't discuss this here, although I'm sure the FSA has rid Baikonur of all those who were disloyal. I'd like to spend an hour with you this evening to show you the apparatus."

Clearly upset, Ligachev argued, "If you plan to add anything to the payload, I must know immediately, unless it weighs virtually nothing."

Tsvigun half smiled. "It won't be a problem."

Ligachev replied angrily, "I assume you had sound reasons for not informing me of this."

Belyaev responded, "When you learn of our problem, I'm sure you'll appreciate the need for secrecy."

***

Belyaev stopped his staff car in front of a small, trailer-like building at the edge of an abandoned tracking complex. As he climbed from the back seat, Tsvigun scanned the horizon, trying to orient himself. Even in the gauzy light of the half moon, he quickly identified the Zenit launch towers and processing buildings. He placed their location about ten kilometers to the north.

"What the hell are we doing here?" Ligachev asked. "This hasn't been used for years."

"Its principal attraction!" Belyaev answered. "Let's go inside. As the group walked toward the building, an army sergeant carrying an assault rifle seemed to appear from nowhere. With a few words, the Defense Minister convinced him of their legitimacy. The soldier unlocked the metal door and pulled it open.

Following Belyaev, Tsvigun stepped up into a windowless, pitch-black room. The air was stifling and he began to feel dizzy as he groped in the darkness. He felt Belyaev's strong hand grab his arm.

Once Ligachev was inside, Belyaev closed the door and switched on a row of fluorescent lights that ran down the center of the ceiling. It took Tsvigun a moment to adjust to the glare.

No larger than a one-car garage, the room was empty except for two large platforms, crudely fabricated from metal supports and wooden beams. On each sat a rectangular container about the size of a half-meter-high stack of wallboard.

"Experiment mockups?" Ligachev asked. "Why did you bring them here?"

"Not mockups, Vladimir," Belyaev said. "This one is the actual experiment."

Not comprehending, Ligachev responded, "There are two of them?"

"No, this is the only one."

"Then what did we load into the lander last week?"

"A replacement. The box on the other platform contains a

mockup."

Ligachev walked around the object, carefully examining every attachment and connector. "It looks identical. What's inside?"

"A laser, Vladimir. Open it up."

After carefully rotating the latching devices in the proper order, Ligachev lifted the covers.

"Just like the experiment."

"Not quite, Vladimir," Tsvigun said. "The mineral-analysis module opens into a tracker and the cylinder is a chemical laser, not the boring machine. The rest of the space is taken up by electronics."

"What the hell is it for?"

"It's a gun, designed to destroy incoming spacecraft."

Obviously disturbed, Ligachev replied, "A weapon? For what purpose?"

Tsvigun listened as Belyaev outlined the government's strategy, assuring Ligachev the gun would never be used, explaining the legalities that made it necessary.

But Ligachev wasn't convinced. "I don't believe this justifies a departure from established policies to bar weapons from space. Any disclosure of this would be disastrous."

Belyaev argued, "Vladimir, when I first told Yevgeni of our plan, he reacted the same way. But I convinced him that, if we don't make a defensible claim, the Americans will and they'll bring whatever weapons they need to enforce it. Do you really believe they'd share any part of the moon's wealth?"

Shaking his head rapidly from side to side, Ligachev answered, "I don't know, but I can't allow this to proceed. I must return to Moscow to confer with the President."

Standing, Belyaev informed him, "I'm sorry, Vladimir, that will not be possible. You will remain in Leninsk until the launch."

Appalled, he stammered, "I'm under arrest?"

"Nothing of the kind, I assure you. You are merely required to observe the same security precautions as others who have knowledge of the weapon."

"You'd have detained me even if I'd supported your plan?"

Belyaev answered haughtily, "To be honest, no. In fact, I had hoped this inconvenience would not be necessary."

"Am I to remain in my room?" he said, his face reddening.

"Of course not, Vladimir," Belyaev responded in a patronizing tone. "You may come and go as you please. However, any communications will be monitored and you'll be escorted by a security agent."

Tsvigun tried to intervene. "Please, Anatoly, don't be hasty. Let Vladimir think things over, ask questions, discuss the problems as he sees them. We needn't make these decisions tonight."

Belyaev paused for a moment, looking straight ahead at the wall. Then he replied, "I quite agree, Yevgeni. Let us say no more of this until tomorrow. Come, it's time we got some sleep."

But a quick glance at Ligachev told Tsvigun there would be no compromise. Unable to look into the eyes of his former mentor, he found the drive back to the lodge almost unbearably painful. He knew they would never speak again.

## Chapter 10

# Sims

**Johnson Space Center**

As Brian reconfigured the Artemis simulator, Brandt sat at the primary control console studying the displays. He didn't see Collen and Hensfeld enter the simulator bay.

"Okay, Colonel," Collen barked. "What do you want?"

Startled, Brandt whirled his swivel chair around, recognized Collen and answered, "Ron, your system doesn't make sense. We've gone through a bunch of emergencies with both the computer and the backup and almost every time the procedures aren't the same."

Collen shrugged. "So, what else is new?"

Trying again, Brandt said, "Show you what I mean. I've got the ship about midway to the moon and I'm going to create a leak in the hydrogen tank of the number two fuel cell." Brandt touched his light pen to an icon at the left of the desired emergency.

"Now, with the primary computer working, here's what we get."

The right-hand display changed to show a diagram of the fuel-cell system with a blinking diamond at the location of the leak. Below it was a list of the actions taken by the computer to correct the problem.

"Okay, I'm going to save this." He transferred the information to the adjacent display.

"Now I'll fix the leak, bring the simulator back to the original condition and then fail the primary computer. Brian will go through the recovery procedure and get the ship working on the backup."

Collen yawned, obviously bored by the demonstration.

"Now, supposedly, we're in exactly the same condition. Watch what happens when I put in the leak."

Another list of required actions appeared.

"See! They're not the same. Backup says transfer all the remaining hydrogen into the number-one system but the computer divides it between one and three."

Stretching, Collen said, "Colonel, the responses will probably never be the same."

"Why not?"

Sounding annoyed, Collen answered, "Because the situations aren't the same. Don't you get it?"

"But they are. I used identical configurations."

"No you didn't. The second time, you failed the primary computer."

Brandt looked back blankly.

Hensfeld tried to explain. "Brandt, when you input a failure, the primary computer examines the status of every associated component and devises the best possible approach to deal with the problem. The backup can't do that."

In a mocking voice, Collen said, "Know what the trouble is, Jerry? These guys want something to do. They want us to display a list of procedures, just like we do with that stupid backup, so they can turn off valves and switches and then worry about what they just screwed up."

"What we want, Ron, is a way out if your distributed-processing wonder screws up!" Brandt replied angrily.

Collen taunted, "No reason to get pissed off, Colonel. Anyway, that's why we agreed to the backup. But you know what worries me? That you idiots will use it to override the main processor just so you'll have something to play with."

"I wouldn't put it that way," Hensfeld intervened, "but I'm concerned about your lack of faith in the primary system. There's no way you can match its capabilities with the backup."

Brandt thought for a bit, then responded, "Truth is, it's weird sitting in the simulator with the primary system working, have the operator fail a major component, and then get a message on the display saying the computer's taken care of everything. How do we know it's done the right things?"

"You can call up a list of every action in the response if you want to."

"Suppose we don't like what we see? You're saying we have to trust the computer."

"You have control of everything in the vehicle. And if you make a mistake, the computer will handle the problem, tell you what's wrong, and advise you of a corrective action."

"Save us from our own folly," Brandt quipped.

Hensfeld smiled. "Something like that. Just remember, the backup doesn't do anything for you. If you have a single failure, you can trust the checklists. Otherwise, you'll have to figure out whether the procedures will lead to more problems."

"Best you can do for us?"

"Hell no, Colonel," Collen interrupted. "It's what you insisted on: the most direct control possible. And that's what you've got."

Brandt tried to sum things up. "Jerry, as I understand it, unless we have a catastrophic computer failure, our best response to an emergency will be to sit with our arms folded and read the displays, is that right?"

Hensfeld nodded. "Essentially. The computer will handle everything."

"So that means the only real training we can get is with the backup, and there's almost no chance of ever using it."

Stroking his chin, Hensfeld answered, "That's going too far, Brandt. I think it's important for you to exercise the primary system; see how it handles different combinations of failures; try to determine the impact on mission performance. Think of it this way. The computer system does the dog work, but that's the end of it. As far as making judgment calls about modifying mission objectives, that's between you and Mission Control, same as always."

Still troubled, Brandt replied, "I get the picture all right, but it means we're wasting time training by ourselves. We should start integrated sims right away. If the primary objective is to analyze mission impact, we ought to be working with Mission Control."

"Couldn't agree more," Hensfeld replied. "In fact, that's one of the reasons we're at JSC: to talk to the flight controllers."

"Talk about what?" Brandt said. "As of last week, Mission Control had barely started generating profiles. Where's the training team? Who's the Sim Sup?"

Hensfeld nodded as he listened and responded, "Don't have any answers, Brandt. But we'll be working the problem."

As Collen and Hensfeld left the simulator bay, Brandt said, "That leave you with feelings of cozy confidence?"

"Shit," Brian answered. "I still don't get that computer stuff. I think we should keep going until we can accomplish the whole damned mission with the backup."

Brandt gave him a thumbs-up.

**Star City**

"My God," Svetlana thought, "it's easier to count the systems still working than the ones we've lost." By the end of the fourth day, she'd grown tired of the endless barrage of malfunctions. Now, nearing reentry, she struggled to bring the crippled descent module toward its encounter with the upper atmosphere.

"Soyuz, this is Flight Control." It was Alex. "Five minutes until lithium hydroxide depletion. Recommend you terminate regeneration."

"Confirm that, Flight Control," Mikhail answered. "Going to emergency oxygen." After pulling up the system diagram, he highlighted the actuators and selected the appropriate commands.

"Soyuz, this is Flight Control. I have your final trajectory estimates based on your last guidance-system alignment and star fix. The uncertainty band still falls outside the maximum-G limit. Recommend you maneuver to control the G-load and ignore the landing location."

"Understand, Flight Control," Svetlana replied. "We're still working on the position update."

With the optical-alignment sight pointed toward the simulator's small porthole, Vadim scanned the computer-generated star field, quickly identifying the designated constellations and manipulating the device until the patterns matched. As quickly as possible, he loaded the derived position coordinates into the memory of the last functioning computer and then transmitted the numbers that fixed the location of the spacecraft. The loss of nearly all telemetry mandated the crude process.

Seconds later, Alex called, "Soyuz, Flight Control. The uncertainty is reduced but you're still close to the G-limit. Stand by for best-estimate touchdown based on maximum load factor."

"Fuel-cell oxygen pressure dropping," Mikhail reported, the tension in his voice increasing. "Checking bus voltage. Increasing load. Voltage constant. Assuming sensor-bias failure." He raced through a batch of system diagrams, found the one he wanted, tagged the errant sensor and reset its alarm limits. "Limits adjusted. Warning light out."

"Good going," Svetlana whispered, concentrating on her display's attitude and velocity information. Her forward speed began to stabilize, then decrease. "We're into reentry," she said. "Vadim, call out the Gs."

"Soyuz, Flight Control. Touchdown offset now one-two-zero kilometers. Recovery operations being directed to the location. Expect arrival within four-five minutes after impact."

"Wish he wouldn't say *impact*," Svetlana thought, then answered, "Understand, Flight Control. Estimate two minutes to S-band blackout."

The next few minutes were an eternity, a period of total inactivity after hours of tumult. Vadim's voice ended it. "G-forces building. Two, three, four..."

Svetlana fired the thrusters to adjust the module's angle, creating a lift force that would control its plunge into the denser atmosphere.

"...five, five-point-five..."

Using the attitude indicator, she made tiny adjustments to the pitch, trying to keep as close to six Gs as possible.

"Getting right at six now. Six, six, five-point-eight..."

"Cabin temperature increasing," Mikhail announced calmly.

"Five-point-eight, five-point-seven, five-point-nine..."

"Fuel-cell temperature increasing." Mikhail sounded more concerned.

Now halfway through the blackout, Svetlana stared at the display, utterly engrossed in keeping two lines in the proper relationship. One line too high, she would drastically overshoot the safe-landing zone; too low, she would burn through the heat shield.

"Cabin temperature forty; fuel-cell temperature forty-four."

"...six, six-point-one!" Vadim's voice rose as she edged beyond the G-limit.

"...six, five-point-nine..."

"Cabin temperature four-five; fuel-cell temperature five zero. Stand by for fuel-cell failure."

"...five-point-eight, five-point-nine..."

"Voltage dropping. Switching to emergency batteries." Mikhail punched the trackball button, then watched as the bus voltage stabilized. "Cabin temperature four-eight."

Still maintaining her intense concentration, Svetlana uttered through her clenched teeth, "Makes you glad this thing doesn't simulate the temperature too."

"...five-point-eight. Sure would be warm in here, Svetlana. Five-point-eight, five-point-four..."

"Okay, we're through it," Svetlana said, still working to maintain a precise orientation.

Alex called, "Soyuz, this is Flight Control, do you read?"

After Vadim acknowledged, Alex continued, "We're predicting impact four-zero kilometers southwest of the target. Excellent work!"

Releasing the controls, Svetlana felt the tension begin to melt away. "Thank you, Flight Control. From here on, we're just along for the ride."

"Unless something else goes wrong," Alex joked. "By the way, I just got the readout on your heat shield. You made it with about two millimeters to spare."

Mikhail continued to follow his checklist. "Jettisoning outer porthole panes."

Shedding the coloring algorithm it had invoked with the reentry procedure, the computer cleared the images on the window display, revealing a sparkling picture of southern Kazakhstan. Moments later, Mikhail announced, "Primary parachute deployment." He opened the simulator's side door, one of the few differences between it and the spacecraft.

"And that, my friends, is that!" Vadim declared as he unstrapped himself.

"I half expected those bastards to throw in a parachute failure," Svetlana said as she followed Mikhail out of the simulator.

"Or maybe both parachutes," Vadim joked. "Be just like them to put us through all that and then kill us."

**Johnson Space Center**

"Man, that was the strangest sim I've ever been through," Brian said as they left the debriefing room on their way to the cafeteria.

"Amen, pardner!" Brandt agreed. "Just sat there the whole dang morning watching everybody else do the work."

"Sure don't feel the way I do after a round of Shuttle aborts," Darrell said. "But you have to admit, the computer system's awesome."

"Brandt, who came up with those malfunctions?" Brian asked.

"I did, Brian—and that's what bothers me the most."

Darrell guessed his meaning. "No training team."

"You got it, buddy. I get real twitchy being both instructor and student. Not much of a test when you get to make up the problems."

"Guess it goes with flying a new vehicle," Darrell said.

Brandt smirked. "Goes with NASA understaffing the program. Andy, what did you think of the pipsqueak control center?"

"Kind of cramped with only eighteen consoles, but the Artemis mission is pretty simple. Not much different from an unmanned operation."

"Except for us," Brian noted. "The excess baggage. Doesn't seem right having the big center doing the Shuttle part while Artemis gets controlled from a weather-satellite facility."

"No way Transpace would give up the CCC," Brandt replied.

"Good news about the ship, though," Darrell said, changing the subject. "Sounds like the final firing test went off by the numbers."

"That's one I'd have enjoyed watching," Brian said. "Too bad we were tied up here."

As they entered the Branch Cafeteria, Andy commented, "We'll have about forty-five minutes for lunch, then fifteen to get into flight suits."

"I hope the dang picture-taking doesn't take all afternoon," Brandt groused.

## Chapter 11

# Target Practice

**Johnson Space Center**

The day's activities had already stretched Brandt's limited patience. Pictures at the duck pond, pictures in their offices, pictures in the simulator. But the photographer wasn't finished. "Gentlemen," he said, "I'd like to do one more series in an open environment—without any buildings around."

Having received a memo from Cushman's office requesting his complete cooperation, Brandt had little choice but to acquiesce. They piled back into the NASA van and headed toward the northern part of the Space Center. A few minutes later, the photographer pulled to the side of the road, picked up his tripod-mounted camera and walked toward a small clump of trees. He set up his camera, then walked forward to pose the crew.

As he adjusted chins and shoulder angles he said, "As you may have guessed, this operation has nothing to do with photographs. My name is Gates. I'm from the CIA—in charge of special weapons development. We've developed a weapon that will provide some basic protection should the Russians take any hostile action."

He dropped back to his camera, made some adjustments and took several pictures, calling out requests to move one way or the other. Then he returned to refine the poses.

"The weapon is quite simple, an electrically-fired, single-shot barrel. It will be mounted under a new layer of cloth on the upper arm of the space suit, completely undetectable. The round is a fléchette with a small explosive charge. It can easily penetrate a Russian space suit and the warhead will guarantee that any hit is immediately incapacitating and quickly fatal. This leaves the problem of training. Col. Strickland, you'll have to request the use of NASA's zero-gravity aircraft for lunar walking practice. You've got two weeks to complete the preparations."

Brandt's eyes narrowed. "Mr. Gates, I'm going to have one tough time convincing NASA we've suddenly developed a critical need for the KC-135."

Obviously not interested in complaints, Gates snapped, "Base your request on the inadequacy of the existing lunar-walking equipment. Stage some incidents if you have to."

Then he continued rapidly, "Because of the need for secrecy, we'll have to keep the flight crew out of the way. Colonel Strickland, you'll need to have the cabin blocked off aft of the forward door. I'll provide a bullet stop that will protect the rear wall. I've arranged a briefing for you tomorrow morning covering the details. Oh yes. I'll come along as the official photographer."

He took one more picture before leading them back to the van.

**Baikonur Cosmodrome**

Svetlana had stayed in the cottages many times before, but never for a month. She surveyed her bedroom, annoyed by its disorder. Even her Spartan lifestyle demanded more clothing than could be fitted into a chest of drawers and one small closet. She'd been forced to leave many things in suitcases.

Her frequent glances through the window were finally rewarded by the sight of a Cosmodrome van pulling up in front. She checked herself in the bathroom mirror, tucked the back of her mauve blouse into the narrow waist of her loose-fitting white slacks and left the cottage.

As Svetlana climbed aboard, she saw that Vadim and Alex were already in the van. A short distance down the road, they picked up Mikhail and headed for the Energia assembly building. The driver escorted them inside where Tsvigun waited beside the transporter erector.

"Thought we could watch the final integration together," Tsvigun said. "But you can't see much from down here. We'll need to go to the top floor."

As he led them to the elevator, Svetlana tried to absorb the incredible scene around her. The transporter erector occupied the same position it had during her last visit. Looking up along its side, she could see only two of the Energia-booster strap-ons and a small part of the core. Far above, a bridge crane moved slowly toward them, the completely integrated spacecraft dangling from its cables.

The group emerged on the ninth floor and found places along the railing at the edge of the walkway. By this time, the crane had moved the vehicle to a position directly above the SL-17's core. Majestically, the precious spacecraft descended toward the attachments on the SL-17. Technicians, standing at the end of a long mobile arm, studied the approach and relayed their observations to the crane operator. Finally, the vehicle settled into its supports and the men on the arm began to insert temporary attachments.

Svetlana became aware of her pounding heartbeat and rapid breathing. She suppressed the embarrassingly emotional response, turned to Tsvigun and said, "I expected to see Doctor Ligachev here. Did he return to Kaliningrad?"

Sounding uneasy, Tsvigun replied, "No, Svetlana. I thought you'd have heard by now. He was taken ill, some sort of intestinal disorder. Nothing serious, I understand, but he'll have to spend some time recuperating."

"That's so unfortunate," Svetlana said, "not being able to see the culmination of all his work. I hope he'll be well enough to watch the launch."

Tsvigun's eyes looked through her as he replied wistfully, "So do I, Svetlana. I know how much he'd enjoy it." Then, seeming to bring himself back, he said, "Not much else to see here. I've got one more thing I need to show you."

***

Tsvigun told the driver to stop about twenty meters from the small building, alongside an army staff car. He opened the van's sliding door and walked toward the soldier guarding the entrance. The sergeant recognized him immediately and opened the door, then descended the three steps and stood to one side. Tsvigun led them in, closed the door and turned on the lights.

"More experiment training?" Svetlana exclaimed, recognizing

the large black containers. "Yevgeni, there's nothing we don't already know about the damned thing."

Sounding amused, he replied, "I promise you won't spend another minute working with the mineralogy equipment." He patted the box on the stand to his left and walked toward the other device. "This is what you'll be working with, and it's not a science experiment."

Sounding confused, Mikhail said, "It looks the same. What is it?"

"Before I tell you," Tsvigun continued, "let me explain some of the problems we've run into with our plan to prevent the Americans from claiming the moon. First of all, under international law, we can't claim it for all nations. If we tried, the Americans could legally ignore us and take it anyway. We must first claim it for the Federation, then grant other nations rights of access. One of the reasons for bringing you here this early is to provide time for briefings from our Foreign Affairs Ministry. They'll tell you precisely what you must do to make a legal claim.

"Our other problem involves supporting a claim once it's been legally made. We could do this by establishing a permanent operation on the moon. That would give us the right to claim some reasonable area.

"If it wasn't for the Americans, we'd follow that course of action. Unfortunately, they're not likely to afford us the time necessary to establish a mining facility. In fact, if we don't stay on schedule, they may own the whole moon in a matter of months."

"From what you just said," Vadim argued, "I don't see how they could do that. Wouldn't they have to set up a mining operation? And wouldn't their claim include only the area they're developing?"

"Allow me to finish, Vadim," Tsvigun responded. "It turns out, there's another way to establish ownership. Basically, you can claim territory you're able to defend. We've uncovered an American plan to launch a series of unmanned vehicles that will land on the moon and set up missile batteries." Tsvigun stumbled over the words.

Svetlana snorted, "I guess that tells us how far they'll go, doesn't it?"

"This has created a dilemma for us," Tsvigun went on. "The only hope we have to thwart the American plan is to establish a valid claim first. As I've told you, this means providing some means of defense. Now let me tell you what's in the container."

He bent over it and began to unfasten the latches. "This is our weapon, a small chemical laser. You'll spend a good part of your time here learning how to set it up and put it into operation."

Fascinated, the crewmembers remained silent.

"The engineers at Akademgorodok did a marvelous job designing it to match the mechanical configuration of the mineralogy experiment. You'll find the basic layout very familiar."

"Yevgeni, excuse me," Svetlana interrupted. "You're saying we're going to do precisely what you just condemned the Americans for?"

"No, Svetlana, although I understand your concern. As I explained, we must set up the laser to substantiate our claim. However, the government has no intention of using it—except, perhaps, to destroy American weapon carriers should that become necessary. As soon as you land, we'll announce our claim to the moon, disclose the despotic American plan, and state our commitment to free and open access. Once we obtain the support of other nations, we're confident the Americans will abandon their objectives. At that time, we'll disable the weapon."

Svetlana walked to the side of the laser and stared down at the device without really seeing it. Her mind raced as she tried to absorb the new situation and catalog the changes it made to the mission. The warlike overtones disturbed her, but Tsvigun's explanation sounded entirely logical, an unimpeachable justification of the plan. Still, something about his voice bothered her—a certain hesitation, as if he didn't quite believe what he was saying.

"Now we come to a most distressful development," Tsvigun continued, sounding sincerely concerned, "one that utterly astonishes me. We have reason to believe the American crew will be armed."

Audible gasps came from each of the astronauts. Svetlana blurted out, "That's beyond comprehension, Yevgeni! Are you sure of this?"

"We are certain they're developing some type of anti-personnel weapon for their astronauts. The work is being done by a unit of their Central Intelligence Agency. Fortunately, we have an agent there. But, at this time, I have no other information."

"Are you saying they plan to kill us?" Vadim stammered in disbelief.

"I can think of no other reason for their actions."

"But Yevgeni," Svetlana protested, "that doesn't make sense.

They've already announced their landing site, and it's far from where we'll be."

"And, if by some miracle, they arrive first, I'm sure that's where they'll go. But they have the ability to change their destination, even during the mission. And remember their President's announcement that they'll try to meet us on the moon. They've already set the stage."

Staggered by Tsvigun's words, Svetlana exclaimed, "Then we must expose them! Tell the rest of the world!"

"If only it was that easy, Svetlana—but they'd simply deny the allegation—say we invented the story for propaganda purposes. They might even allow independent inspections of the spacecraft to disprove it. The only outcome would be embarrassment for the Federation."

Obviously shaken, Mikhail asked, "What can we do?"

"I've already directed the small-arms group at Akademgorodok to begin developing weapons for you. I expect them to be available within two weeks. You'll have to take time from your other activities to practice using them."

"I'm sorry, Yevgeni," Svetlana said, "but this is almost unbelievable. How sure are we of the intelligence? Has there been any verification? The Americans have always been committed to banning weapons from space."

Tsvigun sighed. "Our agents are working hard to obtain better information. For now, we have to respond to what I've told you. But I think it simply demonstrates what the Americans are capable of when great wealth is at stake."

**Over Galveston**

Sitting in the last of the four rows of seats behind the temporary partition, Brandt peered through one of the KC-135's few windows, watching Galveston slip by as they climbed east toward the Gulf of Mexico. Speaking to Gates, who'd taken the adjacent seat, he said, "Hope we didn't blow security doing this flight. The NASA folks sure looked at me funny when I told them what I wanted, especially since we'd lambasted this old wreck when they offered it earlier in the program."

"Chance we'll have to take, Colonel. Are the suits you brought the same as the ones you'll be wearing on the moon?"

"Pretty close. We use them to practice moon walking. Main difference is the fittings for the harness."

"Where are the fittings located?"

"Near the waist ring."

Gates thought for a moment. "Shouldn't be a problem."

As the plane climbed above a layer of thermal turbulence, the ride smoothed out.

"Time to get to work," Gates said as he unbuckled. "I'll need your help, Colonel. We'll start with the big case in the back."

They stepped carefully across what looked like a twenty-foot-long sandbox filled with a thin layer of dirt and rocks, arriving at an open area next to the rear partition. Gates unlocked the case and removed what looked like a large photographer's reflector. He began to unfold it.

Brandt examined the material that appeared to be a half-inch layer of foam covered with silver plastic. "This stuff's going to stop a bullet?"

"The bullets you'll be using, Colonel. I've blunted the noses so they'll flatten rapidly. The Kevlar will absorb the energy."

Cleverly packed, the shield unfolded quickly. A set of lightweight frames sat in the bottom of the case. Brandt removed one and handed it to Gates. He expanded it and quickly snapped it into place. Brandt handed him another, then took care of the last one himself.

"Time to put on your suits," Gates said.

Brandt walked forward to the seats and told Darrell and Brian to get ready. They exchanged their flight suits for cooling-and-ventilation garments and walked toward the two EMU frames on the sides of the aircraft.

After returning to the back, Brandt watched Gates open a second case and remove its upper tray which held a camera, lenses and some film. He took the camera, made some adjustments and walked across part of the soil area to get pictures of the suit-donning process. Then he returned, put the camera down and pulled a stack of black-plastic bags from the bottom of the case.

Gates motioned Darrell and Brian to the back of the plane. "Gentlemen," he began, "this is your weapon."

He tore the top off one of the bags and pulled out a piece of heavy cloth. "I've mounted the guns in these arm bands. For the lunar mission, they'll be attached permanently to the suits but they'll work the same way."

He turned to Darrell, told him to extend his arm and carefully wrapped the band around it, taking time to align some markings with the seams of the suit before pressing its Velcro strips together.

"Underneath the cover is a single-shot barrel with a small laser designator. The impact point will appear as a red dot through the helmet visor. To aim the weapon, raise your elbow and place your hand on the top of the Display and Control Module." He moved Darrell's arm to the proper position while turning his palm down and holding it against the box mounted on the chest of his suit. Then he fitted a second weapon around Darrell's left arm and repeated the demonstration.

"The Display and Control Module is also used to arm and fire. The suits you'll wear on the moon will be modified so the oxygen-mode selector will also be the arming switch. The fan switch will be the trigger."

Gates opened one of the smaller bags. "For today, I'll snap these devices on the front of the control modules."

He removed a plastic box the size of a cigarette pack and fastened it to the module on Darrell's chest.

"To arm it, turn the mode selector all the way to the right or left, beyond the normal stop. Right to arm the right side, left for the left. To fire, just push the fan switch all the way forward, past the *ON* position."

Darrell put on his helmet while Gates connected wires from the armbands to the control box, then pointed toward a small black circle at the center of the bullet stop.

The other crewmembers followed Darrell forward onto the simulated lunar surface, then stood behind him as he wiggled his arm around. Brandt saw him turn the arming switch, then push the firing switch.

A puff of smoke from the front of the armband accompanied a muffled report. Darrell rocked back a bit, then walked toward the target as he removed his helmet. His bullet had punched out the left half of the inch-diameter circle.

"Nice going," Brandt said. "You're a real gunslinger."

"Piece of cake, Brandt. You'll be surprised at how easy it is to hold the designator on the target."

Darrell stepped back to the center of the sandbox while Gates pasted another target circle on the bullet stop. When everyone was in place, he fired the left-side weapon, this time just nicking the target.

Gates worked quickly to remove Darrell's armbands, verify

that the arming switch had been returned to its safe position, and then fit weapons to Brian. He repeated the instructions, placing Brian's hand on the module and pushing his elbow to the correct position.

The crew moved forward while Gates patched the target. Brian's shots were even more accurate than Darrell's.

As he wrapped new guns around Darrell's arms, Gates said, "Now try one with reduced gravity. Just be ready to fall. You won't have as much traction available to offset the recoil."

Finished with the new armband, he asked Brandt, "Can you get the crew to fly an arc?" Brandt nodded, walked to the front of the cabin and put on a headset that had been hanging on the partition. After only a few seconds, he took it off and returned to the group.

"They'll be another couple of minutes. ATC's maneuvering us around some traffic."

"How are they going to hold a sixth of a G?" Darrell asked.

"I found them a digital accelerometer," Brandt replied. "Battery powered. Just stuck it on the instrument panel with foam tape."

"You know," Brian said as Gates replaced his arm band, "there's one teensie problem with these things."

"Only two shots?"

"Kind of a serious limitation, wouldn't you say?"

"No argument. But there's no way to either reload or add more barrels without making the weapon detectable. We've invented a plausible reason for the oversleeve and the barrel, something about needing extra protection in case of a fall. But put in even one more barrel and the technicians are bound to get suspicious."

Brandt shrugged. "With the kind of accuracy you've achieved, we can probably handle all three Russians if worse comes to worst."

"Unless they shoot first," Andy added gloomily as the plane entered a shallow dive.

"Feels like they're getting ready for a run," Darrell observed. "Suppose we use the first one or two arcs to practice walking."

He and Brian put on their helmets, moved to the lunar surface and waited. As the plane pulled out of the dive, reaching almost two Gs, they strained to support the added weight of the suits. Then, when the pitch had increased to about thirty degrees, the pilot pushed the nose over.

The two suited astronauts used the one-minute period of reduced weight to walk back and forth across the dirt-covered area, practicing the loping hop first employed by Apollo crews. Gates took several pictures of their efforts.

"I asked the pilot to continue the arcs until we tell him to stop," Brandt mentioned as the plane leveled out.

Darrell flapped his arm up and down, indicating he wanted to try the gun. After the plane entered the second arc, he hopped around a few more times, then stopped, raised his elbow, armed the weapon and fired. This time the recoil knocked him off his feet. He landed on his backpack but, because of the reduced gravity, didn't hit very hard. He got up immediately and fired the other weapon, this time catching himself as he fell.

His aim was nearly as good as the first time. Gates hurried to replace his weapons while Brian got ready to practice walking.

By their fourth shots, both astronauts had learned to brace themselves so they stayed on their feet. Pleased with their performance, Brandt asked the pilot to stop the maneuvers while they exchanged the suits. Because Brandt and Darrell wore almost the same size, as did Brian and Andy, NASA had provided only two EMUs for walking practice, thus creating the inconvenience. But, by helping each other, the astronauts completed the swap in matter of minutes.

Darrell took over talking with the pilot and, before long, the plane entered another series of dives and arcs. Brandt and Andy easily mastered the odd firing sequence, although it took Andy all four tries before he was able to remain standing.

With the group once again gathered in front of the bullet stop, Brandt said, "Folks, I think we've got ourselves a posse. Anybody need more practice?"

Before the others could answer, Gates said, "We don't want to extend this any more than is necessary. This has already been an unusually long training flight and the crew may be wondering what's going on." He posed them for a few more pictures, then quickly stowed the spent weapons, the control boxes and, with Brandt's help, the bullet stop.

After they landed at Ellington, Gates climbed down the rear air stairs as his van pulled alongside the plane. He asked the driver to remove his camera cases while he walked to the front stairs. As the NASA pilots emerged, he invited them to see the back of the plane.

"Doesn't make much sense for you folks not to see this when it'll be in the newspapers any day."

The captain responded, "Then why all the secrecy?"

"Sir, I'm just a photographer," Gates lied, "but they told me it was because the Russians did this first. Seems that's where we got the idea. Apparently, there was some problem about protecting the source of the information, but I guess that's been resolved. Just the same, you probably shouldn't talk about it until it hits the papers. Officially, it's still classified Secret."

He led them up the stairs and into the back of the plane.

**Baikonur Cosmodrome**

"Yevgeni was right," Svetlana remarked as she helped Mikhail fold up the left-hand solar panel. "Setting up the laser gun is just like the experiment."

"That little radar is incredible," Alex commented as he watched the others work. "Hard to believe it'll pick up a non-cooperative target several thousand miles away."

Svetlana noticed his flushed face. "Alex, you look like you're about to faint."

"You don't know how lucky you are wearing those cooling garments," he replied over the intercom. "It must be more than forty degrees in here."

"Time to stop anyway. Yevgeni will be here in a few minutes."

After shedding their space suits, the cosmonauts stood in their underwear, combing their hair and getting ready to slip into lightweight flying suits.

The guard pounded on the metal door.

Vadim zipped up his coveralls. "Right on time."

The door opened and Tsvigun entered. "My God, Svetlana, it's like an oven in here. Let's talk in the van." They followed the Director out of the building.

The van's driver was a short, stocky man with a stubbly beard and uncombed brown hair. He wiped perspiration from his face with a dirty handkerchief while Tsvigun introduced him.

"This is Yegor. He developed your weapons. We'll be driving to a remote location for the demonstrations."

The van bounced along for a few miles, then turned off the road and drove a hundred meters across an open area. Yegor got out, retrieved a small box from the back of the van and returned to the driver's seat. He opened the box and withdrew an oddly shaped cloth pouch.

"This is the holster," he explained. "It can be fitted to any part of the space suit." He opened the fold-over cover, reached in and withdrew something resembling an automatic pistol. Two cloth ribbons connected it to the pouch.

"We developed the weapon from the MCM-K, the Margo. Short, light weight, high muzzle velocity from a small-caliber cartridge, minimum recoil. Arming and firing mechanisms have been replaced. Everything's electronic. The lanyards release the safeties. One's mechanical, the other's electrical. As long as the weapon stays in the pouch, there's no way it can discharge. The bullets will be shaped to penetrate the American space suits."

He took the weapon and stepped out of the van, implying the others were to follow. When about ten feet away, he stopped, waited for them to gather around him and said, "I'm going to put on this space-suit glove."

With his hand encased, he pried open the pouch, grabbed the gun and pulled it until the ribbons fell away.

"That's the most dangerous part of using the weapon," he cautioned. "If you squeeze it the wrong way after the lanyards release, it can go off."

He put the gun in his other hand and showed it to the astronauts. "Since you can't use a trigger with the gloves on, I developed a firing device that works with thumb pressure. You just grab the weapon by the grip and push down with your thumb."

After placing the gun in his gloved hand, he faced away from the group with the barrel aimed toward the open expanse and pushed. The discharge sounded like a conventional automatic.

"I'd like each of you to try it while I'm here."

Svetlana slid the glove on her right hand and picked up the weapon with her left. Stepping ahead a few paces, she put the gun in her glove and aimed. She pushed down with her thumb, then harder. After a brief hesitation, the weapon fired.

"Takes a lot of force," she noted.

"It can be adjusted. Sir, what about you?" Yegor pointed toward Mikhail.

After each crewmember had fired a round, he reinserted the plugs to safety the weapon and returned it to the pouch.

"You'll have to practice wearing the complete space suit, learning to get it out of the holster, aimed and fired in a short time. I'll be here for another week to help out."

"Even if the bullet penetrates the American suit," Svetlana said, "with the small-caliber it may not stop them from firing back."

"Your concern is justified, Colonel. My recommendation would be to fire at the helmet. The bullet will penetrate both the glare shield and the pressure shell. At the very least, this will destroy the American's vision, but I'd expect it will fracture the helmet and impact the head. This is your best hope for self defense. Of course, it requires a higher level of skill."

Svetlana's lips tightened. "Let's hope the weapons aren't necessary."

**Kennedy Space Center**

"How many ways can you say big?" Brandt thought as he peered up toward the ceiling of the Vehicle Assembly Building some fifty stories above his head, trying to sort out the confusion of girders, crossbeams, piping, balconies and stairways.

"You look like a tourist on his first trip to New York," Hensfeld teased.

"Still blows me away, Jerry."

"Know what you mean, Brandt," Hensfeld agreed. "But what's really incredible is the vehicle, sitting there on the Mobile Launcher Platform damned near ready to fly. Hard to believe it wasn't even an idea two years ago."

"Think of all the things that had to happen," Andy said. "All the millions of pieces, all the drawings, people, tests. It's miraculous!"

"No miracles," Collen grunted. "Just a hell of a lot of work."

"When did they bring in the crawler?" Andy asked.

"Just yesterday," Hensfeld replied. "Brought in the one for the Super Shuttle right afterward."

"Almost forgot about Atlantis being parked next door," Brian commented. "Haven't had time to follow the Transpace mission."

"As far as I know," Hensfeld responded, "they're moving right along. The satellite they're deploying is already in the cargo bay and I heard the crew got through their joint sim without any major screwups."

"Depends on what you call major," Brandt grumbled.

"Are you saying they're not ready for the mission?" Hensfeld responded, sounding disturbed.

Brandt realized his griping could be misinterpreted. "Just that they work toward different standards compared to military crews."

He looked over Hensfeld's shoulder. "Oh oh! Here we go."

The public-relations coordinator led a large group of reporters and television cameramen across the area in front of the open bay doors. Brandt spotted Singleton walking just to the right of the NASA man, talking intently with him.

Hensfeld led the astronauts and engineers toward the group. It reminded Brandt of two medieval armies marching toward each other, ready to do battle.

After an extended round of handshaking and feigned remembrances, the public-relations agent opened the conference to questions.

"I'd like to direct this to Mr. Collen," one of the television interviewers began. "Granted that completing a spacecraft as complex as Artemis in only eighteen months is an outstanding achievement, do you feel the rapid pace has compromised the safety of the astronauts?"

Collen rattled off his standard response about the untiring efforts of the workers at Boeing.

"But, Mr. Collen, it took almost ten years to develop Apollo. How can you possibly do the same job in such a short time?"

Hensfeld intervened. "Sir, this is hardly the same job. For one thing, the entire booster is built from proven Space Shuttle components. Even the spacecraft is based on a previously flown vehicle. But, what really makes the difference is the capability of modern computers. Every aspect of the spacecraft has been thoroughly analyzed."

A woman newspaper reporter cut in. "Colonel Strickland, do you and the other astronauts agree with that?"

Managing to effect a convincing facade, Brandt replied, "I'd sure rather be riding in Artemis than in Apollo. Being an astronaut in those days took guts. Today, you just need a degree in computer science."

Primed to respond warmly, the media people all laughed. Singleton beamed like a proud parent.

"Colonel," a newspaperman probed, "are we going to beat the Russians?"

Answering for him, Singleton stated, "As the President has said many times, getting to the moon first is not our objective. Our goal is to investigate the capability of modern technology to support manned operations on the lunar surface."

Unable to stomach any more deception, Brandt blurted out,

"But we'd sure as heck like to get there first!"

Singleton glared at him, but his anger quickly dissipated as the reporters responded with enthusiastic applause and shouts of, "That's the spirit, Colonel!"

One of the photographers asked the group to move forward, away from the vehicle, so he could frame the Artemis team with something more interesting than one cleat of the crawler's right-front track. The rest of the session was spent rearranging the astronauts and moving them to different locations. Finally, a Kennedy official drove up and told Singleton the crawler was about to start its three-mile journey.

Moments later, Brandt heard a quite rumble radiate from the bay as the crawler's engine-generators started. Almost immediately, the sound was joined by the whir of electric motors. The huge tank-like treads began to move, almost imperceptibly. Its precious cargo kept perfectly vertical by a hydraulic leveling system, the gigantic platform crept through the building's acre-sized doorway.

As it emerged into the glorious fall morning, the hundred-odd invited guests emitted an enthusiastic cheer and followed it with sustained applause. The driver carefully guided his eleven-million-pound vehicle down the tracks of the crawlerway toward its historic rendezvous with Launch Pad 39A.

With the public-relations coordinator and his hoard of media people now occupied with the one-mile-per-hour trek of the crawler, Singleton had an opportunity to speak with the leaders of the Artemis team. First addressing Hensfeld, he said, "Doctor, it gives me great pleasure to convey the President's sincere appreciation for the enormous effort you and all the others have made. He's looking forward to the earliest possible launch, hopefully before the first week of next month."

"Oh for Christ's sake," Brandt thought. "That rotten hypocrite! Pushing us to get off before the blasted election."

Even Hensfeld needed a few seconds to recover. "Mr. Singleton, I'm sure we'll continue to do everything we can to launch as soon as possible."

Collen was somewhat less tactful. "What does that shithead think we've been doing for the past two years, sitting around with our thumbs up our asses?"

Singleton flinched. "Sorry, had to convey the message. Obviously, I know you're doing everything possible to push the schedule. But seriously, do we have a chance to get off within the next few weeks?"

Hensfeld replied, "The Sea of Tranquility goes dark on the third of November. In order to make the window, we'll have to launch by the twenty-ninth. Gives us a little over two weeks."

"And if we miss it?"

"Next window opens about November nineteenth."

Singleton shook his head. "Too late! I mean, the Russians will probably launch before then, don't you think?"

"Depends on where they plan to land," Hensfeld explained. "So far, they haven't told anyone."

"What are our chances for getting off before the twenty-ninth?"

"Hard to say," Hensfeld answered. "We've still got all the on-pad checks to complete. If everything goes okay, we might make it. Just barely."

"Guess all we need is some good luck," Singleton said.

Collen snorted, "Good luck is what schmucks call good engineering."

**Baikonur Cosmodrome**

Yegor walked back toward the firing line after patching the holes in the four human-profile targets and called, "Fire at will!"

Vadim got off the first shot. With a single smooth motion, he pulled open the cover of the holster, slid his gloved hand around the grip and pulled it straight out using his fingertips. As his elbow flew back, the safety lanyards fell away. Immediately, he reversed the direction of motion while bringing up his left hand to steady the weapon. Taking only a moment to aim, he applied a firm, smooth squeeze with his thumb. The bullet hit just to the left of the target's heart outline.

The second round came from Mikhail's gun, hitting almost precisely at the center of the head. Alex's shot was next, followed, after a significant pause, by Svetlana's.

"Still can't get the damned thing out of the pouch," she complained. Yegor took her weapon, replaced the safety pins and loaded another round.

"I think your holster may be a little too much to the side," Vadim suggested, communicating over the intercom. "You're probably not getting your fingers around the gun."

Hearing him over his headset, Yegor quickly finished with Alex's weapon and went back to analyze Svetlana's holster. After moving her arm to different places on the leg of the space suit, he pulled the pouch from its Velcro mount and relocated it to a new position at a slightly different angle. Then he serviced the other two weapons and went forward to paste the targets.

The next series went smoothly, with each crewmember getting a shot off within a few seconds and all the rounds impacting near their intended targets. Yegor seemed pleased.

"I think you're ready to try multiple rounds," he said. "Would you like to start with two or should I put in all three?"

Before anyone could answer, the building's military guard pounded on the door and then opened it for Tsvigun. Looking rather grim, the Director entered and said, "I'm sorry we couldn't find better practice facilities but if we used an outdoor range the American satellites could detect you."

Svetlana shrugged, scanning the unfinished cinder-block walls and leak-stained ceiling. Tsvigun continued, "I came by to give you some information concerning possible launch dates." Then, addressing Yegor, he said, "If you could excuse us for a few minutes."

As he left, Tsvigun called after him, "Please relax in the van." The guard closed the door.

Before Tsvigun could begin, Svetlana said, "Yevgeni, except for perhaps one or two more sessions with the guns, we're ready to go. We can set up the laser in our sleep."

Still wearing the same sour expression, he replied, "Very good. Very good indeed. Unfortunately, your departure will be delayed for a while."

"Delayed? Is there a problem with the vehicle?"

"No, Svetlana. In fact, as you were told in yesterday's briefing, nearly all the checkout procedures have been completed."

"Then what?"

"The President has requested that the landing be postponed until after the American elections."

Stunned, she put her gloved hands on her hips, turned away from him and walked toward the back wall of the building. The others just stared at him, speechless.

"He is greatly concerned that any announcement claiming the moon, however qualified by assurances of international access, may lead to the defeat of their President Torres. The man running against him is openly hostile to the Federation."

Sounding almost unable to speak, Vadim asked, "How long must we wait?"

"The elections will be held on the sixth of next month."

"Sir, we can't land then!" Alex shouted. "The landing site will be dark and the spacecraft has no external lights. There's no way we could set up the laser."

"I know that, Alex, and the President has been informed."

Looking at him anxiously, Svetlana asked, "And?"

"The first opportunity after that starts on the nineteenth."

"Are you telling us to sit here for another month?" Her anger grew with each exchange.

"I'm relaying the President's concerns."

"Yevgeni, tens of thousands of people have labored long and hard for the past two years to get us where we are. Think of the sacrifices that have been made to save even one day. You're going to throw it all away over a political matter?"

"Svetlana, the sole purpose of this operation is political. If America didn't exist, we wouldn't be here discussing launch dates."

"Those same Americans just moved a very capable spaceship to the launch pad. Suppose your estimates of their checkout schedule are wrong? Suppose they launch in time to make the November-third window. Where would that leave the Federation?"

"That possibility has been presented to the President."

"And? What did he say?"

"I spoke to him late yesterday. He asked me whether I thought the risk was significant. I had to tell him that I didn't think there was any chance the Americans could get off that soon."

Now almost out of control, Svetlana screamed, "Did it ever occur to you that you might be wrong?"

Feeling weak, Tsvigun stepped back to lean against the wall. He answered quietly but firmly, "Of course it did, Svetlana, but in my position I must give those superior to me objective opinions, uncolored by personal aspirations."

Now torn between the compassion she felt for her failing old friend and her utter frustration with the insanity of Stakhanov's order, she simply turned away, unable to continue the argument.

As if groping for a way out, Vadim asked, "Would it be possible for us to keep the mission on schedule but wait to announce our claim?"

"The President feels this should be done only if the Americans are ready to launch."

"Sir," Alex argued, "doesn't he understand the risks, the possibility we could have a problem during the countdown? Even if the Americans can't launch until the next cycle, if we wait, they'll have a good chance of getting there first."

"I explained all that, Alex, but I doubt if he really understood what I was trying to tell him."

"Isn't there anyone he'd listen to?" Svetlana asked curtly, having recovered her composure only enough to be civil.

Mikhail interrupted. "Perhaps I should speak to my father-in-law. I'm sure I can convince him of the enormous risk the President's taking and the President needs his support. I think there's a chance they'll be able to work out a compromise."

Tsvigun perked up. "That would be extremely helpful, Mikhail. I sincerely appreciate your willingness to solicit the Chairman's support. It could make the difference."

"Politics!" Svetlana muttered under her breath.

## Chapter 12

# Down to the Wire

**Johnson Space Center**

Recollections of its dilapidated predecessor heightened Brandt's gratitude for the new Astronaut Isolation Quarters. Built on the same site near Johnson's northeast boundary, the small, two-story apartment building kept Shuttle crews away from mission-stopping germs during the last seventeen days before a launch. For the Artemis crew, the quarantine also provided a welcome hiatus in the crescendo of media attention.

The computer in each apartment kept the astronauts in touch with the many activities now converging toward the launch event. While his three colleagues relaxed on the sofa and love seat of his small living room, Brandt scanned the day's news.

"Oh, oh! Look at this." Brandt's heart sank as he continued to read the newly posted information. "I think we just lost the window."

The others crowded around the monitor. Darrell grasped the significance immediately. "Damn!" He shook his head. "Guess that's the gamble they took bringing Artemis to Kennedy before they'd reduced the test data."

"Don't see why it's so important," Brian shrugged. "An unanticipated node in the third stage?"

"It's a resonance," Brandt explained. "Probably an interaction between the third stage and the spacecraft."

"That's a big deal?"

"Can't tell from this, Brian, but it could be. Let me try to catch Jerry at his office." He picked up the telephone next to the computer, selected one of the preset numbers and waited for it to dial through. After a short, one-sided conversation, he put the phone down.

"Jerry says the resonance is serious but Collen's got a solution."

"I heard you say something about fixing it on the pad," Darrell replied.

"That's the plan. Improve the stiffness matrix for the third stage. Collen's going to add some external stringers. Bond them in place with adhesive."

Brian looked concerned. "Won't that add weight?"

"Pulling the secondary video to compensate. Won't be much of problem."

Brian responded with, "Not compared to getting the damned spacecraft fixed."

"Amen to that," Brandt agreed, then grumbled, "Dang it! We finally get close and we run into this crap. Makes me feel like we're snake-bit."

"Why?" Darrell said. "Until the Russians are walking on the moon, we're still in the race."

"Which brings up something," Andy interjected. "The cosmonauts have been in Baikonur for more than a month. They should have launched by now."

"But last night's videoconference indicated they haven't even started fueling," Brandt said. "In fact, no activity on the pad at all."

The crew sat silently for a few moments. Finally, Darrell voiced Brandt's fondest hope. "Hesitate to say this but it looks like they've finally hit a snag."

"Thinking the same thing, Darrell," Brandt responded, "but afraid to say so. Truth is, I'm sittin' here with ants in my pants."

"Kind of what I was trying to get to," Darrell laughed. "Needed you to find the right words."

"I'm itching to get going too," Brian agreed. "Shit, if the damned hardware was ready, we could launch tomorrow."

"Still got some sims to get through," Brandt reminded him. "Need to get everybody up to Andy's level playing CapCom. Then we're off to the Cape."

"Better hustle," Darrell added. "If we're not out of here in a week, we miss the window."

**Baikonur Cosmodrome**

Tsvigun sat behind the simple wooden desk in Ligachev's office as the cosmonauts took their seats at the opposite end of the room.

He began, "I apologize for bringing you out this late in the quarantine. Unfortunately, the information I have cannot be transmitted over the lines to the cottages."

Svetlana thought his voice sounded even more depressed than usual.

"We've obtained a detailed description of the American weapons, thanks to an extremely diligent agent attached to the NASA group that maintains their KC-135 aircraft.

"It seems they copied Svetlana's idea of installing a simulated lunar surface to practice moon walking at reduced gravity. The agent decided to investigate the operation and managed to install a recorder inside the plane. Although we have no photographs or drawings, the conversations during the flight were very revealing.

"The operation had nothing to do with moon walking. It was a practice session for using their weapons. From the conversations, we know the devices consist of a single barrel sewn into the upper-arm portion of their EVA suits and some switches incorporated into the oxygen-control module.

"The weapon fires a sharply pointed bullet, designed to penetrate any part of our spacesuits, with an explosive warhead. The instructor took pride in describing its lethality."

"Miserable bastards," Vadim grumbled.

"To fire the weapon, the astronaut places his hand on the oxygen controller. It's on the front of the suit, in the middle of the chest. He arms the weapon using one switch and fires it using another. To aim it, he raises his elbow and maneuvers his arm until a laser designator appears on the target. From the recordings, we know the devices are extremely accurate."

"They've only got one shot?" Mikhail asked.

"Two. One weapon on each arm."

"At least we've got them there," Alex responded grimly.

Greatly troubled by the report, Svetlana said, "I'm appalled! This is an extremely serious threat."

"I wonder whether the astronauts would really use them,"

Vadim pondered, "really try to kill us. It seems so bizarre."

"You've all read their dossiers," Tsvigun replied. "Every one professional military, three of the four have combat experience."

"I'm convinced their commander, that Colonel Strickland, would enjoy killing us," Svetlana said. "He hates Russians."

"He's a fanatic," Mikhail said. "I wonder how people like that end up in positions of responsibility."

"The American system," Alex stated. "It rewards loyalty above everything else."

"Which may explain the black astronaut going along with the weapons. He's obviously a political pawn. Would do anything to please his superiors."

"He's also a close friend of Strickland's. Owes his life to him, in fact," Vadim reminded them.

"You mean that story about Strickland rescuing him in Chad?" Svetlana laughed. "Obviously fabricated by the American propaganda machine to create heroes and build support for the war."

"You don't think it happened?"

She looked at him condescendingly and said what was really on her mind. "Of course, there's one thing we can do to avoid the whole problem."

After a short pause, she gave them the answer. "Get there, get our jobs done and be on the way back before they arrive."

**Kennedy Space Center**

As they brought their T-38s to a stop, airmen hooked yellow ladders to the canopy rails and helped them remove their helmets and parachute harnesses. The four astronauts climbed down to the ramp, walked to a small platform and gathered around a microphone.

Standing behind a low barrier about fifteen feet away, sixty invited media representatives waited with their questions. A NASA public-relations professional walked among the reporters with a portable microphone. He started with an overweight, middle-aged man in a rumpled blue suit.

"Colonel Strickland, were you and the other astronauts surprised by the decision to launch in three days?"

Brandt grinned. "I'd say elated."

The NASA man brought the microphone to a woman in the center of the crowd.

"Was the President responsible for moving up the launch

date?"

Brandt replied, "Ma'am, we've been committed to flying as soon as the spacecraft is ready. It's ready. We're ready. So it's time to go. Just that simple."

Another woman further back asked, "This is for Major Howe and Commander Yang. How do your wives feel about the mission?"

Brian answered first. "About the same way I do. Relieved that the big day is finally coming. Excited about us going to the moon. Looking forward to my getting back so I'll be able to mow the lawn."

Andy added, "Patty's real happy about the free trip to the Cape. And the kids can't wait to see Disney World."

The questions continued for another ten minutes. For a change, few were offensive and the astronauts managed to keep the answers humorous. Finally, the NASA representative called a halt to it, allowing the crew to board the waiting van and ride to their quarantine apartments.

A half-hour later, Brandt stood next to his bed unpacking his suitcase. "Sure reminds you how simple life can be. Hardly need anything to get by here. Even less when we're in the spacecraft."

"You always wax philosophical before a mission?" Darrell responded as he stood in the doorway.

"Okay, wise guy, since you'd obviously rather talk about something repulsive, try this. The final physical starts at six a.m. tomorrow."

"Why so early?"

"Part of moving up our sleep schedule. They'll be getting us up at about two-thirty for the launch."

"Oh well, it'll make Andy happy. Once we're given the green light, he gets out of quarantine. Wonder what the Russians are doing."

"They must know about us leaving Johnson. And they'll see our interview on TV in about an hour. If that doesn't get them going, they must have one heck of a problem."

"Still hard to believe they're not already on the moon."

"You know Darrell, even if they start the final count right away, it'll put them only about two days ahead of us. If I remember those briefings correctly, the best they can hope for is a joint claim."

"Because they couldn't substantiate controlling more than a small region?"

"Because we'd have launched before they made their claim."

"Brandt, you just made me feel a whole lot better."

"It's my new approach to leadership, Darrell. Motivational, supportive, inspirational, upbeat."

Darrell opened his mouth, put in his thumb and pretended to gag.

"Is that why we got nominal missions on this morning's sims?" Andy asked as he stepped in from the hallway.

"Dang, not only do I have to mollycoddle my crew, I can't get any privacy," Brandt grumbled. "Hardly worth being a commander anymore. Where's Brian? Might as well have a crew party while we're at it."

"Haven't seen him since they dropped us off," Andy replied.

**Baikonur Cosmodrome**

"Settle down, Svetlana!" Vadim held her by the shoulders and shouted in her face. "You can't let Mikhail and Alex see you this way."

"I swear to you, Vadim, I'm going to spit in Yevgeni's face. The damned coward. Two years of work wasted because he didn't have the guts to oppose Stakhanov."

"Svetlana, that simply isn't true."

"You don't think he should have insisted upon launching last week? You don't think it matters that the Americans will lift off before we have a chance to claim the moon?"

"They haven't done it yet and there's a good chance they won't be able to."

She spun out of his grasp. "My God, Vadim, you're still underestimating them. When are you going to learn?"

"I'm trying to deal with the situation as it is."

"The situation? The Americans announced they're going to launch in what?" She forced herself to do the calculation. "Sixty hours! That's the situation. If we leave this instant, we'll still be a day from the moon when they lift off. Everything we've worked for just blew up in our faces."

"Believe me, Svetlana," he said firmly, "I'm just as upset as you are. But there's nothing to be gained by lambasting Yevgeni. The only thing that matters now is getting off the ground."

"What time is it?" She picked up her watch from the end table. "The briefing's in fifteen minutes."

"That's right, so pull yourself together." He looked down at her stocking-clad feet and muttered, "At least finish getting dressed."

She walked back into her bedroom, sat on the bed and slipped on a pair of low-heeled shoes. Her voice trembled with rage as she shouted through the open doorway.

"My God, Vadim! We had it in the palm of our hand and that idiot threw it away. Now there's no way we can make a claim that will exclude the Americans." She pulled a leather jacket from the closet and put it on over her flying suit, then walked back to the outer room.

Vadim had been looking out the window. "Here's the van. Are you ready?"

"Not really, Vadim. I feel beaten—by things I have no control over."

After pulling germicidal masks over their faces, they left the cottage and walked to the van. Although the eastern sky had grown brighter, sunrise was still fifteen minutes away and the cold of the desert night startled Svetlana. She shuddered momentarily but the icy air seemed to clear her thoughts, even subdue her anger.

Svetlana and Vadim climbed into the van, taking the seats behind the driver.

Mikhail asked, "Who'll be briefing us this morning?"

"I assume it will be Director Tsvigun," Svetlana answered, "telling us the President has graciously given his permission and that we may now haul our asses to the moon."

Vadim gave her arm a very hard, almost painful, squeeze. She went back to mentally preparing the tirade she planned to lay on Tsvigun.

The van stopped outside the headquarters building just as the sun broke the horizon. The cloudless sky added no modulation to the faded orange of the refracted light, leaving the Kazakhstan landscape appearing as always: bleak, desolate, unforgiving.

The driver led them inside to a small conference room. Tsvigun stood at the end opposite the door waiting for them to enter. Svetlana thought he looked nervous.

Conspicuously neglecting to greet them he said only, "Please be seated." Then as if deliberately cutting off any discussion, he continued, "Let me start by accepting responsibility for the difficulties we now face. I seriously misjudged the abilities of the Americans. Apparently, they've accomplished what I believed to be impossible. Having said that, I insist we waste no further time discussing decisions that cannot be reversed."

Although his confession brought Svetlana a degree of satisfaction, it didn't make up for being denied an opportunity to voice her carefully structured diatribe. She remained as angry as ever.

"Given the circumstances, it should come as no surprise that the President has agreed we must now launch as soon as possible. Svetlana, is the crew ready for the mission?"

Forcing herself not to remind him they'd been ready for a week, she answered, "Certainly, Yevgeni. We will not be the cause of any further delays." Then, wanting to take control of the dialogue, she asked, "What is the condition of the spacecraft?"

He answered stiffly, "We have already initiated the final checkout procedure." He glanced at his watch. "The launch is scheduled for 1530. That gives us a bit more than nine hours."

Vadim interrupted him. "Yevgeni, that launch time is outside the window."

Tsvigun nodded in agreement. "It's certainly not ideal. The final mission profile is being developed as we speak. You'll get an update later this morning."

He looked down at a piece of paper he was holding. "We'll start to load liquid oxygen at eleven. All the propellant should be transferred by 1330 and you'll be boarding the spacecraft shortly thereafter. Do you foresee any problems?"

"None whatsoever," Svetlana answered. Then, speaking very cautiously, she added, "Not implying any criticism, I wonder if you could arrange a briefing on the status of our ability to claim the moon."

Tsvigun stared at her, harshly at first. Apparently concluding that her face reflected only sincere concern, his reaction softened and he replied, "I'd be happy to do that right now. I spent almost an hour last night talking with the Prime Minister. He feels we can still make a valid claim.

"Assuming the worst happens and the Americans actually launch on Sunday, they'll get to the moon about two days after we start our return to earth. The Minister feels we can claim the entire moon by stating we'll permit the American expedition to land as a one-time exception. We're absolutely confident they're not bringing any regional-control weapons with them. When they leave, they will have, once again, abandoned the moon."

"What if our launch is delayed?"

"From what I've been told, as long as we get there first, the situation is the same. But you're being too pessimistic, Svetlana. It's much more likely the Americans will be delayed. In fact, I believe their announcement to be nothing more than a political ploy, a ruse created by their president to help his reelection prospects. Perhaps I'll be proven wrong once again, but all the information at my disposal indicates their vehicle will not be ready."

Abruptly changing the subject, Tsvigun said, "Alex, you must return to Kaliningrad immediately. The crew at the Flight Control Center will be arriving shortly and they'll need you there to prepare for the mission."

A strange expression came over Alex's face as he absorbed Tsvigun's order telling him his chance to walk on the moon had all but vanished. With a quavering voice, almost overcome with emotion, he said, "Before I leave, I must tell you what a privilege it's been to work with this team. These two years have been the best of my life. I wish you every good fortune on the mission." Then, ignoring the politically preferred philosophy, he added, "May God protect you."

He embraced each of the other crewmembers, then went to Tsvigun and took his hand.

"Sir, you've been a constant source of inspiration. I look forward to seeing you back at the Flight Control Center."

***

Scanning through the numbers on the control room's primary monitor, the senior launch engineer had every reason to be pleased. The automatic test sequences had proceeded without so much as an advisory message. Now, only three hours from liftoff, he watched as the data showed that the SL-17's liquid oxygen tank was nearly full. It was time to begin the chill-down process with the liquid hydrogen.

"Prepare to initiate liquid-hydrogen transfer," he called to the technician. The man replied, "Tank pressurization complete. All parameters normal."

"Begin the transfer."

His finger already on the switch, the technician sent a signal to the microprocessor in a large, remote-controlled valve located at the storage tank's outlet.

The engineer watched his display, waiting for temperature sensors to detect the arrival of the liquified gas. There was no response. He looked at the data coming from a flow-rate meter. The number remained a row of zeros.

"Open the valve, Andrei."

The technician pressed the switch again, this time holding it in the depressed position for a moment. "The command has been sent," he reported.

Grabbing the thick manual that contained detailed information about the test stand's fluid-handling systems, the engineer thumbed through the pages, finally stopping near the middle of the book. He entered a number into the left-hand computer and waited for the requested data to appear. Then he looked back at the manual.

"The damned thing's still closed! Hit it again."

Andrei complied with the request, but the number on the left-hand monitor didn't change.

"Signal must not be getting through. I'll to run the diagnostic."

Once again following the manual's dictates, he entered a series of commands, then waited while a program exercised the valve's processor. Seconds later, the monitor's screen filled with an array of cryptic messages and numerical values. He studied them and said, "Nothing wrong with the processor. Must be the valve itself. Are there any circuit-protection warnings?"

The technician had already checked every indicator on the control panel, but he looked again just to be sure. "Everything's normal."

"Damn! All right, we'll hold at this point. Send a command to close the valve. We don't want to start flowing LH2 when we're not expecting it."

Andrei quickly accomplished the required switch actuations and the engineer verified that, once again, the digital portion of the system had functioned perfectly.

Although he knew all the activities taking place in the bunker were being seen by his supervisors on closed-circuit television, the engineer called to verify that steps were being taken to deal with the problem. He needn't have bothered.

**Kennedy Space Center**

The alarm sounded a few minutes before five. Brandt had deliberately deprived himself of some sleep so he could answer the phone with a cheery `Good morning!' when the crew specialist called to wake him, a practice he'd adopted many years before but couldn't really explain. With just enough time to use the bathroom and brush his teeth, he managed to pick up the telephone on the first ring and greet the caller before he could say a word.

Noting the blinking *Message Waiting* alert at the top of his computer display, he walked to the machine and selected the appropriate menu, then brought the latest information to the screen.

*UNCLASSIFIED*

*Activities Noted at Energia Launch Complex*

*LandSat images taken at 0558 UTC show a distinct vapor plume flowing downwind from the lunar-landing vehicle now on the Energia launch pad. Assume this indicates ongoing propellant-loading activity.*

"Blast dang it!" he reacted to the news. "Looks like they finally got their act together. Can't be more than a few hours 'til liftoff. Dang! Means they'll get there about two days before we do."

He deleted the item and returned to the home page but the alert continued to blink. Repeating the inquiry procedure, he found a second message.

*From: B. Howe*
*To: W. Brandt*

*PERSONAL/CONFIDENTIAL*

Brandt entered his password.

*Would like to meet with you as soon as possible. Have important matter to discuss.*

*Thanks*
*Brian*

Brandt read the request twice and still couldn't figure it out. He muttered to himself, "Why didn't he just call me?"

After taking a few minutes to shave and get dressed, he picked up the phone and dialed Brian's extension.

"Got your message. Come here? If that's what you want."

He'd barely put the phone down when Brian knocked at the door.

"It's open," Brandt called across the room.

Brian entered, closing the door behind him. He looked as if

he'd been up all night. He said, almost in a whisper, "I may have a problem. Had trouble clearing my ears during the letdown yesterday. Almost had to call a missed approach and climb back up."

That got Brandt's attention. "Lordy, you think you've got a cold? That'd mean the whole crew's been exposed."

"Not a cold, Brandt."

"Then what?"

"Allergy. Some kind of pollen. Get it every fall, whenever I'm in Houston. I was taking some antihistamines—and yeah, I know it's against the rules. Hoping to get by until we left for Florida but I ran out while we were in quarantine. Couldn't get any more."

"Far be it from me to lecture you about cheating on the flight surgeons. How are you feeling now?"

"The allergy symptoms are going away, just like I figured. Trouble is, my right ear's ringing."

"Infection?"

"I hope not."

"Hey, pard, we've got a final physical coming up in a few minutes. What are you planning to do?"

"Don't know. Any ideas?"

"Can't mess with a middle-ear infection. You'll have to tell the docs and see if they can fix you up."

"Risk getting grounded?"

"Afraid so. You'll have to get those Eustachian tubes opened up in order to use the EVA suit. And if it develops into a serious infection, there's not much we'll be able to do for you aboard Artemis."

Seeing Brian's expression turn from concern into something close to despair, Brandt tried to reassure him. "Listen, Brian, the medicos will probably shoot you full of something that'll fix up the ear before the flight. Just let them handle it. That's what they're getting paid for."

***

Brian paced up and down the hallway in front of the clinic, wringing his hands, then pounding his fist into his palm.

"Grounded me! The bastards grounded me—for seven God-damned days! Where the hell did this last-minute physical-exam bullshit come from anyway?"

The others stood silently, staring at the floor.

He looked at Brandt. "I'm sure the antibiotics won't impair my performance and the sons-of-bitches told me the ear will be back to normal in two days. There's no reason why I should be bumped off the mission."

Brandt pursed his lips. "Hey, Brian, I won't say you're wrong. But I don't make the rules. Just cuss 'em and abide by 'em, same as you."

"I know, I know." Brian shook his head in despair. "It's just that I'm all primed to do this operation. I'm sure I can do a great job."

"Nobody's going to question that, pal. But I'll tell you, I'm not gonna lose a wink of sleep worrying about you taking over CapCom."

"Second that," Darrell said. "You were smooth as glass during the final sims."

Brian smiled for the first time in two days. "You bullshitters trying to make me feel better?"

Looking seriously troubled, Andy said, "Brian, the question on my mind is whether I'll be able to fill your shoes."

"Oh shit, Andy," Brian said, "I'm just kidding myself thinking I'd do anything exceptional. You've every bit as good and you've got a better understanding of the overall operation."

"Maybe." Andy seemed even more disturbed. "Truth is, doing the mission isn't my biggest problem."

Brandt looked at him, not comprehending.

"It's Patty, damn it! She's gotten used to the idea that I'll be riding this one out. Telling her I'm actually going—it'll be a shock."

"But she knew right along that was a possibility."

"Brandt, you wouldn't understand. Her knowing it and her believing it are two different things."

"Better tell her right away," Darrell said.

"That's another problem. She's already left to pick up Anita in Orlando. Then they're going to run around with the kids getting things together for the cookout. Probably won't even stop by the motel before she heads for the Cape."

"Oh well," Brandt sighed. "Guess you'll have to tell her this afternoon. Gonna' be one heck of a picnic."

"Looks like I'll have to miss it," Brian said, looking dejected. "Really ought to head back to Johnson—get in as much sim time as possible before the launch. Shit, I'd be lousy company anyway."

"Come on, Brian," Darrell said. "You're not going to get anything done today, even if you get a flight out before noon. Besides,

Kim's going to be awfully uncomfortable if you're not there."

"Right on," Brandt agreed. "Wouldn't be the same without you."

Brian sighed, then replied, "Okay, if you say so. I'll see if I can get a flight back tonight. Christ, can't believe I'll have to go commercial."

**Baikonur Cosmodrome**

It had been an agonizingly long day, an emotional roller coaster slamming her from despair to enthusiasm, from excited activity to anxious boredom. Svetlana felt utterly exhausted.

After Tsvigun's early-morning briefing, she'd been able to divert the energy of her rage toward the completion of myriad last-minute details. By the time she joined Vadim and Mikhail for lunch, her spirits had lifted to the point where she was speaking enthusiastically of the launch, trying to assure herself that in little more than an hour, they'd be boarding the spacecraft. Then, just as they were finishing, the call came telling her about the valve.

Tension abraded every moment of the long afternoon as updates flip-flopped between optimism and hopelessness. Dinner went by with barely a word spoken and the evening had been almost unbearable. Try as she might, she could not maintain enough concentration to complete even simple tasks. Even reading was impossible as her mind raced through one scenario after another. Then Tsvigun ordered them back to the headquarters building.

"Thank you for joining me at this late hour," he began. "We're certain the problem with the valve is in the motor. We've tried to locate a new one but so far without success. It was made especially for the valve and there are no substitutes. Not even replacement parts. One of the technicians is fabricating some shims which will allow the existing brushes to function a while longer. Another man is trying to clean the commutator.

"Because the repair time is uncertain, we had to offload the liquid oxygen. As soon as the repairs appear to be nearing completion, we'll initiate a new countdown. This means we should be able to launch about five hours after the problem is resolved.

"I see it's past eleven. I suggest you try to get some sleep."

With that, he turned and left the room.

**Cape Canaveral Air Force Station**

As a beach, it wasn't much, just a narrow strip of sand littered with shattered shells and small pieces of rotting driftwood, separated from the two-lane access road by a belt of ugly grass and scrub plants. But it was private, and that made it special, a piece of the Cape Canaveral Air Force Station reserved for the use of military personnel, astronauts, and very few others.

Because of the quarantine, the cookout had required special approval from Singleton. But, with the proviso that all the children be checked by doctors before they left, he acquiesced and what had, over the years, become a Shuttle-launch ritual became part of the moon program.

As expected, the women had done a first-class job with the food, although it had taken them the entire morning to round up all the cooking gear, charcoal, eating utensils and blankets deemed necessary for the occasion.

A cool breeze and a sky of broken clouds had put everyone in sweaters or jackets, but Brandt appreciated weather that brought some semblance of a fall day to Florida. Feeling pleasantly overfed, he sat on an orange and blue beach towel looking across the beach. The Howes and Yangs were all at the water's edge enjoying the surf. Darrell and Anita had walked north along the shore, occasionally stopping to pry a shell from the sand.

"Sure great getting away from the pressure for a while," Brandt thought. "Hope Andy gets Patty settled down. But she's been a Navy wife for a long time. She'll handle it."

He watched the waves for a while. "Kim's really helping Brian cope with not going. He's lucky to have her."

Trying to suppress the pain, he forced himself to contemplate his own situation. Had the time come for a new relationship? His loneliness sometimes overpowered him, yet he knew he could never recreate what he had lost. But perhaps it wasn't necessary. Perhaps he could find a different sort of happiness. Perhaps when he returned from the moon.

Brandt looked up the coastline to where Darrell and Anita strolled hand in hand. They stopped, embraced, kissed. "Why don't they get married?" he asked himself. "Don't they know love when it hits them in the face?"

Brandt spotted the children heading toward the picnic area. He checked his watch. "Dang, almost time to leave." He walked toward the others as quickly as the sand would allow.

**Kennedy Space Center**

As the alarm went off earlier and earlier, it became harder for Brandt to beat the crew specialist's wake-up call. He'd set the clock for 0355 but managed to sleep through the beeps until almost four so his greeting was less cheery than usual.

As soon as he put down the phone, he went to the computer to check for messages. There was only one.

*UNCLASSIFIED*

*Changes Noted at Energia Launch Complex*

*LandSat images taken at 0517 UTC show that the Federation moon vehicle is still on the Energia launch pad but the vapor plume observed the previous day has disappeared. Assume this indicates termination of propellant-loading activity.*

"Hot dang!" he said aloud and thought to himself, "Wonder what's keeping them on the ground. Must have run into another snag. Puts us only a day behind." Almost afraid to even think it, he whispered to himself, "We might beat them yet!"

The early rise time brought with it an annoyingly long period of inactivity. After he'd cleaned up and dressed, Brandt settled into a review of the updated mission plan that had been loaded on the database. To keep from falling back to sleep, he stood up and walked around the apartment every few minutes. Just as he reached the procedures for the lunar landing, it was time for breakfast.

After weeks of living together, Brandt found eating without Brian a little strange. He talked with Darrell and Andy about him, speculated about his reaction to the freak misfortune and concluded that, once he got into the CapCom routine, he'd be fine.

Finished with his meal, he left with the others to watch the Transpace crew put Atlantis into orbit.

Their van came to a stop at the end of a seldom-used road that ran along a small peninsula on the west bank of the Banana River. Because it afforded a full view of the orbiter, unobstructed by the pad's tower, the location was often touted as the best spot for watching Shuttle launches. However, its primary advantage this morning was the absence of germ-carrying members of the general public.

As for the launch, it was much like any other. Brandt had the van driver turn up the volume on his hand-held radio so they could monitor the proceedings while standing outside looking toward the pad. The countdown went smoothly until T-minus five minutes when a message warned of a pressure drop in one of the helium tanks used to pressurize propellant. Launch control quickly determined that the problem arose from a malfunctioning sensor and switched to a backup. The count resumed and the last stages of the pre-launch procedure passed without incident.

In a short while, the reverse-numbered seconds reached five and the orbiter's main engines roared to life. Drowned out by the sound from the rocket-engine exhausts, the zero count marked the ignition of the solid-rocket boosters and the simultaneous lifting of Atlantis from its supports on the Mobile Launcher Platform.

As the Shuttle climbed away from the tower, the astronauts were raked by the crackling shock waves from the booster plumes. The spacecraft rolled about its axis, then pitched over until it was almost upside down. Darrell tracked the vehicle with binoculars, announcing the separation of the spent boosters seconds before the confirmation blared from the radio.

The trio continued to stare into the morning sky as the spacecraft streaked across the Atlantic, finally becoming a bright dot, then disappearing. They reboarded the van and drove back to their quarters, monitoring the radio to be sure the mission was progressing normally. By the time they arrived, their ride back to earth was safely in orbit. The moon expedition had begun.

## Chapter 13

# Countdowns

**Baikonur Cosmodrome**

Looking at Tsvigun, Svetlana's remaining indignation quickly turned to pity. The old man appeared utterly dejected, his eyes reflecting the sadness of someone who's just lost a child.

"Once again," he began, "I must apologize for bringing you here at this late hour, but the situation remained uncertain until just a few minutes ago.

"The technicians have repaired the motor—at least well enough to actuate the valve a few more times. They've started the reassembly process which will take another six hours. That means we'll be able to start loading hydrogen at five tomorrow morning.

"I've instructed the launch crew to resume preparations. If everything goes normally, you'll be on your way by eight. I see no reason why you shouldn't sleep until five. Svetlana, do you agree?"

Nodding wearily she replied, "If we can get to sleep."

**Kennedy Space Center**

Brandt looked down at the two small pills he'd been given to trick his biorhythms into making sleep possible four hours too soon. He downed them, then went to his computer to read the final list of messages.

*UNCLASSIFIED*

*Atlantis mission proceeding according to profile. Super Shuttle now positioned to recover Artemis crew in case of launch emergency.*

Pleased with the update, he selected the next message.

*UNCLASSIFIED*

*Activities Noted at Energia Launch Complex*

*Latest LandSat images show reappearance of vapor plume flowing downwind from the lunar-landing vehicle. Assume this indicates resumption of propellant loading activity.*

Brandt flopped back in the chair, the hopeful enthusiasm of the previous twelve hours quickly evaporating.

"Should have expected it. Puts us fifteen hours behind them if we launch on time. Maybe they'll glitch again. You never know."

He yawned. The pills were more powerful than he'd realized. He deleted the messages and went to bed.

**Baikonur Cosmodrome**

Svetlana's sleep ended with the first bang. "Good God!" she said aloud. "Is he trying to break the door down?" She staggered into the living room wearing only her bra and panties.

"I'm awake!" she yelled.

"Sorry Colonel. I was instructed to be sure the crew members wouldn't fall back to sleep. The launch is scheduled for 0800."

"Okay, Sergeant," she answered, guessing it was the same van driver who'd awakened her the day before. Through the window curtains, she saw him run off toward the other cottages.

Her final preparation for the trip involved only small, personal items. Everything of importance had been stashed into the recesses of the spacecraft long before. This morning, her responsibilities included only making herself as presentable as she felt necessary for a brief series of publicity photographs and packing a few items into the small plastic case provided for personal belongings.

After a quick shower, she dressed, donning the tan coverall

she'd wear for almost the entire mission.

Into the plastic container she loaded three packages of American tissues, taken from her dwindling personal supply, a favorite hairbrush, a tiny manicure kit, a small jar of skin cream, and a tube of ointment she used to keep her elbows from cracking. She closed the lid, then stopped and walked toward her dresser. She opened the top drawer, took out a wallet-sized photograph and looked at it. Reaching a decision, she reopened the container and slid the photograph down alongside the tissues. She would think of her daughter before descending to the moon.

In the few remaining minutes, she went around the cottage putting things in order. Finally, after one last scan of the rooms, one last glance in the mirror, she was satisfied.

The night air felt even colder than the day before as she walked to the van, her face once again hidden behind the quarantine mask. She looked up to see a black, star-filled sky. "Weather won't be a factor," she thought.

Settling into the back seat to wait for her crew, she asked the driver, "Did they tell you to stop at the Gagarin memorial?"

"Yes, Colonel," he answered smartly. "I was briefed yesterday. Then we go to the headquarters building."

"Wonder if we'll get anything to eat," she thought as Mikhail arrived. He sat behind the driver. Vadim joined them and the driver jumped out to close the van's door. Then he drove toward the oldest part of the cosmodrome and stopped in front of a small house.

Visiting the homes used by Gagarin and Korolev during the Soviet Union's first ventures into space had become a staunch tradition among cosmonauts. Somehow, in the chaos of the previous week, it had been forgotten until Svetlana brought it up at lunch the day before. The tradition was a solemn one and the military photographers completed their work quietly and unobtrusively.

It was only a few kilometers to the headquarters building and they were soon back in the conference room, once again being updated by Tsvigun.

"Everything went well through the night," he began. "The valve repairs were successful and the technicians are completing the propellant loading. The vehicle will be ready for you in about thirty minutes. There have been no changes to the weather briefing you were given last night, nor any to the status of the vehicle.

"Our latest information indicates the Americans haven't

started loading propellant, although they still say their launch will occur in about thirteen hours. The international-law experts have confirmed that our lead will be more than adequate to establish our exclusive right to the moon.

"And so, my friends, the future of our country is now in your hands. Once again, I apologize for the unfortunate delays."

Vadim stood. "Minister, it is ludicrous that you would apologize to us. Without you, a flight to the moon would be a year away. We owe you our deepest gratitude. If one name is to be linked with this endeavor, that name must be Tsvigun."

Svetlana looked into the pitiful face of the once powerful man, rose to her feet and said softly, "Your friendship and encouragement have carried us through many trials. Vadim is right. The mission is yours. Thank you."

Looking happier than she'd seen him for weeks, Tsvigun replied, "Compliments from this group are the most cherished of all. But now it's time for you to go. I'll leave you with a short message from the President."

> *To the glorious crew of our lunar expedition I send the sincere best wishes of a grateful and admiring nation. It is indeed rare to find the hopes and dreams of so many people entrusted to the care of so few. But we all rest confident in your extraordinary capabilities and your proven dedication. Our future could not be in better hands. We thank you.*
>
> *Viktor Yegorovich Stakhanov*
> *President of the Socialist Federation*

Tsvigun placed the message on the table. He looked at each of them, smiling but with a hint of sadness. He finished almost in a whisper. "Good luck!"

The cosmonauts filed from the room, back outside into the night. Their trip to the launch pad took another quarter hour.

The hundreds of spotlights glaring down from the towers surrounding the pad gave the area a surrealistic quality. Partially obscured by the launch tower, the giant rocket thrusted into the black sky, its white paint gleaming in the harsh light. Although she had time for only a glance, Svetlana couldn't help but be awed by the incredible sight as she hurried toward the corner of the pad.

The cosmonauts walked quickly up the stairs of the concrete building, down the now-familiar corridor to a room adjacent to the service tower. There, technicians helped them put on their communications headgear and make a final check of their microphones and headsets. Then they escorted the crew to the waiting elevator for their sixteen-story climb to the swing arm.

They crossed the tower on an open walkway and moved out onto the arm. Greatly extended to wrap around the booster and access the spacecraft from the opposite side, the arm's length now exceeded twenty-five meters. Nevertheless, it was remarkably rigid, oscillating only slightly as the group neared its end.

The cosmonauts removed their shoes, exchanging them for the slippers they would wear inside the spacecraft. Their preparation complete, they began to board.

Vadim went first, crawling on his hands and knees through an open panel in the outer fairing, then disappearing down the hatch at the top of the orbital module. Mikhail followed, then Svetlana. Although she'd practiced the procedure many times in the mockup, she experienced some anxiety as she made the awkward transition from the crawlway into the hatch.

Small rungs had been installed inside the orbital module to serve as both steps and handholds. She carefully lowered herself into the center corridor and stopped. Because she entered last, she had to verify the security of the hatch cover. One of the technicians lowered it into place and closed the locking mechanism. Svetlana checked the three visual indicators, verifying that they showed the desired bull's-eye pattern.

Dropping the rest of the way down the orbital module, through the docking hatch at its lower end and into the descent module, she saw Mikhail and Vadim already in their couches. Standing in the middle of hers, she reached into the orbital module and pulled its half of the hatch system down into place. Then she took a locking tool from her shin pocket and used it to secure the latches. After checking the indicators, she called to Mikhail, "Ready for the docking hatch."

He reached up to release the meter-diameter disk, then brought it down and around so Svetlana could grab it. Completing its motion, she pushed it up into place and moved the clamps into the locked position. With it now firmly supported, Svetlana completed the latching procedure, checked that the seals were properly seated, then settled into her couch.

The cosmonauts strapped themselves in, then attached the connectors from their headsets and spent the next several minutes verifying that their voice links to the launch-control facility at Baikonur and the Flight Control Center at Kaliningrad functioned normally.

"Beginning final guidance alignment," Vadim noted, followed shortly by Mikhail's, "Initiating final systems checkout."

For the next thirty minutes, the spacecraft's computers would conduct the mission. Svetlana relaxed, watching the center display report the status of the recovery areas.

"Vehicle integrity check complete," Mikhail reported. "Pressure returning to normal."

A valve opened to vent the excess air, then remained open as pure oxygen entered the modules, flushing out the air's nitrogen.

"All recovery teams are in place," Svetlana said. "Stand by for final weather update."

Mikhail's display brought up a new message. "Withdrawing crew-access arm." The long structure pivoted slowly away from the spacecraft, stopping in its storage position against the side of the service tower.

"Weather conditions are acceptable in all recovery areas," Svetlana reported.

Vadim continued to monitor the computer-controlled procedures. "Guidance-system alignment complete. All functions nominal."

"Going to internal power," Mikhail declared, beginning to sound more excited. "Service arms being withdrawn." The swing arms that had provided power to the vehicle rotated out of the way.

Svetlana scanned her display. "Coming up on ten minutes. Final communications checks." They completed another series of contacts with the control centers and downrange recovery teams.

"Starting final countdown," Vadim announced. "Strap-on tank pressurization. Propellant umbilicals disengaged."

As many times as she'd gone through such procedures, Svetlana had never before felt this degree of apprehension and exhilaration. Even as the clock decremented steadily toward zero, she had difficulty believing they'd finally reached the end of the agonizing series of obstacles.

"One minute!" Vadim's voice rose with excitement. "Core

tank pressurization. Twenty-five seconds. Engine start sequence. Strap-on engines start."

The huge vehicle shuddered as the rockets came to life.

"Core-engines start!" Vadim was screaming.

"Liftoff at 0202 Universal Coordinated Time!" Svetlana said, expanding the acronym for dramatic effect.

The thundering vibration shook her every cell, the immense power of the engines enhancing her excitement to the pinnacle of elation. She screamed, "We're on our way!"

"Azimuth alignment complete," Vadim called as the vehicle rolled toward the intended direction of flight.

Svetlana watched the velocity and altitude values rapidly increase, straining against the mounting g-forces.

"Stand by strap-on burnout," Vadim alerted them. "At one-four-zero seconds—mark."

The rumbling decreased markedly as the giant engines of the Energia's side rockets shut down. Seconds later the vehicle was jolted by pyrotechnic actuators which cut through the attachments, allowing small separation rockets to push the strap-ons safely to the side.

"Passing seventy-five kilometers, velocity sixteen-hundred meters per second," Svetlana read from her screen.

Mikhail made the first transmission, following a time-honored tradition of Russian manned-space operations by using the call sign of the ship's commander. "Flight Control, this is Tigrytsa."

"Tigrytsa, this is Flight Control. Good morning." The voice was Alex's.

"Good morning to you, Alex," Mikhail replied. "On-board systems checks show nominal operation."

"Telemetry confirms that, Tigrytsa. We have you passing through 100,000 meters. Estimating 212 seconds until core-engine shutoff."

The velocity and distance numbers increased more rapidly.

"Tigrytsa, Flight Control shows nominal trajectory possible on two engines."

"Concur," Vadim replied.

Svetlana checked her numbers again. "Four-thousand five-hundred meters per second. Stand by for core engine shutdown."

"Flight Control has shutdown in twenty-two seconds."

The cosmonauts waited, watching the counter on the center screen.

Vadim announced the event. "Core engine shutdown at 452 seconds."

The G-forces that had pushed them into their couches since liftoff decreased and then disappeared. The spacecraft became strangely quiet.

"Tigrytsa, Flight Control. Stand by for core separation."

Another jolt marked the action of more pyros. The spent booster thrust itself away from the spacecraft on its way toward destruction in the atmosphere.

Seconds passed by while the crew awaited the next crucial event.

"Autosequence for shroud separation," Svetlana called.

The first shocks separated the nose cone and the escape rocket. Another series of explosions broke the cylindrical sides into four sections and pushed them away from the spacecraft. With the outer fairing removed, the windows of the descent module became useful for the first time.

"Take a look, Mikhail," Svetlana said, pointing toward the twenty-centimeter porthole above his head. He loosened his belts enough to bend upward and peer out. "Unbelievable!" was all he had time to say.

A final round of jolts, these rather muted, told them the remaining shrouds covering the third-stage engines and the entire fourth stage had been blown away from the vehicle. Now freed of the weight of the fairings, the spacecraft was ready for the next phase.

"Shroud separation complete," Svetlana declared. "Five seconds to third-stage ignition."

"Tigrytsa, Flight Control. We show normal ignition and acceleration. Estimate orbit in thirty-eight minutes, twenty-four seconds."

Looking over, Svetlana said, "Mikhail, I think you've got time for some sightseeing."

**Kennedy Space Center**

"It's already started," Brandt thought lying in bed. "Brian's on his way to Mission Control, techs are at work all over Kennedy."

He'd already been awake more than twenty minutes. "Two twenty five. Might as well get up."

After a trip to the bathroom, he checked the computer. The message alert was blinking. He brought up the only entry.

*UNCLASSIFIED*

*Launch of Lunar Spacecraft from Baikonur*

The subject line told him everything. He turned away in frustration, pacing the small room and speaking aloud, although there was no one to hear. "After all that they beat us by ten hours. Think of all the places we could have saved a day—gotten there first."

The phone rang with his wake-up call. Although he tried, he couldn't make his response sound as jaunty as usual.

"Wish there was a way we could catch up," he thought. "Not like an airplane race where you can push up the power or cut closer on a pylon. Need to modify the trajectories."

His mind continued to toy with the problem as he returned to the computer to delete the unwanted information. The message alert was blinking again, indicating something had just arrived.

*UNCLASSIFIED*

*Artemis Update*

*Liquid oxygen propellant loading started at 0233 EST.*

"Here we go," he whispered to himself, then cleared the message and went back to the bathroom to clean up.

A few minutes later he wiped the last dab of shaving cream from his face and thought, "Last decent shave for six days." After neatly rearranging his toiletry items in the small medicine cabinet, he went to the bedroom and dressed.

"Nice being able to wear Shuttle garb," he thought as he pulled a navy-blue knit shirt over his head and slipped into his trousers.

"Oops—nearly forgot." He opened the draw of a night stand and removed an unlabeled pill bottle. Taking a piece of paper from the memo pad next to the telephone, he carefully removed ten tablets, placed them in the center of the paper and folded it over several times. He pulled open the flap from the thigh pocket of the trousers and slid the paper all the way to the bottom.

"Probably won't need 'em, but you never know," he thought.

The remainder of the dressing process consisted of putting on his shoes and taking a cobalt-blue Shuttle jacket from the closet.

"That ought to do it," he told himself as he turned out the lights, left the small apartment and walked down the hall to the dining room. Andy was already there. Brandt got a glass of orange juice and took a seat across from him at the small square table.

"Dang, Andy," Brandt moaned. "Just kills me that we only missed by a few hours. Been trying to find a way to catch up."

Darrell arrived, got a glass and poured himself some juice. "Well, they beat us, but not by much."

"Yup," Brandt replied. "I'm trying to find a way to close the gap."

"Come up with anything?"

"We could skip the extra earth orbit."

Momentarily ignoring the proposal, Darrell went to the refrigerator to get his prepared meal. "You guys ready to eat?"

"Sure, Darrell," Andy replied. Brandt just nodded.

The quarantine rules deprived the crew of the traditionally sumptuous pre-launch breakfast, but Brandt was just as happy with the lighter fare.

While setting the timers on the microwave ovens, Darrell said, "Can't see anything wrong with boosting out of the initial orbit. Might not even need the circularization burn—just do the whole thing at one time."

"Probably take more propellant," Andy said. "Moves us out of the window a bit."

"Yeah," Brandt agreed. "Need to have the trajectory guys look at it. Better get them going, though. Only got a few hours."

The bells on the ovens announced their meals were ready. Darrell put them on the table while Brandt grabbed three silverware packs from the pile.

Andy peeled back the thin cover, poured himself another glass of juice, then said, "Wonder how the fueling's going."

"Guess we'll know soon enough," Brandt said as he ate his omelet. "Look, I'm going to run back to my room for a minute—see if I can get Johnson going on the new trajectory."

He hurried back to his apartment to make the call. It took him almost five minutes to convince the Flight Director he was serious about making a major mission change three hours before liftoff. Then he went back to the dining room, got some coffee and returned to his chair. His sweet roll had cooled, but he didn't care.

"Any luck with Houston?" Darrell asked.

Brandt shrugged. "Flight said she'd work the problem. Didn't sound very enthusiastic."

"I'll bet," Darrell said, laughing. "Dropping that on her at T-minus three hours. Must have made her day."

The crew specialist appeared at the doorway. "They're ready for you downstairs."

The trio stood up and followed the technician to the door of the Operations and Checkout Building. As they approached the exit, a party of NASA representatives fell in behind them.

Compared to a Super Shuttle operation, the group emerging into the glare of floodlights was quite small, as was the contingent from the media. Mission guidelines still restricted interactions to the smallest possible number of people and the launch schedule eliminated any chance for a press conference. Consequently, only a few reporters accompanied the photographers and television cameramen.

For once, Brandt's smile wasn't pasted on for the benefit of public relations. Proceeding down the ramp from the building, he walked the short distance to the brown Astrovan. Sized to accommodate Shuttle crews, it looked nearly empty with only the Artemis trio tucked in the back.

The astronauts said little during the twenty-minute drive to Pad 39A. A smaller group of cameramen awaited them, this one made up of NASA and military personnel. With the spaceship in the background, the crew provided the expected number of waves and grins, then walked toward the base of the Fixed Service Structure.

"My Lord, that's beautiful!" Brandt whispered as he turned around and looked up at the vehicle. Forty high-intensity searchlights beamed upward from all directions around the pad, giving the spacecraft an awesome majesty. He'd seen a Shuttle in the same position and at almost the same time of day, but this was different. Artemis had no wings, nothing to link it to the earth. It was built for space.

His reverie lasted only a few seconds. The crew specialist led them to the elevator for the ride to the Orbiter Access Arm. Stepping out on the open walkway, they quickly covered the distance and arrived in the White Room at the arm's end.

Had this been a Shuttle operation, a team of technicians would have been there waiting to help them make last-minute adjustments to their launch/entry suits. Today, however, there was little to do other than don in-flight footwear and thank the members of the closeout crew for the help they'd rendered throughout the program.

Andy moved around the others to the opening at the end of the room, through an accordion-like seal that created an enclosed passage to the spacecraft, then through the open hatch. With a technician's help, he crawled across the left two couches, dropped into his position on the far side and began to strap in.

Brandt moved to the center couch and Darrell settled in on his left. The technician inspected their safety belts and then withdrew from the cockpit.

The astronauts made a quick check of their communications, first with each other and then with Kennedy's Launch Control Center. Their next task, made easier by instructions on their multi-function displays, involved checking the position of every switch in the vehicle. Then Brandt began a series of communication tests with other control facilities. The second item on his list called for contact with Mission Control.

"Houston, this is Artemis. How do you read?"

Brian answered, "Artemis, this is Mission Control. You're loud and clear, how me?"

"Houston, Artemis reads you loud and clear. We're standing by for a reading on our requested change to the mission profile."

"Roger that, Artemis. Be advised, the request has been denied. We're looking into some alternatives. Information will be downloaded to you—estimating T-minus thirty minutes."

Brandt started to speak to the other astronauts but realized he'd be heard by the controllers at Kennedy and Houston. He reached forward and moved a switch just below the center display from *TRANSMIT* to *INTERCOM.*

"Dang!" he said. "Could have saved us ninety minutes."

Andy interrupted. "Need to finish the comm checks."

Brandt switched back to *TRANSMIT* and completed the procedure.

"Time to button up," Darrell said as the technicians came toward him to secure the hatch.

"Artemis, this is Launch Control. Hatch is secure."

"Roger that," Brandt responded, reading the report on his display. "Now we relax while the machines do the work."

But Brandt found the remaining minutes of the countdown

anything but relaxing. Totally beyond his control, thousands of computers, located all over the world and even in orbit, began a final analysis of every item involved in the launch. The results of their tests flowed into the Kennedy Space Center where they were verified, assembled and transmitted to the displays of controllers, administrators and, of course, the astronauts waiting on Pad 39A.

The right-hand display began scrolling through the items. Rescue teams stationed at recovery areas, tracking systems all around the world, satellite communications networks, surface communications, weather conditions—one after another the elements came together. Brandt stared at the screen, dreading the discrepancy that would scrub the launch. Suddenly, the center display went blank, then filled with terms from the obscure language of astrodynamics. At the top was the word *CONFIDENTIAL*.

"Hold on here," Brandt exclaimed as he tried to decipher the information. He checked that the intercom switch would keep his comments inside the spacecraft. "Know what this is?" He answered his own question. "These are our new trajectory instructions. Maybe the NASA cats are trying to cut our flight time without making it show."

"Artemis, this is Houston. Confirm receipt of guidance update readout."

"Roger, Houston, we confirm that."

"Artemis, Houston. We needed to trim up your TLI burn a bit. No action required."

"Roger that, Houston."

Brandt took one last look at the information. He couldn't tell for sure, but he thought the transit time had been reduced.

"Artemis, Control. Ground crew is secure."

Instinctively looking through the hatch window to be sure, Brandt confirmed that the technicians had withdrawn to a safe area. "LCC, Artemis. Roger that."

The events scrolling across the right-hand display became more meaningful. "Okay," Brandt thought, "maneuvering-system pressurization—we're getting there."

"Artemis, Control. Stand by final weather update."

"Roger weather," Brandt replied automatically.

"Artemis, Control. We'd like to give you as much margin as possible on that cold front. All reporting stations are tracking the time line so, unless you have objections, we'd like to skip the scheduled hold."

Brandt slapped Darrell's arm, then transmitted, "Launch Control this is Artemis. Support that."

"Roger Artemis. That puts us at T-minus twenty minutes and counting."

"It ain't much," Brandt thought, "but it might help."

The computers ground on, processing command after command, testing, analyzing, verifying. Brandt glanced back and forth from one display to the other.

"Artemis, Control. Stand by abort check."

"LCC, roger abort check."

The large red *ABORT* light flashed on momentarily.

"Artemis, Control. We've still got everybody on the time line—like to reduce the second scheduled hold to one minute."

"LCC, Artemis. Support that."

"Roger. That puts us at T-minus nine minutes and counting."

"Roger that. We are showing go for launch."

"Roger, Artemis. Go for launch."

Darrell announced, "Crew-access arm retracting."

Brandt looked across just in time to see the White Room slip by as the arm moved away from the vehicle. Their ability to escape had just vanished.

Working one system after another, the computers raced on.

"Artemis, Control. Go for purge sequence four."

Valves opened to allow liquid hydrogen to flow through the turbopumps and nozzle tubes of the main engines, chilling them in preparation for starting.

"Transfer to internal power," Brandt noted. "On our own now."

"Artemis, Control. Go for external tank oxygen pressurization."

"Roger."

"Gaseous Oxygen Vent Arm retracted." The right display told Brandt the last connection to the Fixed Service Structure had been removed.

"Artemis, Control. T-minus two minutes and counting. Have a good ride."

"Roger that—and thank you."

"Artemis, Control. Go for H2 tank pressurization."

"Roger H2."

"Artemis, Control. T-minus one minute and thirty seconds."

The display said the joint heaters on the Solid Rocket Boosters had been deactivated.

"Artemis, Control. T-minus thirty seconds. Go for autosequence start."

"Roger autosequence."

"Artemis, Control. APU start is go. Control to on-board computer."

"T-minus four. Main engine start," Brandt called to his crew.

Liquified gases gushed into the three engines, turbopumps raced, preburners ignited, propellants mixed in the combustion chambers and ignited. Three blasts of hot gas roared out of the nozzles.

"Main engines are go!" Brandt shouted. "SRB ignition."

"Artemis, Control. We have liftoff at 1145 Zulu."

"Clock's running," Brandt announced. "Tranquility, here we come."

"Artemis, Control. Clear tower."

"Roger LCC. Nice going!"

"Houston, Artemis. Roll program."

"Roger roll, Artemis," Brian answered.

Pivoting on its axis, the booster aimed itself along the trajectory path.

"Pitching over," Darrell noted as he watched the attitude-director indicator at the center of his display.

Seeing the power-setting value drop, Brandt transmitted, "Houston, Artemis shows main engines at sixty-five percent."

"Copy that, Artemis."

Suddenly, Brandt felt a pulsating vibration, as if something was beating against the back of his couch. "Darrell," he asked, "you feeling anything?"

"Pogo oscillations!" Darrell exclaimed.

"Houston, Artemis. Experiencing thrust surges," Brandt transmitted.

"Roger, Artemis, we're seeing them."

Buried inside the propulsion segment, a liquid-oxygen valve stretched and compressed the expansion bellows that supported it, creating pressure pulses that moved through the feed system into the thrust chambers. Sensors on the engines detected the changes and sent signals to flow-control valves in an attempt to keep the thrust constant. But the process took time, just enough time to keep the corrections out of phase with the surges. The amplitude increased.

"Houston, Artemis," Brandt called, "ride's getting pretty rough." The concern in his voice had nothing to do with comfort. He knew the surges could break down the layer of cool gas protecting the engine walls, allowing the white-hot flame to burn through.

"Artemis, we're going to push the power up to seventy percent—see if that smooths things out."

Because the huge solid boosters were still burning, Brandt couldn't feel the small thrust increase. But the pulsing stopped.

"Houston, Artemis. Feels like that did the trick."

"Roger, Artemis. We're liking the numbers a lot better."

"What about the tank-ablation numbers?" Brandt thought as the vehicle's speed increased above the baseline values just as the aerodynamic heating reached its peak. The seconds went by ever more slowly.

"Artemis, go at throttle up."

"Roger, Houston, go at throttle up."

Brandt watched the power levels steadily increase toward 104 percent. His voice, although slightly strained by the mounting G-forces, sounded more relaxed as he said to the crew, "So much for max-Q, folks."

Suddenly, the acceleration decreased markedly. "SRB separation," Brandt announced.

As the empty booster cases fell to the ocean, Brian announced, "Artemis, performance is nominal."

"Roger, nominal performance," Brandt replied, then let out a sigh as he watched the numbers on the center display report the increasing velocity, downrange distance and altitude. After a few more minutes, the altitude peaked, then began to slowly decrease. Brandt noted the event. "Setting up for external tank separation."

"Artemis, press to MECO."

"Roger, Houston, press to MECO," Brandt replied, comforted by the knowledge that, even if they lost an engine, they'd still be able to complete the mission.

A few minutes later, Brian transmitted, "Artemis, single-engine press, 104."

"Roger, single-engine press, 104," Brandt repeated.

"Artemis, main-engine throttle down."

The thrust dropped slowly to sixty-five percent, keeping the G-level at a mildly uncomfortable three.

"Artemis, MECO at 38.3"

"Roger, 38.3"

The mission clock at the top of both displays blinked through thirty six, thirty seven, thirty eight.

"Main engine cutoff," Brandt reported.

For the first time, no engines were accelerating the spacecraft. The astronauts were weightless.

"Stand by for tank separation." The event appeared on the right display. "Houston, Artemis shows nominal separation."

"Roger that. We show you go for third-stage ignition."

"Folks," Brandt said, "we're flying a whole new vehicle."

Rapid changes to the right display signified the absence of all Shuttle-related components and the reconfiguration of the computer.

"Stand by third-stage ignition," Brandt alerted them.

The three RL-10s of Boeing's creation came to life, pushing the crew back into their couches, but only with the force of a fifth of a G. Barely half-a-minute later, the engines shut down.

"Artemis, we're with you through TDRS," Brian noted, informing them that communications were now being routed through one of the Tracking and Data Relay satellites.

"Roger, Houston. Read you loud and clear."

"Artemis, show you nominal at third-stage cutoff, perigee 65.1 miles, apogee 152.4 miles."

"Okay, folks," Brandt said over the intercom, "let's get on the systems checks."

Brandt unstrapped, rolled over and squeezed a switch above the head of his couch. Slowly, the couch folded up against the back wall, clearing an opening beneath the center display that led from the cockpit into the nose area. "All yours, Darrell," he said.

Darrell unstrapped and floated through the opening into the nose of the spacecraft to perform a physical check of the stowed equipment.

Floating in front of his folded couch, Brandt worked with the center display, trying to determine the effect of the trajectory modifications, while Andy used the right screen to verify the status of the vehicle's subsystems.

Twenty-five minutes later, they were back in their couches waiting for the engines to put them in a circular orbit.

"Artemis, Houston, your second burn nominal targets—burn time five colon four six, delta-v two two four."

The crew watched the clock approach the engine start time.

"Third-stage ignition," Brandt told them for the second time. In a few minutes, it was over.

"Artemis, show you down the middle on circularization. Trans-lunar injection in 122 minutes."

For Brandt, it was the longest earth orbit in history. The astronauts unstrapped, floated into the nose to reacquaint themselves with the layout, looked out the two side windows at the earth below, and ran through some of the information stored in the computer. Eventually, the waiting ended. They returned to their places and fastened the restraints.

"Artemis, Houston. You're go for trans-lunar injection."

They were the words he and thousands of others had been waiting to hear. He replied happily, "Roger that, Houston. Standing by ignition."

Again, the displays changed to show a countdown clock. When the number dropped to zero, all three engines sprang to life. The acceleration gave them just a bit less than normal earth forces. Seven-and-a-half minutes later, the engines stopped, leaving them weightless once again. The burn seemed to last longer than Brandt remembered from the simulations.

"Artemis, Houston. Seems to be a minor discrepancy in your state vector—probably due to an error in the trajectory update. Looks like you'll be going a bit faster than baseline. It'll take a small mid-course correction and a longer deceleration burn going into lunar orbit. Except for the reduction in propellant reserve, we don't see a problem."

Elated, Brandt responded, "Copy that, Houston. Sure glad the glitch was in the right direction."

"Some glitch," he thought. "I take back all the bad things I ever said about NASA."

Then he cheered, "All right, dang it! If that ain't showin' 'em how I don't know what is. Hang on moon. Here come the Americans!" He'd forgotten to check the communications switch.

## Chapter 14

# Transit

**Soyuz TML-1**

"...and sixty, and one, and two, and three..." Svetlana's legs pushed hard against the springs of the exercise machine. She had set the return force close to its maximum. Strapped tightly to the device's tiny seat, she steadied herself by grasping the grips above her head. "...and eighty, and one, and two ..." Pulling down, she stretched the arm exercisers, left arm down with the right foot, right arm down with the left foot. "...and eight, and nine, and four hundred."

She stopped and panted, "Better let Vadim get on this before we go to sleep." Her breathing returned to normal in less time than it took to unclamp the components of the machine and swing them into their storage positions. She used a pre-moistened towel to wipe off and slipped back into her flight suit.

Feeling refreshed, she floated toward the open hatch and into the descent module. As she emerged, she glanced to her left.

"Mikhail," she chuckled, "if your stomach doesn't settle down, you'll use up all the bags on our first day out."

His face enveloped by the container's tacky opening, Mikhail continued to retch.

"Hard to believe you did aerobatics with that tummy," she teased. "Who cleaned up the plane for you?"

He used the neck of the bag to wipe the vomit from his mouth, then carefully sealed the opening. "Never had a problem," he mumbled. "Don't know what's wrong. Sorry about the smell."

Svetlana turned toward Vadim. When their eyes met, they burst into a fit of laughter. Mikhail looked at them, obviously embarrassed.

"Relax," she reassured him. "Private joke."

As Mikhail left to add another deposit to the wet-waste container, Vadim returned to his display. "Report on the Americans," he announced. "Analysis of their trajectory. Not minimum energy. Must have extended their burn to gain some velocity."

"And they're not racing us to the moon!" Svetlana huffed. "Any estimate of their transfer time?"

"About five hours off nominal."

"Damn!" Her anger resurfaced. "That means they'll enter lunar orbit only five hours after we do."

"Why can't we increase our velocity?" Mikhail asked, his voice sounding rather weak as he floated through the hatch.

"Can't spare the fuel, Mikhail," Vadim replied. "I'm sure the Americans took a serious risk. They'll have to burn even more propellant to slow down again when they get to the moon. Their actions are truly irresponsible."

Mikhail asked, "Anything else we could do?"

"Might be able to reduce our time in lunar orbit. Land on the first pass," Svetlana replied. "Worth analyzing."

"I'll do it as soon as I finish the IMU update," Vadim said. "We'll need approval from Flight Control."

"See what you come up with before we ask them," Svetlana responded. "Right now, I want some dinner."

"Wondered when you'd finally get hungry," Vadim said. "Almost time to sleep. I'm glad I ate earlier."

"But now you get to exercise on a full stomach," she countered.

"Get you anything?" she asked Mikhail as she moved back toward the orbital module.

"Don't think I'll eat until I feel better."

Vadim cautioned, "You'd better drink something or you'll become dehydrated."

Mikhail shrugged and asked, "Would you bring me some tea, Svetlana?"

She looked at him sympathetically. "Cheer up, Mikhail. This

happens to many cosmonauts, even after several missions. Usually the nausea subsides after the first day."

He replied limply, "Please don't say *nausea*."

**Artemis**

Because the EMUs provided the only means for survival should a meteorite pierce Artemis' hull, a daily check of their readiness had been added to the list of duties. Brandt scrolled the last instructions to the top of the pocket computer's LCD screen. Glancing briefly at the familiar words, he completed the checklist, examining the glove connections and the condition of the sleeves, marveling at the skill of the CIA engineer. The weapons couldn't be detected—even by an EMU expert.

To accomplish the last procedure, he opened a flap on the bottom of the Display and Control Module, exposing a small, multi-pin connector. To it, he attached a short cable extending from the top of the computer and pressed the *RUN* button.

The screen became a blur of fleeting comments, each verifying that a test of the space-suit's control system had found no discrepancies. Finally, the messages stopped and the screen read *Test Complete*. Brandt disconnected the device and pressed the flap back into place.

After propelling himself away from the narrow nose region, through the access way and into the cockpit, Brandt addressed the other astronauts. "Everything checked..."

"Hold on, Brandt," Darrell interrupted him. "Got a report coming in from Mission Control. Analysis of the Russian trajectory. They just announced they're also going for the Sea of Tranquility."

He stared at the display as a map of the moon's surface gradually emerged. As soon as the last row of pixels had been drawn, the computer added a red streak, the projected path of the Russian spacecraft.

"Which orbit are they showing?" Andy asked.

"Wouldn't make any difference at this scale," Darrell replied and then asked, "Houston, Artemis. Can you expand the image?"

"Roger, Artemis," Brian replied. "Stand by."

The screen went blank, then another map appeared showing several closely spaced lines crossing the center.

Andy floated over and hovered above Darrell's head. "The last line passes right between the Maskelyne and Sabine craters," he said.

"They could land right on top of Apollo 11."

"Don't think so, Andy," Brandt responded. "That's the sixth orbit. You can bet they'll be down after no more than two. Puts them about four degrees away. What's the distance, Darrell?"

"Closest approach?" He did the calculation in his head. "Maybe twenty kilometers."

"Houston, Artemis. You concur with that?" Brandt asked.

"Artemis, Houston. Sounds about right."

Brandt responded, "Heck, they'll probably do a course correction that'll totally screw up our projections."

"Roger that," Brian replied, reminding him his comments were being heard in Mission Control.

Carefully repositioning the communications switch, Brandt asked, "Where do you think that leaves us with respect to the weapons?"

"Hard to say," Darrell replied. "They might be aiming to land near our site. On the other hand, the Sea of Tranquility's the obvious choice for helium-three research."

"But if they get there first," Andy protested, "there'll be no reason for them to take hostile action."

"You mean if we lose, we're safe?" Brandt responded curtly.

"Tell you something," Andy retorted. "I never believed the CIA crap. As far as I'm concerned, the message could mean anything—or nothing. And how come we never got a follow-up report?"

"Andy's got a point there," Darrell said. "Inferring that the cosmonauts would be armed was really a stretch."

"Think what you like," Brandt replied. "I wouldn't put anything past the commies."

"Wish we could disable those damned things they put in our suits," Andy grumbled. "Just an accident waiting to happen."

"Let's talk sleep," Brandt said, deliberately moving away from what had become an uncomfortable discourse. "Now that we've shaved the transit time, we'll need to adjust our wake-ups so we'll be bright eyed and bushy tailed as we approach the moon. Works out to a twenty-three-hour day, pushing the sleep time up an hour each night. Gets us up about two hours before LOI."

"Think that's enough?" Darrell asked. "What if we want to cut the orbits short?"

"If the Russians are already on the surface, there'll be no need to. Of course, if they get hung up we might have to trim the sleep time a bit. But I'll be so danged tickled I won't even notice."

**Soyuz TML-1**

The computer-generated alarm sounded twenty hours after liftoff, a series of long, loud, monotones, impossible to ignore. Floating in her restraint in the corridor of the orbital module, Svetlana drifted from a deep sleep to hazy awareness. Surprised she'd slept completely through the rest period, she attributed it to the exhausting events of the previous week. She released the restraint's thin straps and slipped free, then unsnapped the harness from its mounting points and returned it to its storage compartment.

Mikhail was awake, albeit still groggy. She waited for him to disengage himself, then packed his restraint on top of hers and slid the bin back into its slot.

She examined Mikhail's face, now puffy from the weightlessness, and asked how he was feeling.

Shaking himself awake, he answered, "Much better, Svetlana. Took me a while to get to sleep but the nausea's gone. In fact, I'm starved."

She laughed. "Well, you've got all of yesterday's food waiting for you. Help yourself while I catch up on the mission."

Svetlana floated down to the descent module, passed feet first through the open hatch and settled into the center couch. Vadim had spent the night in the couch to her left.

Studying the array of numbers covering the left display, she sighed and said, "Vadim, your skill with trajectory software hasn't diminished. The Americans will be there exactly when you predicted."

He nodded and replied, "And they'll probably minimize their time in lunar orbit—maybe go down on the first pass."

Svetlana shook her head. "That would be easier for them. No reconfiguration, no docking. Just fly the whole vehicle to the surface. Makes me furious. No excuse for us being in this situation." Her eyes narrowed. "Vadim, suppose we try to land right away. How much time do you think we'll have?"

"From the end of the insertion burn to de-orbit? About fifty minutes."

"It'd be difficult, but not impossible. We'd have to run through the procedures a few times."

**Artemis**

"Hard to believe how quiet this thing is," Brandt thought, listening to the muffled sound of the ventilation fan. "None of the Shuttle's creaks and moans."

For the first sleep period, he'd assigned himself the cockpit watch, a procedure that assured an immediate response should the computer detect a malfunction. As expected, nothing had gone wrong, but his sleep had been sporadic just the same. Loosely strapped to the left-side couch, he gazed through the small porthole above the hatch at the millions of stars set against the blackness of space. He lined up a star with the edge of the window, then, keeping his head still, watched it slowly change position, proving to himself what he already knew. The computer maintained a one-turn-per-hour roll rate, rotating Artemis to balance the sun's intense heating on one side with the frigid cold of space on the other in what the Apollo astronauts had labeled the *barbecue mode*.

The conical shape of Artemis blocked his view of the earth but, by pressing his head against the porthole, he found he could get the barest glimpse of the moon, its sunlit half brilliant against the ebony. As he twisted, trying to improve the vista, a sharp pain erupted inside his neck.

"Dang," he cursed to himself, trying to rub it away, knowing he wouldn't succeed. He thought about the pills in the pocket of his flight suit but decided to save them for a more severe attack.

He looked at the mission clock. "One minute 'til T-plus-eighteen. Time to get everybody up." A touch of the trackball brought the cursor to life. After making two of the three selections necessary to disable the alarm, he thought better of it and waited out the last remaining seconds.

The opening fanfare of Sousa's *Washington Post March* blared from speakers placed throughout the crew compartment. Andy was the first to express his appreciation.

"Oh shit! Damn it, Brandt, turn it off!"

Darrell's compliments followed shortly. "Jesus! What a hell of a way to wake up!"

Returning to the trackball, Brandt accomplished the silencing procedure. "What's the matter with you guys? Doesn't it get your blood flowing?"

"Boiling's more like it," Andy grumbled. "But what can you

expect from a zoomie? Probably thinks Mendelssohn is a brand of beer."

"I'd sure rather ease into the day with some soft rock," Darrell suggested. "Something romantic."

"Christ," Brandt retorted, "do that and it'll take you the whole morning to finish takin' a crap. Need something with spirit. That's my favorite march."

"What'd you do, load those damned recordings for every wake up?" Darrell asked as he rolled up his bag.

"Nope," Brandt assured him. "Your stuff's still on the computer. When you pull crew-station, you get your choice."

"Now there's a real dilemma for you, Andy," Darrell responded. "I think he's found a way to sleep in a bag for the rest of the trip."

"Better quit bitching and get your act together," Brandt said, still directing his voice toward the forward bay. "We've got serious PR work coming up."

Darrell drifted into the cockpit. "When's the broadcast?"

"We're live on the *Today* show. Eight eastern. Still almost seven hours to go, but we've got some photography to finish first."

"At least we get to see the earth again—and handle the flight controls."

Brandt smiled. "Yup. They still haven't figured out how to make the computer follow instructions from a TV anchor."

**Soyuz TML-1**

"Svetlana, I can't tell you how good it feels to be able to eat again," Mikhail commented as he devoured his breakfast. "This stuff tastes great."

"You like it?" she sneered. "You're still sick. Just not barfing."

Vadim called to them from the descent module. "We need to go over the video taping."

"Two more minutes," Svetlana called back.

She finished her last two containers, put the empty packages into a wet-waste sack and held it while Mikhail deposited his remnants. Then, using her paper napkin, she collected some droplets of juice that were drifting in the air, added the napkin to the garbage, sealed the bag and placed it in the assigned container. Finally, she folded the tiny table back against the front of the galley.

With her crew once again assembled in the descent module,

Svetlana said, "Vadim, this is your project. Tell us what to do."

"Just what we practiced," he replied. "The script says we start with a picture of earth. It'll be just a sliver, but still pretty dramatic. Svetlana, I'll shoot out the left porthole while you position the spacecraft."

Connecting her restraints, Svetlana secured herself to the center couch and took hold of the controls. Guided by the attitude display, she yawed the spacecraft until it was nearly perpendicular to the direction of motion. Then she rolled it to raise the small porthole next to Vadim's head.

"That's good, Svetlana," Vadim said as he peered through the camera's viewfinder. "Roll back the other way about ten degrees to keep the sun out of the view field."

Vadim began a short narrative, telling his audience about the Soyuz's position and the reason most of the earth was in darkness.

Mikhail took over the camera for the next sequence. He positioned himself in the passageway to the orbital module and aimed the camera at his colleagues while they introduced themselves. Then Vadim played cameraman while Svetlana conducted a tour of the modules. At times, he had trouble finding a place in the cramped spacecraft where he could get a decent picture, but the difficulties were handled with a running series of humorous comments.

When it came time to show the exercise machine, Mikhail performed the demonstration. He carefully swung the sections into place, climbed on the seat and fastened the belt. But when he pushed down on the footrests, they barely moved. He pushed harder and harder with no better success. He huffed and puffed, trying to act at ease while explaining the need for exercise. Finally, Svetlana couldn't contain her laughter any longer and Vadim suggested he check the force setting.

"Very funny," Mikhail blurted out. "I hope the people in Moscow enjoy laughing at me." But after Vadim told him the camera wasn't on, his attitude changed and he seemed pleased to be involved in one of the pranks his colleagues were famous for, even as their victim. With the force level reset, he completed the segment in fine form.

Finally, with the camera attached to the top of the instrument panel and the crew back in their couches, they each thanked the people of the Federation for their support and good wishes.

Vadim stopped the camera and asked, "What do you think?"

"It seemed to go smoothly," Svetlana replied. "I'd like to see it through before we send it back."

"Good idea," Vadim said as he selected the file with the digitized video and instructed the computer to display it.

The crew devoted the next twenty minutes to watching themselves play cosmonauts.

Svetlana gave the verdict. "Excellent! I think we all look quite professional."

**Artemis**

"What'd you think of it?" Brandt asked as the transmission from Mission Control ended. They'd just finished watching a rebroadcast of the video from the Soyuz.

"Pretty good," Darrell replied.

The response irked him. "Really? I thought it sounded stiff and rehearsed."

"Sour grapes, Brandt?" Andy probed. "I thought it looked a lot more professional than what we sent out."

"How so, Andy?"

"I liked the format, especially their tour of the spaceship. What'd we do? Same silly nonsense—tossing things around in zero gravity, gobbling up blobs of water and pieces of food. Nothing technical at all."

Brandt shrugged. "Wasn't exactly graduate level, but we gave the networks what they asked for. Short, entertaining segments."

"They must think the American people are brain dead," Darrell said, sounding disgusted. "Frankly, the folks I know would appreciate seeing something like the Russians put together. I think we should do that for tomorrow's broadcast, whether the networks like it or not."

"Suits me," Brandt replied. "Of course, NASA public affairs might get a little testy if the networks complain."

"Screw 'em!" Andy declared, ending the matter.

"You know," Brandt said, "it's really ironic. The only time we're in control of the ship is when we're making commercials for NASA."

"So now you enjoy doing television shows?" Darrell asked.

Brandt knew he was being baited but answered anyway. "You out of your mind? Nothing I like worse than being on stage—makin' nice to the taxpayers so NASA keeps getting their money. Always wondered what would happen if they just told the truth. Told the public that the reason they want to send spacecraft to the planets is simply to find out what's there, not lie about how it'll stop pollution or improve dishwashers."

"Hard to say," Darrell responded. "But as long as they're convinced that exploring the unknown gets you peanuts from Congress, we'll keep hearing the bullshit."

**Soyuz TML-1**

"My God, Vadim. The smell's getting worse. What could be wrong?"

"Don't know, Svetlana, but it takes a long time for the scrubber to get rid of the vomit stench."

Svetlana checked the mission clock. "It's been 45 hours since the last time he was sick. I don't think I can sleep with this."

"Let me check the air composition." Vadim brought up data from the gas analyzer.

"Nothing dangerous, but something's definitely not working," he said. "Trace gas levels are too high."

Svetlana thought through system details. "We've only been up sixty-one hours. Can't have exhausted the cartridge yet."

Vadim pulled up the relevant checklist. "Only one action listed. Check the filter."

"Under the couch?"

"Not too hard to get at. You'll have to move into the orbital module for a while."

Svetlana floated feet first through the passageway, then stopped so she could watch. Vadim selected a new menu from the row of icons and instructed the computer to raise the couches to their landing positions. Valves opened, nitrogen flowed into the shock struts and the Kazbek-Y couches lifted thirty centimeters.

With room to work, Vadim eased himself under the center couch, reached back and located the cover of the filter holder. He flipped the catches back, pulled off the retainer and slid out the cartridge. After extricating himself, he floated over the couches and examined the filter.

"Take a look, Svetlana."

She moved back into the descent module and inspected the cylinder. "No doubt about where that came from."

After doing a slow somersault to put her head through the

hatch opening, she called, "Mikhail, come here when you're through."

He had already stowed the exercise machine and was in the process of wiping himself off. He disposed of the paper towels, slipped back into his flight suit and poked his head into the descent module.

Holding the filter where Mikhail could see the inlet end, Svetlana said, "Take a look."

Mikhail studied the device, took it and turned it over. "Charcoal filter cartridge."

"Look at the inlet end."

He studied it some more. "Something's on it."

"Smell."

"Vomit. How the hell did it get there?"

In a schoolteacher voice, Svetlana answered, "I told you it was important to chase down every last bit. The ventilation system will pull it into the filter every time."

"Sorry. Thought I had it all." Mikhail's expression showed his frustration and his voice sounded discouraged.

"Not that important," Vadim responded. "Just wanted you to see what can happen. Here, take this and get a replacement."

Mikhail moved back into the orbital module, trying to remember the location of the cartridges. He pulled open several storage compartments but couldn't find the right one.

"Okay," he moaned. "I give up. Where are they?"

"Two stacks this side of the exercise machine. Bin next to the top," Svetlana answered.

In a few seconds, Mikhail had extracted the component and removed its protective cover. He used the cover to wrap the contaminated filter, then put it in the bin and pushed the drawer closed.

"Here it is. Couldn't remember where they stored them."

Vadim took it, slid back under the couch, inserted it in the holder and replaced the retainer.

**Artemis**

"Guys, we're one up on Apollo," Brandt said, announcing his favorable reaction to the group videoconference.

"Much better than a one-way conversation," Andy agreed.

"Even with Mission Control looking in, I think the gals seemed pretty relaxed," Darrell added. "Nice of the people at Johnson to set it up."

"I'm sure it took some effort to tie the sites together," Brandt said, "but there was no other way to do it. Couldn't expect Anita to go to Houston."

"The links worked great," Andy said. "Expected it for Patty, since she was right in Mission Control, but the transmissions from NASA Headquarters surprised me. Really couldn't tell the difference."

"Nope," Brandt agreed. "Just like a group meeting."

Andy said, "Only thing missing was someone for you to talk to, Brandt."

Brandt took a deep breath. "Hard for me to think about another close relationship."

"What's the problem?" Darrell asked.

Speaking very softly, Brandt said, "You know how it was between Nancy and me. I can't imagine that happening twice."

"I'm sure it won't, Brandt. But that doesn't mean you can't be happy with someone else."

"Worried I'll make comparisons. Wouldn't be fair. Need to be sure I'm ready."

Darrell nodded. "See your point."

"What about you, buddy? You gonna marry Anita?"

"If she'll have me. You know I already asked her?"

Brandt was surprised. "No. You never mentioned it. What happened?"

"Turned me down."

"What? That's hard to believe. She's absolutely bonkers in love."

"Not absolutely. She's afraid I won't make it back. Refused to be committed until the mission's over."

"I can relate to that," Andy said, joining the conversation. "Patty's terrified. Certain something awful's going to happen."

"That surprises me, Andy," Brandt responded, "especially after being a Shuttle pilot's wife. She did a super job handling the media."

"Put up a brave front, just the way she was supposed to, but the fear was always there. Never told this to anyone before, but she started using alcohol to help her get through."

"Jesus," Brandt said. "Never would have guessed."

"Covered that up too, just like the terror. Finally had to get her some help."

"She's okay now?"

"Off the booze, if that's what you mean. But the moon mission pushed her fear factor right off the scale. She's convinced she'll never see me again."

"Understand why you weren't happy about filling in for Brian."

"Wasn't me, Brandt. Just concerned about Patty."

"Wonder why she thinks the moon operation's so dangerous," Darrell probed.

"Nothing rational. She's been a bit off center since the baby died. Thinks it's some sort of punishment. Hard to deal with."

"Makes me feel bad about getting you into this. Wish you'd said something during the training program."

"No reason to, Brandt. As much as I care about Patty and the kids, there are some things I just have to do, whether she likes it or not. Besides, everything will be fine after we get back."

"Well, she looked great today. If that's her brave front, it's a beauty."

"Thought they all looked super," Andy replied. "Especially Anita."

Darrell's voice became wistful. "Same dress she wore the afternoon I proposed."

"She's an angel," Brandt said. "You're a lucky man."

"She's even taking time off to work with my Houston kids. Can you believe she's flying back and forth from Washington?"

The low-level alarm tone ended their discussion.

"Looks like a high current," Andy said as he scanned his display. "For some reason, the computer hasn't been able to isolate and correct the problem."

Extracting electrical-system data from the memory, Andy traced the overload back through the bus architecture until he'd eliminated all but a single group of devices as possible culprits. After selecting manual control, he switched the items off and on one at a time, checking for changes in the current load. When he got to the backup pump for the crew-compartment's main cooling loop, nothing happened.

"I've found it, but I'm not sure what to do. Somehow, the secondary coolant pump's telling the computer it's off when it's still running. And it doesn't respond to a manual *Off* command."

"Artemis, this is Houston," the speaker squawked. "We

observe your actions with respect to the cooling pump."

Brandt replied, "Houston, Artemis. Any suggestions?"

"We've got people on it, but if the computer couldn't devise a workaround, I'm not sure we'll do any better."

"Understand, Houston. Any problem with having the thing run continuously?"

"Artemis, Houston. The engineers advise against it. If the bearings go out, the overload will increase."

"Any action we can take, Houston?"

"Not at this time, Artemis. It'll take an EVA to disconnect the thing."

Brandt fumed, "Darrell, the last thing we need is an unscheduled EVA this close to LOI."

"Concur with that, Artemis." CapCom reminded him, once again, that his microphone was hot. Brandt shrugged it off.

After a few more minutes, Mission Control transmitted, "Artemis, this is Houston. Looks like the risk in letting it run for a while is pretty small so we recommend postponing repair operations until the return trip."

"Roger, Houston," Brandt replied, feeling very relieved. "We support that."

This time remembering to disable the transmissions, Brandt said, "Close call! I was afraid they'd make us fix it in lunar orbit."

## Chapter 15

# Lunar Orbit

**Soyuz TML-1**

"Svetlana," Mikhail called from the orbital module, "the toilet stinks."

Annoyed by the interruption, she responded, "I assure you, Mikhail, that smell is the thing you'll miss most on our trip back. Vadim, shall I review the use of feces bags during weightlessness?"

"Words can't do it justice, Svetlana. But that reminds me. We should switch to minimum-residue food. Last chance to use the toilet comes in less than sixteen hours."

Svetlana replied with an emphatic, "Ugh!"

"Mikhail, if you're finished, I'd like to get in one more round of exercise," Vadim said, releasing his restraining straps. The trio had adopted an etiquette that kept interactions with the waste-disposal system private ordeals.

"All yours," Mikhail answered as he floated into the descent module, settling on his couch as Vadim went the other way. He checked the mission clock and asked, "When do we put on our EVA suits?"

"As soon as Vadim's finished exercising," Svetlana answered.

Sounding excited, Mikhail said, "My God, Svetlana, we're about to walk on the moon. Wish we could see it."

She smiled. "We'll get a good look when we pivot around for

the orbit-injection burn."

"Svetlana," Vadim called, "I need some help."

"Sounds like he's ready. Vacation's over, Mikhail."

She pushed off and glided through the hatch. Vadim stood at the center of the corridor making final adjustments to the ventilation garment. His EVA suit floated between them. Svetlana grasped the waist and spread the back opening apart so he could wriggle his feet down the legs of the suit and into the boots. He attached the hoses from the ventilation garment to the supply connectors and made a few comfort adjustments to the suit's lower half. Then he bent over and worked his hands through the sleeves and his head through the neck opening.

With the hardest part finished, he turned away from Svetlana so she could close the back. She connected the pressure seals and fastened the retainers. Finally, after mating its hoses to the suit, she attached the new backpack Ligachev's engineers had developed for the lunar mission.

The remaining steps were easy in comparison. Vadim pulled on the communications headset and waited while Svetlana connected its cable to the suit. After a few more adjustments, he departed for the descent module with Svetlana behind him.

As she reached the hatch, she said, "Your turn, Mikhail. Let me know when you've got the undergarment on." He pushed away from his couch and drifted into the orbital module.

"Starting to get busy," Vadim said.

"Wait until we're in orbit," Svetlana replied. "I hope we got enough practice last night."

"I'm sure we did, Svetlana. Everything went very smoothly. But not much time for fumbling."

"Or checking the landing site, or handling malfunctions."

"The Americans aren't making this any easier."

Her anger reemerging, she responded, "We did this to ourselves, Vadim."

"Ready, Svetlana." It was Mikhail.

She returned to the corridor and repeated the suit-donning process, checking a bit more carefully this time to be sure her rookie had maneuvered everything into its proper place. Then, after he left to join Vadim, it was her turn.

She eased out of her flight suit, folded it and stored it in her clothing compartment. Then she exchanged her panties for a urine-collection device, removed her bra and worked her way into the tight-fitting cooling garment. She removed her suit and backpack from the storage area near the open hatch and called for Vadim.

With his suit on, he couldn't be of much help, but her skill in snaking her limbs and head into the proper cavities required only minimum assistance. However, her dexterity couldn't help him close the back, a task he accomplished only after a few false starts. With her backpack installed and communications headgear connected, they made their way back to the descent module.

The cosmonauts connected umbilicals from the sides of the couches to their suits. The bundles of tubes and wires would bring them cooling water, electrical power, oxygen and communications until they arrived on the lunar surface. Only then would they activate the systems in their backpacks.

The next transmission added to Svetlana's growing excitement.

"Tigrytsa, Flight Control. Twenty-eight minutes to ignition. You are approved for LOI and spacecraft reconfiguration. Anticipate resumption of communications at 0228 UTC."

The spacecraft arced around the moon, racing closer to the portion forever hidden from the earth. For the next half orbit, the crew would be unable to communicate with the Flight Control Center.

Svetlana's right hand grasped the rotation controller. She made a tiny movement, directing the service module's yaw thrusters to put the spacecraft into a slow turn.

Mikhail's head filled the small porthole to his right. After they'd turned only a few degrees, he shouted, "There it is! We're almost there."

She touched the stick again, checking the attitude display on her screen to verify that the spacecraft had stopped its rotation.

Mikhail continued to stare, enthralled at the sight. Finally, Svetlana asked, "Aren't you going to let the rest of us take a look?"

As he pulled his head back, he stammered, "Of course, Svetlana. Guess I got carried away."

"Vadim?" she asked.

Busy with a final review of the reconfiguration sequence, he replied, "Why don't you swing it around to my side after you're finished."

Svetlana leaned toward the porthole. Because the trajectory aimed at the advancing face of the moon, they now looked down at a surface still bathed in sunlight. Neither her many months in Earth orbit nor the long hours looking at simulations had prepared her for the sight.

"My God!" she exclaimed. "It's incredible!"

"What is?" Vadim asked.

"The mountains, Vadim. The mountains of the moon."

She stayed there, transfixed, studying the strange gray landscape jutting out in a harsh clarity, its pattern of ridges and craters traced on the pock-marked valleys as crisply edged shadows. She rationed herself another few moments, then returned the porthole to Mikhail and his video camera.

He scanned the surface, zooming in on one feature after another, adding his comments to the fantastic pictures.

"Twenty minutes to LOI," Vadim interrupted.

"Better let him have a look before we run out of daylight," she told Mikhail as she yawed the spacecraft around a half turn so Vadim could see the moon through his own porthole.

He examined it, saying nothing. Finally, he remarked, "I see what you mean, Svetlana. It's awesome, but everywhere gray. Like a beach of ashes after a massive shelling. Certainly not attractive."

As they moved beyond its sunlit half, the moon became a black emptiness, an arc-edged cutout in the universe of stars.

Svetlana yawed another quarter turn to aim the engine of the upper stage opposite their direction of motion. Satisfied with the alignment, she instructed the computer to resume control.

As it completed its long, S-shaped trajectory, the spacecraft flew in front of the advancing moon, a safety measure that allowed the crew to swing around it and return to earth in case the fourth-stage engine failed to fire. Of course, this assumed that the guidance system had led them to a narrow window, a tiny slit in space barely a hundred kilometers above the moon's surface.

Svetlana knew all this, knew the phenomenal reliability of the upper stage, knew that the combination of Soyuz systems and telemetry analysis made a navigation error virtually impossible. Yet, her heart pounded just the same. Although she'd faced far more threatening situations, never before had so much depended upon the operation of a single rocket engine.

"One minute to ignition," Vadim noted.

The cosmonauts tightened their restraints, forcing their backpacks down into the cutouts of their couches, watching the countdown clock.

Fifteen meters behind them the Korolev 58M roared to life. Its thrust gradually reduced the spaceship's speed until the centripetal acceleration of the orbit exactly balanced the acceleration of the moon's gravity.

The lack of noise surprised Svetlana. Only the barest vibration and a list of reassuring numbers on her display confirmed what the pressure on her back continued to tell her. The 58M was doing its job and one of the most critical phases of the mission was progressing according to plan.

"And shutdown!" Vadim announced as they once again became weightless.

"All right, gentlemen," Svetlana said firmly, "let's show them how well we can function."

"Stand by for upper-stage separation," Mikhail announced in response to the message on his screen. A second later, the firing of four explosive bolts jarred the modules. Behind them, springs pushed the freed stage away from the rest of the spacecraft. Once safely distant, commands from the Flight Control Center would restart its engine and use its remaining propellant to push it further from the moon where it would remain for eternity.

"Time to close the hatch," Svetlana ordered. "Mikhail, get the helmets and gloves."

He unstrapped and pushed himself into the orbital module, then pulled the remaining spacesuit components from the storage area. He pushed a helmet and two gloves into a slow flight across the module. Vadim grabbed them and immediately started to complete the assembly of his suit.

Svetlana's components arrived a second later but she handed them to Vadim. In the event of an automatic-system failure, she did not want the helmet's restricted vision or the glove's stiffness to impair her ability to maneuver the spacecraft.

She collected Mikhail's equipment as it drifted toward her. Then his feet emerged through the opening. The next task fell to him.

The docking hatch, a masterpiece of Soviet engineering, consisted of two separate covers. Each supported one piece of a sophisticated mechanism that guided modules together during a docking operation.

As a safety precaution, the covers had been closed during the launch from Baikonur to allow the rapid disassembly of the spacecraft and the safe recovery of the descent module in case of an emergency. Once in earth orbit, Mikhail had opened the covers to create the integrated spacecraft. Now he had to reverse the procedure.

Using the fingers of his left hand, he grasped a handhold that protruded from the domed wall of the descent module, then stretched into the orbital module to grab its cover with his right hand. He pulled the cover towards him, swinging it on its hinges until it closed. Then, using a tool Svetlana had handed him, he wound the locking system into place.

He took hold of the mating cover resting against the wall of the descent module. Employing tricks he'd taught himself in the neutral buoyancy tank, he placed his other palm against the wall, then spread his hands apart to move the cover around until it also clicked into place. With a few more turns of the tool, he finished the job.

"Ready to undock," he announced.

Svetlana handed Mikhail his helmet and gloves and watched as he fastened them in place, then helped him reattach his umbilical and set the oxygen flow.

Vadim verified that the hatches had properly latched and the pressure seals now isolated the modules. His next message brought Svetlana another moment of apprehension. As it appeared on his screen, Vadim said, "Auto-undocking sequence initiated."

With a mild thump, the orbital module separated and drifted slowly away. Using its small thruster set, Flight Control would ensure it remained close to its preplanned orbit, ready to join the descent module one last time before being abandoned to an unknown future circling the moon.

Vadim's screen listed the next sequence of events. He read them in order.

"Transfer to internal power—Normal."

"Transfer to internal life support—Normal."

"Service Module undocking sequence start."

Another mild jolt announced their separation from the module and its store of fuel cells, cooling systems, batteries and oxygen as well as the only rocket engine capable of thrusting them back to earth. For the moment, the descent module had become their world.

"Reorientation maneuver starting."

Svetlana heard the clacking of the descent module's thruster valves. Spurts of pure hydrogen peroxide shot through catalyst beds and into the nozzles of monopropellant rockets, pushing the module sideways, away from the remainder of the spacecraft, then slowing it. Svetlana kept her hands on the manual controls.

"Look at this," Mikhail exclaimed, pulling his head back from the right-side porthole. He'd taken the portable light from its holder and pointed it outside.

Svetlana craned her neck to follow the lamp's beam. Then she saw it, playing on the side of the service module as they drifted slowly backward towards the lander.

"Looks different in space, doesn't it?" Mikhail said. "Must be the light."

Indeed, the meager illumination gave the module a ghostly character against the star-filled blackness. He ran the lamp over the thermal blanket and radiator rings. Tinged by the porthole's filters and the yellow tint of the lamp, the distorted colors gave the module an eerie, aged appearance.

As they slid toward the flared base, the gray titanium legs of the lander came into view.

Beyond the base of the service module, the lander's engines could be seen protruding from the doughnut-shaped propellant tanks. The descent module puffed its thrusters, adjusting its velocity to follow the programmed path, keeping an exact distance from the lander as it moved back past the bay carrying the laser weapon.

"This is incredible, Svetlana!" Vadim exclaimed. "There's no way we could maintain this precision manually."

Once past the lander, the descent module began a slow rotation, turning 180 degrees to point the probe of its docking system toward the lander's upper platform. More clattering from the valves, more gentle pushes by the thrusters put the modules into perfect alignment. Now the Kurs rendezvous system brought the segments closer until the capture mechanism on the lander engaged the descent module's probe. A second later, a decisive thump told the cosmonauts the operation had succeeded.

"What a performance!" Svetlana said, still not quite believing what she'd just experienced. "Does this make us obsolete?"

Vadim replied, "The computer can't claim the moon—or put your helmet on for you." He handed her the remaining pieces of her suit.

"Tigrytsa, this is Flight Control. How do you hear?"

Just emerging around the edge of the moon into view of the earth, the spacecraft's antenna barely detected the transmission.

"Flight Control, Tigrytsa. You're weak but readable."

"Tigrytsa, this is Flight Control. We hear you normally. We show you in orbit, fourteen minutes to descent burn with all systems nominal. Approved for lander separation."

Vadim read the next message as it reached the top line of his display. "Stand by for leg extension."

The computer commanded the four motors attached to the lander's legs to push them outward, away from the sides of the service module. Their first movement would open the overcenter locks that held closed four metal clamps.

The clamps disengaged almost simultaneously: number three leg, number one leg, number four leg.

A red warning symbol flashed at the top of all three screens, below it the message, "Number-two leg-extension motor overload."

"Damn!" Svetlana exploded. "I knew this was too good to last. Vadim, get going with Flight Control—and start coding our transmissions. Let Tsvigun decide whether the rest of the world should know we've got a problem."

She went into action, searching for procedures that would tell her how to overcome the malfunction. She found only one.

"Recycle system," she read to herself. "Not very helpful."

She ran through menus, searching for one containing instructions for closing the legs. She found nothing.

"Damn!" she fumed, hunting for direct-control commands. After a few seconds, she found them under *Lander-Leg Motor Extension*. Once again, Ligachev's engineers had failed to include retraction procedures.

"Vadim, I can't find a way to reverse the motor command. How do we recycle the thing?"

"Flight Control's on it, Svetlana," he replied.

"Tigrytsa, Flight Control," the radio snapped. "Recommend you recycle the system."

"Good God," Svetlana thought, then transmitted, "Flight Control, Tigrytsa. What are the recycle procedures?"

The earphones in her headset remained silent.

"Flight Control, Tigrytsa. Repeat, what are the landing-leg-recycle procedures?"

"Tigrytsa, this is Flight Control. The engineering team's working on that."

"How much time?" she asked, then answered her own

question by looking at the countdown clock while Mikhail replied, "Nine minutes, twenty-three seconds."

"Mikhail, see if you can pull up the circuit diagrams."

She returned to her computer, racing through a hierarchy of documents to find the motor specification. "Got it," she said under her breath. The information she wanted jumped out from the top of the page: *DC Gearmotor.*

"It's DC, Vadim," she said. "We can reverse it by switching the polarity."

"Mikhail, have you got the circuits?" she asked.

"On the screen," he replied.

"See if there's a way to switch the polarity to the actuator motors."

"Tigrytsa, this is Flight Control. The engineers say there's no way to recycle the command. They think the problem is mechanical. Probably the overcenter lock."

"Flight Control, Tigrytsa. We have exactly four minutes to get it fixed. Any suggestions?"

"Still working on it, Tigrytsa."

"Shit!" She spewed out the word in disgust. "We just lost the immediate descent."

For the next ten minutes, Svetlana scanned procedures while Mikhail searched the computer's memory for the secret to reversing the direction of the motor.

"Found anything yet?" she barked, her frustration evident in the words.

"Nothing, Svetlana. Looks as if the engineers designed it to work only one way."

"Are you sure?"

"Absolutely. No way to reverse the polarity."

"Flight Control, this is Tigrytsa." Svetlana snapped out the words. "We have less than thirty minutes until loss of communications. What is your recommendation?"

"Tigrytsa, this is Flight Control. The engineers would like to try unloading the motor by pulsing the thrusters while you remove and restore power."

Svetlana barked, "Vadim, which way do we thrust to unload the damned thing?"

Vadim pulled up a diagram of the lander with the descent module attached.

"For the number two leg, thrust negative y."

"Okay, then. On the count of three. One, two, three!"

She slammed the translation-control stick left to the stop. Her exertion made no difference, the electrical switches needing only the lightest touch to send their message to the propellant valves.

The thrusters fired simultaneously, pushing the spacecraft left. Svetlana could barely detect the acceleration. Certain any benefit had already been attained, she moved the stick right to stop the motion.

"Any luck?" she asked, almost sure of the answer.

"No," Vadim replied as he checked the sensor readouts. "Leg angle hasn't changed."

Svetlana repeated the procedure.

"Still no change," Vadim reported.

"Flight Control, this is Tigrytsa. No success with the thrusters. What's next?"

"Tigrytsa, Flight Control. No further actions required at this time."

"Flight Control, may I remind you we have barely twenty minutes remaining before signal loss?"

"Tigrytsa, Flight Control." The controller's voice sounded angry. "Thank you for the time check. We have several mission clocks available. They all confirm your report."

"No use harping at them, Svetlana," Vadim said.

"Tigrytsa, Flight Control. The engineering group has concluded that the only way to fix the problem is to go outside and pry the leg loose."

"Do an EVA?" Svetlana yelled, not bothering with the call signs. "Now?"

"That's affirmative, Tigrytsa. Recommend you begin immediately."

"Doesn't give us much time, Svetlana," Vadim noted. "Want me to take care of it?"

"No, Vadim. Keep working with Flight Control. I'll do the EVA. Didn't think I'd be into the emergency tool kit quite this soon."

"What are you going to use to loosen it?" Mikhail asked.

"Suppose I start with a screwdriver?" she snapped as she called up the menu for depressurization.

"Let's get these suits checked. Mikhail?"

"All tests are normal."

"Vadim?"

"All normal."

"And mine's normal."

Vadim commanded a vent valve to open and monitored the cabin pressure. The suits gradually expanded against the vacuum.

Svetlana released the straps of a cargo net fixed to the cabin wall and pulled a toolbox free. She unfolded its hinged trays and scanned their contents. She lifted a small pry bar from its holder and removed a rolled lanyard.

"We're below a kilopascal," Mikhail called. "Hatch coming open." As the seal broke, the last of the module's oxygen rushed into space.

Svetlana attached one lanyard clip to a handhold near the opening and the other to a ring on her suit, then eased herself outside the module.

She gazed down at the moon through her helmet visor. Now in a different frame of mind, she agreed with Vadim. It was a portrait of desolation. Endless craters. Massive, tiny, every size in between. Craters blown into craters. With the sun beating down from directly above, the moonscape lacked definition but the color had taken on a beige tint, like a sun-bleached, rock-strewn desert.

Using the external ladder, she moved herself quickly along the green-blanketed descent module toward the lander. "Number-two leg," she mumbled to herself. "Next to the laser."

With a few quick tugs on the external handholds, she moved to the other side. "There it is," she sighed, seeing one leg still pressed tightly against the lander's structure. She pulled herself to the mid-station structural ring and located the overcenter clamp.

"Looks normal," she thought as she gently pushed and pulled on the leg. "But it sure is stuck."

Failing to move it with her gloved hand, she pushed the pry bar into the clamp and carefully pushed on the leg. The clamp held fast. She tried striking the top of the pry-bar handle, but the force propelled her in the opposite direction, necessitating a grab for the lander's structure.

A chill came over her as she realized that, with the lander clinging tenaciously to its side and covering its engine, the service module couldn't thrust them back to earth. If she failed to free the lander, they would die orbiting the moon.

With renewed vigor, she rammed the tool back into the space between the clamp and the leg, held on to the structural ring and shoved down hard. The leg bent slightly, then jumped free about a centimeter. The clamp snapped to its open position.

"Okay," she puffed, "where the hell are the deployment springs?" Then she remembered. The springs that pushed the modules apart wouldn't work while a leg remained folded.

"Have to separate them myself." With her feet on the flared base of the service module and her hands around the lander's center ring, she pushed, trying to move the modules apart while being careful not to damage their fragile structures. Almost imperceptibly, she imparted a tiny relative velocity. The foot of the closed lander leg bumped against the service module's base, necessitating another push, but the separation gradually increased. The lander was free.

"So," she panted, almost completely out of breath, "we will live. But will we walk on the moon?"

She moved back to the location of the actuator and studied its attachments. After making a few futile attempts at shaking it into action, she transmitted, "Vadim, patch me to Flight Control." A moment later he replied, "Done, Svetlana."

"Flight Control, Tigrytsa. I've disengaged the clamp but the leg remains folded. Please advise."

"Tigrytsa, Flight Control. Confirm your report. We show three legs in the open position and the number-two leg still closed. Once the lander is clear, we suggest you again command the legs to open. That may restart the drive motor."

"Flight Control, Tigrytsa. Understand. Vadim, did you copy?"

"Affirmative, Svetlana. Advise when clear."

"Lander's clear," she reported, checking to be sure her safety lanyard wouldn't create any additional problems.

Vadim replied, "Leg position going to *Open*."

From her location, she could clearly see three of the four legs. Those to her left and right had fully extended, their linkages properly unfolded and locked into place. But the number-two leg hadn't moved.

"I show number two still closed," Vadim reported.

"Confirm that," she replied grimly. "Flight Control, did you copy?"

There was no response.

Vadim said, "I think we've lost them, Svetlana."

She turned to put her face as close to the actuator as possible, studying the mechanical connections. "Basic ball linkage." She tried to wiggle it around, but the connections wouldn't budge. "Tight tolerances," she thought. "Nice stuff. Wish it worked."

"Look at this thing," she said to herself as she examined the motor. "Completely encased. No way to get at anything."

Moving back to the hatch as quickly as she dared, she rolled up the lanyard, pushed herself down on her couch, reopened the small tool kit and rummaged through the items. "Damn!" she muttered. "Nothing to cut the shaft with."

Finished for the moment, she closed the box, eased back on the couch and reconnected her umbilical.

"Any ideas?" Vadim asked.

"Don't see any way to disconnect the thing," she replied. She glanced at the mission clock. "Was I really out there forty minutes?"

"EVAs always take longer than you expect."

Her anxiety mounting, Svetlana fumed, "What the hell are those idiots at the Control Center doing?"

**Artemis**

"Wha?" Brandt blinked. Darrell continued to push his sleeping restraint back and forth. "Oh, it's you. What's up, buddy? Reveille already?"

"Not quite. Thought you'd want to know right away. The Russians are in lunar orbit."

Brandt yawned, "Yeah? Well, we figured on that."

"Didn't try for an immediate landing."

"Don't say?" Now interested, Brandt slipped out of the sleeping bag and moved through the passageway into the cockpit.

"Just got the message. Left it on the display."

Rolling to get face up, Brandt grabbed the bottom edge of the instrument panel and pulled himself into the center area. He scanned the information on the left display, nodding his head.

"Doesn't mention why they didn't head down right away. Any ideas?"

Darrell floated in alongside him. "They have a lot to do. Completely reconfigure the spacecraft—just about pull it apart and put it back together. It's possible they're just being careful, checking everything before they descend."

"Yeah," Brandt groused, "a luxury that comes with being ahead. But they'll de-orbit on the next pass."

"If they don't, I'll bet they're in trouble."

"Oh, don't say it unless you mean it."

"Want me to get Andy?"

Brandt checked the mission clock. It read 63:55:18. "Still five minutes left in the sleep period. Might as well let him enjoy it."

He moved toward Andy's empty couch and peered through the window at the moon. "A little more than two hours to LOI," he sighed. "Look at that thing, Darrell. Getting bigger while you watch. Eerie, isn't it? Utter desolation. No air, no water, no life. Never has been, never will be—except for us humans. Makes you wonder why anyone would want to come here. But here we are, chasing some crazy gas."

Darrell groaned. "You getting philosophical on me again?"

"Just mad 'cause they got here first. We'll probably land maybe two hours after they do. Don't think I'd feel so bad if they'd beat us by a month. Nothing we could have done about that. But two hours! Doesn't it frost you?"

"Don't know, Brandt. I think we did our best. Truth is, I'm amazed they didn't beat us by a month—or a year."

Ten minutes later, as he was extracting his breakfast-food packets from the galley, Brandt heard Darrell's voice. "Hey, look at this!"

"Now what?" he muttered to himself as he abandoned his meal and drifted to the cockpit.

The center screen had turned red. A white-lettered message blinked at the top, *CONFIDENTIAL.*

"Got some classified coming in," Brandt noted.

As they watched, the decoded words streamed onto the display.

> *Coded transmissions between the Soyuz TML-1 and TsUP indicate occurrence of significant malfunction. One of the legs of the landing system has failed to deploy properly. Recovery attempts, including an EVA, have not been successful.*

"Yahoo!" Brandt yelled. "Sounds like they're stuck in lunar orbit until they get this thing figured out. Darrell, you know what this means? If they miss coming down on this pass and we make a direct descent, we might just beat them. Let's see, what've we got?" Brandt checked the mission clock, then did some subtractions. "An hour forty five until LOI. Plenty of time."

He put on his headset and selected *Transmit*. "Houston, this is

Artemis with request."

"Brian answered, "Artemis, Houston. Go ahead."

"Roger, Houston. Request descent to lunar surface immediately after completion of LOI."

"Artemis, Houston. Understand. The people here thought you might want to give it a try so they've been working on the burn parameters. It'll take a little more fuel to compensate for the trajectory offset, but they don't see any problems."

"Houston, we'll need a go for both LOI and descent before the first LOS."

"Roger that, Artemis. It's giving some people here heartburn, but they're working the problem."

Brandt slapped Darrell on the leg, then caught himself as he flew across the spacecraft. "Buddy, I think they're gonna go for it."

"No reason why they shouldn't. The sims we ran at JSC showed there weren't any show stoppers. And if things don't look right after we get into orbit, we can always abort the descent burn and wait until everything's okay."

"We've got a few things to do before the burn, mostly nailing down stuff that's floating around."

"Plenty of time for that."

"Got a thought, Darrell. Suppose we suit up before the descent and try to beat them down to the surface, even if they land first."

Darrell pondered the implications. "Should get approval from Houston. It's a deviation."

"They'd never be able to decide in time. No contingency plan, no risk analysis."

"When would we put them on?"

"After LOI, on the back side of the moon. When we're out of contact."

"Brandt, you must have been one hell of a teenager."

"Should have seen me at the Academy."

"Walked a lot of punishment tours?"

"Nearly set a record."

Andy's head popped through the passageway. "Man, if my muscles are atrophying, it's not the fault of the damned machine."

Brandt got out of the way so he could move into the cockpit. "Might want to check the display, Andy."

He read the message, his eyes growing wider and his eyebrows pushing up lines across his forehead. "I'll be damned. Looks like they might be circling the moon for a while."

"My thoughts exactly," Brandt grinned. "Could give us a chance to beat them after all."

Andy nodded. "We'd need to descend right away."

"Darrell, the man's positively psychic. Thought of something else we could do, Andy."

Apparently sensing from the tone of Brandt's voice it might be a bit shady, Andy responded hesitantly, "Oh yeah?"

"Get into the EMUs right after LOI. Wear them through the descent, then pop out as soon as we land and scramble for the surface."

"Why the rush?"

"If they get down after one more orbit, we'll land at pretty much the same time. I'm betting they'll wait a while before they go outside and actually walk on the surface. But if they're going to claim the moon, that's what they need to do. We could beat them to it."

"Good plan. What's Houston think of it?"

"Tell you what, buddy. I thought we might leave it as a little surprise."

"I don't have a problem with that, Brandt. Just give the order." He snickered, "It's your ass."

**Soyuz TML-1**

To appease Svetlana, Vadim had started his calls to the Flight Control Center five minutes before the predicted resumption of contact. His efforts gained a minute of broken communications.

"Tigrytsa, Flight Control. The engineers still haven't found a way to extend the leg. We're investigating other options."

Furious, Svetlana responded icily, "Flight Control, we do not need options, we need a solution. Have you contacted Dr. Ligachev?"

"Tigrytsa, Flight Control. Negative on Dr. Ligachev. We have the Energia engineers here, the group that designed the landing legs."

"Flight Control, Doctor Ligachev designed the entire spacecraft. Please contact him immediately and arrange a communications link so I can speak with him myself."

Tigrytsa, Flight Control. Have your request. We'll get back."

"Don't those idiots understand?" she raved. "If we miss this burn and the Americans do a direct descent, we'll land at virtually the same time. They might even beat us!"

Even Vadim's voice tensed with frustration and anxiety. "Which would eliminate any hope for making a valid claim."

"Where the hell is Director Tsvigun?—or Minister Belyaev?" Mikhail asked angrily. "They should be pressuring Flight Control to save the mission."

"I'm sure they are," Vadim replied. "And I'm equally sure they're as upset as we are at the lack of progress."

"Tigrytsa, this is Flight Control. The engineering team is confident there's no way to extend the lander leg. They believe the problem is a fused power transistor."

"Flight Control, Tigrytsa. Have you contacted Doctor Ligachev?"

"Tigrytsa, that is affirmative. He's evaluated an alternative approach and agrees with the engineers' recommendations. They've just completed a series of simulations that indicate the spacecraft can be landed safely with the leg in its present position."

"Flight Control, Tigrytsa. Did you say land with the leg folded up?"

"Tigrytsa, that's affirmative. The automatic landing system will compensate for the change in configuration."

"Flight Control, did these simulations include terrain variations?"

The reply came only after an uncomfortable pause. "Tigrytsa, that is affirmative. All necessary features were included."

"Flight Control, Tigrytsa. Stand by."

The proposal staggered Svetlana. It involved enormous risk and left no margin for handling other malfunctions.

"Vadim," she said, flabbergasted, "did I hear them correctly? Did they actually tell us to land with the leg folded?"

"Didn't tell us, at least not yet, but they certainly said it would work."

She shook her head inside her helmet, trying to clear her thoughts. "What do you think? Is it possible?"

"The engineers think it's okay."

"I wonder, Vadim. I really do."

"What do you mean?"

"Were they pressured by Yevgeni?—or Belyaev?"

Vadim didn't respond immediately. When he did, he spoke deliberately.

"Svetlana, it's not like you to be suspicious of our superiors. I don't believe that either Yevgeni or Minister Belyaev would intentionally risk our lives."

Svetlana contemplated his reply. "You're right, of course. It's not our place to question. But I have the feeling they're keeping something from us."

Then she said, "Mikhail, Vadim and I are military officers, obligated to carrying out the orders of our superiors. You, however, are not. What Flight Control recommends is obviously dangerous—a completely untested mode of operation. As you know, we can, if we wish, undock from the lander, reassemble the Soyuz and return to earth. Should you prefer to do this, neither Vadim nor I will bear you any ill will. Vadim, you will recall that my orders from Director Tsvigun included Mikhail's safe return."

Mikhail replied immediately and emphatically. "Svetlana, I will not be the cause of failure."

After a single nod toward Mikhail, Svetlana said, "Vadim, we have nine minutes until the descent burn. Do you know of any reason we shouldn't attempt a landing?"

He answered, "None."

She pushed her microphone button. "Flight Control, this is Tigrytsa. With the exception of the lander leg, all systems are functioning normally. With eight minutes until ignition, we are ready for descent."

"Tigrytsa, this is Flight Control. Confirm ignition in eight minutes, nine seconds."

## Chapter 16

—

# Landings

**Soyuz TML-1**

"Mikhail, get the hatch closed so we can repressurize," Svetlana ordered. "Vadim, load the descent instructions."

The computer generated the burn parameters for the modified trajectory in less than a minute and then turned the spacecraft around, directing its rockets to reduce the speed. Finished with pre-descent activities, the cosmonauts returned to their couches and watched the countdown clock.

The lander's four KDTU engines fired smoothly.

"Tigrytsa, Flight Control. We show ignition and normal function for all engines."

"Confirm that, Flight Control," Svetlana replied. She kept her hands firmly clasped around the manual controls, ready to take command should the computer falter. But the display in front of her showed a bright blue diamond precisely centered on the black line that represented the ideal flight path.

The orientation of the descent module placed Vadim's porthole on the side next to the moon. He managed to steal a brief glimpse of an incredibly rough terrain rippled with enormous cliffs.

The flight path bent downward, describing a flattened ellipse that intercepted the surface near their designated touchdown point. Vadim reported, "Approaching the Sea of Tranquility. Looks smooth, like wet clay."

Mikhail glanced out his porthole. "Earth!" he exclaimed. "I can see the earth, more of it than the last time."

"Pay attention to the numbers," Svetlana replied.

The engines burned on. Except for the G-force, the only indication of their operation was a buzzing vibration.

"Descent camera on," Mikhail said as a panorama of the moon crept into the lower-left quarter of each display.

"Standby for throttle back," Vadim said as the timer appeared on his screen. "Shutdown for two, three and four."

The computer sent commands to close the propellant valves feeding three of the four engines. The vibration level dropped and the G-force became barely noticeable.

"Tigrytsa, Flight Control. We show transition to single-engine. All systems normal."

"Through three-thousand meters," Vadim noted. "Pitching vertical."

On the quarter-screen images, the horizon slid up off the top and details of surface features became evident.

Now nearly vertical, the spacecraft dropped toward the surface, its descent rate controlled by the throttled thrust of the center engine. Vadim studied the information streaming onto his display, watching for anomalies. This close to the surface, only his immediate action would save them should the automatic system fail. Frequently, he glanced up at the red *ABORT* switch, its guard now raised to allow instant actuation.

"Through one-thousand meters," Vadim announced.

The descent module's thrusters began to clatter and the spacecraft rolled a few degrees one way, then the other.

"Landing system's identifying the touchdown zone," Svetlana said.

As the descent continued, Vadim called out the altitude. "Five-hundred meters. Three-hundred meters. One-hundred meters. Fifty meters."

The vibration level increased as the engine reduced the descent rate.

"Thirty meters. Ten meters."

"Contact!" Vadim yelled as the strut sensor icons appeared in a diamond-shaped array.

"Flight Control, we show contact on four pads," Vadim

transmitted.

"Confirm that, Tigrytsa. Touchdown at 0458 UTC, seventy-four hours and fifty-six minutes after liftoff. Congratulations!"

"Okay," Svetlana exclaimed, "I'm impressed!"

Guided by their individual laser sensors, the legs of the lander reached for the ground, adjusting to sensed variations in surface height. The computer shut down the rocket, allowing actuators in the legs to lower the spacecraft to its final position.

As the weight on the foot of the folded leg increased, the rock it had rested on, a half-meter boulder, rolled out of the way. The leg motor immediately tried to make up the gap, but the delay caused the spacecraft to tip. Now sensing both the gap and the inclination, the control system commanded the motor to run much faster, just as the foot struck the surface. The leg extended, tilting the spacecraft in the opposite direction.

"What the hell?" Svetlana yelled.

The lander tilted first one way, then the other. Five meters above the footpads, the cosmonauts rocked slowly from side to side, each oscillation slightly greater than the one before.

"Limit cycle!" Vadim shouted. "Control system's entered a limit cycle between number two and number four legs."

As she braced herself, Svetlana cried, "Can you do anything?"

"Negative, Svetlana. Lander control is completely independent."

"We're going to fall over!" Mikhail screamed in terror.

"It's okay, Mikhail," Vadim reassured him. "The amplitude seems to have stabilized. It should start decreasing."

But the rocking continued, each cycle seeming to bring the spaceship to the edge of disaster as it teetered on the unextended leg.

"Tigrytsa, Flight Control. Are you experiencing lateral oscillations?"

"That's affirmative," Svetlana replied tensely, trying to control her growing anxiety. "Stand by."

"Control system must be out of its operating range." Vadim blurted out the words.

"When will it stop?"

"Hard to say, Svetlana. May continue until a motor burns out."

"It's going to capsize. I can feel it!" Mikhail shrieked as the spacecraft once again tilted towards him. "Have to stop it!" He began to release his restraints, fumbling as he tried to rush.

Although riveted to the attitude display, Svetlana caught his movements out of the corner of her eye.

"What the hell are you doing?" she shouted. "Stay strapped in, for God's sake!"

"I'm not going to lie here and wait to die," he proclaimed, sounding strangely determined.

"Remain where you are," she screamed. "That's an order!"

Suddenly Mikhail shoved himself out of his couch. Yelling, "I'll save us!" he rolled over her, ending up face down on top of Vadim just as the spacecraft reached its maximum tilt in the opposite direction.

"Like a sailboat! Don't you see?" he shouted in terrified elation.

The amplitude of the tilt seemed to decrease slightly. "It's working!" he screamed. "It's working!"

Reversing its motion, the spaceship tilted back toward Vadim. Mikhail prepared to execute his next leap.

"Here we go!" he cheered. He pushed away, but a lanyard connector on his chest snagged Vadim's oxygen control. He struggled to get free. Vadim tried to help but, with his limited vision field, he groped ineffectively.

The spaceship tilted towards them, teetered, then began its move in the opposite direction.

"You're pushing the wrong way!" Mikhail shouted. He put his hands on Vadim's helmet and shoved himself down. The connector popped free. Another push sent him back over Svetlana. He landed face down on his couch just as the spacecraft tilted his way.

For what seemed like an eternity, the lander remained balanced on one leg, as if deliberating the fate of its occupants. Then, surrendering to the moon's gravity, it slowly fell to its side.

At only a sixth of its earthly weight, the spacecraft took nearly five seconds to hit the surface and the descent module struck the thick dust layer at the speed of an easy jog. The noiseless collision sent a small cloud of gray particles streaming outward through the vacuum. They settled to the surface, creating an insignificant alteration to a landscape long accustomed to abrupt visits by foreign objects.

The impact yanked Vadim and Svetlana from the backs of their couches and left them dangling from their harnesses. Unprotected by his restraints, Mikhail smashed into the side of the module. His face hit the inside of his helmet, causing a profuse nosebleed.

Hanging over him, Svetlana screamed, "Damn you, Mikhail! You've killed us! Do you know that? You've killed us!"

Barely had she voiced the words when she regretted the outburst. But it was too late. Mikhail sobbed uncontrollably, "Oh God, I know! It's my fault!"

Her mind racing, Svetlana realized that her suit had not inflated. The crash had not fractured the shell of the descent module. It remained pressurized. Not only that, Mikhail had heard her. That meant the intercom still worked and the electrical system was providing power. She twisted her head around to see the displays. They were all functioning.

Suddenly she remembered Vadim. Twisting in her restraint, she tried to see him. "Vadim, are you hurt?"

He replied groggily, "I don't think so, Svetlana. The side of my head hit the helmet. Dizzy for a moment. Are you all right?"

"As far as I can tell. Mikhail, what about you?"

He continued to sob. She assumed that as long as he was making noise, he couldn't be seriously injured.

"Let's get our suits checked. Vadim?"

He grunted, trying to read the status display. "Still normal."

"Mikhail?"

He didn't respond. The sobbing had turned to a quiet whimper.

"Mikhail!" she yelled. "Check your suit!"

After a moment, he replied weakly, "It's okay."

"Good," she replied. "Now switch over to the backpack and unfasten the umbilical."

"Vadim, can you reach your trackball?"

"Afraid not, Svetlana," he answered. "Have to get myself out of the straps."

"Probably better if I get free first. Mikhail, can you get out of the way?"

He used the instrument panel to help pull himself up, then stood on the wall of the module.

"Give me a hand with this," Svetlana said. When he didn't move, she muttered, "Forget it!" and unfastened her harness, falling clumsily across Mikhail's couch onto the porthole. Turning herself around, she managed to stand and support Vadim while he released himself. They quickly transferred their life support to the backpacks.

"Incredible that the module remained intact," Vadim said, his faculties returning. "Don't see any damage to the interior."

"Neither do I," Svetlana agreed, "but I think we should get outside right away and check for propellant leaks."

"Right," Vadim said. "Let's see if we can depressurize normally."

He leaned back across the couches, reached down and began to manipulate Svetlana's trackball. Fumbling as he adjusted to the display's sideways orientation, he selected the instructions that opened the vent valves.

As the pressure dropped, Svetlana felt her suit stiffen. She remembered the hatch tool clipped to a mount on the side of her couch. She found it, still in place.

With most of the oxygen vented, she pushed Mikhail out of the way and unlocked the hatch, then pulled it in and looked out at the moon. Now in the last tenth of the lunar day, the setting sun cast long shadows across the rough surface.

"Well, we're here," she thought bitterly. "Probably forever."

Having the module on its side made it easy to get through the opening, a convenience she'd gladly have done without. She crawled out backwards, dropped her feet through the opening, then her waist, and finally eased herself down the meter distance to the surface. Vadim followed immediately, then, after a while, Mikhail.

Had the circumstances been normal, she'd have stepped carefully to the surface and cautiously attempted to walk. Instead, she gave the matter no thought, and immediately attempted to move toward the lander at a rapid pace. Predictably, she stumbled and staggered, nearly losing her balance.

"Loping jog," she reminded herself. Each step launched her on a short trajectory, ending in a spray of black dust as her boots gouged the powdery surface. Her skill developed quickly as she covered the five meters from the top of the descent module to the lander's tanks.

She'd already dismissed the possibility of massive leaks. The hypergolic propellants would have exploded on contact and burned them alive. But any leak into the moon's vacuum would create a spray of propellant. Hindered by the blackness of the shadows, she examined the tanks as best she could, saw nothing and decided there was no immediate problem.

Vadim joined her and spoke through his suit radio. "Surprising how well everything held up. The only major damage is to the leg structure."

"No propellant leaks, as far as I can tell," she replied. "Did you check the descent module?"

"Didn't see any serious damage except to the interstage section. Looks like the attachments fractured."

"Guess we'd better tell Flight Control about our situation."

On their way back to the descent module, they passed Mikhail practicing his moonwalk, aimlessly wandering about. Svetlana decided to leave him alone.

"Flight Control, this is Tigrytsa. How do you read?"

There was no reply.

"May have a problem with the high-gain antenna," Vadim said. "I'll check it."

His inspection took only a few minutes. "Must have jammed when we hit. Jumped free as soon as I touched it."

"Flight Control, this is Tigrytsa. How do you read?"

"Tigrytsa, Flight Control. Transmission is normal. What is your status?"

Vadim described the condition of the spacecraft. The controller made no comment until he'd finished his report.

"Tigrytsa, Flight Control, the engineers are already working on a recovery plan."

"Understand, Flight Control. We're going back outside to evaluate the damage."

Once back on the surface, Svetlana looked for Mikhail. Not seeing him, she walked to the opposite side of the module but had no better luck.

"Where the hell did he go?" she fumed, scanning the landscape for hills or boulders that might be hiding him. She tried calling on the radio but got no reply. "Must be out of my line of sight, she thought.

Walking back toward the lander, she heard a sharp snap through her earphones, then a hissing sound. "What on earth is he doing?" she wondered.

As she drew nearer, she saw him lying on his back, next to the number-two leg. "Mikhail?" she called.

Reaching him, she looked down. "Oh God!" she called. "Mikhail?"

Red droplets speckled his white suit and a red liquid oozed from a hole in the middle of his helmet visor. The brilliant colors erupted from the gray background like a macabre abstract.

"Mikhail!" she screamed. "Mikhail!"

She looked down at his right leg, saw the open cover of the weapon carrier. The gun lay in the dust about a meter from his hand.

"Oh no!" she shrieked. "This can't be happening!"

Vadim bounded toward her from the descent module. "Svetlana? What's wrong? What happened?"

"Mikhail. It's Mikhail. He's killed himself!"

"Good God, no!"

Vadim knelt down to examine the lifeless cosmonaut. Small pieces of pink flesh dotted the helmet, blown out when the bullet released the high-pressure oxygen inside the suit. He mumbled, "Horrible!"

Unable to look any longer, Svetlana wandered away from the spacecraft, wishing she could wipe her eyes, not just to clear the tears but to rid herself of the image that throbbed in her brain.

After a few minutes, Vadim returned and said, "I reported the matter to Flight Control."

"You told them what happened?"

"I said Mikhail died trying to roll the spacecraft so we could deploy the laser."

Svetlana looked toward him, wishing she could see the face hidden by the golden mirror of his visor. "Vadim, you think of everything," she sighed. Then she added slowly, "I've failed you, Vadim—failed in my mission. You deserved better."

"You're being too hard on yourself, Svetlana," he said. "I'm convinced you were correct in your assessment of Flight Control's responses to your questions."

She answered absently, "What do you mean?"

"I don't believe they conducted the simulations. And I don't believe they contacted Ligachev. I doubt he'd have approved the operation. I think Tsvigun and Belyaev knowingly risked our lives, hoping we'd arrive before the Americans, still able to claim the moon for them.

"As for poor Mikhail, who knows why he took his life? He may end up being the lucky one. We both know there's no possibility of our survival. If the descent module continues to function, we may be able to live a few more days. But very soon we must face the inevitable—and decide how we're to die."

Svetlana squeezed her eyes shut and shook her head rapidly.

"I can't deal with that yet, Vadim. But I'll tell you this. I'm not going to sit inside the module and wait for it to happen. If there's a way to get out of this, I'm going to find it. Let's look over everything, see what we have to work with and then get back to Flight Control. They may come up with something."

**Artemis**

"Got some more classified coming in, Brandt," Andy said. "Holy shit! Look at this." The words rapidly filled the display.

*CONFIDENTIAL*

*Coded messages from the Soyuz TML-1 indicate the vehicle has crashed on the lunar surface at a point 96 km NE of the crater Molkte, approximately 80 km ENE of the Apollo 11 landing site. One cosmonaut has been reported killed in the accident. The condition of the other two crew members is unknown. However, they are continuing to transmit messages.*

Brandt drifted up from below the instrument panel. "Tell me they're still in orbit."

"They're down, Brandt. Take a look."

As he read the words, he mumbled, "Oh Jesus! Heaven help 'em."

"Doesn't say anything about the condition of the spacecraft," Andy said. "Big question is whether they can get off again."

"Big question is how long they can stay alive," Brandt said. He yelled toward the nose, "Darrell, come take a look."

Darrell's voice came back, "Have to finish checking the suits."

"Forget it for a minute. Big problems on the moon."

Darrell quickly moved to the cockpit. "What's going on?"

"Read, buddy."

With his left hand over his mouth, Darrell shook his head slowly as he read. "They're in deep shit, Brandt."

"Hold on, here comes some more," Andy said.

*CONFIDENTIAL*

*Analysis of coded communications between the Soyuz TML-1 and TsUP has disclosed that the vehicle fell on its side after an apparently successful landing. The cause of the accident is unknown.*

"Fell on its side?" Darrell gasped. "Even if they survived the crash, they're as good as dead."

"Bet they attempted to land with the leg retracted," Andy said. "Sure paid a big price for beating us by a couple of hours. Wonder if there's any way to get the thing back on its feet."

"Probably hopeless," Darrell replied. "It may not be as big as Artemis, but it still weighs a hell of a lot—even on the moon. Unless they've got some very unusual equipment with them, they're not going back."

Brandt had remained motionless, staring at the message, not saying a word. He turned around to put his back against the center of the instrument panel and faced his crew. He looked first at Andy, staring straight into his eyes, then at Darrell.

"We're gonna rescue 'em!"

Darrell looked at him, incredulous. "You can't be serious, Brandt. Even with all of us working, we'd never get the Soyuz back on its legs. And if we could, it's very unlikely the ship's still flyable. Must have suffered extensive damage when it toppled over."

"We'll bring 'em back with us."

"In Artemis?" Darrell yelled. "Are you crazy? How are we going to get six people off the moon?"

"It's five, remember. They lost one."

"All right, five then."

"Don't know just yet, but by God we're gonna find a way."

"Brandt, think about it," Andy said. "I'm sure we'd all like to save them, but two cosmonauts in space suits weigh at least eight-hundred pounds."

"More like six-fifty. We'll remove their backpacks—use the oxygen inside their suits to keep them going while we dump the packs overboard and repressurize. And they're pretty small people."

"What's the difference?" Andy protested. "We still can't lift that much extra weight."

"We've got a hundred pounds allocated to moon rocks. Now it's five-fifty," Brandt continued, becoming impatient. "But whatever it is, we're going to rip that much out of this spacecraft. I don't care what it takes. If those people are still alive, we're giving them a ride home."

Brandt moved the communications selector to *Transmit.*

"Houston, this is Artemis."

"Roger, Artemis, go ahead."

Darrell switched off the transmissions. "Brandt, if you're going to discuss the accident, you'll have to activate the scrambler."

"Oh yeah. Thanks Darrell."

Brandt had to search through several menus before he found the path that led to the coding instructions. He entered the necessary commands and transmitted, "Houston, Artemis. How do you read?"

A half minute elapsed before the reply. "Artemis, Houston. You're loud and clear through the scrambler, how me?"

"Loud and clear, Houston. Be advised, it is our intention to land near the site of the Soyuz and attempt to provide assistance."

There was no reply.

"Houston, this is Artemis. Did you copy?"

"Artemis, Houston. We sure did. Stand by."

"Brandt, we've only got nine minutes until LOS," Andy reminded him. "There's no way to change the landing site."

"Artemis, this is Houston. That request is denied."

"Houston, Artemis. Brian you tell those clowns the last transmission was not a request. Tell them we're prepared to generate trajectory data with the onboard computers using current location estimates and complete a manual landing to locate a suitable touchdown site."

Mission Control used up three of the remaining minutes to formulate a response.

"Artemis, this is Houston. Brandt, you've got the people here going crazy. They say you shouldn't, under any circumstances, attempt a manual landing at an unevaluated site."

"Brian, I suggest you remind them that their leaders signed a treaty some time back obligating us to provide whatever assistance we can to astronauts in peril. That's precisely what I intend to do."

"Artemis, Houston. I think that got everybody's attention."

"Houston, Artemis. Listen, Brian, I need some help with this—accurate trajectory data as soon as we pop out on the other side. Heck, buddy, we ain't asking for much, just a minor revision in the touchdown point."

"Artemis, Houston. Have your request. You're beginning to break up. Talk to you after LOS."

"Gents," Brandt said, "we've got twenty-nine minutes until LOI. About thirty-six minutes after that we burn for descent. In between we need to generate complete descent profiles, study the landing area data and review manual-landing procedures. Let's get crackin'."

"What about getting into the suits?" Andy asked.

Brandt thought for a minute. "Probably be a good idea to get you and Darrell ready—cut down the time it'll take us to get to the cosmonauts. But I'm not about to try a manual landing with the suit on."

"Pardon, sir," Darrell interrupted. "Wouldn't that be my job?"

Brandt looked at him poker faced. "Not this time, pal. Command decision."

**Sea of Tranquility**

As the module's oxygen pressure approached thirty-four kilopascals, Svetlana removed her helmet and gloves. "I'd like to get out of this damned suit for a while," she grumbled.

"No reason not to," Vadim responded, setting his helmet down between them, "once we finish working outside."

"Let's get the backpacks recharged while I talk to Flight Control. Guess we know as much about the spacecraft as we're going to. Still have to do what we came for."

"Claim the moon?"

"Of course," Svetlana replied firmly.

"But without the laser, the claim can't be defended. Tsvigun made that quite clear."

"Then we'll have to deploy it—somehow."

"Need to roll the spacecraft."

Svetlana nodded. "But six-thousand kilograms? That's like a ton on earth. Seems impossible."

Vadim replied, "Maybe not. I've been giving it some thought. And I'm hoping Flight Control will have some ideas."

"At least it'll keep us occupied for whatever time we have left." Intending to be ghoulishly humorous, Svetlana succeeded only in reinforcing her despondency. Choking, she said, "Let's get started with the report."

"Flight Control, this is Tigrytsa with a status report."

"Tigrytsa, Flight Control." It was a new voice. "You are instructed to complete your mission before conducting any further activities. A statement will be transmitted and you will respond without coding."

"Not much doubt about their priorities," Svetlana said caustically.

Vadim raised his eyebrows. "Not surprising, considering our status."

"Here it is." Bending her neck over to align her eyes with the display, Svetlana watched the words scroll across and down the screen. The text appeared unchanged from the version she'd reviewed at Baikonur.

"You know, I thought I'd feel some sense of historic importance reading this," she said, "but now it seems almost meaningless." Svetlana began to read, carefully pronouncing each word, her voice sounding almost imperial.

> *To the peoples of the earth, I bring you greetings from the moon. I, Engineer Colonel Svetlana Zosimova of the Socialist Federation, as the commanding officer of the spaceship Soyuz TML-1, do claim for the peoples of the Socialist Federation, their offspring and all generations to come, the moon in its entirety including all surface areas, mineral deposits, regions below the surface to the center of the orb, and regions above the surface to the distance of gravitational dominance.*
>
> She added,
>
> *I dedicate this claim to the memory of Cosmonaut Mikhail Alexeyevich Bakatin who valiantly gave his life that his people might benefit from this achievement.*

"Well done, Svetlana," Vadim said softly.

"Tigrytsa, this is Flight Control. I have a message for you from the Federation President."

> *My sincere congratulations and heartfelt best wishes to the crew of the Soyuz. Your achievement has opened a new chapter for the people of the Socialist Federation. My thoughts are with you as you struggle with the challenges ahead. Be assured that every effort will be made to bring about your safe return.*
>
> *Viktor Yegorovich Stakhanov*

*President of the Socialist Federation*

"Tigrytsa, you will now resume transmission of telemetry."

"Back to coding," Vadim remarked. "Apparently they haven't released information about the accident."

Svetlana instructed the computer to convert their audio transmissions into coded digital words and said, "Flight Control, we've examined the spacecraft and find..."

The controller cut her off. "Tigrytsa, Flight Control. The engineers are evaluating the status of the modules and are attempting to devise a method for your return. However, they say the first step must be the removal of the experiment to reduce the weight of the lander. To accomplish this, you must roll the vehicle through an angle of at least sixty degrees. We show the vehicle resting on legs one and two. You must roll it so it rests on legs two and three. The engineers are evaluating alternate approaches and will have recommendations in a few minutes."

"What do you think?" Vadim asked.

"They're right about getting the laser unloaded. Don't know how we'll roll the spacecraft."

"I've been thinking about looping an EVA lanyard around number four, then trying to pull the spacecraft over. We'll have to get our feet well planted—maybe dig cutouts into the soil."

"Tigrytsa, this is Flight Control. We have important information concerning the American spacecraft."

"Flight Control, Tigrytsa," Svetlana answered. "Go ahead."

"Tigrytsa, we've decoded secret messages sent from the Artemis vehicle to the NASA Mission Control Center indicating the crew intends to land near your position, supposedly to offer assistance. They have broken our coding and know of your situation."

"Understand, Flight Control. Do you have an estimate of their landing time?"

"Tigrytsa, the current estimate is 0654 UTC, one hour and two minutes from now."

"Understand, Flight Control. We've been evaluating our ability to rotate the spacecraft and believe we can attach an EVA lanyard to the number four leg and possibly apply enough torque to accomplish your objective."

"Tigrytsa, our engineers came up with a similar proposal. Request you attempt the procedure as soon as possible."

"So, the Americans are coming to save us," Svetlana sneered. "Do you believe that?"

"No way of knowing, Svetlana. Remember some months ago when they kept pressing the Space Agency for the location of our landing site, saying they wanted to meet us here. I always questioned their motivation, especially after we found out about their weapons."

"You have a remarkable way of understating things, Vadim. Frankly, those exploding bullets gave me the chills. Absolutely diabolical!"

Vadim remained quiet for a moment, then said briskly, "But we're wasting time. Let's see if we can make a success of this mission after all—give the Russians something to cheer about for a change."

**Artemis**

"Okay gents, one minute until we roll for all the marbles."

The astronauts were back in the cockpit, strapped into their couches, waiting for lunar-orbit injection.

"Andy, final systems check."

"Still go for LOI."

"Darrell, navigation?"

"Down the middle, Brandt. Burn parameters still right on baseline."

"Five seconds," Darrell called. "Three, two, one."

"Feels good!" Brandt grunted.

"Three engines normal," Andy reported.

The spacecraft continued to slow, its path bending to match the curvature of the moon. Tiny adjustments to the gimbal angles of the engines corrected any deviations from the desired path.

"Right down the pipe," Darrell said, straining against the unfamiliar weight. "Got to hand it to Collen's programmers."

"Let's not get hasty with the praise," Brandt retorted.

"Stand by for shutdown. Three, two, one."

The heavy hand lifted from their chests. They were in orbit.

"What've we got, Darrell?" Brandt asked.

"Looking good; 109 kilometer perigee, 110 kilometer apogee."

"Ready with the descent trajectory?"

"Almost, Brandt, for the position they gave us. Still pretty rough."

"I'm counting on Houston coming through with an upload."

Brandt checked the mission clock. "We'll know in twenty-six minutes. Let's get into the suits."

He unstrapped and folded the center couch so Andy could get to the passageway and into the nose section. Meanwhile, furiously working his trackball, Darrell loaded the trajectory data into the active memory.

"Okay, Brandt. We're ready to go it alone, if that's what you want to do."

"Thanks, buddy. Nice work."

"Would you really try it?"

"If that's the only choice. Can't let those people just die down there. Don't you agree?"

"Brandt, I'd be the last person to tell you not to try a hair-brained rescue. Thought any more about how to get them in here?"

"Matter of fact, I've been doing just that while you were working on the descent. No end of stuff we can get by without. Problem is getting it unbolted and dumped in the time available."

"We'll need a lot of support from Houston—tallying the weight reduction, recomputing the liftoff."

"Could do it on our own, if we had to. It's all in the computer."

Darrell looked at him disapprovingly. "Can't afford to turn down help."

"Just contingency planning, pard, like a good commander."

Darrell sighed.

"But Houston's not my biggest problem."

"What is?"

"Being able to take only one of 'em."

Nodding his head slowly, Darrell replied, "Yup. That'd be a bummer."

Andy emerged from the passageway, eased around Darrell and stopped over his couch. He connected the life-support hoses to his chest.

"Your turn, buddy," Brandt said. Darrell disappeared under the center of the instrument panel.

"Working on some weight-reduction estimates, Andy. You can help. Pull up the data pages as I call out the components, then give me the mass values."

While Darrell donned his suit, Brandt examined one component after another, trying to determine whether it could be removed quickly and how much it would contribute to the life-or-death calculation. By the time Darrell returned, he'd saved one cosmonaut plus 154 pounds.

"Contacted Houston yet?" Darrell asked.

Before Brandt could answer, the speaker crackled, "Artemis, this is Houston. How do you read?"

"Houston, you're four by four. You got some trajectory data for us?"

"That's negative, Artemis. Your request is still under consideration. NASA has decided to go for another orbit before descending. That'll give us a chance to verify the data files before transmitting—give you a safety margin should we get the okay for the revised landing site."

"Load of manure," Brandt thought. "Damned politicians will never make up their minds."

Then, with no emotion in his voice, he told Mission Control, "Roger that, Houston. Understand one more orbit before descent."

"That's affirmative, Artemis," Brian droned. Then in a more animated tone, added, "We've got some additional information concerning the Federation mission."

"Roger, Houston. Go ahead."

"Artemis, Houston. At 0546 UTC, the crew commander, Colonel Zosimova, made an open transmission that was broadcast around the world, formally claiming the entire moon for the Federation."

Brandt replied, "Understand, Houston. It'll take us a few minutes to absorb that one."

"Roger, Artemis. Got everybody here going too."

"Houston, where does that leave us with respect to our planned statement?"

"Artemis, Houston. We'll have a new version for you, probably before LOS."

"Roger, Houston."

Andy said, "So you were right after all."

"Can it, Andy," Brandt growled. "We've got eight minutes 'til ignition."

The words floored Darrell. "You're going for it?"

"Believe it! Those people may not have another two hours. You got that trajectory loaded up?"

"Over the mission baseline, just like you said."

"Andy, get strapped in. I'm gonna need you to ride the

systems all the way to the ground.

"Darrell, you can monitor the profile until we get within visual range. Then I'll need you to hunt for the Soyuz. That position we backed out could be off by several kilometers."

"You planning to bring it down manually?" Darrell's voice had a noticeably anxious edge.

"Course not. But we'll have to designate a landing zone high enough for the computer to work out a descent strategy."

"Artemis, Houston. We have you into the sunlight."

"Roger that, Houston," Brandt replied casually. "Guess we'll have time to do a little sightseeing."

With their EMUs on, strapping in became a much more challenging enterprise. The backpacks lifted them almost a foot off the couches and placed their faces awkwardly close to the instrument panel. But the many hours in the simulator had taught them to function in the less-than-ideal conditions.

Brandt brought up the commands needed to take control of the spacecraft. He went through the initial command, verified it, then brought the last instruction to the top of the display.

"Okay, here we go." He entered the final verification.

"That's it, guys. We own the spacecraft."

"Computer is tracking the descent file. Countdown clock is running at fifty-four seconds."

"Artemis, this is Houston. We show you assuming control. Acknowledge."

"Houston, this is Artemis. We're getting some funny messages on our display. Trying to sort things out. Stand by." Brandt swallowed his laughter.

Once again, the countdown clock seized their attention. The numbers decreased, finally hitting zero just as the computer commanded the propellant valves on the RL-10s to open. The ignitors fired and the engines began the five-minute-long process that would place them in a final, near-vertical path to the surface.

"Artemis, this is Flight," a woman's voice barked. "Do not! Repeat, do not attempt a manual landing!"

Brandt chuckled. "Probably the first time NASA's ever talked directly to an astronaut. She sure sounded pissed."

He pushed the mike button. "Houston, Artemis. Understand your instructions. We seem to be having some sort of malfunction here. Looks like the computer's locked on to a descent profile and doesn't want to let go."

Mission Control made no response.

As the altitude decreased, surface features became easier to identify, especially in the low-angle light.

"Right down the middle," Darrell observed from the graph on the center display.

"Houston, Artemis. Passing through fifty kilometers."

"Roger that, Artemis." Brian was back. "Got some real unhappy folks around here."

Brandt ignored him. "Houston, we sure could use an update on the position of the Russian spacecraft. Looks like this screwball trajectory is going to bring us down pretty close and it'd be nice not to have to hunt around manually."

"Understand, Artemis. I'll see what I can do."

"Can you imagine what's going on down there?" Darrell said, only half laughing. "They're probably figuring how much jail time they can drop on us."

"Houston, we're through forty kilometers."

"Roger, Artemis. Stand by."

"They'd better hurry up or we'll have to shift into the recon mode."

The spacecraft decelerated rapidly, the G-forces building as the mass decreased.

"Houston, Artemis. Thirty kilometers."

"Roger, Artemis. Confirm that."

"Are those jerks playing with us, or what?" Brandt fumed.

"Could be they just don't have the coordinates," Darrell suggested.

"Ah horse puckey!" Brandt roared. "They must have had trackers on the Soyuz from the git-go. They know where it landed."

"Houston, we're through twenty."

"Roger, Artemis. Should have some numbers for you in just a bit." Brian sounded anxious.

"Tilting up," Brandt noted. "Picking up the surface video." The top of his display showed the lunar landscape stretching across the Sea of Tranquility.

"Darrell, crosscheck the video. I want four eyeballs looking for that ship. Andy, if you pick up any problems, just yell 'em out."

Brandt placed his hand on the manual control, half wanting Mission Control to make his intervention unnecessary, half hoping they wouldn't.

The engines throttled down while the attitude-control thrusters brought the spacecraft vertical. The scene on Brandt's display looked like a relief map, filled with jagged features.

"I think I've got the Soyuz, Brandt," Darrell said, the intensity of his concentration making his words terse. "Check the upper left corner. Bright colored area, small, oblong."

Brandt studied every pixel of his display but saw nothing. "No joy, Darrell," he said, dragging out the words.

"Looking a bit greenish now," Darrell said.

Brandt yelled, "Got it, buddy. Mark it!"

Darrell used the trackball to put crosshairs over the tiny spot, then pressed the button to record the position. "Keep watching it, Brandt. Image is pretty small. Could be something else."

"Artemis, Houston. We have the coordinates for you. Advise when ready to copy."

Now less than five kilometers from the surface, Brandt ignored the transmission. "Darrell, try to designate on that location. Let's see if the automatic system can get us there."

Darrell selected an icon from the toolbox, tapped the trackball button twice and read the verification. "Done, Brandt."

The thrusters tilted the spacecraft, directing the rockets to move them closer. But almost immediately, the thrusters fired again, rotating them in the opposite direction, then to the left, then back again toward the target.

"System's hunting. Must be outside the capture envelope."

Brandt let the autopilot go through one more gyration before selecting the manual override. An attitude-indicator image filled the top of his display with the terrain picture below it.

"Gonna get us in closer. Keep watching that spot, Darrell."

Brandt used the manual control to maintain the pitch angle. The display showed the target slowly moving from the corner, across the screen, down and to the right. When it reached the center, Brandt gave control back to the computer.

"Givin' the software another crack at it," he muttered as he stared at the display. This time the autopilot made only minor attitude changes. The target remained centered. Brandt announced, "It's locked on!"

"That's the Soyuz, all right," Darrell replied.

"Gotta choose a landing zone," Brandt said. "Right of the

Soyuz and uprange looks best."

"Got it designated," Darrell replied.

The engine vibration became more noticeable as the thrust increased to slow their descent.

On his display, the image of the surface began to translate, first from side to side, them from top to bottom as the computer searched for a suitable landing point. All the time, the surface features grew larger. Suddenly, the motion stopped and the image rotated back and forth.

"It's got a spot," Brandt shouted, his hand now gripping the control stick. "Come on, baby, bring it down."

Only by watching a specific crater could Brandt detect their approach to the surface. Finally, the image began to blur.

"Into the dust!" Brandt yelled, his excitement mounting.

"And contact!" Darrell responded. "We're down!"

"Houston, Artemis has landed." As Brandt got out the words, the engines stopped.

"Roger, Artemis, we have you down at 0657 Zulu. Everybody here's feeling a lot better. By the way, the coordinates were two degrees, twenty-one minutes north; twenty-six degrees, five minutes east."

"Darrell, what'd we get?" Brandt asked.

He gave the trackball a few more pushes and reported, "Two degrees, twenty-one minutes, nineteen seconds north, twenty-six degrees, four minutes, fifty-one seconds east."

Brandt added, "And that, Houston, is accurate!" He switched back to *Intercom* and said, "Gents, no time for patting ourselves on the back. We've got work to do."

## Chapter 17

# Sea of Tranquility

**Sea of Tranquility**

"Blast!" Brandt's voice bellowed back into the cockpit.

"What's the problem?" Darrell shouted up the passageway.

Brandt lowered himself from the nose. "Oxygen! My suit's almost out of oxygen. Didn't you check it?"

"Never finished. You stopped me. Brought me back to read the messages about the Russians."

"Better start filling it," Andy said.

Brandt shook his head. "That won't do it. There's a leak someplace. Don't know how bad. Might take a day to bleed down, might take an hour."

"Or a minute," Darrell added. "We'll have to test it. Fill it up and see how fast the pressure drops."

"Means we'll have to wait to go outside."

"You'll have to, Brandt. The two of us can get started."

Brandt thought about Darrell's comment and said, "Wanted all of us to go out together. But we need to find out what gives with the Russians. Let's see if the suit will hold me long enough for you to get outside."

He put on his helmet and gloves, then attached the chest-mounted umbilical and set the control switches. Finally, he opened the valves that routed oxygen to his backpack and watched the pressure increase.

"Filling up okay," he observed, then, after a minute, said, "Should be enough for a quick test."

He shut off the fill line and watched the reading on his helmet display. "Holding pretty steady. I won't die in the time it takes you get through the hatch. You guys ready?"

"Suit checkout's complete," Darrell said.

"Same here," Andy added, "but there's something we forgot.

"Yeah?"

"How are we going to communicate with the cosmonauts? We can't work their frequencies."

"We know the woman speaks English," Darrell reminded them. "Probably reads it too. Why not use the scratch-pad screen on the pocket computer?"

Andy replied, "Tough to write with the gloves on, but we can make it work."

"Okay," Brandt said. "I'll tell Houston you're heading out." Using the suit's *push-to-talk* switch, he transmitted, "Houston, this is Artemis. Because of a minor suit problem, the commander will not be participating in the first EVA. We're ready to depressurize and open the hatch."

"Roger, Artemis." Brian sounded tired. "You're on your own mission plan now. Keep us informed."

"Wilco, Houston. You ready to receive video?"

"That's affirm, Artemis. We'll be taping for later broadcast. Not many people interested in space activities in the middle of the night."

"Okay, guys," Brandt said. "We'll have to modify the procedures a bit. Darrell, suppose you get the depressurization started while I fetch the ladder and the pocket computer. Then you pop the hatch, drop the ladder and start down first while Andy handles the camera."

Still lying on the left-side couch, Darrell used his trackball to bring up the vent commands and started releasing the ship's oxygen.

Brandt climbed into the forward area, retrieved the equipment and dropped back to the cockpit.

"Camera checks normal," Andy said, scanning the cockpit while monitoring the picture on his display.

"Point two psi," Darrell said. "Hatch coming open."

He directed the computer to release the latches and pushed the hatch outward. Using tricks developed at Marshall, he deftly released the ladder's metal strap, clipped the safety tether to the hatch and maneuvered the cylinder through the opening. Then he aligned the side rail supports with the lower edge of the hatch and shoved them down until they locked. Carefully adjusting the ladder to be sure it would unroll straight down, he called nervously, "Okay, here goes."

With Andy recording the event, the cylinder dropped smoothly along the side of the spacecraft as if in slow motion, popping its latches into the receptacles as it unfurled. Fully extended, it stretched to the top of the mating ladder on the lower stage.

"Looks okay," Darrell said. "Let's see if it works." He unplugged the hoses from his chest.

"Don't forget this," Brandt said as he slid the pocket computer into the equipment pouch on Darrell's right thigh.

Darrell tucked himself up, pivoted a quarter turn and poked his legs through the hatch. Then he grabbed the edge of the opening and eased himself out, dropping his feet to the second rung of the ladder.

Watching Andy's video on the right display, Brandt saw Darrell carefully step down, one rung at a time, then start to kick the latches into place, holding fast to the slender side rails. Twenty feet lower, he transferred to the sturdier ladder on the side of the third stage.

The remainder of the descent went more quickly. Darrell soon stood on the last rung, about three feet above the surface. He hesitated there for a moment as if unsure what to do next. "Just a little hop, buddy," Brandt thought to himself. "Use your arms to control the drop."

As if he'd heard, Darrell jumped gracefully off the ladder and landed softly in the dust, sending a small spray outward from his boots. Andy's video got it all.

Brandt saw Darrell reach for the *push-to-talk* switch on the suit's display-and-control module. In a clear and powerful voice, he said, "America proudly returns to the moon to open a new era of peaceful exploration."

"Well said," Brandt replied, clapping his gloved hands. "You ready for Andy?"

"Everything worked as advertised except for one latch. Right side, a little less than halfway down. Doesn't seem to have locked. Shouldn't be a problem."

Brandt took the portable video and recorded Andy's departure through the hatch. Then he picked up the ground camera from where Andy had placed it, eased it through the opening and handed it down. Andy took it in his left hand, then slowly descended to the last rung. After giving the camera to Darrell, he hopped off the ladder. Brandt recorded the historic meeting on the surface.

"Houston, Artemis. You get that?" Brandt asked.

"Artemis, it came through beautifully. Can you get some pictures of the lunar landscape?"

Leaning on the edge of the hatch, Brandt took a slow panoramic sweep of the terrain.

"Artemis, Houston. Can you see the Russian spaceship?"

"That's affirmative, Houston. Have to lean out a bit—shoot around to the left. You should be able to see it just above the hill."

"Roger, Artemis. Definitely on its side."

"Artemis, Wilkins on the surface. It's just as the Apollo astronauts described it. Thick layer of tiny black particles. Small to medium-sized boulders strewn about. Lots of small craters. Some larger, maybe twenty-feet across. I'm going to try a few steps now. Work on my walking technique."

"Roger, Darrell," Brandt replied.

"Artemis, Yang here. I've got the camera ready. Thought I'd start with some shots of the spacecraft."

"Okay, Andy. You copy Houston's request for pictures of the Soyuz?"

"Got a look at it coming down the ladder, but I can't see it from here. Low ridge in the way."

"Roger, Andy, understand. Picking up your video now. Picture looks good."

"Artemis, Wilkins. I'm ready to head over to the Soyuz."

"Artemis, Yang. Ditto that."

"Roger," Brandt responded. "Keep me posted."

"Artemis, Houston. Statement is ready. You should be seeing it on your screen."

"Roger, Houston. Coming through now. Advise when you're ready for the reading."

"Artemis, Houston. Ready any time. This isn't going out live, so don't worry about getting it perfect on the first try."

"Roger, Houston. Here goes."

*As the commander of the spaceship Artemis, I, Colonel Brandt L. Strickland, United States Air Force, do claim, for the people and the government of the United States, all rights pertaining to the development of natural resources on and beneath the surface of the moon as permitted under international law and in accordance with those covenants, treaties and agreements duly ratified by the present and previous governments of the United States of America.*

He paused, then said, "That do it for you, Houston?"

"Just fine, Artemis. Should make the folks here feel a bit more kindly toward your new mission plan.

Brandt dropped back into his couch, glad to have the legalities out of the way but wondering about the statement. "Sure didn't sound like claiming something for all mankind," he thought. "Must have something to do with the Russian statement. Wish I could get outside but I'll need to check the suit for at least an hour."

***

Svetlana looked across the desolate terrain at the white cone jutting upward from the top of the rise. She and Vadim had watched Artemis approach, descending on a billowing plume of barely visible gas expanding into the vacuum. As it dropped behind the ridge, a large dust cloud had bubbled up and settled again. It had been an awesome display.

"Wonder how long it'll take them to get here," Vadim said.

"Wonder what they'll do when they arrive," she replied.

"Still worried about the weapons?"

"Can't help it. But I keep telling myself they'll probably try to help us. Not that there's much they can do."

"They could help roll the spacecraft—get the laser unloaded," Vadim said.

"They wouldn't if they knew what it was," she snickered.

"Considering our first attempts, I'm almost sure we can do it ourselves. Just need better footholds."

"Then what?"

"Have to try to get the spacecraft vertical, or at least close to it."

"But that's impossible, Vadim, even with the Americans

helping."

"Perhaps not, Svetlana. I've been thinking about digging out a large hole under the lander and tipping up the spacecraft. Put the pivot point near the center of gravity."

"You're talking about an awfully big hole, Vadim. And we don't even have a shovel!"

"Still hoping Flight Control will have some ideas. Suppose we walk up on the hill toward the Americans. Perhaps we can see them coming."

They set off, covering the hundred meters to the top of the rise at a remarkable speed. Svetlana's moon gait proved more effective and she arrived just before Vadim.

"There they are," she exclaimed. "Coming right toward us."

With Andy bounding along about ten meters in front of Darrell, the astronauts had already moved to within the width of a football field. Just as Vadim reached the crest, Andy stopped and raised his right arm as if to block the sun, then reached for his *push-to-talk* switch with his left forefinger.

"Watch out, Svetlana!" Vadim yelled. "He's going to shoot!" As he ripped open the holster cover and yanked out his gun, he snarled, "You bastard! Why would you kill her when she's already dead?"

Svetlana whirled her head around and saw him take aim. She screamed, "No, Vadim! No!" But her plea went unheeded. A flash erupted from the barrel.

She looked back in time to see Andy thrown backwards as the bullet smashed through the center of his visor. Vadim had learned his lessons well.

The plastic bent inward under the impact, finally yielding and allowing the projectile to complete its task. Then it rebounded outward and broke apart. The gas in the suit blew out and with it the air in Andy's lungs, hurling the wreckage of his face through the gaping hole, a grotesque cloud of pink droplets and small pieces of flesh and bone. It expanded into the lunar vacuum, some vaporizing, some freezing, finally drifting to the surface a dozen yards from where he fell.

Mesmerized by the horror, Svetlana forgot about Darrell. By the time she looked in his direction, it was already too late. The laser designator had found its destination in the middle of Vadim's chest. As the flame shot from Darrell's elbow, she screamed once more,

"Vadim!"

The fléchette sliced cleanly through the protective layers of the suit, leaving only the smallest hole. Its warhead detonated just below Vadim's heart. The explosion of pain snapped his legs straight, launching him three meters through the vacuum. He fell slowly and crumpled in the dust. Svetlana knew that the sound of his scream would haunt her as long as she lived.

She whirled and, in a single motion threw open the holster cover and yanked out her gun. As she brought it up and aimed it at Darrell, she saw him throw up his arms. She tried to stop herself, but her reflexes only allowed her to move the aiming point above his head. Her tightening grip caused the gun to fire, throwing her back and nearly ripping it from her grasp. She lunged for it, but again squeezed too hard. The second shot wrenched it out of her hand. She looked up to see Darrell's left elbow pointed at her heart. He had his right hand on the side of the control module. The moon war was over.

He inched toward her, examining her spacesuit, then squatted down, still keeping his elbow aimed as he snatched up her gun and hurled it away, immediately returning his finger to the firing switch.

Apparently satisfied she had no other weapons, he backed away and pointed toward the Soyuz. Then, waving his hand, he indicated she should move toward the wrecked spacecraft.

Confused at first, she slowly loped in the direction he'd ordered and then realized what he wanted. "Worried about the third cosmonaut, are you?" she muttered, picking up her pace. Minutes later, she reached the base of the toppled lander.

"Take a good look," she snarled to herself as she pointed to Mikhail's body. "He's no threat to you."

She watched the American as he glanced down, then quickly up again, always keeping his weapon trained on her. Then he waved her back toward Artemis.

When they reached Andy, he stopped. After several rapid looks at the gory spectacle, Darrell aimed his elbow directly at her chest. He stood there with the weapon pointed at her for nearly a minute before continuing on.

Nearing the base of the spaceship, she spotted the video camera on its stand, pointing at them. "Why don't you murder me to entertain your bloodthirsty American audience?" she thought. Then she noticed him hesitate.

She stopped, crossed her arms and glared at him through her

visor, daring him to fire. He pointed toward the ladder, then dropped his arm to his side. Pleased with her tiny victory, she walked to the spacecraft and began to climb.

***

The alarms continued to flash and Brandt's display filled with recovery procedures. The computer had detected a loss of hydrazine from Artemis' propellant tank and had dumped the helium that maintained tank pressure in an attempt to conserve the precious fuel.

And there was that aborted transmission from Andy, a loud bang that cut him off in the middle of a word.

"Heck with the oxygen," he grumbled to himself. "Gotta find out what's going on out there." He disconnected his umbilical and looked out the hatch to check the position of the ladder.

Surprised to see a cosmonaut climbing toward him, he pushed himself back inside. As the Russian commander reached the opening, he took her arm and guided her to Andy's couch.

He returned to the hatch to see Darrell stepping up from the third-stage ladder to Artemis. A minute later, he tumbled through the opening onto the left-side couch, immediately connected his umbilical and pointed to Brandt's chest, indicating he should do the same. Then he turned the communications switch to *Intercom*.

"Darrell, what going on? Where's Andy?"

Darrell didn't answer. Instead he took the pocket computer from the pouch, wrote a message on it, handed to Brandt and said, "For her. Give it to her."

Brandt looked at it. Its block letters said simply, *DO NOT MOVE*. He passed it to the cosmonaut. She took the stylus between her gloved fingertips, wrote something on the screen and shoved it in front of Brandt's helmet. It read, *MONSTERS*.

"Darrell? You all right?" Brandt probed.

In a trembling voice, he replied, "Andy. They killed him. Shot him for no reason. Blew his head to pieces."

"Jesus Christ!" Brandt roared. "Andy? You're telling me they got Andy?"

"Never saw it coming, Brandt. One second he was there in front of me, waving at them. Next thing I knew he was hurtling backwards with his face spewing out of his helmet."

His rage becoming uncontrollable, Brandt screamed, "Then

what's this piece of trash doing here in his couch? Help me throw the garbage out the hatch!"

"Too easy, Brandt. I want to take her back. Put her on trial. She tried to kill me too, but the gun flew out of her hand when she fired it."

"What happened to rest of them?"

"I shot the one who killed Andy. Warhead blew him apart. The third one was already dead. Made her show him to me."

"Died in the crash?"

"That was bullshit. Somebody shot him. Nice neat hole in his visor. Must've done something they didn't like. Nice people these Russians."

"Jesus! I can't believe this." Brandt pointed to the display. "We've got other problems. Computer's detected a leak in the hydrazine tank. It dumped the helium. Haven't been able to figure out whether it's real or just a bad sensor."

"It's real, Brandt. Saw it climbing up. We've got propellant coming out the side—about a yard to the right of the ladder."

"Dang! Must have taken a meteorite hit."

"Nope. Slug from the bitch's gun. She got two off before it flew away. Artemis was right in the line of fire."

"We've got to get that thing plugged up. Could you tell how fast it was leaking?"

"Not very fast, but that's another problem. When I went by, it was barely arcing out enough to clear Artemis, hitting on the third stage. If the flow decreases, it'll hit the thermal layer. Probably destroy it. At least loosen the adhesive."

"All the more reason to get it plugged."

"If there was a way to do it. The fumes from that stuff are deadly. If we splash any of it on us, even our gloves, we can't bring the suits back inside."

"Which means we have to stay outside with them."

"That's about it."

"Darrell, are you telling me we're dead—that the witch killed us?"

"Depends on where the slug hit. If it's high enough, the leak will stop before we lose too much propellant. If not, you're right. We've had it. But the leak seemed pretty high up. If that's the case, the best thing we can do is restore the pressure. Push out whatever else is going to leak. Get it away from the ship. Then dump the pressure again."

"Okay. Do it."

Darrell raced through tiers of toolbox icons, found the right menu and made the selections. The ullage pressure, which had been displayed continuously since the alarm went off, rose rapidly. Then he put his head through the hatch.

"Looks much better. Really streaming away from the side."

Back inside, Darrell watched the value of the remaining propellant slowly decrease, then stabilize. "That's it, Brandt. I'm dumping the pressure again."

"Blast!" Brandt exclaimed. "We lost a lot of hydrazine."

"Afraid so. And we still have to figure out how we're going to stop the leak. It's okay here, where we've got some gravity to keep the stuff at the bottom of the tank, but once we're weightless, it'll blow right out again. Won't have any left for orbit circularization."

"If we ever get back to earth," Brandt mumbled. Then he said, "We'd better talk to Houston. Get them up to date. They're not gonna believe this."

"Thought about that walking back to the ship. Decided not to contact you."

"What do you mean?"

"Brandt, what the hell are we going to tell them? That we had a gunfight with the Russians? That they shot an astronaut? That we shot a cosmonaut?"

Brandt nodded. "See what you mean. Could start a war."

"Exactly, with each side saying the other guys shot first."

"So what do we do?"

"Brandt, right now the main thing is to get the hole patched."

"Fair enough. But Houston must be out of their minds wondering what's going on."

They've still got telemetry coming through. They know the status of the spacecraft—even that someone's back on board. In fact, they know we've got three people here. Should keep the panic level under control."

"Okay. What about fixing the leak."

"Thought I'd go back on the ladder. Evaluate the problem." Darrell released himself from the umbilical and backed out the hatch.

Brandt realized they'd forgotten about the Russian. He looked over at her. Her eyes glared back at him, filled with hatred. "What an animal!" he thought. "Cut your throat as soon as look at you." He picked up the computer, printed, *SERIOUS PROBLEMS DEAL WITH YOU LATER* and handed it to her. She read it, then threw it back at him.

"Real sweetheart," Brandt muttered.

Darrell crawled back inside and reconnected. "Leak's stopped. Should be safe to work. Have to find something that will cut through the thermal tiles. Need to get at the tank skin."

Brandt had the answer. "What about the lanyard cutter?"

"Worth a try. Need to prepare a clean area around the hole for the patch."

"Patch?"

"Only thing we've got is the meteorite patches for the pressure wall."

"Not sure they'll work, Darrell. Designed for having the pressure pushing them into the hole. Tank pressure would be pushing them out. Besides, we don't know how that stuff would hold up to MMH."

"Any better ideas?"

It took Brandt only a few seconds to mentally search the options. "Nope. Not a thing."

"Listen, Brandt, our best hope is to do as good as job as possible with a pressure patch, then smear several layers of the sealant over it. Once that stuff cures, it's really rugged. And we're talking about a half-inch hole."

"Okay. I'll get on it."

"I'll take care of this one, Brandt. Doesn't make sense for you to be working outside with a suit that's got an oxygen leak. But you could get me a wet-waste bag."

***

"Gees, that's a son-of-a-bitch!" Darrell winced as he stretched as far as he could without falling. He worked the blade into the tough, fibrous, thermal-protection covering. Then, holding the cutter in his fingertips, he pushed it through another quarter inch. Every three of four cuts, he had to lie back on the ladder to give his arm a rest.

Finally, he freed a section about half-a-foot square, pried it from the tenacious adhesive and slipped it into the waste bag, carefully avoiding the hydrazine-soaked center. He folded over the top of the bag and jammed it into the space between the ladder rail and the side of the spaceship. Nearly exhausted, he climbed back into the cockpit and flopped on the left-side couch.

Reconnected to the intercom, he panted, "Need the scraper from the patch kit."

Brandt disconnected, pulled himself up into the nose area, and reappeared with a small container. He squeezed the cover between his fingers and carefully peeled it back. The scraper sat right on top. Darrell took the tool and immediately returned to work.

Reaching as far as he could, he pushed the blade against the gummy surface, creating little worms of adhesive. He pulled himself back to get balanced on the ladder, clipped the scraper to his suit, then stretched again to pick the rolls off one by one, sticking them to the outside of the waste bag.

He had reached the end of his endurance. Although not entirely satisfied, he decided to accept the less-than-perfect result and get on with the repair.

Back in the cockpit, he rested on the couch for a few minutes, letting the cramps in his arms, legs and back return to tolerable levels. Then he removed a tube of resin from the patch kit, crushed a separator to connect its two chambers and kneaded it to blend the components. Finally, he took one of the squares of graphite-fiber cloth and returned to his task.

He smeared the resin over the scraped area. Then he reached across as far as he could and carefully draped the cloth patch over the hole. Using the blade, he poked the material into the resin. Then he emptied the rest of the tube over the cloth and smoothed the surface. He wiped the scraper on the side of the cutout, then clipped it to his suit and returned to the cockpit.

"Tell you, Brandt," he puffed, "stretching to reach the hole is no fun."

"You done?" Brandt asked.

"Need to put the piece of thermal material back."

"Aw, forget it, Darrell. Can't be that important."

"Have to smear another layer of sealant over the patch anyway. Pushing the square into the stuff won't add a thing. Need another tube of goo."

Brandt retrieved it from the container and handed it to him.

Darrell blended the adhesive then backed out of the hatch, climbed down the ladder and returned to work.

After smoothing the last layer of sealant and wiping off the scraper, he pulled the waste bag from its perch, extracted the piece of tile and leaned away from the ladder, trying to fit it back into place.

His first attempt left it tilted in the hole with the farthest edge sticking up from the surface. "Damned thing!" he thought as he tried unsuccessfully to push it down. "Must be wedged in. Have to pull it out again."

His reach wouldn't quite allow him to get a grip on the protruding corner. With his left foot on the right edge of the ladder rung, his left hand gripping the right rail, and his right foot dangling in space, he stretched his right hand as far out as he could.

Bending under the strain, the ladder's unsecured latch popped out and the right rail twisted away from the surface of the spacecraft. Darrell's foot slid off the rung. For a moment he hung from his gloved hand. Then his grip failed and he hurtled into space.

***

In the vacuum, the impact made no sound but Brandt felt the jolt as it traveled up the structure. "Darrell?" he called as he jumped toward the hatch, his heart pounding. He looked down the ladder and saw him hit the side of the third stage, rebound off and land on his back. He didn't move.

"Oh, God!" he choked. "Hold on buddy. I'm coming for ya!" He yanked out the umbilical, launched himself out the hatch and scrambled down the ladder. Bent away from the spacecraft where Darrell had wrenched it from the latches, it twisted precariously as he leaped from rung to rung. He didn't notice.

Five feet from the surface, he jumped off and fell to the ground in a cloud of dust. Skidding on the loose surface, dropping to his hands and knees, he staggered toward his friend.

He raised Darrell's visor. A face distorted in agony stared up at him. Pressing his *push-to-talk* switch, he said, "Hang on, buddy. You're gonna be fine. Ol' Madman's gonna take care of everything." Darrell remained motionless, his eyes filled with pain and terror.

Brandt pleaded, "Talk to me, buddy," and gently depressed the switch on Darrell's control module.

"Can't move, Brandt. Must have broken my back. Landed on a boulder. Christ, Brandt, this hurts."

"Okay, pal. I'll get you back. Just gotta figure a way. Hang on a minute."

Darrell blinked his eyes rapidly. Brandt took it to mean he wanted to say something and pressed the switch again.

"Nothing you can do this time. If you try to move me, you'll kill me."

Brandt stood up, unable to accept what had happened. He walked in circles, his mind racing, wondering if he could carry Darrell up the ladder, pull him up on a tether, anything to get him into the spacecraft. But then what? How could he get him out of the suit? How could he keep from killing him?

Returning to Darrell, he saw his eyes blinking again. He touched the switch.

Although still gnarled by the pain, Darrell's words came slowly, deliberately, with resolution.

"Brandt, need you to do me a little favor here." His breathing had become labored. "You see—pressure in the suit—getting awful uncomfortable. Need you to—ease it down—just a bit. Do it myself—just can't move—you know." His eyes closed hard against the pain.

Brandt kneeled beside him, resting on his knees and elbows. He beat his fists into the black dust. For the first time in his adult life, his eyes filled with tears. But he knew what he had to do. He pushed his switch again.

"I'm hearing ya, buddy. Gotta get the dang pressure down."

Brandt took Darrell's hand, squeezed it and whispered, "Bye, buddy." He rotated the joint but held the glove as it tried to blow off.

"That doing it for you, pal?"

He pushed Darrell's switch. "Oh yeah, Brandt. A lot better. Hey..." He winced in pain. "Another thing. Gotta tell Anita..."

"Yeah buddy, I know. Don't worry."

Darrell cried in pain, then forced himself to speak. "No, Brandt. Tell her—tell her—she was right." He said no more. A minute later he dropped into unconsciousness.

Brandt released the glove. He stumbled around the spacecraft, doubled over from cramps. As he passed the camera, he kicked it to the ground, trying to release the rage inside.

"Ah dang," he sobbed to himself. "What am I gonna do? Heck, might as well finish it. Me and Darrell together." He raged, "My God, it's so easy to die here."

It took another ten minutes of aimless wandering before he could begin to think rationally. He looked up at the open hatch.

"That bitch! I'm gonna kill her. Throw her out. Let her bust her back. Show her how Darrell felt."

He walked to the ladder and started to climb. "But what'd Darrell say? Take her back. Put her on trial. I'd feel better putting a bullet in her gut. But he wouldn't want that. Gotta think. Gotta think."

When he reached the location of the leak, he examined the patch. The repair appeared flawless. "Oh God, buddy," he wailed, "why couldn't you have left well enough alone? But that wouldn't have been you, would it, pal?"

He climbed through the hatch and dropped on the couch, unable to move. A warning flashed on his helmet display, telling him his oxygen supply had reached a dangerously low level. He ignored it, staring ahead at the instrument panel but not seeing it.

His prisoner picked up the pocket computer, wrote something on the scratch pad and held it in front of his eyes. It read, *TWO HOURS OF OXYGEN*. Brandt grabbed it from her, erased the screen and wrote, *STICK IT!* She took it, wrote a reply and handed it back. She had written, *DO NOT UNDERSTAND*.

Brandt started to laugh, an uncontrollable, hysterical laugh mixed with wails and screams. The incongruity, the absurdity. Trapped in this tiny world with a beast he wanted to slaughter, the monster who'd killed his dearest friend, and she couldn't understand his curses.

The alarm finally caught his eye. Instinctively, he grabbed his umbilical and slapped it to his chest. "All right!" he yelled at himself. "Time to function. See if I can get this sack of slime back to earth. Do it for Darrell." He continued the self-motivation, trying to get his brain working again.

"Fuel state. Most important. What's the fuel state?"

He began to work frantically with the computer, setting up an analysis of the return profile. Within a few minutes, it had confirmed his fears. The remaining hydrazine could not possibly boost them into a transfer trajectory.

He reran the analysis, trying to estimate how much weight he'd have to remove. The number staggered him. He thought through the list of items he'd considered during his evaluation of the rescue plan, laughing bitterly at the irony.

"Got to get the big pieces off first," he thought. Then he realized he hadn't deployed the JPL experiment. "Dump it. Lots of weight," he muttered as he checked his oxygen supply to be sure it had filled enough for a quick trip up into the nose. He returned with a large yellow container.

"Just shove it out," he thought, then quickly dismissed the idea, concerned it might hit the spacecraft on the way down. "Okay, do it the right way."

He released a tether from the side of the container, clipped the safety fastener to the hatch and pushed the experiment out, dangling it alongside the ladder. Hand over hand, he lowered it, down past the base of Artemis, along the third-stage ladder, down the landing leg and to the surface. He unclipped the tether and tossed it away from the spacecraft, watching to be sure it arced safely to the side. "Just like Brian figured it," he thought.

He returned to the nose, got a trash bag and started to fill it with food, medical supplies and other loose items. After dropping it down the passageway, he rounded up all the filled waste bags and dropped them on the pile.

Back in the cabin, he started to throw the bags to the surface when he recalled the need to avoid contaminating the moon. Then he remembered. "Christ! We're leaving four corpses behind. Guess we've already done as much damage as anyone possibly could." He hurled the bags away from the vehicle.

Now almost frantic, he said to himself, "Gotta get something heavier!" He pulled up the list he'd developed earlier. It included almost every piece of electronic equipment inside the pressure vessel. After another trip to the nose, he had the tool kit in the middle of the cockpit and a torqueless screwdriver in his hand.

As the heaviest single item, the telemetry interface earned its place at the top of the list. Brandt pondered cutting off the last flow of information to NASA but quickly decided he had no choice. "No use sending 'em a highly accurate account of us failing to get back," he muttered, then turned off the device and began to attack its mounting fasteners.

But, wearing the suit, he couldn't work fast enough. "Have to repressurize," he thought. "Get the stuff unbolted, then dump it."

He leaned toward the hatch and then realized it couldn't be closed without dropping the ladder. As he began to release the rail clamps, he looked down and saw the experiment far below.

"Might as well have something good come out of all this," he mumbled to himself as he maneuvered around to get his feet through the opening. Taking it a bit more slowly this time, he stepped down to the surface.

Deploying the rover took little time or effort. The JPL engineers had done a marvelous job keeping the procedures simple and the fittings easy to manipulate. Within minutes, the ungainly device, looking like a child's Erector-set fantasy, sat on its wheels, its small antenna extended like a sail. Brandt aimed it towards earth, gave it a pat, then climbed back up to the hatch.

After releasing the rail attachments, he watched the ladder jerk down the side of Artemis, rolling itself up, hesitating at each set of latches. It wobbled badly when it reached the broken fitting, but straightened out and continued its awkward operation. Finally, when it reached the last receptacles, it popped free and rolled down the third-stage ladder to the ground.

"Goodbye moon," Brandt thought as he closed the hatch, "and good riddance!" He told the computer to fill the vehicle with oxygen. As soon as the pressure reached the suit's value, he removed his helmet and gloves.

Now he worked quickly, like a man possessed. One piece of electronic equipment after another joined the growing pile in the hatch-side couch. As he removed the large, multi-function displays, he thought, "Hope the center display can handle everything." At the moment, its screen was filled with alerts, alarms and warnings as the computer tried to digest the loss of one system after another.

With every communication radio removed, he returned to the nose area and unbolted the suit mounts, experiment mount, treadmill, galley, and the microwave oven. He kept a minimum number of food packets for the return journey, none of which required heating. As soon as he removed an item, he dropped it down the passageway into the cockpit.

Finally, nothing remained that could be unscrewed, unbolted or pried loose. He considered the toilet, but had no idea how to disassemble it.

He had to kick a pile of equipment out of the way to get back into the center area. Pushing open a path to the hatch, he replaced his helmet and gloves, checked his suit and dumped the pressure. He assumed the Russian had taken care of her own needs. If she hadn't, he didn't care.

After getting the hatch reopened, he began to hurl items away from the spacecraft. One after another, they landed in the dust, creating a bizarre garbage dump alongside the vehicle.

Getting the items from the center of the cockpit to the hatch took an exhausting round of pivots, tucks and bends. The inflated suit fought every movement and the work went slowly. As he made yet another turn toward the pile, the Russian held the pocket computer in front of his face. It read, *I WILL HELP*.

Wanting to hit her, Brandt compelled himself to act rationally. He pushed the few remaining items from the couch, squatted on it and let her hand him the scrapped equipment, one or two pieces at a time. The pile dropped rapidly and soon Brandt was able to return to the computer to evaluate the consequences of his work. The trajectory analysis said he had a long way to go.

He went over his lists. The few items remaining amounted to a trivial reduction in mass. He thought of the equipment in the unpressurized area between the cockpit and the propellant tanks. Batteries. Fuel cells. Plenty of opportunities. But with the ladder sitting next to the landing leg, sixty-five feet away, he couldn't get to them.

Of course, he could always eliminate his prisoner. Her three-hundred-plus pounds would go a long way toward making the return possible. He could have a trial, like a ship's captain at sea. Find her guilty of war crimes. Execute her. Finding the prospect at the same time appealing and revolting, he purged it from his mind. But what else could he do?

"Go through the ship," he told himself. "Every bit of mass. Find something expendable." He started at the tip of the nose and envisioned each section, progressing downward through the cockpit.

"The couches! Didn't get the couches. Can't fit the side ones through the hatch, but the center." He filed away the item and continued his mental search. "Already looked at the unpressurized bays. Can't get at them. Next down are the tanks. Can't get rid of any propellant, obviously. That's why I'm working the problem. That leaves..."

He had it! He didn't need all the nitrogen tetroxide, only enough to react with the remaining hydrazine. Punching up the remaining mass of MMH, he quickly calculated how much NTO would be needed and subtracted it from the total. Even throwing in the center couch, it didn't quite make the requirement, but it was close. He reran the trajectory analysis program.

In the few minutes it took the computer to complete its work, he unbolted the fold-up couch, disassembled it and added its pieces to the junk pile. Then he checked the results.

"Still won't make it!" His mind raced. "What else can I do?" He looked at the burn figures. Liftoff to orbit. Trans-earth injection. Circularization.

It hit him. "Direct transfer! Go right into TEI." But that would mean lifting off at a specific time, the exact second that would match his position on the moon with the entry window above the earth's surface. He had to determine the next opportunity.

He loaded the problem into the computer and thought about dumping the excess NTO. The Russian held another message in front of his face. It read, *TWENTY MINUTES.*

The note reminded him of her backpack. He pulled a roll of duct tape from the tool kit and wrote on the computer, *REMOVE BACKPACK.* She looked at him, not knowing what he wanted. He slapped the life-support unit. She seemed to understand and rolled on her side so he could remove it.

"Amazing," thought Brandt. "Figured I'd have to coldcock her to get the thing off."

The classes at JSC had covered only the basic configuration of the new Russian suits, not the details. Nevertheless, he found the backpack attachments and released them. It dropped into the center of the cockpit and dangled from its hoses. "Now comes the tricky part," he thought. "Have to get these things folded over—sealed pressure tight—then cut them."

Because they were rather short, he had difficulty bending the oxygen tubes. "Probably ought to forget this," he thought as he fumbled with the sticky tape. "But we're talking close to 150 pounds. Could make the difference." Finally, he squeezed the folded hose in one hand, touched the dangling end of the tape to it and quickly wrapped several layers over it to keep it from unfolding and venting the trapped gas from the suit. It looked as if it would hold.

"Gotta hurry now," he said anxiously. The second gas line surrendered to his technique with less of a struggle and the thin cooling tube was no challenge at all. With everything sealed, he took the tool kit's utility knife and sawed through the tough hose material. The backpack fell away.

He hurled it out the opening, quickly closed the hatch and repressurized the spacecraft. Then he removed his helmet and indicated that his prisoner should do the same. Her attack began immediately.

"Colonel Strickland! You have decided to let me live. How

generenerous."

Despite the accent, Brandt found her proficiency in English remarkable. But it delayed his response only a second. He roared, "Shut up! Do you know what that means? You murdering commie bitch! Thanks to you, there may not be enough propellant left to get back. In any case, I'd sure have a better chance without you being here. So if the numbers I'm running don't work out, I promise you, you're going through that hatch. Understand?"

Her hate-filled eyes burned into his. Then she turned her head and stared at the empty holes in the instrument panel.

Shrugging off the distraction, Brandt returned to the problem of the nitrogen tetroxide. Working through the menus, he found the commands that dumped the remaining propellants prior to the Shuttle rendezvous, but they opened both sets of propellant valves. It seemed the programmers hadn't included a procedure for getting rid of just the NTO. But Brandt knew everything could be operated manually, if only he could find the command.

Searching through the system diagrams, he found the valve, put the cursor on it and punched the trackball button. A list of commands appeared, including one labeled, *Open for dump*.

"Got it!" he thought. "Just need to get the quantity displayed."

That posed no problem and he shortly found himself watching the number decrease, wondering what effect the caustic liquid would have on the engine components as it flowed over them on its way to the surface. Allowing a small margin for error, he closed the valve just before the quantity reached his calculated value.

"Check the trajectory analysis," he remembered. Changing screens, he displayed the results of the calculation. The first number jumped out at him.

"Gees! Liftoff at 1007 UTC! That's less than ten minutes. Not enough time to do the calculations." But the number rang a bell. He checked the equivalent mission time. "Seventy hours, twenty-two minutes. Hearse mode!"

Someone in the NASA hierarchy had insisted on it, an automatic-return routine that would fly Artemis back to earth on a direct trajectory some period of time after the scheduled liftoff. It had been justified as a last-ditch emergency measure, something that would bring the crew back even if they were completely incapacitated. But NASA hadn't fooled them. The astronauts knew it would take control only if they were all dead.

"I'll be," Brandt thought. "The software's gonna bail me out. Profile's already programmed." He quickly cleared the analysis problem and brought up the primary message page. Right at the top the warning flashed. *NINE MINUTES TO AUTOMATIC LIFTOFF.*

"Just enough time to get out of the suit," he mumbled as he released the waist connection. Even with the moon's gravity, doffing the torso without the holder took a goodly measure of squirming. The Russian watched for a while, then grabbed the glove connectors while he pulled his arms free. He pushed himself out the rest of the way and looked at her. "Guess you'll be needing some help with yours too." He pointed to the message. "We lift off in eight minutes." She stared back, her face expressionless.

The lower-torso segment presented no problem once he worked his feet out of the boots. Now clad in only the cooling-and-ventilation garment, he stowed the suit as best he could in the center of the cockpit, hoping it wouldn't create a problem when they became weightless.

"I must remove mine," his prisoner said. "It is too hot."

Brandt knew that without the cooling system, she could die from heatstroke. He recalled the need to open the back and motioned for her to turn so he could reach the fasteners.

"A lot easier working without gloves," he thought as he released the seals. As soon as the air entered the suit, she began to wriggle out of it. Brandt tried to help, but her dexterity required no assistance. In a minute, she was free.

"Lie down," he commanded as he draped the restraining straps across her waist. "Fasten these."

"Okay, so much for her," he thought. "Gotta check systems. Hope the software doesn't shut down because of all the malfunction messages."

He brought up the status screens for one system after another, clearing the warnings as quickly as possible, trying to tell the computer that everything was all right. But the failure messages went on and on. Finally, he came to the hydrazine tank. A blinking line reminded him he had vented the helium.

As he instructed the computer to restore the pressure he thought, "That would have stopped the show."

"Let's hope Darrell's patch holds." Thinking his name brought a wave of nausea. "Dang, buddy, if it doesn't, it's no fault of yours."

He strapped himself in. At the end of the countdown, the

computer sent propellants to Artemis' three engines. As the thrust boosted them away, Brandt choked, "Goodbye, buddy. And you too, Andy."

With the G-force pushing his head into the couch, he squeezed his eyes shut, pounded his legs with his fists and screamed, "It wasn't supposed to end this way!"

## Chapter 18

---

# Transitions

**Artemis**

After six minutes and sixteen seconds, the burn ended.

"So much for that," Brandt thought. "But where are we? Where are we headed? How much fuel have we got left?"

He cleared the screen and told the computer to find the answers.

"Not too bad," he thought as he studied the numbers. He scanned the rest of the data. "Trouble is, it's just checking itself. Without the star tracker, I won't really know where we are until we pick up the GPS. Maybe I overdid it tossing all the nav equipment. Oh well, worst that'll happen is a big course-correction burn—using propellant we don't have."

"Speaking of which." He instructed the computer to calculate the fuel remaining after the orbit-circularization burn.

"Close," he muttered to himself. "Nothing left for course corrections. Where am I gonna find some more fuel?"

He already knew the answer. More mass would have to be stripped from Artemis. But he had other problems to deal with first.

He turned to his passenger. Still strapped in, she stared straight ahead, ignoring him, seemingly deep in thought.

"Colonel Zosimova, the engines operated normally and we are now on a trajectory that will place us in earth orbit."

She didn't respond.

"You may unstrap if you wish and move about the spacecraft. I'll show you where things are and instruct you in their use."

She continued to stare at the instrument panel. Brandt lost his temper.

"I feel bound to inform you that I'm bringing you back to face charges. Charges that you are guilty of war crimes."

"War crimes?" she exploded, ripping her straps off so she could face him. "War crimes? Your crew member tried to kill me! My dearest friend, a hero of the Socialist Federation with a wife and a young daughter, saved me. Then the other American pig shot him with that hideous weapon. And you accuse me of war crimes?"

"Kill you?" Brandt screamed. "We were coming to save you. Take you back with us. Even if it meant risking our own lives."

"Pig!" she spat. "Stop your lying. We knew about your weapons. Your man—he raised his right arm. Put his left hand on the firing switch. In another second I would have been dead."

Astonished, Brandt blurted out, "The weapons. How did you find out?"

Gloating, she snarled, "Ha! You admit it. You did come to kill us—to keep us from using the moon."

"Don't be ridiculous," he huffed. "The man you shot was probably waving at you—pushing his microphone switch to tell me you were still alive."

"Microphone switch!" she repeated scornfully. "I am very familiar with the American spacesuit. You do not need a switch to talk."

"He needed one!" Brandt yelled. "The suits were changed for the moon mission. As for the weapons, we developed them only after we found out you'd be armed."

"Another lie!" she snorted. "What you say is impossible. We decided to develop the pistols after our intelligence discovered your filthy plan. We did nothing until September."

Brandt narrowed his eyes, flared his nostrils and spat out, "Horse dung! Which means I don't believe you. We found out you were carrying weapons back in May."

Her expression changed to a deadpan. She stared through him as if searching for an answer on the far wall of the spacecraft.

"Gotcha that time, didn't I?" Brandt taunted. "Lying bitch! God, I'm going to enjoy watching them execute you. Watching you retch in convulsions just before you die."

She ignored his ranting, continuing her unfocused gaze, pondering his information. "Май," she muttered. "Май."

"That's right, May!" Brandt knew enough Russian to recognize the word.

"They told you we would be carrying pistols?" she asked.

"No, as a matter of fact," he replied haughtily, "We only knew you'd have a weapon. I'm afraid our American spies aren't quite as effective as the FSA."

Her face took on a look of incredible sorrow. Her cheeks sagged and her mouth turned down as she said slowly, "That report. It referred to something else. A different weapon. Not the pistols."

"Another weapon?" Brandt roared. "What were you carrying? Missiles?"

Her expression once again hardening, she retorted, "You are stupid, Colonel."

He waited for her to continue.

"The weapon was a laser gun—to attack spacecraft if they invaded our moon territory. Necessary to make a legal claim. We never intended to use it."

"This was on the Soyuz?"

"On the lander part. We never unloaded it."

"And the pistols?"

"Developed only when we were sure—absolutely sure—the information about your spacesuit weapon was true. We were horrified about the type of weapon—about the CIA being the designer. It proved everything we'd heard about the Americans."

Now it was Brandt's turn to contemplate, to digest what she'd told him. "Can't believe this," he thought, his fury turning to turmoil. "The whole thing. Andy dead. Darrell gone. Because of bad intelligence. But it's still their fault!"

Watching his face, she sensed his misgivings. "You believe me, yes?"

Brandt responded quietly, "You know, the man you murdered all but refused to carry the weapons. Yes, he was armed when you shot him, but only because he couldn't figure out how to get the things out of his suit. He couldn't believe a cosmonaut would ever fire on him. We're talking about a family man with a wife he loved and two young children."

Struggling to keep his emotions in check, he went on. "The

weapons. Let's talk about the weapons. If you people hadn't decided to take the whole moon for yourselves—brought up a laser to shoot down peaceful spacecraft, for God's sake—this never would have happened. You spat on every treaty. Doesn't that matter to you?"

"Don't lecture me, Colonel Strickland," she hissed. "Your disgusting hypocrisy. Treaties. Agreements. All written to give everything to the capitalists. We welcomed you to our country. What did you do? Exploited us. Nothing but exploitation. Took everything. Left us nothing. We are starving—really starving. Our people are dying. What do you do? Impose sanctions because we defend the free people of Kazakhstan against fanatics. You give us weapons to fight them, then impose sanctions."

Barely pausing to catch her breath, she continued her diatribe. "Americans must have everything. Cannot leave anything for someone else. The capitalist way. Take all the wealth. Crush every country trying to improve conditions. This is why you are hated."

Brandt countered, "We tried to help you. You greeted us with corruption, lawlessness and bureaucratic insanity. Our executives were murdered by your gangsters. Any wonder why our companies began to lose their enthusiasm?"

"Corruption and crime came with—how do you say it? Free enterprise. Never a problem under the Communists."

"And the ridiculous procedures? Dozens of agencies with conflicting regulations. Years to get simple approvals. Was that our fault too? Don't you people take responsibility for any of your problems?"

"I am aware of our faults, Colonel." She paused, then said, "I must the use the toilet."

Suddenly forced to think of her as a human being, Brandt's chivalry momentarily overcame his loathing. "Of course. I'll show you how to use the equipment."

"That is not necessary," she said arrogantly. "I studied your spacecraft." With that, she adroitly pushed herself into the passageway and disappeared.

Brandt thought, "Gotta hand it to 'em. Really thorough. And their intelligence puts ours to shame. Hard to believe they picked up on the weapons when even the President didn't know."

Her head appeared at the passageway entrance. She glanced at Brandt as she drifted back to her couch. Saying nothing, Brandt moved past her into the nose area. He stripped off the space-suit undergarment, took one of the half-dozen body wipes he'd retained, cleaned up, then retrieved his clothes from the storage compartment and dressed. "Feels good to get rid of the EMU crap," he thought as he pulled the knit shirt over his head. With everything tucked in, he moved back to the cockpit.

"Colonel Zosimova, I kept a set of clothing for you. It's in a compartment just beyond the toilet."

She looked at him quizzically, not sure how to interpret his small act of thoughtfulness. "Thank you, Colonel Strickland. That will be a great comfort."

"Oh yes," he added, "the bag on top contains a moistened paper towel. You can clean yourself with it, if you wish."

"I will find it," she said curtly as she drifted forward.

While she took care of herself, Brandt went through a few more alarm messages, trying to clear them so they didn't keep cluttering the display each time he pulled up a new page. Because the software had a network of interlinked crosschecks, each trying to evaluate the ramifications of the dozens of failed systems, the work went slowly.

Returning from the nose, Svetlana looked far more comely. Except for her hair, which remained a bit tousled, she appeared quite neat, perhaps even attractive. Her face, however, still carried the burden of sadness.

"Colonel Strickland, I am tired. I would like to sleep."

"Of course," Brandt replied. "I'm afraid there are no sleeping bags. I threw them overboard. We'll have to use the couches. They flatten out." He pressed the lever that caused the chair-like folds to extend.

As she fastened a strap loosely over her waist, she said, "This is fine," then turned her back to him.

He returned to the computer, but found it hard to concentrate. His mind drifted back. Back to the moon. To Darrell's face looking up at him. Pleading.

"Screwed up. I screwed up. Must've been a way to get him up the ladder. Bring him back. Oh, buddy. I'm so sick. So sick."

The cramps in his stomach brought his knees almost to his chin. He held his legs, curled up tightly, trying to shut out the pain. He sobbed quietly, hoping the Russian wouldn't hear.

**Johnson Space Center**

"Louise, the information doesn't support your conclusion." Brian had spent the past fifteen minutes trying to convince her. "Look at it! The telemetry clearly indicates that they're still on board."

"Sorry Brian," the Flight Director argued, "I don't interpret it that way at all. Everything points to an empty spacecraft." She had cleared the Instrumentation and Communications support room so they could talk in private.

Brian studied her face as she spoke. "Just like her," he thought. "NASA-approved solution. Won't even consider possibilities that might muddy the waters."

He'd met her before. Louise Ehlers. Eighteen-year NASA veteran. Pushed and shoved her way to the top. He didn't think she belonged there. Not sitting in the Flight Director's chair.

"But the telemetry," Brian protested. "We have voice up to 0744 when Andy screamed and Brandt said he was going to look through the hatch to see what was going on. And just before that, Andy said, `There they are!' so he must have seen at least two cosmonauts. That means five people were alive."

Ehlers' face reflected the strain of the previous four hours. Her trademark power suit, dark green with a mid-calf skirt, bolstered the image of a deadly serious professional in the midst of a major career crisis.

"We've been over this, Brian. What matters is what happened afterward."

"Which we can figure out. That's what I've been trying to tell you. Here. The first sign of a problem is the drop in hydrazine followed by a loss of helium pressure when the computer opened the vent valve."

"Which supports the analysts' conclusion that they were hit by a meteoroid."

"Yes it does. We agree on that. Fortunately, we continued to get telemetry for a while longer, and that's what proves the astronauts survived the meteor shower."

Getting impatient, Ehlers said, "You're talking about the foot-pad sensors again?"

"Right. Look at the sequence of weight changes. Now we know Brandt was still in the cockpit because of the transmission." He pointed to a hard copy of the processed telemetry. "That means this weight increase here and the second one right after it put all three of them back inside, still very much alive. So whatever happened to Andy, it didn't keep him from climbing up a sixty-five-foot ladder."

"Unless it wasn't Andy," Ehlers said grimly.

Brian looked puzzled. "What do you mean?"

"Could have been a cosmonaut."

"Okay, that's a possibility. Anyway, then we have a sequence of weight reductions, then an increase."

"Where is this taking us?" Ehlers asked, checking her watch.

"All I'm asking is that the telemetry people analyze the weight changes. Go back to known events—Andy and Darrell leaving the vehicle. Get accurate sensor responses. Then compare them to the events after the loss of voice communications. Find out who got on and who got off. At least that will give us a for-sure status at the time of telemetry termination."

Sounding as if she'd agree to anything that would end the discussion, Ehlers said, "Very well. I'll take care of it." She turned to go.

"Louise, all I'm trying to do is make sure we don't give up too soon."

She managed a half smile. "Understand how you feel, Brian. Listen, I have to get back."

**Artemis**

Brandt woke with a start. "The dream!" he thought, almost panicked. He wondered if he had cried out again. Turning toward his passenger, he saw she'd been watching him.

"You are troubled, Colonel Strickland."

"Did I say something in my sleep?"

"Could not understand it. Just yelling. You are thinking about the moon?"

He didn't know why, but he had an overpowering need to tell her—tell her of his turmoil. Not quite believing what he was doing, he answered curtly, "Of course, but not in the dream. I am deeply saddened by the deaths of my two crew members. I feel that, as their commander, I am responsible. I should have insisted upon going to the Soyuz—recognized the risk and put myself in the line of fire. I also should have done the repair to the spacecraft. For that matter, I should have refused the weapons, especially given the limitations of our intelligence."

Hardly sympathetic, she sneered, "So! You admit your guilt.

You admit we acted in self defense. You Americans are the aggressors, not the Federation."

Brandt turned away and looked through the window at the stars.

"But, as a military officer," she continued, "you must accept the death of a subordinate. It is weakness to indulge in sentimentality. Your men died performing their duty. It is not..."

She stopped. For a moment, the spacecraft remained absolutely silent. Then she screamed. Like a banshee from hell she screamed, a blood-curdling howl from the depths of her soul. She turned away and buried her face in her hands.

Covered with goose bumps, his neck hairs standing on end, Brandt asked, "What is it? What's wrong?"

"I killed him!" she sobbed. "Don't you understand? I killed that poor boy."

"Who?" Brandt asked. "Who did you kill?"

"Mikhail. I killed Mikhail."

"The other cosmonaut? You're the one who shot him?"

She didn't answer for a while. Finally, she said, "No. I did not shoot him. He shot himself. But it is my fault."

In bits and pieces, she told him the story. Told him of the relentless browbeating, how she frustrated Mikhail's every effort to gain her approval, how she observed his growing instability, his obsession with proving he was worthy of her admiration. Then, with obvious discomfort, she related the events leading up to the accident and her outraged rebuke.

"It is the same as if I shot him," she said quietly.

Neither spoke for quite a while. Then she said, "I do not know why I told you this. It does not concern you."

Brandt replied quietly, "I've been lying here thinking about what you said—how I do the same thing—demand that my pilots reach impossible levels of perfection."

"Why do you do this?"

"Don't know. Never gave it much thought. I have this concept of perfection—how a plane would be flown by someone with ultimate skills. When my pilots don't fly that well, I get frustrated—even angry—as if it's an attack on me somehow."

"Yes," she responded, clearly identifying with what he had said. "That is exactly correct. Exactly the way I feel."

"I say it's essential that my pilots develop the highest possible skill level, that I'm pushing them so they'll end up better. But it's just rationalization—making excuses for behavior I know is wrong."

"And your pilots. Do they perform well?"

"Oh yeah, they sure do. But it's out of fear. Heck of a way to motivate!"

"I think it is an excuse for not knowing a better way."

"Yup. That's right." Brandt contemplated what he'd just discovered. "You know, I'm lucky none of my actions ever led to the kind of tragedy you experienced. Could have happened any one of a dozen times."

"When you trained the astronauts, is it the same?"

"Completely different. As far as space flight was concerned, they had more experience than I did. I was scrambling to catch up. We worked together as equals."

"It was same with Vadim—Colonel Ippolitov—and Dubinin, my other cosmonaut. All experienced. As you say, equals."

"What will happen to you when you return—to Russia?"

"You said you will put me on trial in America."

"That was before I knew about the weapons. It's obvious you weren't responsible for Andy and Darrell getting killed. And I was very angry."

She thought about his question. "In Russia, I will be a hero for a while—to make people think the mission was a great success. Then, when people forget, I will have an accident. Disappear. Something like that."

"Why?"

"I failed! My mission was to claim the moon, set up the laser gun and bring Mikhail back safe. I failed two of the three. That is not permitted. Also there is the problem of the weapon. I would not be allowed to live knowing about the plan."

"They'd execute you?"

"I don't know. Something. What will the American government do to you?"

Brandt had already given the matter some thought. He replied, "It depends. If I'm willing to say nothing about what really happened—go along with whatever cover story they concoct—they'll probably make me into some sort of a hero."

"You would do this?"

"Not sure. I want people to know the truth. To know how and why Andy and Darrell died. To make those responsible pay for their mistakes. That includes me, by the way. On the other hand, it's not worth starting a war over. Too many people have died already. In any case, I'll probably be forced to retire. After that, I could go on the lecture circuit. Get paid for speaking to colleges, civic organizations. Maybe even write a book. Probably could make a lot of money if I wanted to."

"It doesn't matter what you do, you come out good."

Brandt snickered, "That's the way it is in America. If you get enough publicity, whether it's for doing something good or doing something terrible, you can get rich."

She grumbled, "It is part of the evil American society."

"Certainly one of our idiosyncrasies. But, considering what you have to look forward to, I prefer our brand of irrationality."

She had no answer.

Brandt decided to turn the discussion toward something less traumatic. "How about something to eat? I'm afraid the choices are pretty limited. Threw out all the hot food."

"It is not a problem," she replied. "If it is like Shuttle food, it will be good."

**The White House**

"Twenty-four hours since this thing started," Torres thought to himself. "What a hell of a day." He rubbed his eyes, trying to focus on the stack of memos that had turned his world upside down. "First the Russians, now this." He rocked back in the heavy, tan-leather executive chair, staring across the Oval Office at the marble fireplace.

His personal secretary knocked once on the door to his right, allowed enough time for him to get to his feet, then entered. "Mr. President," she said, sounding remarkably alert after a long and trying day, "Dr. Nguyen is here with Mr. Herrera." Torres stretched and shook his head rapidly, trying to clear his mind. "Have them come in."

Accustomed to Nguyen's invariably neat appearance, the President flinched as he entered. His tie hung loosely, a good inch below the collar of his rumpled white shirt, his suit looked as if he'd worn it to play tennis, and he needed a shave. Frances moved him toward a fussy peach love seat, part of a small conversation grouping in front of the President's desk.

Herrera stood facing him from the opposite side of a square wooden coffee table. He too looked rather rumpled, although more presentable than the NASA Director.

Torres dropped into a wooden arm chair at the end of the table closest to his desk and motioned to the others to take their seats.

"My greatest concern, of course, is the condition of the astronauts. I understand some people at NASA are saying they're all still on the moon, presumably dead. What's your opinion?"

Nguyen squirmed in his seat, obviously troubled by the question. "Mr. President, I've reviewed the data and I believe that conclusion is justified."

"Everyone died? All three of them?" Herrera asked.

"That appears to be the case." Shaken by his own words, Nguyen choked, "It's the saddest day of my career."

"Phong," the President said, "I share your grief to the fullest measure, but I'm also angered by the wasteful loss of life on a misdirected escapade I opposed from the very start."

"And we at NASA shared your misgivings, Mr. President."

"Yes, that's true," Torres admitted, "isn't it Marty."

Herrera raised his eyebrows. "Absolutely, Mr. President."

Something about Nguyen's response bothered the President. He probed, "Are you absolutely certain the spacecraft is empty?"

"Mr. President, I can't be that confident. However, all the information points in that direction."

"When will we know for sure?"

"For sure? Not until the spacecraft is recovered by the Shuttle crew in about two days."

"Mr. President," Herrera interrupted, "given the circumstances, I'd recommend we continue with our present position with respect to the media."

"Keep telling people we're still hoping some or all of them are alive?"

"Yes sir. As you know, the media's going crazy. Screaming for information. Saying we're stonewalling them. If we change our story now, it'll only feed the frenzy."

The President stroked his mustache. I see what you're driving at Marty, but what happens when they recover the spacecraft?"

"Mr. President, if even one of the astronauts is alive inside, the nation's going to celebrate. I'm certain the effect on the polls will be positive."

"And if it's empty, or they're dead?"

"We're no worse off than we are now and two days closer to

the election."

"Phong," the President asked, "what about the Russians?"

"As far as we know, Mr. President, they also perished. Their spacecraft is still transmitting telemetry but there hasn't been a voice message for about eighteen hours."

"Incredible!" the President muttered. "How could such a thing happen?"

Nguyen leaned forward and placed his hands on the table. "Extremely unusual meteor shower. Unlike anything we've ever seen before. It's the only explanation."

"Shouldn't we have protected the astronauts?"

"Their suits were designed to absorb impacts from small meteoroids, the sort we encounter occasionally during Shuttle operations. So was the spacecraft. The ones that killed them must have been much larger, something very rare."

"And the first cosmonaut who died? What happened to him?"

"An accident, trying to right their spacecraft."

Torres raised his eyes, looking toward the oil painting on the opposite wall but not seeing it. After a short while, he said, "Marty, I agree with you. The truth is, we still don't know for certain whether or not the astronauts are dead, and we owe it to the American people to be straight about this. I'm going to continue asking for their prayers, telling them we must all keep hoping for a favorable outcome while realizing the awful potential for tragedy."

"That sounds excellent, Mr. President," Herrera responded, clearly pleased. "I did have one other idea."

"Yes?"

"Dr. Nguyen, how long could the cosmonauts survive in their spacecraft?"

"They were supposed to ride back inside the descent module, so I presume it has at least a few days of life-support."

"Mr. President, I wonder if we could feed that information to the media—give them a picture of the two cosmonauts, slowly dying inside their spacecraft. Might divert attention away from our own problems."

The President's head twitched in a barely detectable nod. "That's a thought, Marty. That's a thought. But not for this evening's news conference. Let's keep it until we really need it."

**Artemis**

"Blast!" Brandt cursed to himself. "Just too close." He scanned the numbers one more time to be sure.

"Trouble?" Svetlana asked.

"Nothing new. Short of propellant. If we have to make a course correction, we won't be able to enter earth orbit after the aerobraking. I'll have to go outside. Dump some more stuff."

"That is a problem. I have no life-support."

"I know. You'll have to get by on what we can trap inside your suit while I get through the hatch, then close up and repressurize."

"And when you finish?"

"Put your helmet on, open the hatch and let me in. Should have enough time before the carbon dioxide in your suit becomes critical."

"You'll have to teach me the procedures for the hatch and the pressure control."

"I won't leave until I'm sure you're proficient. You can bet on it!"

"Bet on it?"

Brandt muttered, "I'll explain later," then returned to the display, scanning system components in the unpressurized areas of Artemis.

"Dang," he thought, "we need most of this stuff. Except for things I can't get loose in the time I've got. Oh yeah. Need to check the backpack. Might be able to fix the leak.

"Let's see. Fuel cell. Check the weight. Worth trying." He displayed the installation drawing. "Have to cut the tubing. Valve everything off. Check mechanical. Piece of cake. Just slips into the retainer.

"What else?" He looked at the list of weights. "Could pull a battery. Means cutting the current to nearly nothing if the other fuel cells drop out. What the heck? Almost nothing left in the spacecraft. Have to do it."

He continued the hunt. "Pickings getting lean. Could pull a set of fuel-cell tanks. Dang. Don't hardly weigh anything."

Then he remembered the cooling pump. "Geez! Have to chop the cable to that thing. Could drain the fuel cells in a big hurry."

"Okay. Let's think it through." Brandt envisioned each step of the upcoming EVA, every motion, every piece of equipment. The few tools he'd saved for the cooling pump repair would have to suffice. "All right," he said to himself. "Think I've got it."

He turned to his passenger. "Colonel Zosimova, I'd like to go through the procedures now."

Even with the minor language barriers, it took only fifteen minutes for Brandt to feel confident in her ability. "No doubt about it," he thought, "she really knows spacecraft. And she absorbs information like a sponge."

Finished with the lessons, he told her, "I'm going to check a problem in my EMU. While I'm doing that, I'd like you to get your suit on."

"Very well," she replied.

He went forward with her, retrieved the upper-torso section with its backpack and returned to examine the oxygen system. After connecting it to the spacecraft's supply and partially filling the tanks, he smeared saliva on the flow path. It didn't take long to find the problem, a tiny crack in the connection between the Portable Life Support System shear panel and the primary oxygen regulator assembly. He had none of the tools needed to repair it.

"Doesn't look like it'll get worse in the time I'll be outside," he thought. "Just watch for the low-level warning and then beat it back."

Svetlana returned from the nose wearing her butchered spacesuit and carrying her helmet and gloves. "I'll pump the suit through the glove connection before you drop the pressure," she said.

"Good idea," Brandt replied as he sealed the back of her suit, wondering how she'd do it.

He pushed himself through the passageway, holding the torso section in front of him, exchanged his comfortable clothing for the undergarment and donned the EMU.

After he returned to his couch and plugged himself into the umbilical, he told her, "Have to fill my oxygen tanks. Takes a few minutes." She nodded and looked out the right-side window.

"That's about it," he said to himself when the tank pressure reached the full value.

He turned toward her. "Time to get ready."

She put on her helmet and left glove, then blocked as much of the right-glove's wrist opening as possible. After taking several deep breaths, exhaling fully each time, she puffed rapidly into the sleeve. He suit expanded noticeably.

"Pretty clever," Brandt thought as he watched.

After slapping the second glove into place, she nodded her head vigorously.

Brandt started to vent the oxygen. He looked over at the cosmonaut. Her suit had inflated against the dropping pressure. "Guess the crimped tubes are holding," he said to himself. "My God, what an abortion this turned out to be."

When the pressure had dropped to a safe level, he opened the hatch and moved into space. Even before he'd attached his tether, she'd closed the hatch behind him. He watched through the window as she entered the commands needed to refill the spacecraft, then saw her suit slacken as the pressure equalized. She waved her hand as she removed her helmet.

He moved rapidly toward the base of the spacecraft, to an area between the crew compartment and the propellant tanks where the electrical power systems were located. When he was sure he had the right segment, he went to work with a torqueless driver, releasing the fittings that held the cover in place. Even with the spacecraft oriented to provide direct sunlight, he had trouble fitting the tool to the fastener heads. They were at the bottom of small holes cut in the thermal protection.

When he felt the last fastener release, he slipped the tool back into a cloth caddy attached to his chest. Then he pushed his index fingers into the access holes and tried to remove the cover. Nothing moved.

He slid the cutter blade into the crack between sections of thermal-protection material, and gently pried. Certain he'd seen something move, he replaced the saw and again tried to remove the cover. This time it worked.

"That's step one," he whispered as he eased the cover away from the spacecraft. To keep it from drifting off, he clipped one end of a tether to its edge and the other end to a ring on his waist.

Peering into the equipment bay, he spotted his first target, one of three rectangular fuel cells. To release it, he would have to cut through its power cable, gas supply lines, and thin mounting braces. He started with the most dangerous item.

Touching the power cable to its grounding bus would produce enough of an arc to burn a hole in his glove. He sliced through it and bent it back to prevent the bare end from shorting.

Next, he cut through the thin metal tubes that carried oxygen and hydrogen to the device. Upstream valves, which he had previously closed, prevented the gases from leaking out.

Finally, he attacked the composite structure that held the fuel cell in place, using the saw to cut through the thin flanges. Certain he'd severed all connections, he popped the saw into its holder and began to work the fuel cell from the bay.

Except for having to bend the cable out of the way, he got through the operation without a hitch. He gently pushed the mass away from the spacecraft. Like everything else being removed, it would burn up in the earth's atmosphere.

Replacing the cover went quickly and in a matter of minutes he'd started the second task.

Brandt found excising the number-two battery from its bay no more difficult than his first endeavor. "Getting the hang of this now," he said to himself. "Might have a whole new career here. Sawing up spacecraft and dumping the pieces."

With the battery distancing itself from Artemis, he replaced the cover and addressed his third task. As planned, the spacecraft had rotated enough to move the cooling-system bay into the sun.

It took a bit more prying to free the third cover but the work involved only cutting the wires that brought current to the errant pump. The saw took care of the matter and Brandt again folded the wire ends back for safety. Finished, he replaced the cover.

Although he'd been outside only an hour, Brandt's display showed that his oxygen supply would be exhausted in a few more minutes. He pulled himself back toward the crew compartment and peered through the window.

Svetlana had been watching for him. She immediately donned her helmet, went through the suit-filling procedure, clamped her glove on and vented the spacecraft. Brandt couldn't see the pressure reading on the center display but the process seemed to be taking longer than usual. He checked his oxygen. "Down to ten minutes," he told himself.

Finally, he saw her enter the command to release the hatch. She moved toward him to push it open. Brandt watched her struggle, much as Brian had at Marshall.

"Blast!" Brandt scolded himself. "Should have made her open it the last time—given her some practice." He motioned to her through the window and tried to indicate how she could get a bit more leverage. She seemed to understand.

Working feverishly, she went through the procedure again, putting as much force as possible on the hatch. It refused to open.

He pointed toward the center, hoping she knew about the manual release. Immediately, she reached down and seemed to be trying to rotate the lever.

"Gotta help her," Brandt thought, although he knew he could do little without having something to brace himself against. He pounded on the window to get her attention, then rhythmically slapped, *one, two, THREE; one, two, THREE.* He grabbed the external release, tried to get some friction by pressing his other hand against the hatch, and kicked the side of the spacecraft, *one, two, THREE.*

With perfect timing, she moved the handle in unison with him. The hatch flew open. Startled, he let go and began to drift away. He grabbed the tether and reeled himself in to stop the motion, then dove into the spacecraft and shut the hatch.

As soon as he found a handhold, he pushed himself to the panel-mounted trackball and started the repressurization.

Brandt checked his oxygen quantity. It read zero. He looked at the Russian and saw her eyes fluttering rapidly. The pressure seemed to creep upward. He felt panicked and wanted to pull off his helmet but the pressure hadn't reached a safe level.

He waited until the display showed 150 kilopascals, then vented the EMU and pulled off his helmet and gloves. His head swam from the effects of carbon dioxide and low pressure. Forcing himself to think, he remembered his passenger.

She appeared to be unconscious. He pulled off her helmet but couldn't tell if she was breathing. Turning her over, he ripped apart the fasteners and tore open the seals on the back of her suit. After throwing off the top of his EMU, he reached through her suit opening and worked his arms around her chest and under her diaphragm.

"Oh God," he cried to himself, "I can't let her die too! Squeeze. Relax. Squeeze. Relax." He forced the oxygen into her lungs. "Squeeze. Relax." She began to gasp and choke. He continued until her breathing seemed assured, then pulled his hands out. He panted to himself, "Okay! She seems okay!"

After pulling off the rest of his suit, he tried to calm down, but his heart continued to pound. He floated in the center of the cockpit, watching her, wondering why he cared so desperately that she should live.

Moaning softly, Svetlana gradually reacted to her surroundings. She looked over at Brandt. "Close call, as you say."

"Too close. How are you feeling?"

"Head is spinning. Eyes hurt. Feel I might get sick."

"That'll pass as you get rid of the carbon dioxide. Let me know when you want to get out of the suit. I'll give you a hand."

"Now. Get me out now," she said weakly.

Brandt held the ends of the sleeves while she worked her arms and head out. She managed the rest by herself, but immediately returned to her couch, holding her head.

"Headache?" Brandt asked.

"Yes," she answered. "Do you have something?"

"Sorry. Dumped the medical kit." Then he remembered. "Hold on a second."

He went forward, retrieved his trousers, reached into the thigh pocket and removed the folded piece of paper. He selected two pills, refolded the paper and returned it to the pocket. After filling a water pouch, he glided back to the cockpit.

"Try these," he said, handing her the tablet.

She swallowed them but pushed away the water. "Not now," she said, sounding nauseous. "Maybe later." Then squinting at the display, she asked, "You finished the work?"

"Removed a fuel cell and a battery."

"Is that enough?" she asked.

"Gives us a small amount of propellant for course corrections."

"That's good," she sighed. Then, hesitantly, she said, "You helped me breathe, yes?"

"Yes."

"You are a good man, Colonel Strickland."

**Johnson Space Center**

Quang Doan, the lead controller for instrumentation and communication, spread a long graph across the table. "Okay, Brian. Here's the complete time history of the weight from touchdown to the loss of telemetry."

Brian, along with the other six people in the small support room, leaned over the strip of graph paper as the analyst pointed out the events.

"As you see, nothing changes until here." Doan pointed to an obvious drop in weight. "This is Yang stepping to the surface. And this is Wilkins. Those changes give us reliable markers for identifying them later."

He moved down the chart to the beginning of a gradual decrease. "This is where they start to lose hydrazine. Coincides exactly with the readings from the tank. Continues at about this rate for quite a while.

"Now here's Yang getting back on, so we know he wasn't killed. Then Wilkins gets on. At this point, we're back where we started.

"The next part matches their attempts to control the hydrazine leak. Here's where they increase the helium pressure. Leak rate increases. Here's where they vent. Leak stops. That pinpoints the location of the hole in the tank."

Pointing to the next drop, he said, "Then Wilkins leaves."

Moving his finger to a smaller drop, he explained, "Next change is the JPL experiment being offloaded. Weight matches exactly and it's a logical thing for the crew to do. Then there's this change which doesn't match any of the others so it must be Strickland leaving. That means Yang's still aboard, possibly because he's injured.

"Finally, we have Strickland returning, and that's it for the telemetry."

"Which means someone dumped the telemetry system," Brian concluded. "I think Brandt was trying to decrease the weight."

Ehlers frowned. "Hardly the most probable explanation. More likely it was hit by another meteoroid. Tanya, your turn."

The trajectory specialist dropped a page of printout over the chart.

"These are the results of the latest reconstruction. We're using regression analysis to back out the mass of the vehicle during the ascent burn. Here's the fit." She pointed to a table of values. "As you can see, the residuals are very small."

"Which means," Ehlers interrupted, "the analysis is extremely reliable."

Doan picked up the presentation. "Bottom number is the best-estimate mass. It happens to match the final value measured by the pad sensors less the mass of Strickland and Yang—almost exactly."

Ehlers turned to Brian. "There are a thousand ways these numbers could have ended up disagreeing, but there's only one way they could end up equal. Artemis is empty."

Brian examined the data, moved it to one side, went over the graph, then back to the data, hoping to see something different.

"Doesn't look good," he said with resignation. "But there's

always the chance they dumped equipment to make the Artemis lighter. If they ran trajectory profiles, they'd have determined that the weight would have to be just about what you calculated in order to get back. I'll grant you, it's a stretch, but I don't think we can just write off the possibility."

Ehlers said patronizingly, "Brian, I doubt if there's any way I, or anyone else, can convince you your friends are still on the moon. Right now, I have to give my superiors an unbiased appraisal and, from what I've heard, it seems very unlikely that any of the crew survived. As for NASA's response, we're going to recover the spacecraft in any case, so what we tell the press makes very little difference. Now, we have to get on with the job and quit wasting time on speculation that doesn't go anywhere."

Nodding his head, Brian replied, "Guess you're right."

## Chapter 19

# A Joint Operation

**The White House**

"Mr. President," Herrera said, "they're ripping us to shreds. The way we're dropping, the election's a tossup at best."

Pushing away from his enormous pecan desk, the President turned around and looked through the tall, paned window out across the west lawn. The backlit silhouettes of leafless trees framed by the somber drapes of the oval office created a surreal mural. It deepened his depression.

He turned to face his Chief of Staff. "What do we do, Marty?"

"Get it off the front page. Redirect the story. Lower the level of interest."

The President replied grimly, "Won't happen until they recover the spaceship."

Nodding, Herrera said, "I'm afraid you're right, Mr. President. We'll have three days to repair the damage."

"More like two. The day after it gets back, the media will be filled with Shuttle activities. And heaven help us if one of the astronauts is inside—dead or alive."

"Speaking of which, isn't Nguyen supposed to give us an update?"

"He's waiting outside."

Torres picked up a telephone and told his secretary they were ready for the NASA Administrator, then stepped around his desk to the small meeting area. Greetings were abbreviated to quick handshakes as the three took their seats.

Herrera began, "Your report says NASA is certain there's no one on board, is that right?"

Looking at the floor, Phong replied, "That appears to be the case."

Torres' head sagged. "Terrible," he mumbled. "Lost all three of them." Looking up, he asked, "There's really no hope?"

His lips pressed together in thin line, the Administrator seemed reluctant to reply. After a moment, he said, "Mr. President, the astronaut who's been CapCom for most of the mission believes the crew might have removed equipment from Artemis, trying to make it lighter so they'd have enough fuel to get back."

Herrera asked, "Is that possible?"

"They might have done something like that. But removing just enough equipment to match their own weight? That's extremely unlikely."

"See what you mean," Torres sighed.

"Mr. President," Herrera interrupted, "much as I hate to say it, I think this may be what we've been looking for."

Sounding irritated, Torres replied, "Don't follow you, Marty. On top of everything else, we'll have to backtrack on our story. Not only are we stuck with the tragedy, we end up looking as if we don't know what we're talking about."

"We'll handle that, Mr. President. Get statements from NASA saying they couldn't be sure until they'd analyzed all the data. Basically the truth. But once that's over and everyone accepts that the astronauts are dead, we get our chance to bombard the opposition. Blame them for forcing the operation down our throats. Announce a thorough investigation. Even encourage Congress to investigate."

"That's going to help us?"

"Absolutely! It'll put the campaign back on the front page. The astronaut stories will drop down to interviews with families, background stories. Stuff nobody cares about."

The NASA Administrator shuffled through some papers he'd brought with him, obviously uncomfortable with the politics.

After pondering Herrera's comments, Torres responded, "You may have something there, Marty."

Then, turning to Nguyen, he said, "Phong, I'm very saddened

by the information, but I want you to know how much I appreciate the sacrifices the NASA people are making to keep on top of this. Thank you for coming by."

After getting up and heading toward the door, Nguyen stopped. "Mr. President, before I go there's another problem I should tell you about."

Torres scowled. "Does this ever end?"

"Mr. President, if Artemis continues on its present course, it will enter the atmosphere at too steep an angle to allow recovery."

"We're going to lose the spacecraft? All things considered, that doesn't sound very serious."

"I'm afraid it's a bit more complicated. You see, with its thermal protection, there's a very good chance Artemis will survive to impact."

"It'll hit the ground!" Herrera exclaimed. "Where?"

"We don't know exactly. We've never evaluated a complete reentry so we're not sure what path it will take. In fact, it may break up somewhere along the way. This makes the analysis extremely difficult. However, most of the final path will be over Australia. There's a very high probability it will land in an uninhabited area."

"Australia?" Torres jumped in his chair.

"Much of which is desert. Virtually unpopulated. There's a good chance the impact will do no damage whatsoever."

"But you can't be certain of that," Torres responded.

"Not at this time. We've got a team of analysts at Johnson conducting detailed simulations. I hope to have some results in a few hours. I'll inform you immediately."

Herrera opened the door for the Administrator, then returned to the peach love seat.

"Jesus, Marty," Torres fumed, "we barely get our noses above water when these SOBs hit us with another kidney punch. What the hell are we going to about this one?"

"Can't act yet, obviously. Wouldn't know who to warn even if we wanted to. Trouble is, I think Phong was playing it down. Might be worse than he said."

**Artemis**

"Food bars. Almond crunch or granola raisin. Canned pineapple or apple drink. Chewy sweet roll. Looks like that's it for breakfast." Brandt held up the food packages for the cosmonaut to see.

"Thank you, Colonel Strickland," Svetlana replied, sounding rather formal. "I'll take this one." She selected the granola bar. "And an apple drink."

"Have to apologize for the food," Brandt said as he squeezed his drink container. "Didn't have time to choose things that would go together."

Her teeth sticking together, she mumbled, "Food bar is good. Better than on Mir. It is not a problem."

Chuckling, Brandt replied, "Not compared to the other things we've got to worry about. Wish I knew where we are."

"When will we do the course correction?" she asked, still chewing.

"Won't know until we pick up GPS signals. Briefings at Johnson said maybe thirty thousand miles out. But the accuracy will be poor until we get closer."

"So we wait until one hour before entering the atmosphere?"

"May want to wait even longer. I've set up a program to do propellant-consumption optimizations. Problem's really complicated because if we enter wrong, we'll use more fuel steering the ship through the aerobraking. On the other hand, if we wait for good signals we may need a larger course correction."

"It is risky either way."

"To say the least. It's possible we simply don't have the propellant needed to get into orbit. The whole exercise may be a waste of time."

"But we hope it works, yes?"

Brandt shrugged his shoulders. Her unfounded optimism brought back the turmoil and pain, the feeling of emptiness and failure he'd been able to suppress only for brief intervals. He said with resignation, "Frankly, I don't much care. I'm not sure it's worth going on."

Looking into his eyes, she rebuked him, "That is—how you say?—self indulgent. You must accept responsibility. Deal with the situation. Giving up is not acceptable."

Her simplistic lecture didn't help. After a period of silence he asked her, "Do you believe in fate?"

"You mean that things are already decided?"

"Yes."

"It is foolish. An excuse for mistakes."

"I'd always thought so—until Darrell died. Now I wonder."

"It is silly," she huffed.

"You know I saved his life during the Chad war? No way he could have gotten out alive from where he went down. And it ends up that I have to..." He choked. "...to kill him."

"You did not tell me."

"Had to. He broke his back. Fell off the ladder. In terrible pain. Couldn't let him suffer until he ran out of oxygen. Dropped his suit pressure until he passed out." Brandt mouthed the words, trying to convince himself he had no choice, but it only rekindled his doubts.

"You did the right thing. Could not have saved him a second time."

"But that's the point, don't you see? It's as if, by saving him the first time, I'd cheated fate. And now it's all come around. I ended up having to carry out fate's plan myself. My punishment for interfering." His emotions taking control, Brandt sobbed openly.

"I'm sorry. Can't get it out of my mind—the picture of him dying there. Darrell and I—we were more than good friends. Went through the war together. Worked on Super Shuttle. He had so much going for him. In love with a wonderful woman. Planned to get married when he got back."

Svetlana listened sympathetically. "I heard about the rescue in Chad. Thought it was propaganda. I see why you might think you are destined to do something. But it is foolishness. These things—they come from bad decisions. Fate has nothing to do with it."

After a while, she said, "I told you I also lost a good friend."

"Ippolitov. Yes."

"We went through the Moscow Aviation Institute together. Became very close. Worked together for many years. Spent months together in Mir. Many times he kept me from making mistakes. Always patient, sensible. He was great man, maybe the best cosmonaut ever."

"Were you lovers?"

Svetlana laughed loudly at the suggestion. "Me and Vadim? It is funny. He was a very devoted family person. Loved his wife very much. Also his daughter. He told me on the moon that, if he died there, he will miss most his daughter." She turned away, muttering something in Russian. Brandt thought he could hear her stifled sobs, tiny cries of despair from someone unaccustomed to showing any sign of human weakness.

"I'm sorry," Brandt apologized. "Don't know why I asked you

that. Knew you were divorced so it seemed logical."

Back under control, Svetlana replied, "It is all right. Your wife. I read she is dead."

Brandt looked out the porthole at the star-filled blackness. "Yes. Perhaps another act of fate. I killed her too."

"You killed your wife?"

"Traffic accident. Driving on a two-lane road approaching the top of a hill." Brandt hesitated, afraid to relive what he had long suppressed.

"Car came right at us, in our lane. Don't know why I did it. Should have gone right, into the ditch. But I went left. Tried to go around him on the other side. He reacted at exactly the same time. Hit us head on—in his lane."

Brandt stopped, mentally envisioning the nightmare, feeling the panic, the terror.

"The sound of the crash. It was terrible. Then the air bag exploded in front of me. Couldn't hear anything afterward. Everything was absolutely quiet. I remember yelling Nancy. Looked over and there she was. Sitting straight up in her seat. Funny smile on her face. Eyes wide open. Peaceful. I said to myself, `Thank God! She's all right!' Then her head twisted around. Flopped over on her shoulder. Dead. Broken neck."

"It is a terrible thing," Svetlana said quietly, "but not your fault."

"We'd stopped for lunch. Just sandwiches—and beer. Had two beers. Just two beers. But if I'd skipped them, had a coke. Maybe I'd have reacted differently. Been just a hair sharper. Might still have Nancy."

"You torture yourself Colonel Strickland. It is a bad thing."

"I've told myself that ten thousand times. Still can't help feeling the way I do. I loved her so much. We were expecting our first child. All the light went out of my life that day. Just going through the motions ever since."

Svetlana studied his face while expressing in hers a penetrating sense of understanding. "I say you must forgive yourself. But I have the same trouble. Too much guilt.

"I did not kill my husband, but I did kill my marriage. He was a fine man, my husband. I think he loved me very much. Also very proud. We had a baby daughter."

After an awkward pause, Brandt asked, "What went wrong?"

As if waiting for the prompt, she answered immediately, "Another man. I was a young cosmonaut, very impressed with the space program. It was a time when Shuttles docked with the first Mir, when all the Mir modules were in place. Russia was having problems, but for a cosmonaut, there were no problems.

"I met a brilliant engineer—manager of Mir module programs. Twenty years older. Very well known. His name is Tsvigun. You might know this name."

"The Space Agency Director?"

"Yes, Tsvigun. We fell in love, but not really in love. More—how do you say?—infatuation. The affair continued for two years. But then, disaster."

"Your husband found out?"

She replied matter-of-factly, "I told him."

"Really? Why?"

"You do not understand the Russian. It is part of our culture. Eventually you must confess wrongdoing. Cannot live any other way. My husband was a good man. Did not deserve my behavior. Besides, I truly loved him."

"And Tsvigun?"

"He told his wife."

"Your husband divorced you?"

"Of course. He was right to do it. Was badly hurt by my actions. Humiliated. But he took my daughter. I did not see her for many years."

"Do you see her now?"

"Only once in a year, perhaps less. She hates me. Sees me only when forced to. She is very bitter. My fault. I feel very bad about this."

"Don't you blame Tsvigun? Sounds as if he seduced you."

"We seduced each other. After it was over, we agreed never to speak of it again. In the moon program, we worked together very closely. Even fought—many times." She chuckled at some of the memories. "But we never spoke of the affair."

"Do you still love him?"

"Very fond of him, but not love. He is dying of cancer. About this I am very sad."

"Strange how it all works out, isn't it? The things that shape our lives most profoundly don't ever seem to be the things we've planned. That's what I meant about fate."

"It is true the way you say it. But we make decisions. Always there is opportunity to choose."

Floating in the cockpit, Brandt tried to sort it all out, to identify the rationality, accept the randomness, find his place. For a moment, everything would seem terribly clear. But the illusion evaporated and he returned to confusion and disorder. Only one thing emerged with any consistency. He'd developed a surprising empathy for a remarkable Russian woman.

**The White House**

As Nguyen droned on, Torres scanned the Situation Room, wondering who he could count on to handle the crisis. "Bunch of second stringers," he thought. "My own fault. Chose every one of them. Political necessities. Didn't think we'd ever face anything like this."

Pointing to the map image on the right screen of the display, Nguyen continued, "At this point in the reentry path, Artemis will experience heating rates far beyond its design specifications. Although the latest simulations predict it will retain structural integrity, there is still reason to hope it will break into several pieces and burn up. If that occurs, the hazard diminishes to routinely accepted levels."

"But, as I understand it," Torres cut in, "you feel the spaceship will most likely stay together, is that right?"

"Yes, Mr. President, that's our best estimate." He returned to the display. "Given that outcome, the potential impact zone includes most of the Brisbane metropolitan area, as you see, although it's more likely to hit further north."

"And when’s the thing supposed to come down?" Herrera asked.

Nguyen took a moment to do the time conversion. "About nine thirty tomorrow night."

"Twenty-two hours?" Torres fumed. He turned to his new Joint Chiefs Chairman, Gen. Eduardo Dominguez. "Ed, you want to try a worst-case scenario?"

"Not much to go on, Mr. President, but given the weight of the vehicle and the impact velocity, you've got something close to a small nuclear weapon. If it impacted in the center of Brisbane—densely populated, worst time of day—it could produce a hundred-thousand casualties."

The President flopped back in his chair and glared at the

NASA Administrator. Then he searched the faces of the other seven people in front of him. Each sat rigid, staring at the table.

"All right," the President barked, "what are we going to do?"

The Secretary of State spoke first. "Mr. President, we have a clear obligation to notify the government of Australia. They must be given every opportunity to protect their population."

The National Security Advisor disagreed. "Pete, that can't possibly do any good and it might well lead to an even worse disaster. What the hell will the Australians do? If they issue warnings, they'll have a panic—millions of people trying to escape from cities, possibly right into the path of the spacecraft."

"Dr. Nguyen," Torres asked, "isn't there anything NASA can do?"

"I'm afraid not, Mr. President," the Administrator replied meekly. "We have no communication with Artemis. No telemetry. No command capability. But there's still a chance the spacecraft's computer will correct the course automatically."

"But you said it should already have done that," Cushman protested.

"Yes, General, but the programmed corrections required normal functioning of the navigation equipment. If it was hit by a meteorite, Artemis might not know its trajectory was incorrect until it got close enough to pick up GPS signals."

"When will that be?" Cushman asked.

"About an hour before entering the atmosphere."

This seemed to make Herrera happier. "So we'll be able to say—honestly say—that we didn't know the spacecraft would reenter until an hour before it hit the ground. Sounds like the justification we need for keeping this quiet."

"Christ!" Torres swore. "Damned if we do, damned if we don't." He noticed that his Secretary of Defense had been quiet throughout the discussion. "Jeff, got any ideas?"

Farrand responded reluctantly, "Possible solution, Mr. President. Long shot with lots of drawbacks."

"Can't be worse than what we've got," Torres responded.

Sounding nervous, Farrand said, "If you'll recall, we've been working on a new interceptor missile to deal with military satellites in geosynchronous orbit. I believe it may have the capability to destroy the spacecraft or at least damage it enough to assure breakup on reentry."

Chan jumped out of his chair. "What the hell is this," he shouted, "an antisatellite weapon? That's a violation of several signed treaties."

"And, as a matter of fact," Torres exclaimed, "I can't recall hearing about it. Sounds like another damned weapons program that someone started behind my back."

"I'm sorry, sir, but I briefed you about this myself," Farrand replied, "more than a year ago. We initiated the development when the CIA uncovered a similar program being conducted by the Federation. To the best of my knowledge, they're still ahead of us. Possibly even operational."

"All right, all right," Torres said, exasperated. "But I want it clearly understood that I will not tolerate having military activities kept from me. I hope I don't have to remind anyone that I'm still the Commander in Chief."

Out of the corner of his eye, Torres noticed Cushman squirm in her seat. He filed it away as a matter for future investigation.

"Jerry," he continued, "what's the status of this thing?"

"Sir, the missile replaces the upper stage of a Minuteman III. Instead of a nuclear warhead, it has a high-performance rocket motor, a sophisticated terminal-guidance system, and a shrapnel-generating kill device. I'm guessing it could do enough damage to the thermal protection to assure that the spacecraft won't survive reentry."

"How many of these things do we have?" Torres asked.

Grimly, Farrand answered, "As far as I know only one, the test article. Because of the treaty problems, we've never been able to fire it."

"Is it ready to use?"

"No sir, I'm afraid not. It's still at the development facility in Tucson."

Torres fumed, "I thought you said it might be the solution."

"Mr. President," Farrand replied, "if we rush, I believe we can get it on top of a Minuteman in time to do the intercept."

Seeing his hesitation, Torres asked, "Then what's the problem?"

"Sir, the only Minuteman IIIs we have available are in alert silos."

"You're telling me we have to fire one of our regular missiles?'

"That's right, Mr. President."

Chan jumped up again. "Mr. President, we can't do that! The Russians and Chinese might think we're launching a weapon. I'm not sure we could keep them from retaliating."

"Not only that, sir," Herrera interjected, "this would mean firing from the middle of the country, over populated areas. If you think we've got media problems now—well, you can just imagine."

Torres got up and started to walk around the table, his eyes aimed at the carpet. Four slow revolutions later, he stopped behind his chair.

"Jerry, round up whatever military people you need and start moving the missile to a Minuteman base. Get as far away from populated areas as possible. Montana! I think we've got missiles there. If it works, use Montana. Be ready to launch on a minute's notice.

"Pete, put together a plan for informing other nations about what we're doing. I want a low-key approach—precautionary action on the outside chance the spaceship screws up. I want a complete package, information tailored to each country.

"Marty, let's get ready for the media. We'll talk more after this meeting. All right, let's get going. I expect none of us will get much sleep tonight."

As the President departed, Cushman approached Herrera.

"Marty," she said, "I need to speak to the President. Right away."

"Linda, I don't think this is a good time," Herrera replied. "I'll be happy to convey any message."

Quickly becoming stone hard, she replied, "I said, Marty, that the Air Force Chief of Staff must confer with the President on a matter of national importance. Is that understood?"

He looked at her quizzically. "Whatever you say, General. Give me a minute."

**The White House**

"Christ, Marty, what the hell do you make of that one?" Torres asked as he leaned back in the large executive chair and rested his feet on the desk blotter.

"Mr. President, as they used to say, it just blows my mind!"

"You know, I'm tempted to trash the whole lot of them. Joint Chiefs, Deputy Chiefs. Down three or four levels."

"Mr. President, once we're through this election, that'll probably be the right thing to do."

"Trouble is, Marty, when they keep even one thing from you, it destroys trust, the trust you need to function. Know what I mean?"

"I do indeed, Mr. President."

"Think there's any importance to those weapons?"

Herrera stopped to think. "Probably not, unless they had something to do with the disaster. If you let your imagination run wild, you can postulate gunfights on the moon. Our guys killing their cosmonauts. Them killing our astronauts. If the right-wing idiots ever got wind of that, we'd be at war with the Federation inside of a week."

"My God, Marty, is there anything else these people can do to hurt the country? I'd like to charge every damned one of them with treason."

"And you'd be justified, Mr. President. But right now, we'd better work on the spacecraft problem."

"Any ideas?"

"This may sound overly optimistic, but I think we can come out ahead on this reentry business."

"Ahead?"

"That's right, sir. Think of it this way. We have a problem, but not of our making. Our spaceship got hit by meteors, for Christ's sake. Now it's hurtling toward earth without a crew, out of control. Once again, we did our job. It's designed to correct for any problems, come back safely and get snagged by the Shuttle. But we're concerned it just might—not much chance, mind you—just might pose a threat to someone on the ground. So what do we do? Courageously, we take the wraps off a one-of-a-kind experimental missile developed to counter possible threats from space. And we use our one-and-only missile to knock out the spacecraft."

Torres managed a half-hearted laugh. "I'll have to admit, Marty, you make it sound pretty good."

"For one thing, Mr. President, it puts an end to the moon crap. Crew's dead. Bandit spacecraft's destroyed. Act of God. Tough luck, but what the hell? On top of that, it discloses a sexy new military gadget. Takes the starch right out of the damned warmongers. See what I mean? Bet it's good for ten points!"

"We'll still have to tell the Russians—and the Chinese. Can't risk nuclear war over this."

"So we tell them. What's the problem?"

"Treaty violations, Marty. They'll wipe the floor with us, especially the Federation. How can we justify the sanctions against them if we're also violating UN agreements?"

"If the Federation tries that, we reveal the information about their system. The hawks will love us for retaliating and our friends will understand that we had no choice."

"They'll just deny it."

"Listen, Mr. President. You know what we ought to do? Contact Stakhanov. Tell him the situation. Exactly what's happening. Tell him we want to use the missile but don't want to get into a pissing contest with the Federation over it. Then ask him to fire one of their missiles at it, timed to arrive just as ours does. Make the destruction of the damned thing a joint effort."

Torres rocked back in his chair, both amused and intrigued. "Why the hell would they agree to anything like that?"

"Because it'll give them the same favorable image I just described. *Russian technology saves world from ultimate calamity!* It's exactly what they need right now."

"And if they say no?"

"We bring out the stick. Tell them if we miss and the spacecraft takes out a city, we'll say we asked for their help and they refused."

Things had moved terribly fast and Torres wasn't quite sure he should trust his instincts, much less his flamboyant Chief of Staff. But he didn't have time to dissect every nuance, either.

"Okay, Marty. Let's say we give it a shot. How do we know the Russians can get something in the air that fast?"

"Jerry said he thought their system was operational, didn't he?"

"Whatever that means. Let's see. Eight thirty in Moscow. Might be able to get Stakhanov. Guess it's time to try the red phone business. At least we'll find out if it works."

He picked up the telephone on the right side of his desk. The special operator answered.

"This is the Kremlin direct line, Mr. President. Do you want me to establish a connection with President Stakhanov?"

"Yes I do, ma'am. Right away."

"Thank you, sir. I'll call back."

Torres returned the handset to its old-fashioned red receiver and looked toward his Chief of Staff.

"Marty, I'm still worried about the astronauts—wondering if it's possible they're still inside the damned thing."

Sounding irritated, Herrera replied, "Mr. President, the best people at NASA say there's no chance."

"Not *no chance*, Marty. They're never that certain."

"You're right, sir. Those people should have been lawyers. But, you know, in light of the weapons, it's probably just as well none of them made it back."

"Be serious, Marty. If there's a chance in a million they're alive, we have to do everything possible to bring them home."

Herrera backpedaled. "Oh, of course, Mr. President. I couldn't agree more. But we have to be realistic, don't we? Nguyen really didn't hold out any hope."

"Certainly not much, Marty. But I remember the business about the spacecraft correcting itself. I wonder if we could wait until after the time that's supposed to happen before we fire the missiles."

"Sir, it sounded to me as if NASA didn't know when that would be. And I assume we'll want to hit the thing as far out as possible."

Torres pushed up his lower lip. "I suppose you're right. Just the same, I want the missiles set so that if the spacecraft does make a correction, they won't hit it. If the Air Force can't do it, then forget the whole thing. I'm not going to risk killing an astronaut."

Herrera hesitated, as if constructing a reply. Then he responded, "Just as you say, Mr. President. I'll take care of it. But what about the Russians?"

Torres responded, "Let me handle them."

Pressing his temples with his palms, Torres said, "I wonder if anyone could find out how the astronauts died. Suppose they were killed by the weapons. Do you think someone with a telescope would be able to see that?"

"Sir, I doubt if even the best telescope would be able to see that much detail. Besides, I heard that the area is dark now and will stay that way until after the election. Don't think we have a problem."

"Marty, I'm looking at the longer term. If anyone ever finds out we armed the astronauts, even if the weapons were never used—or if they find out about our real intentions for the moon—or if, heaven forbid, they discover that one of the astronauts was still alive on the spaceship—well, there'd be one hell of a row. Might get me impeached. I imagine some of our people would end up in prison."

Looking shaken, Herrera replied, "Mr. President, no one's ever going to find out any of that. And even if they did, our hands are clean."

"Not any more, Marty," Torres replied sharply. "Not since Cushman walked through that door. Can't say we never knew about the weapons."

The red telephone sounded its unique buzzing pattern.

"This will certainly be a first, Marty. An American president asking the Russians to help shoot down an American spaceship. Wonder what they'll say—after they regain consciousness."

Herrera looked him in the eye. "Mr. President, I think they'll go for it."

**The White House**

"They want $165 million? Mr. President, that's highway robbery!"

Sounding very tired, Torres replied, "Granted, Ed, but there's not a whole lot we can do about it. Frankly, I'm surprised they agreed to help us at all. Jeff, how are we doing with our missile?"

"Mr. President, it arrived at Malmstrom an hour ago. We've got a video link to the silo site."

Torres had managed to get a few hours of sleep, but it hadn't done much for his acidulous stomach or tension-numbed brain. He raised his eyebrows, as if trying to get his eyes opened all the way. "Okay, Larry, let's take a look."

The National Security Advisor walked to the display system and punched in a code number. Immediately, the right screen lit up with a pre-dawn view of the denuded flatlands east of Great Falls. In the foreground, the massive concrete covers of a Minuteman silo had been pulled to the side and a large crane hovered over the opening. As they watched, the cylindrical shape of a missile stage emerged from its underground lair.

" Colonel McCallister, this is the White House," Chambers said, addressing the display panel. "How's it going?"

A frigid-looking officer appeared in front of the scene. "Sir, we completed warhead removal and storage at 0345. At this time, we're pulling out the third stage. Soon as that's finished, we'll be ready to mount the ASM. Expect to have the missile ready by ten hundred hours."

Chambers seemed quite pleased. "That gives you twelve hours to spare."

"Not hardly, sir," the colonel's voice replied. "We haven't been able to generate the trajectory files for the mission. Still waiting to get a track file for the target so we can project a launch path. We're not set up to do intercepts, so we have to fool the bird into thinking it's going for a surface target. That'll take care of the guidance for the first two stages. After that, it's up to the ASM."

Chambers asked, "Do you foresee any problems?"

"No, sir. Sets up like a routine launch, except for the problem of the first and second stages. Modified the trajectory slightly to assure impacts in isolated areas. Crews are on the way to take care of the recoveries."

Chambers discontinued the transmission and verified that nothing else would leave the Situation Room.

"All right," Torres said, "that seems to be going as planned. Marty, what're we getting from the press?"

"Surprisingly supportive, Mr. President. The tone of the stories has changed abruptly, accepting the meteorite explanation, painting it as a tragedy, plain and simple. Almost as if they can't think of anybody to blame. How's that for a change?"

"A welcome one," Torres said dryly.

"The attention seems to be shifting away from the moon mission toward the spacecraft," Herrera continued. "Lots of dramatic headlines. *Out of Control Spaceship Plunges Toward Earth.* But nothing that will panic anybody. They seem to have accepted NASA's latest predictions that it'll impact near New Caledonia—and who the hell cares about New Caledonia?"

"New Caledonians, I presume," Chan replied coldly.

"What about Montana?" Torres asked. "Anyone protesting?"

"Hardly a whimper," Herrera replied. "Remember, Mr. President, that's red-white-and-blue country. And lots of the locals work at the base. They're probably looking forward to the fireworks."

"Let's hope so," Torres responded. "Peter, how's the rest of the world taking it?"

"About as expected, Mr. President," the Secretary of State replied. "Having the Federation on board certainly helps."

"Australians?"

"Officially, they bought our story about the spacecraft overshooting the country and ending up in Pacific. I'm sure their analysts produced the same impact predictions we first got from NASA, but the government probably figured that if they sound the alarm they'll do more harm than good."

Torres addressed the Air Force Chief of Staff. "General Cushman, what are we doing to ensure that the missiles arrive at the same time?"

"Sir, we'll be launching about forty-five minutes after the Russians. Their missile will go into orbit, fly half-way around the world, then fire again somewhere west of South America to accelerate toward the spacecraft. We'll know exactly where it is at all times, but to coordinate the intercepts we'll need the transit time from when it leaves orbit to the point of impact. I'm not sure the Russians will tell us."

Becoming angry, Torres snapped, "Why not? We're paying for it!"

"It gives away too much information. Tells us how they plan to use the system."

"That's unacceptable!" Torres declared. "It's imperative that the missiles arrive together. We can't have arguments about who actually destroyed the damned thing, whether this turns out well or otherwise."

"Yes, sir," Cushman replied. "I'll try to coordinate the operations through military channels, but it may take pressure from higher up."

"If it does, you'll have it," the President promised.

**Artemis**

"Trajectory is still good?" Svetlana asked as she watched Brandt studying the latest projections.

He cleared the screen, returning the display to the systems-monitoring program.

"No significant change. Calling for a small course correction. Think I'll override it."

"You worry about the navigation, yes?"

"That's right. All the computer's telling us is that its own calculations are accurate. If we let it complete the course correction, we may end up worse off, not better."

"Still a long time before we receive the satellite signals?"

"Could be ten hours. No use worrying about it now."

His depression returning, Brandt rambled on. "Never felt this way before. As if everything I've ever done was wrong. Disaster on the moon. Entirely my fault. Demanded we land near you. Try a rescue. Darrell and Andy tried to stop me. Just arrogance. Thought I knew best. Maybe I'm really no good. Hard for me. Admitting I could be so wrong. Always been so sure of myself. Don't know what I'll do now."

After a while, Svetlana said quietly, "It is same for me, Colonel Strickland. Always I am confident of my ability. I know it is unsafe to land the spacecraft, but I want to be a hero. I could have refused. Saved Vadim and Mikhail. Now I can never again be a cosmonaut. I think maybe now I have dreams like your dream. Cannot forget seeing Mikhail and Vadim. Poor Vadim. How I am going to face Natalya, his wife? I can never go back." Her voice trailed off.

Brandt moved toward her and gently took her hand. For a while, she didn't move. Then she rolled herself toward him. Instinctively, he put his arms around her, carefully, tenderly, and felt hers encircle him. He buried his face in the hollow of her neck and she pressed her head against his chest. Desperately needing solace, he tightened his embrace. She pulled him closer.

Cautiously, she drew her head back so she could see him, then softly stroked his face as she studied it. Speaking not a word, she ran her fingers through his rumpled hair, gently, as a mother would a child.

Brandt looked into her tear-filled eyes and saw in them the same dreadful pain that tore at his heart. Her short, gray-streaked blond hair floated out from her face, framing her angular features with a wispy halo. He carefully brushed the tears from her cheek with his finger, then placed his hand behind her head and pressed it to his chest.

He felt her lift the bottom of his shirt and slide her hand beneath it. She caressed his back, using her strong fingers to ease the tension in his muscles. He let his mind wander so his body could drink in the dreamy sensation.

He eased up her loose-fitting shirt and stroked her back with both hands, then reached to grasp her shoulders, softly massaging the firm bands of muscle. She moved with his touch, slowly rolling her neck into his fingers.

Her hands drifted to the small of his back, then to his hips. More and more, he gave in to the feeling, trying to blot the agonies from his mind. He barely noticed as she slid the clothing from his thighs.

As she guided him into her, he closed his eyes and buried his face. Lost in her arms, he moved slowly, easily, rolling, spinning, undulating in the tiny weightless world. Tears flowing from his eyes, he whispered, "Nancy, Nancy."

The ecstasy mounted to a peak of rapture, a surging expulsion of all the pain, all the torment. She pressed his head to her breast, her fingers tensing as she whispered something in Russian, then "Natasha, Natasha."

She gently rolled away from him, taking his hand. He touched the spacecraft to stop their motion and floated next to her, wishing he could forever prolong the delirium. Turning his head, he saw her face, tear-streaked but peaceful, the anguish all but dissolved. She looked at him, smiled and pressed her fingertips into his palm.

**The White House**

At the end of his patience, Torres raged, "Would someone please explain what this argument is about?"

"Mr. President," Farrand said, "this is another example of the Federation's commitment to enhancing their military capabilities and the consequences of our failure to keep pace."

Torres glared at him. "Right now, Jeff, I don't give a damn. What's important is that their missile's on the way."

Chagrinned, Farrand replied, "Yes, sir. Of course."

The President snorted and turned to his Chief of Staff. "Marty, any word from Montana?"

"They're ready to launch, Mr. President. Just waiting for the data from the Federation's Flight Control Center. Should come any minute."

"What happens if we don't get it?" Torres asked.

"We'll launch on our tracking data. We've known the position of their missile since it lifted off from Baikonur."

"Then we'll arrive at the same time anyway," the President surmised.

The JCS Chairman replied, "Only if we estimate their trajectory correctly, sir."

The left display showed Col. McCallister walking to the podium of a small briefing room. "This could be it," Cushman announced, quieting the discussion.

"All right, people," the colonel began, "we just got the intercept time from the Russians. We have exactly six minutes to get the bird away. I have launch approval from the President and the codes have been delivered to the launch team. Is there any reason why this mission should not proceed?"

The room remained silent.

"Okay. Let's get the job done."

"Sounds like they've got everything under control," Torres said. "Good work, General Cushman. When this is over, I'd like some recommendations for presidential citations."

Sounding surprised, Cushman replied, "Of course, Mr. President. It will be my pleasure."

"Sir, I've got the Air Force camera on the right screen showing the silo. We'll see the missile leave, but nothing afterward."

"Larry," Herrera interrupted, "the local TV stations are putting up helicopters to cover the launch. We'll probably get the best view watching commercial channels."

"Worth a try," Chambers replied as he punched the necessary instructions into the control console.

On the left screen, a reporter appeared, dressed in a striking blue-and-silver gown. She stood in front of a large group of people, many of them wearing party hats and sipping from champagne glasses.

"We're here in the penthouse ballroom of the new Riverfront Hotel," she sparkled, "waiting for the big event that will highlight this gala celebration."

"Christ!" Torres exclaimed. "They're making a party out of it!"

"Happening all over Great Falls, Mr. President. And it's getting nationwide coverage. Big plus for the election."

"I've just been told that the missile will go up in one minute," the reporter announced. The camera swept around to show people crowding toward the wall of picture windows. "Hal," she asked, "are we ready for the roof cameras?"

"We're already getting the feeds, Marla," a male voice answered. "Just a few more seconds."

The picture changed to a view of the lights from the east side of Great Falls with darkness beyond.

Suddenly, the right screen exploded with a flash of light followed by a blast of orange flame jutting from either side of the silo. Almost immediately, a missile shot upward and the screen filled with its bright exhaust.

On the other display, an orange spot appeared and the camera zoomed in to catch the Minuteman leaping into the air, accelerating rapidly on a tongue of brilliant flame. Seconds later, it entered a cloud layer, turning it into an iridescent umbrella.

The scene switched to a view above the clouds. The news helicopter's camera caught the missile as it emerged, streaking upward into the star-filled sky. Then the show was over.

Cushman called to Chambers, "Need to bring up Cheyenne Mountain."

"Right, General," he mumbled as he entered the commands.

On the right display, the scene changed to show a room that looked like a small launch-control facility with four screens covering the front wall and two rows of consoles, each equipped with four computer monitors. The left-center screen showed a map of the Unites States with a bright white marker moving across the northern tier.

"General Cushman," Chambers said as he walked away from the displays, "perhaps you'd better handle this."

She pushed away from the table, walked to the display control and spoke into its built-in microphone.

"Cheyenne Mountain, this is General Cushman. Do you read?"

"Roger, ma'am," a deep voice answered. "This is General Brown. We have good track on the vehicle from two satellites. First-stage separation occurred exactly as predicted. We should have second-stage separation in four seconds."

"Good so far," Cushman said. "Advise on ASM ignition."

"Happened while you were talking, ma'am. First stage impacted approximately one-quarter mile northeast of the predicted point and the second stage appears to be heading a bit northeast as well. Looks like the winds were off just a tad."

"That's fine, Duane. Keeps us within the cleared area."

A blue X appeared on the right-hand display's map of the northern states. The white line continued to extend eastward.

"Getting the first track file on the ASM, ma'am," Brown's voice boomed. "It's right on course."

"That's good," Cushman replied. "We'd like a reading on its coordination with the Federation missile as soon as possible."

"Yes, ma'am. Should be coming right up. Data show no chance of ASM impact on land."

"Glad to hear it. What about the second stage?"

"Getting the report now, ma'am. First estimate puts it about half-a-mile northeast."

Cushman turned around to face Torres. "Mr. President, the

operation poses no threat to people or property."

"Excellent, General Cushman, excellent!" he replied. "Marty, let's shade the press coverage to emphasize how this was accomplished without endangering any of our citizens."

"General Cushman," Brown's voice called, "second-stage impact point confirmed and we detect burnout of the ASM. Intercept estimate should be coming right up."

Moments later, Brown informed them, "Tracking data predict we'll arrive at the designated point 1.1 seconds after the Federation missile."

Cushman turned around. "Mr. President, at this time I can report that the missile launch was entirely successful. Only the actual detonation of the warhead remains uncertain."

Torres narrowed his eyes. "And when will we know the outcome of that?"

"Intercept will be at twenty one past the hour, as stated earlier."

"And then we'll know if the spaceship's destroyed?"

"Our tracking systems should be able to detect any changes in its trajectory caused by the warheads but there'll be no way to ascertain the extent of the damage they've caused or whether it will affect the reentry."

"You mean to tell me that despite all this we still won't know whether Brisbane will be destroyed until just before it happens?"

"Probably about fifteen minutes before, sir. When the reentry begins.

"Good God!" Torres sighed.

**Artemis**

"Want anything else?" Brandt asked as he began to stow the few remaining items.

"If you have a drink, yes," Svetlana answered.

Brandt added water to the last two grape-drink pouches, shook them up and handed her one. After breaking the seal on his, he took a sip and looked around the front of the spaceship, wondering how he managed to remove so much equipment in such a short time. "Motivation, I guess," he thought to himself.

"Colonel Strickland," Svetlana said hesitantly, "I must apologize for my behavior."

"What?" he asked, not grasping what she referred to.

"Last night. It is my responsibility. I apologize."

He took her free hand and pressed it gently. "Colonel... Oh, this is ridiculous. Call me Brandt—Svetlana."

"I like it. Sounds good to a Russian."

"I needed you last night. And you helped me. That's all there is to it."

"I needed you also," she said, speaking barely above a whisper as she squeezed his hand. I am afraid. For the first time."

Brandt looked into her eyes, the palest blue. He first thought of them as cold, even hard. Now they seemed frightened, perhaps sad. He explored her face, its skin so tight she had hardly a sign of the bloated appearance that went with days of weightlessness. Her high cheekbones and sharp features made her look strong, even striking in a way, surprising considering the lack of makeup. Tiny wrinkles at the corners of her eyes only hinted at her age. He had to accept it, the remarkable fact that he'd come to love this woman. As a comrade. As he'd loved Darrell.

"Svetlana, from what you've told me, I don't believe you should return to the Federation."

Her expression turned curious. "How is this possible? Where can I go?"

"Stay in the United States. Join me doing lectures, interviews. Let the American press make you a celebrity. Protect you from the Federation. When it's safe, you can return."

"Your government would allow this?"

"I'm sure you could get a visa. Probably stay for years with it."

"This lecturing. My English is not very good."

"Your English is fine. Most people will find your accent charming. Please think about what I've said. Why risk your life if you don't have to?"

"Very well—Brandt. I will think about it."

Brandt smiled, took her empty drink container and placed it in the last waste bag. Another look around convinced him everything had been stowed. He started to push toward the cockpit when Svetlana said, "Brandt, I need something."

"Yes?"

"It is the clothing. Too large. It will fall off with gravity."

He chuckled and said, "I've got just the thing. Saved some for the EVA and didn't need it."

After opening the tool container, he pulled a strip of silver-colored fabric from the side. "Duct tape. Works for everything."

She studied it for a moment. "It is perfect. Thank you."

Carefully tearing the piece into four narrow strips, she made folds in the waists of her underpants and trousers and secured them with the tape.

Brandt closed the tool kit and moved back through the passageway. As expected, the Global Positioning System had detected its first satellite.

"Shouldn't be too long before we pick up some signals," he thought. "Get an idea of where we are." Within seconds, the display presented a position. Brandt quickly compared it with the computer's value.

"Blast!" Brandt said it out loud, then thought, "Way off course. Gotta get an analysis."

As he loaded the instructions, he thought, "Hope it's wrong. Could be, this far out. Only three satellites."

The computer displayed its predictions.

Brandt mumbled to himself, "Barely enough propellant to do the correction. Nothing left for circularization."

Four, five, then six GPS satellites added to the information. The position estimate changed, but not by much.

Svetlana drifted in from under the display. "Something is wrong?" she asked.

"Large position error. Must have been caused by the weight reduction."

"Is it a problem?"

"Not enough propellant. Can't do the circularization."

"Not at all?"

"Not enough."

"So we will die." Svetlana spoke the words without emotion, as if stating they would miss a meal.

"Unless we can figure out a way to get the perigee high enough for the Shuttle to reach us. I'm looking at the residual delta-v we can get from the attitude thrusters."

She waited patiently while Brandt completed the analysis.

"It'll help, but not much."

"What are you doing now?"

"Setting up an optimization scheme. Trading off propellant for position accuracy. Need to find the best burn time."

"Brandt..."

"Just a minute. Need to get this finished."

As he spoke, the screen filled with numbers.

"That's a surprise. Says we should delay the burn for another ten minutes."

"You believe this?"

"It's all I've got, Svetlana."

"Brandt, I think you should try something else."

"Yes?"

"The spaceship. It produces lift?"

"Of course."

"Use the lift to do some trajectory correction. Save propellant."

Looking over at her, Brandt realized she'd come up with their last hope for survival.

"Good idea, Svetlana. Let's see what it does."

He worked frantically to load the problem, but could only try one case at a time. "Need to bound it," he thought as he entered the information.

"Son of a gun! Look at that!"

"It is good?" Svetlana asked, interpreting his inflection rather than the words.

"A lot better. But I didn't use enough lift."

As he finished entering the next case he mumbled, "Do it, baby. Do it!"

"Hah! Through the aerobrake with propellant to spare. But still not enough."

The next attempt produced better results, but only by a small amount. "Getting close to optimum." He checked the real-time clock.

"Gees!" he said aloud. "Better decide on something pretty quick."

"It is almost time for the burn?" Svetlana asked.

"About five minutes. Listen, Svetlana, I can't make the computer control this. Have to do it manually. But I'll need both the attitude and trajectory displays and what we've got left will only show one at a time."

"It is no problem, Brandt. I will switch displays while you fly."

"Great. You just need..."

"I watched you." She moved herself to the right-side couch. "It is like this." With a few movements, she cleared the trajectory data from the screen and brought up the attitude- indicator display.

"Then this." She switched to the graphs showing trajectory errors, then back again.

"You've got it." Brandt shook his head in amazement. "I'll instruct the computer to track the new entry angle." He selected the manual control program and entered the burn time and final state vector.

“Svetlana, you’d better strap in. I'm going to swing around to get us closer to the initial burn orientation."

Using the attitude indicator, Brandt turned the spacecraft to aim its engines nearly perpendicular to the direction of motion. As they rotated, the earth appeared, almost completely filling his window.

"Looks close, doesn't it? But if we can't pull this off, we might just as well be back on the moon."

"We will be on earth soon," Svetlana said confidently.

As the seconds ticked away, Brandt directed his attention to the deviation graphs.

"Here we go. Four, three, two, one." He felt the engines ignite, pushing him into the couch.

"Drifting left. Attitude."

Svetlana switched the displays.

"Try one degree. Deviation."

He studied the trends. "Going high. Still left. Attitude."

"Another degree right, one down. Deviation."

The corrections continued for another ten seconds. Then the engines stopped. Brandt checked the final values.

"Pretty good. Need to rerun the aerobraking analysis with the final state vector."

***

The Russian missile streaked upward from the southern hemisphere, its vernier engines making small velocity corrections to keep it moving toward its objective, a collision with Artemis some twenty-thousand miles above the earth. With seconds to go, it armed its warhead and made final course corrections. It would explode precisely at its programmed destination, precisely on time.

Nine miles behind, the American ASM armed itself and activated its terminal guidance system. Detecting the change in its target's path, it fired thrusters to bring it closer but it could not completely close the gap. Ahead, the Russian warhead blew out a spherical cloud of shrapnel, confusing the ASM's trackers. The American rocket turned toward the explosion, encountered its debris and detonated.

## Chapter 20

---

# Earth Orbit

**Artemis**

"What the heck?" Brandt caught the flash out of the corner of his eye as he yawed Artemis around. He released the stick and got to the hatch window just in time to see an expanding orange sphere envelop them, no more than the briefest burst of light. The spacecraft jumped, as if slapped by a giant hand, and a rapid staccato of thuds, so close together they could barely be distinguished, reached his ears. It was over in an instant.

"Gees! What was that?" he yelled. He let his mind recreate the image, as if painted on his retinas, a strange aberration of a perfect circle, brilliant against the black sky but laced with arcs of brown.

Unable to see the phenomena from her side of the spaceship, Svetlana asked, "Is there a problem with the ship?"

"Explosions, Svetlana. Fireballs expanding toward us. Some kind of warheads. Must have been meant for us."

"For us?" she shouted.

"What else would they be doing out here?"

"Who would do this? Why?"

Wondering the same thing, Brandt guessed, "Must be the entry angle. Worried about the ship reentering. Can't imagine what they threw at us."

"They would try to kill us?"

He considered the possibility, tried to process the equation that related his own life to the safety of thousands but dismissed the exercise as futile.

"Don't think so, Svetlana. Whoever fired those things must believe the ship's empty."

Brandt would have preferred not continuing the discussion, but Svetlana denied him the option.

"They may not bring us back from orbit."

"They fired the missiles before we did the correction burn. With my delaying it for so long, they probably figured it wouldn't happen. But they've sure detected it by now. They know we're in here."

"The sounds. They were from the explosions?"

"Yup. But whatever hit us didn't penetrate. We'd have heard alarms by now."

"It may have damaged the engines," she said, still sounding apprehensive.

"I'll check." Once again, he knew nothing catastrophic had occurred. A severed propellant line or a punctured gimbal actuator would have triggered a warning message. But what if a piece of shrapnel had hit a nozzle bell or a thrust chamber? He brought up the engine diagnostic and waited while it performed a series of integrity checks.

"Number one looks okay. Try number two."

The computer repeated the process and, once again, concluded there were no discrepancies.

"Okay!" Brandt felt a lot better. "Might as well do the last one. He watched the test results as they scrolled down the screen.

"Failed the leak test! Must have punctured a cooling tube."

He pointed to the offending lines of text. "Lost number three, Svetlana. No big deal. Only need one for circularization. But it proves something hit us. Probably shrapnel from the warhead."

She read through the report on the display. "The other engines were not hit?"

"Diagnostics didn't pick up anything. Have to keep our fingers crossed."

"Fingers crossed?"

He formed the sign with his hand. "Like this. For good luck."

"That is good luck?"

"Just a saying."

She looked at him blankly. "When is the aerobraking?"

"Still have about forty minutes before we hit the atmosphere. Maybe I can finally get through the analysis—if nobody else shoots at us."

**The White House**

"This is General Brown with a situation report." The voice from the speaker echoed across the Situation Room. "We have confirmation of two detonations at the designated target points. At this time I can report that the missile-intercept operation achieved all objectives."

Torres looked across the table at the image on the left screen. The white tracks that had inched their way across the world-map display at Cheyenne Mountain's Command Center had converged, terminating in a single red circle.

From his seat, the Defense Secretary shouted, "General Brown, this is Jeffrey Farrand. I want to say how much we appreciate your support throughout this operation. Please extend my personal thanks to your officers and men."

Cushman asked through the microphone, "Did you hear that, Duane?"

"Yes, ma'am," he replied immediately, "and rest assured, I'll pass along the Secretary's comments to my people."

"General Cushman," Torres called across the room, "would you mind asking General Brown whether the damned things did any good?"

Cushman said, "Duane, you copy?"

"Yes, ma'am. Been working the problem right along. Still waiting for the analysis of the target's trajectory."

The President asked, "General Cushman, isn't there anyone else who could help with this?"

Dominguez answered for her. "Sir, we've got every tracking resource looking at the spaceship—NASA, all the military services, intelligence agencies. But all the data goes to Cheyenne Mountain. Hands down, it's the best source."

As Dominguez uttered the last word, the speaker boomed, "Mr. President, this is General Brown with the information you requested. The analysts have confirmed their preliminary findings. The spaceship performed a course correction just before the intercept. By the time the warheads detonated, it had moved several miles from the designated intercept point."

"Which means?" Torres shouted.

"Excuse me, sir?" Brown's voice replied.

"Did it hit the damned thing?"

"Sir," Brown responded, "I'm sorry but there's no way to determine the effect of the munitions. Not at this time."

"Jeff," the President snapped at his Defense Secretary, "what's he trying to say?"

"Mr. President, it seems the computers in Artemis determined it needed the course correction, just as Dr. Nguyen predicted. It changed direction before the missiles arrived and they missed."

Herrera called out, "General Brown, I don't understand why our missile didn't track it down." His voice trailed off as he finished the sentence.

Farrand answered before anyone else had a chance, speaking much more loudly than necessary. "Marty, our instructions from the President stipulated that the missiles should fly to the predesignated point. As I recall, the intent was not to damage Artemis if there were any indications it could be recovered."

Seeming anxious to drop the matter, Herrera replied, "Of course, Jeff. Forgot about that."

"But the space ship's working again, right Jeff?" Torres asked. "Won't hit Australia?"

Farrand replied, "That would be my guess. General?" He looked at the Air Force Chief of Staff.

Answering cautiously, Cushman hedged, "The course correction seems unusual to me, sir—delaying it that long. Indicates the spacecraft had no navigation capability until it got fairly close to earth, probably until it picked up GPS signals. Even then, I'd have expected the correction to come earlier. But if the systems are functioning normally, the spacecraft should be set up for aerobraking and then a recovery orbit."

Becoming ever more frustrated, Torres yelled, "Australia! Will it hit Australia?"

Cushman blurted out, "No! I don't believe that's a problem anymore."

"Thank God!" Torres replied as he rocked back in his chair. "For Australia—and for a straight answer!"

"Mr. President," Cushman said as she selected an item from the display's control screen, "we have something coming in from the

NASA feed."

The right display showed the front of a control center with a woman standing between the first row of controllers and the wall of display screens. "Mr. President?" The voice sounded very nervous.

"This is General Cushman at the White House. Please go ahead."

"Thank you, General. I'm Louise Ehlers, Flight Director at the Johnson Space Center. I have a preliminary report on the current trajectory of the Artemis vehicle for you." She coughed.

"It seems the course correction hasn't vectored the spacecraft to an ideal entry angle, although it's certainly better. If Artemis continues on its present trajectory, we predict it will slow to a velocity less than that required for the designated recovery orbit."

Torres muttered, "More technical crap."

"This means," Ehlers droned on, "unless corrective action is taken, reentry is likely at some future time."

That got the President's attention. "What? I thought we were out of this?"

"Ms. Ehlers," Cushman asked, "are you saying Artemis will still impact the earth?"

"Unless it corrects its trajectory."

"Can it do that?"

Ehlers hesitated. "I'll have to say I don't know. It's possible the spacecraft has exhausted its propellant supply."

"Which means?"

"It won't be able to circularize the orbit, even if it performs perfectly during the aerobraking."

"Translation, please!" Torres demanded.

"Mr. President," Cushman explained, "she's saying the Shuttle won't be able to recover Artemis. That it will reenter."

"Good God!" the President fumed. "Here we go again. Where's it going to hit this time?"

Obviously having heard the shouting, Ehlers replied, "Right now there's no way to predict an impact point. We're confident the spacecraft will emerge from the aerobraking but it's possible the vehicle will reenter during the perigee of the ensuing orbit."

Before Torres could complain, Cushman made the bad news perfectly clear. "Which means, Mr. President, we may not know the projected impact point until about forty minutes before Artemis hits the earth. And that event may occur in less than two hours."

Almost frantic, Torres cried, "What the hell are we going to do about it?"

Cushman responded coolly, "First of all, Mr. President, NASA is saying there's nothing you can do. Second, they're saying it probably won't happen."

Displaying a degree of frustration known only to the extremely powerful at a time when they are utterly powerless, Torres squeezed the front of his head between his hands and closed his eyes.

**Johnson Space Center**

Unable to communicate with Artemis, Brian had little to do and could come and go as he pleased without anyone noticing. But, except for side trips to maintain his caffeine level with shots of almost undrinkable black coffee, his departures from the main floor of the control center usually brought him to the place he now sat in the flight-dynamics support room.

He studied the computer display. Somehow, it didn't look right. The course-correction pattern didn't follow anything he'd seen before, not in all the simulation runs in all the months of training. He toyed with the workstation's software, but lacked the proficiency to get meaningful results.

Totally absorbed by Ehlers' mandate to explore all reentry contingencies, every analyst worked feverishly, loading different starting conditions into the trajectory generators.

Brian's eye caught one of them stretching between runs. "Jim? Is it Jim?" he asked.

"I use James, Major Howe."

"James, I need your help for a minute."

Looking very weary, the young engineer replied, "Still have a batch of runs to get through."

"Yeah, I know, and I'm sorry to ask. But it'll only take a minute."

Plodding his way across the room, the analyst stood behind Brian looking at the computer screen.

"Jim—James, look at these deviations from the course-correction burn. Ever seen a pattern like that before?"

"No. But to be honest, I haven't seen many cases."

"Well, I've seen plenty and these don't look right. See the random corrections. No cyclical pattern. I don't think these were commanded by a computer."

"Still looking for evidence that someone's on board?"

"Making sure we don't dismiss anything."

"That's fine, but what I can do?"

"Need you to do some runs. See if the computer can generate these deviations."

"Jesus, major, that'd take an hour and I don't even have a minute. I have to get back to work."

"James, just see if you can squeeze it in for me. That's all I ask."

Looking to the side, he replied, "Okay, but don't expect anything soon."

He'd seen Ehlers enter the room. She walked straight toward Brian. "Major, I'd appreciate it if you didn't interfere with the work here."

Acting surprised, Brian replied, "Louise. Didn't see you there. Just going over these deviations from the burn. Look kind-of funny, don't you think?"

"Frankly," she said haughtily, "I wouldn't know. That's what we have analysts for."

"Exactly, Louise," Brian replied. "And I need a little of their time to check it out."

"Wonderful idea for the mission report. We'll get started next week."

Not being the sort one speaks to with disdain, Brian hissed in her ear, "Listen, bitch, you get people on this right now or I'm going straight to the press area. Tell them you know the astronauts are alive inside Atlantis. Tell them you're deliberately planning to kill them. Tell them you're doing it to cover your screwup that led to firing missiles at them. Now how do you want to spend tonight's wee-small hours?"

She pulled away from him, dumbfounded. Gasping for breath, she said, "Major, you just trashed your career as an astronaut!"

Brian stared hard into her eyes. "You'll do it?"

Glaring back she sneered, "Yes!" then stormed out.

**Artemis**

"Okay, Svetlana," Brandt said as he entered the final commands, "it's loaded."

"The computer will make the lift corrections?"

Brandt considered the question, thinking about the system's

performance since their liftoff from the moon. "To be honest, I'm a little worried about it. We're so far off baseline, the software's having trouble compensating. Could run into more problems—hunting, oscillations. And this time we can't afford it."

"Because we need maximum lift, yes?"

"Exactly. We'll have to maintain just the right angle all the way around. Wish I could set up to take over manually."

"We did it with the course correction," she reminded him.

"This is different, Svetlana. We'll be decelerating at better than one G, sometimes close to two. Toward the nose! If I had all the displays, I'd just strap in tight, hang from the harness and keep my hand glued to the control stick."

"I'll switch the displays for you. Like before."

"Can't do it this time. Need both deviation and attitude continuously." He thought through the problem, wondering if he could find a way to fly with just the one-page screen, but came up empty. "Gotta have that second display," he thought. Then he shouted, "Backup!"

"Backup?" Svetlana didn't understand.

"Last-ditch control computer. Plugs into the connector at the bottom of the display." He peeled off a rectangular piece of plastic to reveal a multi-pin plug. "Be right back."

Brandt moved quickly into the nose, opened one of the few remaining compartment drawers and removed something resembling a notebook computer. Back in the cockpit, he mated its cable to the plug and turned it on.

"Supposedly," he explained to Svetlana, "this thing will run the whole ship, but I sure wouldn't want to try it. Question is whether it'll work as a dummy monitor." He scanned the toolbar on the main screen, tried a few icons but couldn't find any simple display modes.

He mumbled to himself, "I know they said something about using it to replace a broken MFD." Back with the main screen, he tried the pull-down menus. "Ha!" He touched the *Remote Display* tag and generated a list of page options. He chose *Attitude* and the screen changed to a reasonable rendering of the attitude indicator.

"Not as crisp as an MFD, but it's usable," he said. "Have to find a place to put it." He checked the mission clock. "Gees! Running out of time."

Trying different locations on the gutted instrument panel, he soon realized that the number of empty holes precluded anything as simple as taping the computer into place. Every option promised to drop it through an opening under a two-G load.

"I'll hold it," Svetlana said, moving from her couch and placing her back against the perforated panel. She took the computer from his hand and held it below the center display.

"You'll be getting pushed against the instrument panel. No way to strap in."

"It is not a problem. Like lying on it."

"Talking about maybe two Gs for fifteen minutes."

"I can do that. We will start soon, yes?"

"Just about right now," Brandt said as he pulled the harness straps down tight.

Still on the automatic system, Artemis began to make small orientation changes as the acceleration sensors detected the first signs of atmospheric drag. Within seconds, Brandt felt himself ease forward from the couch. Svetlana wiggled around against the panel, trying to avoid protruding bolts.

For several minutes, the deviation display showed the blue diamond centered perfectly on both the azimuth and elevation graphs. But, as the G-load began to increase, it drifted off a bit, then moved back, then drifted off again.

"Beginning to wander," Brandt said aloud. "Still doing the job, though."

With the deceleration now pulling him into the straps, Brandt stayed glued to the deviation display. He spotted what he'd feared. The elevation error increased, came back, but then increased again in the same direction.

"Starting to hunt!" he called out. "Can't afford much of this."

The deviation returned to zero, but then began another cycle, moving the spacecraft below the desired path.

"That's enough." Brandt disabled the automatic control, grabbed the control stick and increased the pitch attitude. The deviation slowly dropped back to zero.

"Okay!" The tension momentarily eased. "Back on track. Had enough lift left to pull us up."

Svetlana rested the top of the backup computer's display against the instrument panel but, as they descended, the vibration level increased markedly and she had trouble holding it steady.

Artemis slammed through the upper atmosphere, shuddering, banging, jumping as it tore through regions of varying density and velocity. Brandt glanced to the right and saw Svetlana struggling to remain in one place.

"Try holding on to one of the cutouts," he yelled over the noise.

"Need both hands for the computer," she called back as she rolled on her side, ignoring the protruding bolts that jabbed into her ribs. Tucking her legs behind her, she found some support on the side wall while she held on to the increasing weight at the end of her outstretched arms.

Intensely concentrating on the shaking displays, Brandt felt the straps cut into his shoulders and groin. Pulled away from the couch, he had to reach backward to hold the control stick, forcing his arm into a cramping twist. He ignored the pain and stared at the graphs.

For the first time, the azimuth began to drift. He caught it immediately. "Right drift, right roll," he told himself as he made a small adjustment to the direction of the lift force. As the correction took effect, Brandt noticed the pain from belts decrease. Then the display became a bit less fuzzy as the vibration eased.

"Coming out of it," he called, hoping to encourage Svetlana. He stole a quick look and saw her face twisted in pain, yet seeming to smile.

As Artemis climbed back through the upper layers of the atmosphere, the forces disappeared and the cockpit became quiet once again. Brandt took a last look at the graphs. "Zeroed out!" he cheered. "Hot dog!" Then he checked Svetlana.

Taking the computer from her, he helped her roll over and float back to her couch. As she did, he saw a streak of blood on the instrument panel.

"You're hurt!" he said.

"Is nothing," she said wincing as she lifted her shirt. "Bolt cut me. Did we do okay?"

Seeing she'd suffered a deep puncture wound, Brandt tried to help but she brushed him away. "Did we do okay?" she repeated.

"Looks about perfect," he said, accepting her Stoicism but still worried about the injury. "If the software's telling the truth, we should hit the apogee right on the money."

"Then we burn again?"

"Right, but we don't have enough propellant to circularize. Last perigee prediction was about sixty miles."

"It is too low," she responded sounding resigned.

"Doubt if Atlantis will go down that far. Too much risk of unintended reentry. I'll burn the OMS engine dry, then use the attitude-control thrusters to add some extra delta-v. Don't know how we'll come out. Have to see."

"Have to see," she repeated quietly.

**Johnson Space Center**

"Here they are, Major Howe. Looks like you were right." The exhausted analyst dropped the computer printout on the table. "Tried every combination of failures we can think of. No way the computer commanded that correction burn. Has to be someone hand flying it."

"All right!" Brian allowed himself the briefest moment of triumph before tackling the awesome ramifications. "That proves it. Someone's inside."

The analyst interrupted. "And there's more." He pushed the top sheets aside. "Look at this. It's an analysis of the required aerobraking—attempting to recover to the nominal orbit. If you run right near max lift, you just about make it. That convinced me. Somebody worked the problem—trying to conserve propellant. It's an optimum solution, but nothing like this was ever programmed and it sure as hell didn't happen by accident."

Brian scanned the plots and tables. "Fantastic! Hard to believe you tucked this in between the reentry sims."

The analyst replied, "We quit that shit as soon as we saw these results. Waste of time."

Brian nodded. "Really appreciate you sticking your necks out. Need to get Ehlers up here."

"Lotsa luck, Brian," a second analyst responded. "She's been talking to the President. She's not about to spend time listening to you."

Not pleased with the reply, Brian growled, "Tough shit! Get her up here!"

"Brian," the first analyst responded, "all I can do is ask Fido on my support loop. He'll have to get her on the Flight-Director's loop, if he wants to."

Brian smiled and patted him on the arm. "Understand. Let me handle it." He walked out of the support room back to his CapCom console on the main floor.

Ehlers, sitting in the chair just to his left, ignored him and continued to study the numbers on her monitors. After waiting a minute, he leaned over and whispered in her ear, "Need to talk to you. Now!"

She jerked her head around and looked at him. "Later, Brian. Much later!"

He whispered again, "Now!"

She responded loudly, "Major Howe, I've been directed by the President of the United States to determine when and where the spacecraft will reenter. I believe that task takes priority over your concerns."

Brian stood up and stared down at her, his square face hardened into the glower of an angry Marine ready to do battle. "Lady," he yelled in a command voice that rang through the control center, "you don't have a reentry problem. You have a recovery problem. Someone is inside Artemis. Alive! Now we can thrash this out here, or you can come up to the flight-dynamics support room and look at some God-damned data."

Although obviously intimidated, Ehlers managed a fairly firm, "How dare you raise your voice at me? Do I have to remind you that I'm the Flight Director for this mission?"

"What you are," Brian continued, increasing the decibel level, "is an egotistical incompetent!" He looked toward the back of the control center to verify the expected pandemonium in the press area. She got the message, stormed down the aisle and out the door.

Half running to keep up with her, Brian dashed into the support room, hoping the guards could contain the media mob. "Okay, Louise," he said, "these are your people. Listen to them."

The analysts went over the data but she didn't seem to pay attention. When they finished their rushed explanations she said, "This changes nothing. It's obvious they haven't worked long enough to determine how the computer generated these commands."

"Good God!" Brian said, looking at her with revulsion. "You'd kill an astronaut rather than admit you're wrong."

James had been talking on the phone, his finger pressed into his open ear. He put the down the receiver, then called across the room. "Aerobraking analysis. Just got the results. They're set up perfectly for the rendezvous point."

Brian sneered at Ehlers, "Ready to start thinking about recovery?"

**Artemis**

"Sixty-one meters a second. Program says that's all we need," Brandt sighed as he completed a final update. "But it also says we won't make it."

"Thrusters will help," Svetlana reminded him.

"Maybe a little, if they don't burn out." He checked the clock. "Should start now."

"Are you going to fly the circularization?"

"Computer should be okay this time. We're right on track. Of course, it'll run out of fuel somewhere along the way."

He aligned himself with the couch and loosely fastened the straps, still sore from the aerobraking. The center engine fired for the last time.

Svetlana held herself off the couch, protecting her sore back and side from the light G-force. Thirteen seconds later, Artemis returned to weightlessness.

"System should get rid of the propulsion section for us," Brandt said, reading the status reports. Seconds later, two closely-spaced jolts told him the pyrotechnic bolts had fired.

Taking control, Brandt pushed the control stick forward, firing the four rearward-facing thrusters. He counted, "One thousand one," then relaxed the pressure. "One thousand one." Push forward. "One thousand one." Relax.

He continued to pulse the small rockets while the computer analyzed the effect. With the propellant nearly depleted, the screen presented him with the discouraging result.

"Perigee altitude 101.6 kilometers, about sixty-three miles." He read it to himself.

"The Shuttle will come to us?"

"It's pretty low," he admitted, knowing he couldn't fool her, "but they'd get through it okay. Right on the edge."

"Brandt," she said firmly, taking his hand, "they will save us. It is not American to let us die."

**The White House**

Passing the twenty-one-hour mark since his last sleep, Torres felt as if someone had thrown pepper in his eyes. Rubbing only aggravated the burning itch.

"Worst part of this nonsense is the damned Vice President carrying the whole campaign," he thought bitterly. "Be a miracle if we pull it off. Unbelievable! Trashed a twenty-two-point lead."

He massaged his forehead. After too many cups of coffee, his brain wallowed in a jumpy stupor of chemically stimulated awareness and his stomach regurgitated a steady trickle of acid.

The others in the Situation Room looked a little better, having managed to steal short naps at various lulls in the long ordeal, but the relentless tension had taken its toll.

A green light flashed at the top of the display. "General Cushman," the President called, "I believe Johnson wants to tell us something."

Looking tired, but still reasonably crisp in her dress uniform, she checked the screen and saw Ehlers step into the view field. She walked to the control console and activated the audio.

Ehlers' voice sounded even less confident than it had during her previous reports. "I have some information concerning the results of the spacecraft's circularization burn. After a thirteen-point-two-second operation of a single OMS engine, the vehicle raised the perigee of its elliptical orbit to an estimated sixty-three miles. This is significantly lower than the NASA-recommended minimum Shuttle operating altitude. Assuming the vehicle is not recovered immediately, the orbit will decay and, at some future time, reenter the atmosphere."

Torres shouted at the display, "Ms. Ehlers, this is the President. You've told me everything but what I need to know. Can the Shuttle pick up the spacecraft? If not, when will it come down and where will it hit?"

Ehlers paused to catch her breath. "Sir, as I said, the altitude of the spacecraft is below what we consider safe for the Shuttle."

"Can it get the damned thing down?" Torres yelled.

Blinking, Ehlers stammered, "I can't answer that, sir. Any decision to violate established safety limitations would require higher-level approval."

Realizing he was listening to a flunky, Torres replied in a cordial voice, "Of course, Ms. Ehlers. Didn't mean to put you on the spot. What about the reentry?"

"Mr. President, the analytic capabilities available to me cannot predict those parameters."

"Okay, Ms. Ehlers." Torres wanted to stop wasting time. "Thanks for your report."

Cushman killed the audio before Ehlers could mouth her goodbye.

"Marty," Torres sighed, "sounds like same song, third verse. What are our options?"

"Mr. President, you could order NASA to recover the spacecraft, but it'd put the risk of an accident entirely on your back."

"Three days before the election."

"Not something I'd recommend, sir."

Chambers had been sitting with his chin on his palm, his eyes barely open. But he sat up, looked at Herrera and asked, "Isn't the Shuttle manned by the contractor's people?"

Before the Chief of Staff could reply, Farrand answered, "That's right, Larry. Couldn't justify using a military crew."

"Then they could refuse to do the recovery if it's outside normal operating procedures."

"I guess that's right," the Defense Secretary replied.

Finding the discussion unproductive, Torres ended it saying, "All right, Marty. Let's do what you recommended. Ask NASA to recover the spacecraft unless they think it's too risky. If the Shuttle people refuse to go along, I guess there's nothing we can do about it. General, get that woman back on the screen—or whoever else has the authority to get this thing going."

**Johnson Space Center**

As Brian watched from the CapCom console, he noticed the change in Ehlers' demeanor as she spoke to the White House. The confidence, the arrogance, had completely evaporated leaving her looking hesitant, almost frightened.

"Finally realizes what she's up against," Brian thought. "About time."

He listened to the discourse, waiting for her to tell the President the good news. But she never did. Brian couldn't believe his ears.

He stormed up the center aisle, but before he got within five feet she announced firmly, "Don't say a word, Major. Not one word! I have my instructions and I intend to carry them out."

"Louise," Brian pleaded, "think what you're doing! You've got to put the trajectory results into the equation. Tell Transpace they're rescuing an astronaut, not an empty hulk."

"I said not one word!"

She made some selections in the communications window on her left monitor, removed a telephone receiver from its cradle, covered her mouth with her hand and turned her back to him.

"I don't believe this!" Brian exclaimed out loud. He waited for a minute, hoping Ehlers would talk to him, then stood up and walked to the back of the center, through the controlled entrance and into the hall. He'd forgotten about the media people. Since his altercation with Ehlers, they'd been nearly hysterical, trying to contact someone inside the center to get an explanation. They pounced on him, screaming questions at him, shoving microphones and television cameras in his face.

He tried to bull his way through but ended up in the middle of the throng, unable to advance or retreat. Finally, he held up his hands, waited no more than five seconds and began to speak softly. The clamor stopped immediately.

"First, the discussion between Ms. Ehlers and myself, which probably sounded pretty heated to you folks, was about a technical disagreement. Sort of thing that goes on all the time."

The uproar began again, louder than before. Brian used the raised-hands ploy again and said, "The real story is what you heard me say. There's pretty good evidence that someone's on board Artemis, still alive. It's what we've been hoping for all along. Now I've got to start working with the Transpace people to see how we're going to bring the ship home."

Seemingly appeased, the mob backed off. Brian made his way through, then raced down the corridor to the Consolidated Control Center, bluffed his way past the guard and slipped his access card into the reader. Somewhat to his surprise, the door opened.

"Good luck for a change," he muttered to himself. "Haven't changes the codes."

Entering near the front of the center, he meandered his way through the rows of consoles, trying to seem relaxed, almost casual. No one paid any attention, even as he slipped behind the Transpace Flight Director and CapCom, then eased into a chair behind an unmanned console to their right. Reasonably certain he recognized her, Brian leaned toward the CapCom and said, "It's Cindy, isn't it?"

She rotated her swivel chair and studied his face. "Aren't you one of the military astronauts?"

"Brian Howe. Got bumped off the moon mission. Met you at an integrated sim."

She smiled warmly and extended her hand. "Nice to see you again. What brings you to the sweatshop?"

"Guess NASA hasn't gotten the word over here yet. Seems they're going to try recovering Artemis after all."

Surprised, she said, "Really? Last I heard it ended up in an elliptical orbit, too low to get to."

"Not all that low, actually. Perigee's about 63 miles."

"Way outside contract. Not a prayer getting Transpace to buy into that one."

"Seems the President wants to try anyway."

"President of Transpace?"

"President of the United States."

Getting the picture, Cindy replied humbly, "Oh! Is that why you're here?"

"To be available in case the operation goes. Provide technical support if anybody needs it."

She nodded. "Glad to have you."

Brian saw the Flight Director put his telephone receiver back on the console-mounted holder and turn toward Cindy.

"You won't believe this," Flight began. "They actually want us to grab the damned thing just on the outside chance it'll impact in a populated area after it reenters. Got any idea what the odds of that happening are? Just got off the phone with the duty manager. Says he's going to get the CEO out of bed. Dump it in his lap."

Cindy replied, "If they screw around with it long enough, the problem will take care of itself. By the next orbit the perigee altitude will be totally unacceptable."

"My guess is that's what they'll do. Just wait it out. Never know, though. Request came straight from the President."

Looking toward Brian, Cindy said, "Sounds like what you were talking about."

Brian nodded while continuing to look straight ahead. Out of the corner of his eye, he saw Flight pick up the receiver, listen intently, then put it down.

"Up to the crew," he said to Cindy. "Management cop-out. Should have figured."

"So what do I tell them?" she asked.

"Explain the situation. Tell them the ball's in their court."

She raised her eyebrows and wrinkled her nose. "Fair enough, I guess." Then she touched the transmit icon.

"Atlantis, Houston."

She had her earpiece inserted too snugly for Brian to overhear

Monica Guerrera's response.

"Roger, Atlantis. Glad to hear everybody's up. Have a message from management. The company's been requested by the President…"

She paused, then said, "That's affirmative, President Torres. He requested we recover Artemis to prevent possible reentry into a populated area. Company says it's up to the crew. Needs a response."

After a moment, she replied, "Roger, Atlantis. Confirm. Way out of contract. Probably why they decided to leave it up to you."

The next pause took a bit longer.

"Atlantis, Houston. No information on the projected impact zone. I'm not sure anyone knows at this point."

Then, almost immediately, "Understand, Atlantis. Don't blame you. I'll put in the request, but by the time NASA finishes an analysis, it'll be too late. I'd guess even one more orbit will put it out of reach."

Cindy turned to Flight. "You heard her. Tossed the monkey right back."

Brian waited while Flight completed another telephone conversation. He tried to look bored while his anxiety level climbed to the stratosphere.

Shrugging his shoulders, Flight said, "Management doesn't give a shit. Just as happy Guerrera said no. Now they get to dump it right back on NASA."

Brian looked at the clock at the top of the mission-data display. "Ten minutes to burn time. Can't wait any longer."

"Cindy, forgot about something." Brian slid around the small workspace that extended between the console stations and sat in the chair next to hers. "I'm supposed to give them some information about Artemis."

"What is it?"

"Easier to tell them myself than tell you to tell them," he said as he put on the headset that had been hanging next to the right monitor."

"Can't do that, Brian. Have to communicate through an astronaut," Cindy protested.

"So what do I look like?" Brian laughed. "Bugs Bunny?"

"Atlantis, Houston," he called, turning away from Cindy and the Flight Director. "This is Brian Howe. Artemis astronaut. Met you at the Cape before the aerobraking test. Listen, I'm supposed to give you some information about the spacecraft. Trajectory analysis proves there's someone aboard making control inputs. Absolutely no doubt. NASA's been sitting on the information because they screwed up yesterday. Told the President the ship was empty. President ended up shooting a missile at it. Whoever's on board has only one more chance. You've got to snag Artemis on the next orbit. After that it's all over. Gives you seven minutes to the retro burn. You ready to copy some numbers?"

Flight yanked the headset's cable out of the socket. "What the hell do you think you're doing?"

"You heard me, didn't you?" Brian yelled. "You've got seven minutes to get a set of burn parameters up to them. If you don't, you've killed whoever's inside Artemis."

"How do I know you're telling the truth?" Flight bellowed.

Brian pulled out his access card. "That's me. Major Brian Howe. Military astronaut. This isn't bullshit."

Flight checked the card, looking carefully at Brian's face. "Just a minute while I check with my management." He returned to his telephone.

"Christ, Cindy! We've got to get those burn parameters up to them."

"Already done, Brian. NASA's been sending over all the Artemis information. Covering every contingency. Every time we get a new set of data, our trajectory people work the intercept problem and transfer the data files. Just need management approval." She gave him a curious look, then asked, "Is it true? What you said?"

"Every word of it!"

"NASA would deliberately kill an astronaut?"

"Of course not."

"Then what?"

"They don't want to believe the data. Convinced themselves that their original conclusions are correct."

Horrified, she replied, "Glad it's not me up there."

"In Artemis?"

"In Atlantis. Tough decision!"

"Cindy." It was Flight. "Tell Guerrera that management's disapproved the operation. No contractual obligation. Unlimited liability risk. No offer of a work-statement modification. The whole thing doesn't make sense."

Cindy dutifully obeyed while Brian stood up and walked in tiny circles inside the console station, pounding his fist into his hand.

Then he heard her say, "Roger, Atlantis, if that's what you want." She touched some icons on her communications window.

Guerrera's throaty voice rang from the center's loudspeakers.

"Houston, this is Monica Guerrera, Atlantis commander, with a message for the center controllers and any attending management personnel. Please give me your attention because I only have time to say this once."

She paused. The center hushed into an eerie silence as she continued.

"The crew of Atlantis has carefully weighed the moral imperative of protecting the life of a fellow astronaut against both the risks of a rescue attempt and the unprecedented violations of our contractual obligations. After a hurried deliberation, we have reached a unanimous agreement." Then her voice blasted across the great hall.

"Fuck the contract!"

For an eerie moment, the center remained absolutely silent. Then a controller in the second row rose to his feet and began to clap, very slowly. Another controller joined him. Then, as a wave sweeping across the room, others jumped to their feet and cheered, shaking hands, slapping each other on the back, shouting, "Go get 'em, Monica!" Even the Flight Director broke into a face-splitting grin.

"Seems like you've got a popular revolt on your hands," Cindy laughed.

**Atlantis**

"Stand by for retro burn," Guerrera said, once again all business as she sat in the commander's seat. "Three, two, one, ignition."

"We have two lights," Le reported, pointing to his display.

Guerrera watched the time tick away. "Must be out of my mind," she thought. "Probably in deep doodoo even if it all works out. Hope Howe knew what he was talking about."

"Thirty seconds," Le noted.

"Got one shot at this, Le," Guerrera called across the cockpit. "Have to complete the rendezvous by the time we're back up out of the atmosphere. Then forty-five minutes to get the thing into the bay."

Le nodded as he watched the clock. "Shouldn't be a problem. No engine section to unbolt this time." Responding to a message, he called out, "Shutdown. Should be seeing it any time now."

"Got a visual," Guerrera replied. "Coming up at us. Just off to the right."

"Tallyho," Le confirmed. "Better get turned around."

With Atlantis' top facing the earth, Guerrera looked through the windshield and saw the white cone against the blue of the Pacific.

Le twisted the yaw rate control while watching the attitude display. When the nose pointed down the flight path, he stopped the rotation.

"Should be popping up in the top windows," Guerrera said calmly.

**Artemis**

Brandt looked down toward the earth as the view from his window swept across Bermuda, wondering whether their struggles would finally pay off. He knew they'd played their last card, that Monica Guerrera and her crew would decide their fate. With nothing left to do, he couldn't keep his mind from evaluating their chances, over and over again.

"Couldn't blame Guerrera if she decided not to try it," he thought. "Any screwup could force 'em into a reentry. For all I know, they may still think the ship's empty. Sure wouldn't risk a Shuttle to save a piece of junk. But maybe they figured out we're alive. Maybe they analyzed the burns or the mass. Wonder what we'll do if they don't come. Could just wait and burn up with the ship. Probably be better to drop the pressure."

The last thought brought another vision of Darrell and another wave of nausea. "Can't think of that now. Drive myself crazy." He forced it from his mind.

Svetlana grabbed his shoulder. "The Shuttle! It is there!" she shouted.

His pulse racing, Brandt pushed across the cockpit and peered out her window into the dawn sky. He searched but saw nothing.

"Can't find it. Are you sure?"

"Yes! Yes! Space Shuttle!"

He looked back, but by this time, Artemis' slow roll had changed the view.

Almost afraid to believe her, he stared out his own window, waiting for the picture to match what she'd seen. Then there it was, floating above them. Unable to speak, he took Svetlana's hand, pulled her close to him and held her. She murmured into his ear, "You see. I told you Americans would not let us die."

He rumpled her hair as she moved away. "Wish we could do something that would show them we're alive."

"You could maneuver. Perhaps stop the rotation."

"Afraid we'll run out of propellant. Need to save it for the recovery."

She thought for a moment. "Your waste system. It ejects urine, yes?"

Brandt looked at her in awe. "Svetlana, you're incredible!"

**Atlantis**

"Damned shame," Le said as he looked through the observation window at the top of the flight deck.

"No way to capture it with those rotation rates," Guerrera agreed.

"Guess one of us will have to use an MMU to fly over to it. See if anyone's alive."

"And if they are?"

"Have to get them out. Fly them back to Atlantis. Let Artemis burn up."

Guerrera nodded. "Yup. No other way. But even matching those rates with an MMU won't be easy."

"What the hell was that?" Sanden shouted as he looked through the other window.

"Where?" Le asked.

"Coming from the side of Artemis. Like a cloud."

"God damn!" Guerrera laughed. "Somebody's trying to signal us with the urine dump!"

"What's going on?" Tyson asked as she emerged from the interdeck access.

"Just got a signal from the people inside Artemis."

"There's really someone alive in there?"

"Yup!" Guerrera answered. "And if it hadn't been for Howe, we'd have let them burn up."

"My God!" Tyson muttered.

"We've just been talking about getting them out of there. Can't recover the ship with those rotation rates."

"But if someone's on board, won't they get them stopped?" Sanden asked.

"Probably out of fuel," Le surmised.

"Will we have enough time?"

"Should be okay," Guerrera replied. "No harder bringing them back with an MMU then putting the ship into the cargo bay, assuming they're suited up and ready for the transfer."

"Considering their situation, I think that's a reasonable assumption," Le said, chuckling. "I imagine they're damned anxious to get out of that thing."

**Artemis**

"If they were looking this direction, they should have seen it," Brandt said, trying to sound hopeful.

"Why are they not coming to us?" Svetlana asked.

"Can't open the cargo-bay doors until we're higher," Brandt replied. "Aerodynamic forces would damage them. Should see some activity in about twenty-five minutes."

"We should put on space suits, yes?"

"Been giving that some thought, Svetlana. I think it's best if we ride down to the surface inside Artemis. If there's any delay getting you into the airlock, or if you have trouble getting it pressurized..."

"I will be all right, Brandt. Remember, I flew in the Shuttle when I worked on Space Station. And we must be in space suits in case they cannot load Artemis into the Shuttle."

"They'll get us loaded. I went along on the mission where they recovered a test vehicle. Virtually the same operation."

"You think we can stop the rotations?"

It was a question Brandt didn't want to consider, the possibility that he'd consumed so much propellant he wouldn't be able to stop the rolling and yawing.

"Hope so. But we should talk through the airlock procedures just to be sure you're up to date."

Brandt knew she'd have little chance of survival if the Atlantis crew couldn't load the spacecraft. The time needed to get from Artemis into the Shuttle's airlock would exceed the ability of the trapped oxygen to sustain her. He wished he could exchange suits, but knew he couldn't get into hers. He also knew she wouldn't let him try.

"Svetlana, I think we'll be able to stop the rotations, but if we can't, the Shuttle astronauts may still be able to load Artemis. If we're wearing suits, they may not try as hard and you'll have to risk the space walk to the airlock. If it turns out there's no way to handle the rotations, we can always put on the suits at the last minute. Do you understand what I'm saying?"

She looked into his eyes, her face expressionless, processing what he'd said. "I understand. We will not wear suits. But you will teach me about the airlock, yes?"

**Atlantis**

"Hey!" Le shouted. "They're firing thrusters."

Guerrera looked up. "Good. Not out of propellant after all. Looks like they've got the yaw stopped. If they can kill the roll rate we've got a baseline operation."

"Roll thrusters are firing. They're getting the rate reduced. Oh oh! They stopped."

"Shit!" Guerrera exclaimed. "Bet that's the end of their fuel. Rate's still too great to handle with the arm. We'll bring them over with an EVA. Is Hank ready?"

"In the cargo bay waiting for us to open the doors."

"Let's go," Guerrera ordered.

Responding to Le's command, the long, curved covers slowly pivoted, revealing Sanden, already wearing the Manned Maneuvering Unit, ready to move toward Artemis. The conical spacecraft floated fifty feet away, spinning slowly about its axis, its nose hovering above the docking fixture at the end of the cargo bay.

"I'm heading over," Sanden said as he thrusted away from the Shuttle. Once at Artemis, he used the MMU to reduce his relative velocity, then grabbed the hatch handle and peered through the adjacent window.

"They're in there!" he shouted. "Colonel Strickland and a woman. Not wearing space suits."

Sanden's few words filled Guerrera with a battery of conflicting emotions. "Only one American," she muttered. "Woman must be the Russian commander. What the hell happened up there?"

She snapped out of her contemplation. "Hank, get them to suit up."

"Strickland's holding up a note. It says, *Woman's suit has no life support!*"

"Damn!" Guerrera exclaimed, wondering what to do next.

"We'll have to find a way to bring the thing in," Le said. "Let them ride down in the cargo bay."

"With that spin rate?" Guerrera responded, feeling very nervous. "There's no way we can get the arm on it."

"What about maneuvering Atlantis to match the motion?"

Guerrera had already considered the option, knowing it offered the only hope. But looping the Shuttle around the helpless vehicle required extraordinary skill, more than she thought she possessed.

"Got to be kidding! You're talking about doing barrel rolls around the damned thing."

"It'd be a bitch, Monica. More than I could handle. Remember that black astronaut, Wilkins? Bet he could have done it."

Guerrera replied gruffly, "Except he's not here, Le. In fact, he's dead!"

"Guess that leaves you."

"You know what you're asking? I have to fly circles around it while Janice gets the arm attached, then reduce the roll rate until it stops. Best way I know of to break the arm. Maybe even rip it off."

"And not be able to close the bay doors," he reminded her.

"Janice, you following this?"

"Yup," the Mission Specialist replied.

"You up to working the arm?"

"Face it, Monica, we don't have a choice. Let's get it over with."

Taking a deep breath, Guerrera said, "Get the arm deployed."

Tyson used the Remote Manipulator controls to move the end effector toward the surface of Artemis. She watched the grapple drift across the screen of the television monitor.

"I'm lined up, Monica. Have at it."

Guerrera worked the controllers, trying to fly a circular path around Artemis, matching its rotation rate. Her first attempts described paths more like squares, too irregular for Tyson to attempt a connection. But she quickly mastered the tricky combination of commands, matching the roll rate while keeping a uniform distance.

"That's good, Monica," Tyson shouted, her voice tinged with apprehension. "Going for the grapple."

Guerrera concentrated on keeping an exact position while Tyson brought the end effector toward Artemis. After what seemed like an eternity, she heard her announce, "Capture! We got it!"

Now Guerrera had to gradually reduce the roll rate, using the arm's force to slow Artemis. Too rapid a reduction would break the arm or tear it from its mount. She twisted the hand controller, commanding a slower roll. Not seeing any effect, she commanded another torque. This time, the Shuttle's roll rate decreased noticeably and the arm began to bend.

"Work it, Janice!" she yelled.

Frantically twisting and pushing the controls, Tyson let the arm extend to follow Artemis' motion and then carefully pulled back to match the roll rates.

Breathing heavily, Guerrera commanded another torque, still trying to keep a fixed distance. This time Tyson accommodated the change more smoothly. "I think we've got it, Janice!" Guerrera shouted.

After three more cycles, the rolling stopped with the Shuttle's cargo bay facing the earth. Artemis floated below at the end of the arm.

Still trying to catch her breath, Guerrera said, "Okay, Janice. Nice work. Bring it in."

Twenty minutes later, as Atlantis once again dropped into the upper fringes of the atmosphere, Artemis lay safely within the cargo bay, the doors closed over it.

"Hell of a job!" Guerrera told her crew, now reassembled on the flight deck. "I'm proud to be your commander."

**Artemis**

"They did it!" Svetlana exclaimed. "Just as you said."

"Have to admit, they amazed me. After we ran out of fuel, I figured our chances for riding back in Artemis had dropped to zero."

Brandt now realized how badly he'd underestimated the difficulty of the recovery and how close they'd come to being forced into a dangerous scramble for the airlock. Finally able to relax, he cherished these last few minutes alone with Svetlana in the dark silence of the cargo bay. He had so many things to tell her—ask her—discuss with her. He searched for a place to start.

Hoping the question would open a discussion and not a wound, he asked, "Have you made a decision about staying in the United States?"

She looked away, her head tilted to the side, her eyes seeming to stare off into space. After a while, she answered, sounding irresolute, "I think there is no choice. If your government will allow it, I would like to stay for a while."

Enormously pleased, Brandt replied, "I'll help you with the arrangements. Find you a place to stay. Introduce you to people."

She smiled. "Thank you. I would be most grateful."

"Think you'll eventually return to Russia?"

"When it is safe. Could be a long time. I have thought about the government—their true goal for this mission. I no longer believe they can be trusted."

"What changed your mind?"

"Lies. Lies about the weapon. Lies about the lander leg. It makes me question other things, things they told us about the United States, about claiming the moon. They said we must claim it to keep it from the capitalists. That the Federation would claim it for all countries. But the statement—the one I read. It claimed the moon only for the Federation. I believe they want to keep it for themselves."

Brandt thought about the wording of his own claim. "I had the same feeling when I read our statement. At the time, I thought it was a response to your claim. Something required by international law. But not any more."

"I do not know of your claim. Do you think America will try to take the whole moon?"

Her question cut to the core of his doubts, his wrenching examination of his attitudes, prejudices, naïveté.

"I don't know, Svetlana. Perhaps that's what they had in mind."

"Then they are no better than the Federation."

"The government? I won't argue with you. I think something happens to people when they reach positions of power. Russians, Americans, anybody. They all end up pretty much the same. The only thing we've got going for us is a system that keeps them fighting with each other. Doesn't sound like much of a difference, but it seems to help."

Brandt felt himself being pushed into his couch. "Starting to reenter, Svetlana. Almost home."

**Kennedy Space Center**

He deemed it a glorious jolt, a bouncing impact announcing their return to the only world that nurtured and sustained their existence. As Atlantis braked to a stop, Brandt vented the spacecraft, released his restraints and put his feet on the wall. After almost six days weightless, he had trouble standing erect.

He turned to help Svetlana but she'd already freed herself. Far less impaired, she bent and stretched, adapting herself quickly to the new environment.

Sanden appeared at the small window. The lights of the cargo bay had been turned on and Brandt found the familiar face a welcome sight. He told the computer to release the latches and listened while the mechanism obeyed the command. The hatch opened to his touch.

"Welcome back, Colonel," Sanden said grinning. "Can you get down okay?"

Brandt replied, "I'll work it out," as he lifted himself to a sitting position on the opening, then dropped to the bay floor.

He looked back inside, intending to assist Svetlana, but she'd already followed his example, swinging her legs through the hatch.

"Hank, I'd like you to meet Colonel Svetlana Zosimova from the Socialist Federation."

Sanders shook her hand and led them down the cargo bay, through the open airlock and up the ladder to the flight deck. After a round of introductions, Guerrera said, "Colonel Strickland, you've got about a billion people ready to listen if there's something you want to say."

Brandt glanced at the television camera aimed at him, thought for a moment before looking into the lens.

"Ladies and gentlemen, I'm Colonel Brandt Strickland, the commander of the American mission to the moon." He took Svetlana's hand and drew her to his side. "And this is Colonel Svetlana Zosimova, my counterpart from the Socialist Federation.

"I must start by thanking the crew of Atlantis for their courageous actions that led to our safe return. They've set a new standard for innovation, skill, and just plain guts." He took Guerrera's hand and shook it vigorously.

"Colonel Zosimova and I return from failed missions, tragedies that cost the lives of our crews. Those wonderful people died not because of technical failures or unforseen hazards. They were sacrificed on the altars of greed, prejudice, and the lust for power.

"It is our hope that we'll learn from these failures. We want to bring our nations together in a spirit of cooperation and understanding. I can think of no greater tribute to our fallen comrades."

He walked from the camera's view to the front of the flight deck followed by Svetlana and Guerrera.

Guerrera looked at him, seemingly stunned. She stammered, "Sounds like you had a rough one, Colonel. Damned shame about Wilkins and the other astronaut. We heard your broadcast—the one where you claimed the moon for America. Kept the damned communists from getting it. At least you can say that, in the end, we won."

"Won, Monica? I left two close friends back there. So did Colonel Zosimova. For what?"

Bewildered, she mumbled, "For the moon, I guess. And the stuff that's up there."

"You think that's winning?"

Sounding frustrated, she replied, "Well, if we didn't win, who did?"

Brandt started to say no one, then thought of a better answer.

"The moon won, Monica. Took revenge on everyone who dared to violate its sanctity. It was the moon, Monica. The God-damned moon."

Made in the USA
Columbia, SC
03 October 2018